The House

on

The Hill

A Ghost Story

By Irina Shapiro

Copyright

Table of Contents

Prologue

If walls could talk, what a story they'd tell—a story of love, betrayal, and murder, the woman thinks as she stands at the top of the stairs watching the newcomer, who is completely unaware of the woman's ethereal presence. The newcomer is moving around the house with the uncertainty of someone who's trespassing in someone else's space, trying it on for size to see if she could make a life for herself there. Many others have passed through the house over the centuries, but this one is different. She's young, by modern standards, but she's known the pain of loss and the heartbreak of betrayal. It's right there in her shadowed eyes and the unhealthy pallor of her face.

Maybe this one will be able to help me, the woman at the top of the stairs thinks. *Maybe she'll succeed where others had failed, and finally set me free so I can fulfill my promise at last.*

Chapter 1

Lauren
The Present

The morning was bright and brisk, with wispy clouds racing across the aquamarine sky and playing peek-a-boo with the pale orb of the sun. It was mid-March, but there wasn't a hint of spring in the air, winter stubbornly clinging on. The roads were clear, but snow still covered much of the ground since the temperature refused to rise above freezing, and the icy breath of the ocean held the shoreline in its thrall.

Lauren peered at the GPS as it instructed her to make a right. The road she turned onto was narrow and surprisingly steep, flanked by ancient trees whose branches moved eerily in the wind. The house was about a mile away, perched on a hill that overlooked Pleasant Bay and the Atlantic Ocean beyond.

Lauren hoped she was going to like this one. She'd seen several potential rentals over the past few weeks, but the ones she liked were too pricy and the ones she could afford were little more than shacks that smelled of mildew and had such low ceilings she could reach up and touch them. She hadn't planned on leaving Boston, but the desperate need to escape her apartment and spend a few months in a place that held no painful memories overwhelmed her.

In two weeks, it'd be a year since Zack died, killed by a sniper's bullet during the spring offensive in Afghanistan. It had been his third tour and would have been his last. They'd made plans. They were going to sell their apartment in Brookline and buy a house in the suburbs, start trying for a baby, and live a wonderfully boring life where Lauren didn't lie awake night after night waiting for him to call from overseas or avoid watching the news for fear of hearing something that would send her into a tailspin.

While Zack was away, she'd concentrated on her work, finally completing the last book of the military romance series she'd been writing. She'd often heard the advice "Write what you know," and this was something she knew—the heart-wrenching goodbyes followed by tearful reunions, the worry, the fear, and the pure joy of those first few weeks of togetherness after Zack finally returned to her, safe and sound. Those first few days were like a second honeymoon, but more intense, more precious. Zack had joked that the months of separation kept the marriage strong because the romance never fizzled out. It stoked their desire for each other and transformed the mundane details of their lives into something magical. They'd talk nonstop, their words tripping over each other and falling like a waterfall from their parched lips, and the need to touch, to feel, to worship each other's bodies was so strong, they barely got out of bed.

Zack had often remarked how lucky he'd been in his life, but his luck had run out a year ago on a windswept mountaintop just north of Kabul. Their life was like a record that had screeched to a halt, the song left unsung, the melody interrupted. Suddenly, Lauren was alone, widowed, a status people tended to associate with elderly women who'd lost their husbands to illness or old age, not with someone who was still in her twenties. She couldn't bring herself to utter the word; it made her loss all too real. The rational part of her brain understood Zack was gone, but the emotional part, the loving part, still looked for him everywhere she went. She still spoke to him, sometimes out loud, and slept on her side of the bed, unable to move to the middle for fear of acknowledging that he'd never sleep next to her again. She needed to have pictures of him, but looking at them tore at her heart. She wanted to be in the place he'd called home, but every piece of furniture, every picture, every item of clothing reminded her of the husband she'd lost. Seeing his favorite mug for the first time after he died had led to a two-day cryfest that resulted in her hiding the cup from view lest she fall apart again.

She'd put off clearing out his side of the closet, unable to get dressed in the morning without touching his shirts and sniffing desperately in the hope that a hint of his smell still clung to the laundered fabric. She'd finally done it a few months ago, but she hadn't thrown anything away. Getting rid of Zack's things seemed too final, too real. Despite her valiant efforts to cope, her life became reduced to eating, sleeping, watching TV, and reassuring everyone that she was fine, a lie no one really believed.

She'd stopped writing. She simply couldn't form an original thought as she sat day after day, staring at the blank screen of her computer. Her agent had been able to get her several ghostwriting gigs. It was much easier to organize someone else's thoughts and turn them into a narrative than deal with her own. Her clients were happy, and her reputation as a ghostwriter grew, resulting in more commissions. She was glad; it was imperative to keep busy in order to keep the worst of the pain at bay. But after a long, snowy winter spent mostly indoors, she needed to get out. She had to get away from the ghost of Zack, to inhabit a new place, to try to put the pieces of her life back together and come to terms with a truth that had come knocking on her door several months ago and shed a new light on her life as she'd known it. She had to get away, to spend a few months in a place that made her feel peaceful and whole.

Cape Cod had naturally come to mind. She'd loved the place as a child. Her parents had rented a house on the beach for two weeks every August, and they'd spent their days tanning and swimming, followed by burgers and grilled seafood eaten on the deck as they watched the sun sink below the horizon. It was a golden memory of her childhood she still clung to and had hoped to recreate with her own children someday.

The summer season wouldn't officially start until Memorial Day, but if she found the right place, she'd be ready to move in as soon as the first of April, eager to watch spring arrive in a place that was nearly free of memories—her own rebirth, for lack of a better word. She owed it to Zack. She'd made a promise.

"Promise me you won't grieve for me should anything happen," he'd said that last morning at their apartment.

"I couldn't bear it if anything happened to you," she'd replied, clinging to him amid the rumpled sheets.

Zack had kissed her tenderly and brushed her tangled hair away from her face. "Lauren, promise me you'll move on. I need to know that you'll be happy; that's the only way I can leave and get on with my job. Promise me," he'd demanded, his gaze anxious and intense. "Promise me."

And she'd promised, even though she'd been lying through her teeth. "Yes, I promise. I will get on with my life if the worst happens." But she'd never imagined that anything could be worse than death, or that some secrets lived on, haunting those left behind from beyond the grave.

Lauren's eyes widened in surprise when the house finally came into view. She hadn't bothered to look it up online, preferring to see it for the first time in real life and form an impression. It was a lot grander than she'd expected, the type of house one saw in advertisements for a holiday on the seashore. It even had an actual name, rather than just an address—Holland House. She parked the car and got out, smiling at Susan McPherson, who'd been waiting in her car but was now coming to greet her.

"Sorry I'm late. Traffic out of the city was monstrous."

"It always is," Susan replied breezily. "No worries. I caught up on some calls while I was waiting for you. It was too cold to hang around outside anyhow."

"Susan, are you sure this place is within my budget? It looks too—I don't know—glamorous."

Susan gave a dismissive shrug. "Glamorous is not a word I'd use to describe this house. The location is perfect for someone who wants to spend the summer in blissful isolation, but it's not overly appealing to families who prefer to be close to the beach. There's a private dock, but no boat," she added as she led Lauren around the side of the house to show her the breathtaking view. Beyond Pleasant Bay, the Atlantic stretched like a blue-gray quilt toward the horizon, its surface decorated with foaming whitecaps whipped up by the wind. Several small islands were visible from their vantage point on the hill. According to Susan, they were uninhabited, being too small and steep to build a summer residence to rival the one she was looking at.

A wide patio hugged the back of the house, complete with wrought-iron furniture and a covered grill. A narrow wooden staircase led to the water's edge, where a short dock extended into the bay. Both the stairs and the dock looked old and rickety, unlike the house, which appeared solid, if windswept, by comparison. It had the pleasing proportions often found in homes of colonial design, but Lauren didn't think this house was a modern-day replica—it looked like the real thing.

"When was this place built?"

"The original house was constructed in the eighteenth century. It had two rooms downstairs and two bedrooms above. I believe the widow's walk dates to the nineteenth century," Susan said, glancing at the white-painted rooftop platform that was such a common feature of houses on Cape Cod. "Over time, the owners added indoor plumbing, several rooms, a patio, a sunroom, and, of course, the driveway and the garage. However," Susan shook her head in dismay, "it's not wired for cable or internet. Another nail in the coffin for the current owner. Families want TV and internet. Kids don't spend their free time reading and playing board games as they did when I was a kid."

"No, I don't suppose they do. Why doesn't the owner just bring in the cable company?"

"I think he just forgets about this place until it's time to rent it out again, and then it seems like too much of an expense, or too big a hassle. I honestly don't know. He lives in L.A., where he makes movies."

"He's a film producer?" Lauren asked, curious.

"No, he does special effects. One of those artistic types," she added, as if that were the worst thing a person could be. "I think he'd happily sell the place if he could be bothered to deal with all the details of putting it on the market. As long as he gets a few tenants in each summer, he's content to let the property sit empty for the remainder of the year."

"So, the isolated location and the lack of internet are enough of a drawback to keep renters away?" Lauren asked, amazed that anyone would pass up such a wonderful place.

Susan looked furtive for a moment, then exhaled loudly, as if she had no choice but to tell the truth. "This house has a bit of a reputation."

"A reputation for what?"

"Look, it's an old house. It creaks, doors slam shut, probably because there's a draft. Lights occasionally go on by themselves, but the wiring hasn't been updated since it was put in, whenever that might have been. It's nothing to worry about."

"Are you saying, in a very no-nonsense, dismissive kind of way, that the house is haunted?" Lauren asked, amused by Susan's desire to explain away the 'reputation.'

"I'm saying it's old, and it gets buffeted by winds from the Atlantic. I don't believe in ghosts."

"Neither do I," Lauren replied. She wished she did because then maybe Zack would come to her. She needed closure, something she'd never have now. "Can we go inside?" she asked as she huddled deeper into her coat. The house's location ensured it would be cool in the summer, but in the middle of March, it was arctic on that hill.

"Sure. Sorry. I always tend to pontificate about the view. I must emphasize the sellable points."

"So, the house is a dump?" Lauren asked with a chuckle.

"No. It's nice." *Passable*, in real estate speak, Lauren thought as she followed Susan toward the front door.

The inside wasn't too bad. The place could use a good airing out, but aside from the stagnant smell, it was more than passable. There was a sofa and comfortable-looking chairs arranged before the fireplace, several lamps, and a colorful rug that made the living room look cozy and inviting. The windows faced the bay, a major plus as far as Lauren was concerned. The kitchen was outdated, but she had no plans to do any serious cooking, so it would do.

"This is the office," Susan said as she threw open the door of a room that faced the front of the house and held a desk, several bookshelves, and a swivel chair. The white walls were bare, and the window faced the side of the garage. "You could write in here."

I doubt it, Lauren thought as she sized up the unappealing room. No inspiration would strike her within its utilitarian confines. Whoever had used this room in the past had left nothing of their personality behind, not even a picture on the wall or a tattered paperback they no longer wanted.

"Shall we go upstairs?" Susan chirped, clearly happier now that she thought Lauren was interested. "There are four bedrooms: two kids' rooms, a guest room, and a master bedroom. The master bedroom is not exactly in keeping with the rest of the house, but it's very quaint."

"Sounds ominous," Lauren joked.

"Not at all. See for yourself."

The three smaller bedrooms were reminiscent of any B&B Lauren had stayed at. Flowery quilts thrown over twin beds with scratched wooden headboards, neutral carpeting, and colorful curtains to brighten the space. The master bedroom, however, was a surprise. A four-poster bed dominated the room, its massive mahogany posts intricately carved. The seafoam-colored quilt appeared to be made of thick damask and decorated with silver braid that matched the delicate pattern. A heavy wardrobe stood in the corner, the design matching that of the bedposts, but the item of furniture that really grabbed Lauren's attention was the lovely secretary desk that faced the window, which opened onto the vista of tall pines and shimmering sea. The desk was mahogany, its surface smooth and satiny despite years of use. There were three drawers on each side, plus several small drawers in the top section. Each drawer had a polished brass knob and a fanciful pattern carved into the wood. The desk was reminiscent of something

Charles Dickens or Jane Austen would own, but it had probably been crafted before their time.

"All the furniture in this room is original to the house," Susan said. "Eighteenth century. This room belonged to the last owner of the house, Mrs. Lacey. She was the current owner's aunt. Died five years ago."

"Not in this bed, I hope," Lauren said.

"No, in a hospice in Chatham. She was a nice lady. My mom knew her well. So, what do you think?"

"I think I love it," Lauren said, already picturing herself at the desk, her computer in front of her as she began a new project, her own this time.

"Great. Let's get the papers signed, then, shall we? Why don't we stop by the office, take care of business, and then grab some lunch? I'm starving."

"I don't know," Lauren replied lamely. She'd actively avoided social situations since Zack's death, but Susan looked so crestfallen, she felt mean for refusing.

"Come on. It's on me," Susan tried again. "I hate eating at my desk."

"Okay. Sure. Thank you."

"No, thank *you*," Susan replied, smiling broadly. "Jerry will be thrilled to have rented this place so early in the season. When do you want the lease to start?"

"April first through Labor Day," Lauren replied.

"Perfect," Susan said, already heading toward the stairs. "I'm already spending my commission in my mind." She laughed merrily. "I think you'll be happy here."

"Billy will love it."

"Oh? Who's Billy?" Susan's arched eyebrows made Lauren laugh. She obviously thought Billy was her boyfriend.

"Billy is a puppy. My brother, Xavier, gave him to me for Christmas." *He thought a dog would make me less lonely*, Lauren added in her head. And he had. Billy was a joy. A brown furball with limpid brown eyes and a velvety nose. "Pets are allowed, aren't they?" Lauren asked, realizing she'd never thought to inquire.

"Yes, the owner has no issue with pets. What breed?"

"Chocolate lab."

"I love those. They're so cute." Susan locked the house behind them and headed for her car. "Just follow me back to the office, and we can walk to lunch from there."

"Sounds like a plan," Lauren said.

As she got into her car, she felt lighter than she had in months. "You'd like this place," she said, addressing Zack, her vow to stop talking to him momentarily forgotten. "The view is stunning, and it's nice and private, away from the mob of tourists. I think I can write here," she added, her voice tinged with hope. "What do you think?"

I think it's time you let go, Lauren, Zack's voice replied in her head. Lauren ignored him and drove down the hill.

Chapter 2

Moving into Holland House didn't take long. Susan McPherson had had the house cleaned and aired out before her arrival, so the rooms smelled pleasantly of pine cleaner and the sea. Lauren brought only the essentials: two suitcases of clothes, Billy's crate and toys, her Kindle, which had at least ten books she had yet to read on it, and several framed photographs.

She set her favorite picture on the nightstand next to the four-poster. It had been taken at Xavier's graduation party nearly ten years ago, the night she'd met Zack. Xavier had caught them unawares, gazing at each other with all the desire and wonder of two people who'd made a sudden and intense connection. They looked young and carefree, and already halfway in love. Looking at the picture always made her happy. It served to remind her that something wonderful could happen when you least expected it and change your life forever.

Lauren threw open the curtains and opened the window a crack to let in some fresh air, unpacked her clothes, and placed some personal items on the old-fashioned bureau, claiming the previously impersonal space as her own. She'd known she'd pick this bedroom before she even signed the rental agreement. She'd always been something of a history buff, and the colonial decor had appealed to her on sight, but it was the four-poster and the lovely writing desk that sealed the deal. Lauren positioned her laptop on the polished surface of the desk, then stowed some office supplies in the drawers, running a gentle hand over the pattern carved into each mahogany rectangle. She couldn't help wondering about all the people that had used the desk before her, especially its original owner, who must have written all their correspondence as they gazed out over the bay, a quill suspended in their hand as they considered their next words.

Her reverie was interrupted by Billy, who pushed his nose into her calf, making her laugh out loud. He'd been nosing around the second-floor bedrooms, yapping excitedly, but now he probably wanted to get outside and explore. Lauren scooped up the puppy and carried him downstairs. He was too small to navigate the stairs on his own, which was a blessing in a way since that would ensure he'd stay put instead of running all over the house, but she'd have to install a security gate soon to keep Billy safe. The little dog ran toward the sliding door and pressed his nose to the glass, his eyes wide with curiosity as he took in the placid bay and the open space beyond the patio.

"All right, all right," Lauren said as she reached for her coat. "We can go outside." She grabbed Billy's leash and pulled on a pair of gloves before opening the door. It was warmer than it had been when she came to see the house, but not by much. The wind lifted Lauren's hair and whipped it around her face, momentarily blinding her. She loosened her grip on the leash, and that was all it took for Billy to take off. He raced toward the wooden steps to the dock and had managed to clear the first two on pure inertia before falling headfirst down the rickety staircase.

"Billy, no!" Lauren screamed as she plunged down the steps after him, hoping she wouldn't follow his example and tumble headlong down the hill. The puppy looked like a brown ball of fur as he rolled toward the bottom, then landed with a hollow *thunk*. Lauren was beside him in moments, crouching next to him as she reached to stroke his head. Billy whimpered pitifully but didn't get up. His gaze was glazed, and his back leg was folded at an odd angle beneath his body.

"Billy?" Lauren called to him. "Billy, get up."

But the dog didn't budge. His head lolled to the side as he rested it on his paws, his eyes closed against the glare of the sun. His breathing was shallow, and his whimper was carried away on the wind. Lauren pulled off her gloves and yanked her phone out of her pocket, searching for the nearest vet. She called two numbers, but both offices were closed, the recording advising her to leave a message. She didn't want to leave a message; she wanted Billy looked at immediately. The third call was answered by an actual person.

"Good morning. How can I help?" a perky female voice asked.

"Hi. My dog fell down some steps. I think he's badly hurt."

"Are you a current patient?"

"No, I just moved to the area. Is there any way you can fit me in?" Lauren pleaded.

"Please hold," the young woman said. She came back a few moments later. "Dr. Kelly will see you at noon. Can I have your name, address, phone number, and the name and breed of your dog?"

Lauren provided all the information, her gaze never leaving Billy's face. He was perfectly still, lying there as if unconscious. "I'm afraid to cause him more pain," Lauren said to the receptionist as she considered the logistics of getting him to the vet.

"Is he bleeding?"

"No, but he's not moving."

"Pick him up very carefully and settle him in the back seat," the woman advised.

"Okay. Thank you."

Lauren glanced at the clock on the phone. It was almost eleven and the drive wouldn't take longer than fifteen minutes. There was no sense disturbing Billy twice, so she sat on the step next to him and waited, hoping he'd miraculously come around, but Billy didn't stir. At eleven thirty, she picked up the puppy and carried him to her car, settling him in the back seat. He whimpered but never opened his eyes and put a paw over his face as if to block out the light.

"We'll be there very soon," Lauren told him as she got in the driver's seat and put the key in the ignition. "You'll be all right. You'll see."

Lauren drove to the vet's office, parked, and carried Billy inside. The young woman at reception looked even younger than she'd sounded on the phone. She had to still be in her teens. She checked them in, took down Billy's medical history, since in her agitation Lauren had forgotten to bring along his medical records, and asked Lauren to have a seat.

There was no one else in the waiting room, so Lauren looked around, studying the framed prints on the walls. Some of the prints were black and white, and the light made the subjects leap off the paper, particularly a photo of a lighthouse in a gathering storm.

"The doctor usually takes lunch at twelve," said the young woman, whose name plate proclaimed her to be Merielle Kelly. "But he could never leave an animal in pain."

"That's very kind," Lauren said, wondering if Merielle was the doctor's wife or daughter. Daughter, most likely.

"He's really sweet," she said, nodding toward Billy. "I'm more of a cat person myself, but I can appreciate a cute puppy. Oh, you can go in. First door on the left," she said when a woman with a French bulldog came out into the reception area and approached the desk.

Lauren cuddled Billy as she followed the corridor to an examining room. The doctor smiled as she walked in and asked her to place Billy on the examining table. He appeared to be in his mid-to-late thirties, with unruly dark-brown hair that brushed the collar of his doctor's coat at the nape, and dark green eyes, so like Merielle's. He was tall and fit with strong, capable hands, Lauren noted as he pulled on a pair of latex gloves and bent over Billy.

"Hello, little guy," he said gently. "Let's see what's wrong with you."

Lauren waited anxiously while Dr. Kelly examined Billy. He was thorough and didn't waste time on small talk, but asked several questions, which Lauren answered to the best of her ability. Billy, displeased at being prodded, opened his eyes and glared at the doctor, who took the opportunity to shine a light into his eyes, making him growl.

"I'm sorry, Billy," Dr. Kelly said as he shut off the light. "I know that's bright."

Billy relaxed once the offending light had been switched off and rested his head on his paws, lying quietly and watching the doctor with obvious suspicion.

"Will he be all right?" Lauren asked anxiously.

"He'll be just fine. Nothing is broken. He's bruised and has a mild concussion. He's scared himself silly more than anything," Dr. Kelly said, pulling off the gloves.

"Concussion? What should I do?"

"Nothing. Allow him to set his own pace. He might be a little lethargic for a few days and will probably be in some pain from the bruises, but he's young and strong, and his body will heal itself. I'd like to see him in about three days to make sure he's recovering."

Lauren nodded, relieved Billy hadn't broken anything or suffered serious brain damage. "Thank you for seeing him. And giving up your lunch hour."

Dr. Kelly shook his head. "Merielle talks too much," he said with an indulgent smile. "So, you moved into Holland House?" he asked, his surprise evident.

"Are you going to warn me that it's haunted?" Lauren quipped, noting the amusement in his eyes.

"No. Is it?" he asked, smiling down at her.

"I couldn't say. I've only just arrived."

"I've heard the stories, of course, but I was always more interested in Hog Island myself." He pointed to one of the pictures on the wall. The island was nothing more than a heavily forested clump of land rising from the sea, with nothing on it to attract attention.

"Did you take these photos?" Lauren asked.

"Yes. I love photography and history, so I spend my free time photographing places of historical interest. Or at least I used to," he amended.

"You're very good," Lauren said, suddenly realizing that one of the photographs behind him was of Holland House. "So, what's so special about Hog Island?"

He was about to reply when the intercom buzzed and Merielle's voice announced that his next patient had arrived. It seemed Dr. Kelly didn't take long lunches.

"Thanks, Merielle." He laid a gentle hand on Billy's head. "Don't hesitate to call me if you have any concerns, and I'll see you in a few days. Bye, Billy."

Lauren thanked him and carried Billy back to the waiting room, where she paid for the visit and made a follow-up appointment. She stole another peek at the wall, noting that there was a picture of Hog Island in the reception area as well, taken from a slightly different angle, which didn't make the island any more photogenic.

Having returned to the house, Lauren settled Billy on his bed in the living room and sat down on the sofa, watching him sleep. She'd picked up a breakfast sandwich on the way from Boston early that morning but hadn't had anything since, and she was getting hungry. The plan had been to run out to the grocery store and pick up some supplies after she unpacked. There was nothing to eat in the house except for the bag of dog food she'd brought for Billy. Lauren went to the kitchen, shook some puppy chow into a bowl, refreshed Billy's water, then returned to the living room. Billy was still asleep.

"I'll be back soon," she said softly, and left him to rest.

She drove to the nearest supermarket, stocked up on the basics, and returned to the house. She'd expected Billy to start barking when she unlocked the door, but he still lay on his bed, his gaze brightening when he saw her. Lauren glanced at his bowl as she came into the kitchen. He hadn't eaten or drunk any water.

Not a great first day, Lauren thought as she put away the groceries. With Billy so quiet, the house was silent around her, and she suddenly wished she had a TV to keep her company. At home in Boston, there was always noise. She could hear the hum of conversation from neighboring apartments, the blare of a TV from across the hall, and the traffic beneath her windows, but here, it was eerily quiet.

She looked out the window, her attention fixing on the island in the distance. Was that the same island she'd seen a photograph of in Dr. Kelly's office? Hog Island, he'd called it. She really couldn't understand the fascination, so she filled a pot with water and set it to boil, took out some chicken, and began to slice celery and carrots. She'd make a big pot of chicken noodle soup, she decided. She needed comfort food but didn't want to have anything too heavy like mac and cheese, or fried chicken. Soup would do her very nicely.

"Tomorrow will be a better day, buddy," she told Billy as she ate her soup on the sofa in the living room to keep him company. He still hadn't moved, so she brought his bowls of food and water closer to the bed in an effort to tempt him. Billy lifted his head and sniffed at the food but didn't touch it.

"Come on, you have to eat," Lauren pleaded with him. "Just a little bit."

Billy closed his eyes and went back to sleep, leaving a worried Lauren to eat alone.

Chapter 3

Lauren came awake slowly, her thoughts crowding in long before she opened her eyes. Her first concern was for Billy, whose warm body was pressed to her side, his breathing even in sleep. He'd finally eaten a little last night, a hopeful sign, in her opinion. Lauren lay very still, taking a moment to recall exactly where she was and why. A gusty wind blew off the Atlantic, and the house creaked, the wooden walls sighing like an elderly woman pining for her youth. A soft half-light crept toward the bed, its gentle fingers stroking the comforter and caressing Billy's round bottom.

Lauren turned toward the window, hoping to watch the sunrise, but the sight that greeted her left her breathless with terror. Her heart pounded in her chest as she clamped a hand over her mouth to stifle the scream that caught in her throat. She sank deeper into the mattress in order to make herself less visible, but she needn't have bothered.

The woman seemed completely unaware of her presence. She sat at the desk, the soft light of dawn illuminating her pale face. Her back was ramrod straight, her hands clasped in her lap, and her troubled gaze fixed on the horizon. A blank sheet of paper lay before her, a quill left forgotten in the inkwell as if she were about to write a letter but had changed her mind. Lauren lifted her head slightly to get a better look at the woman's profile. She was young, mid-twenties Lauren guessed, and attractive. Her old-fashioned gown was sober, and a modest lace-trimmed cap covered her dark hair. Her only adornment was a necklace, the pendant resting just above the V of her lace tucker. It shimmered in the pearlescent light, the fiery stone reminiscent of an opal.

Billy raised his head and looked at Lauren, then turned toward the window. She expected him to let out a bark of alarm, or growl at the intruder at the very least, but he rested his head on Lauren's hip and drifted back to sleep, as if completely unaware of the stranger. He hadn't seen her or caught her scent because she wasn't real. She was an apparition, an echo of a time gone by.

Feeling less frightened, Lauren sat up and leaned against the pillows, watching the woman with interest. After a time, she replaced the paper in a drawer, stood, and turned toward the door. Lauren could have sworn she saw tears in the woman's eyes as she walked across the room, but with her face turned away from the window, it was difficult to be certain. As the light changed from pearl-gray to salmon pink, the woman's silhouette grew fainter until she vanished altogether, leaving nothing but an unnatural stillness in her wake. Lauren laid a gentle hand on Billy's head, needing to feel a connection with a living being. He lifted his head and looked at her, his brown gaze clear and alert.

"Good morning," Lauren said, but made no move to get up. She was in no rush to start her day. As she watched the sun come up, Lauren reflected on what she'd seen. Had the woman been a figment of her imagination, or had she seen an actual ghost? She didn't believe in ghosts, but she also didn't believe that a person simply ceased to exist. Zack was physically gone, but she had often felt his presence, especially for the first few months, and when she spoke to him, sometimes an answer simply dropped into her brain, as if he'd whispered it in her ear rather than saying it out loud. Perhaps it was wishful thinking and she wasn't ready to let him go, but she had felt him close, especially when she was alone, and when Xavier first brought Billy over, the dog had growled at something, baring his teeth and staring into nothingness. He hadn't done it since their first week together, so perhaps he'd grown used to Zack's otherworldly presence, and he seemed oblivious to the woman Lauren had just seen.

At long last, Lauren got up, took a shower, and dressed in a pair of leggings and a warm sweater. She lifted Billy off the bed and carried him downstairs, where she set him on the floor. He trotted over to his water bowl and drank deeply before turning his attention to his food. It seemed Dr. Kelly had been right, and Billy just needed a little time to recover.

After taking him out for a wee, Lauren made herself a spinach and cheese omelet and a cup of coffee, then returned upstairs, sitting down at the desk where the woman had sat only an hour before. There was no trace of the letter she'd been writing or the implements, only Lauren's laptop, which hummed accusingly as soon as she powered it up. She hadn't done any work in nearly a week and it was time to get started. She was working on an autobiography of a popular reality star whose life was of little interest to Lauren, but it was a job, and she would do it to the best of her ability. Once she finished the project, she'd devote some time to her own writing.

"How about writing a ghost story?" Zack's voice whispered in her mind. "You always said you wanted to try a different genre."

"I don't think so," Lauren replied. "Ghost stories are really not my thing."

"Okay, how about a historical romance, then? You used to love reading those. Remember that series you gobbled up about the woman who went back in time to eighteenth-century Scotland? You couldn't buy those books fast enough."

"All right. I'll think about it," Lauren replied grudgingly. "Now I must concentrate on my client's meteoric rise to fame. She wants to devote an entire chapter to Twitter and how a nude selfie she posted went viral."

She could almost hear Zack's chuckle as she pulled out her notes and began to type.

Chapter 4

When Lauren took Billy back to the vet on Friday, he got a clean bill of health and nearly leapt off the examining table headfirst in his desire to get away. Dr. Kelly caught him deftly and handed him to Lauren, who held him close, terrified he'd hurt himself again.

"It's like having a child," Dr. Kelly said, correctly interpreting her expression. "You might want to puppy-proof the house. As he gets bigger, he'll try to climb the stairs and drink from the toilet."

"Eww. Gross," Lauren said, making a face.

Dr. Kelly shrugged. "That's what puppies do. Is he your first dog?"

"Yes." Zack had wanted to get a dog, but Lauren had argued that their apartment was too small and they should wait until they bought a house. Her gaze slid toward the photograph of Holland House. "You mentioned that you like history," she began, instantly wishing she hadn't said anything.

"Yes, local history in particular. Why?"

"I'd like to learn more about Holland House."

Dr. Kelly leaned against the examining table and crossed his arms, his head tilted to the side as he considered her request. "Have you experienced something odd?"

"How do you mean?"

"I've been hearing stories about that place since I was a little kid: weird creaking noises, candlelight flickering in the window, the sound of a woman crying… It was the ultimate act of bravery to go there on Halloween," he said, a small smile tugging at his lips. "Are you afraid of ghosts?" The smile broadened into a full-on grin.

Lauren's cheeks heated with embarrassment. First, she'd brought up that the house was said to be haunted, and now they were once again speaking of ghosts. She averted her gaze, staring at Billy's silky head instead, but Dr. Kelly wasn't fooled by her sudden aloofness.

"Tell you what. Meet me for a drink, and I'll tell you everything I know."

Lauren's head shot up, her eyes opening wide. Was he asking her out? Wasn't it unethical to fraternize with one's patients? Well, technically, she wasn't his patient; Billy was. And what was the harm? She'd spent less than a week in the house alone and already she felt the heavy weight of loneliness pressing down on her restless mind. Getting away and changing her surroundings had seemed like a great idea, but now that she was installed at Holland House, she felt even more lonely and unsettled. She didn't know anyone in Orleans and wasn't likely to make new friends if she didn't come out of her shell, at least once in a while.

"All right," she said, wondering if she was going to regret this. "Where and when?"

"Tonight? Unless you have big plans for your first Friday night in town."

"I don't."

"How about the Blue Fin Bar and Grill? Say, seven? Do you know where it is?"

"I'll find it. See you later, Dr. Kelly."

"It's Ryan," he called after her, making her smile.

**

Lauren's nervousness increased as the afternoon wore on. Why had she agreed to meet Ryan Kelly? She hardly knew him. Just because he was Billy's veterinarian didn't mean she should trust him. Maybe he made a pass at all his female clients. And how did he know she was single? Maybe she'd moved into Holland House with her husband and children, she reasoned as she stood in front of the antique wardrobe, looking for something to wear.

"Wear something pretty," she heard Zack say. Lauren felt the prickle of tears and turned away from the wardrobe, unnerved.

Zack's spirit was urging her to move on, to open herself up to new experiences, but was it his guilt that prompted this encouragement, or her own need to come to terms with the loss she'd suffered? For the first nine months after his death, she'd felt nothing but impenetrable grief, but her feelings had shifted, going from sadness and hopelessness to anger and hurt. Her mother assured her that she was just going through the stages of grief, but her mother didn't know the whole story; no one did. She had to work through her feelings on her own, without involving family or friends. Perhaps it was childish to feel ashamed, or misguided to keep their memories of Zack untarnished, but that was what she'd decided to do when she committed to this period of exile. She had a decision to make, and once she knew how she intended to proceed, she'd tell everyone the truth. But not yet. She wasn't ready to shed light on something she'd kept hidden for the past few months, or to hear everyone's opinions on the subject. This was between her and Zack, and it would remain that way, at least for now.

Suddenly upset, Lauren whipped out her phone and dialed Dr. Kelly's office, hoping it wasn't too late to cancel, but Merielle's voice informed her that the office was closed and gave a number to call in case of emergency. It seemed wrong to call the emergency number simply to weasel out of having a drink with the man, so Lauren disconnected the call and turned back to the meager selection of clothes hanging in the wardrobe. She hadn't brought any of her dressier outfits. She hadn't worn them in ages, and there had seemed no point in lugging extra clothes when she'd be spending most of her time on her own.

She finally selected a cashmere V-neck in hunter green and paired it with the black slacks she'd brought along in case she needed to meet with a client. She hadn't worn any makeup when she saw Dr. Kelly at the office, but some vestige of feminine vanity ushered her into the bathroom, where she applied eyeliner and mascara and dabbed a little lipstick onto her pale lips before releasing her heavy blonde hair from its ponytail.

The sky was full of stars, and a nearly full moon hung majestically over the inky water of the Atlantic by the time Lauren arrived at the waterfront bar. A part of her desperately wanted to turn around and drive away, but she forced herself to leave the sanctuary of her car and walked up the gravel path toward the door. The dining room was spacious and well lit, with waiters weaving between the tables and the hum of conversation spilling through the open doors, but the bar area was surprisingly intimate. Comfortable armchairs and couches stood grouped around small tables that afforded the perfect view of the moonlit bay, and soft music played in the background.

Ryan, who'd been occupying one of the armchairs, got to his feet and came over to greet her, giving her a casual peck on the cheek. "You came," he said unnecessarily.

"I did," Lauren replied, suddenly glad she'd overcome her reservations. It'd been a long time since she'd been out, and it felt nice not to be alone on a Friday night. She took the other chair and Ryan summoned the waiter.

"What will you have?" Ryan asked Lauren.

"Prosecco, please."

"And a glass of Pinot Noir for me," Ryan said. "Are you hungry? We can get a couple of appetizers."

"I'm okay, thanks."

"Maybe later," Ryan said to the waiting waiter. "We'll start with the drinks." He leaned back in his armchair and crossed his legs, looking casual and relaxed. He wore a dark-blue button-down shirt, jeans, and a pair of comfortable-looking suede loafers, making Lauren glad she'd decided to change out of her leggings and sweater.

"You look nice," he said, smiling shyly.

"Thank you," Lauren muttered, disconcerted by his praise. "It's beautiful," she said, gazing out over the moonlit bay to distract him from watching her. "The stars never look this bright in Boston. There's too much light."

"The sky probably looked much the same when the first settlers arrived on Cape Cod," he replied.

"Have you lived here long?"

"All my life. My mother's ancestors settled on Cape Cod in the sixteenth century. The first Hayworth to arrive on these shores was a master builder, and he passed on his skills to future generations. The Hayworths built many of the houses in this area. My paternal great-great-grandparents came here from County Cork in Ireland and settled in Orleans, spawning several generations of fishermen. My dad was the first Kelly to go to college. He taught high school level history. He was the one who got me interested in local lore."

"And who got you interested in photography?" Lauren asked with a smile. Was she flirting?

"My mom, actually. She likes to take pictures. The walls were always covered with family photos and nature shots she'd taken while I was growing up. She especially loves photographing lighthouses."

"Did she take that photo of the lighthouse in a storm I saw in your waiting room?"

"Yes, she did. I love that one. It's one of her favorites, but she gave it to me as a gift when I opened my own practice."

The waiter returned with their drinks, and Lauren took a sip of her Prosecco, nodding in approval. It was delicious. "So, what do you know about Holland House?" she asked, reminding him why they were there.

"Not much," Ryan replied, grinning sheepishly. "I invited you out under false pretenses. I just wanted to have a drink with you."

"Do you have drinks with all your clients?" Lauren asked, miffed at being duped.

"Only the ones I want to get to know better." Ryan's expression grew serious when he realized she was angry. "Look, I am sorry if I made you uncomfortable. You're actually the first client I've ever seen outside the office—by design, that is. I run into my clients all the time. This is a small town."

"It's fine. I'm glad I came," Lauren admitted.

"Ah, so you did want to see me again," he said, his eyes twinkling with amusement. "Either that or you're starting to feel lonely in that big, empty house."

Lauren glanced away. Was it that obvious that she was lonely? Some women wore their widowhood like a shield, using it to keep out the world that refused to stop spinning despite their loss, but although she wasn't ready to embark on a new relationship, she didn't want to come off as someone who was wallowing in grief, giving off waves of loneliness and impenetrable sadness.

"It is a bit quiet," she agreed. "I've lived in Boston all my life. I'm used to traffic, noise, and crowds."

"I went to school in Boston, but I was glad to come home. I love it here, especially in the off-season. There are some mornings when it's overcast and the fog still hasn't burned off and the beach feels completely deserted, as it must have been before anyone settled here. There's an eerie stillness that envelops you in its embrace, and the waves lap at the shore, rolling in faster and faster as the tide comes in. It's perfect. And then Jack, my dog, spots a squirrel and it all goes to hell in a handbasket."

Lauren took a leisurely sip of her drink and reflected on what Ryan had described. It had been foggy and silent only that morning, the mist moving stealthily between the trees and shrouding the dock in a thick blanket of white. She'd heard the blast of a foghorn somewhere in the distance and had looked away from the vast emptiness beyond, feeling uncomfortably isolated. Had the woman she'd seen that first morning felt the same when she'd looked out the window of her house on the hill?

"Surely you must know something about Holland House, having lived here all your life," Lauren said.

"Only that it's said to be haunted, which is nonsense, of course. Any house that's seen several generations of people carries some footprint of their lives; it's only natural, but that doesn't mean their spirits are actually hanging around, spooking the current residents."

"Tell me about Orleans, then," Lauren invited. Learning about the town would give her a starting point in her research if she decided to pursue her idea.

"That I can do," Ryan replied. "This area was first settled at the end of the seventeenth century by Pilgrims who left the Plymouth colony in the hope of securing arable tracts of farmland. It was sparsely populated, and its industry revolved around fishing, whaling, and farming. Most houses were very modest, which made Holland House an oddity when it was built, since it was quite sizeable. The inhabitants of the house didn't farm the land, nor did they join the ranks of men who went out to fish, which set them apart from the community. Over time, the Holland family became one of the most prominent in Orleans."

"That's a French name, isn't it?"

"Yes. Orleans was named after Louis Philippe II, Duke of Orleans, in honor of France's support of the American colonies during the Revolutionary War, but at the time Holland House was built, this area was considered the southernmost parish of Eastham. To be honest, I never really looked into the history of the house. My interest always lay in Hog Island, which is clearly visible from Holland House."

"Are you going to tell me what's so special about this island, or will I have to guess?"

Ryan laughed softly. Lauren thought he might have blushed, but the lighting was too dim to tell for certain. "When I was a boy, I went through a prolonged pirate phase," Ryan said, smiling at the memory. "My grandfather told me the story of Captain Kidd and his treasure, and it captured my imagination."

"And who, exactly, was Captain Kidd?" Lauren asked, giggling when Ryan gave her a stare of mock horror.

"You've never heard of Captain Kidd?"

"Not that I can recall, no."

"Captain Kidd was a seventeenth-century Scottish sailor who became a notorious pirate. Legend has it that he buried part of his treasure right here on Hog Island. The greater part of his loot was said to be buried on Gardiner's Island off the coast of Long Island. He was arrested and eventually executed. The treasure he left behind was never unearthed, either here or on Long Island, but it wasn't for lack of trying. People have been looking for it for centuries. If you row out to the island, you can still find broken shovels and dug-out pits where treasure hunters tried their luck. It's believed that he revealed the exact location of the loot to his wife in one of his letters, but no such letter ever came to light. When I was a boy, I was convinced that I would be the one to find the treasure and become rich and famous."

"And how did that work out for you?" Lauren asked, trying to imagine Ryan as a boy.

"Not well. Like many others before me, I failed to find any trace of the booty."

"That's a shame," Lauren replied.

"Don't I know it. When I was about ten, being a pirate seemed like the most romantic of occupations. Had someone told me I'd be neutering dogs and putting beloved pets to sleep, I would have had them walk the plank."

"Life has its own plan, doesn't it?"

"It certainly does."

"And what does your daughter want to do? Would she like to follow in your footsteps and become a veterinarian?"

Ryan looked momentarily blank, then smiled and nodded as if he'd just gotten the punchline of a joke. "Merielle is not my daughter. She's my little sister. She'll be going to UMass in the fall, but she's helping me in the office until then. She says I'm a great boss," he added smugly. "Really understanding."

"Is a lot of understanding required?" Lauren asked, curious what he meant.

"She's an eighteen-year-old girl who likes to party. Need I say more?"

"No, I guess not. I haven't had any dealings with teenagers since I was a teenager myself, but I can imagine."

"So, what do you do when you're not skulking around historic houses?" Ryan asked.

"At the moment, I work as a ghostwriter."

"What does that entail?" he asked.

"Ghostwriters are usually hired by people who want to write a book but don't have any writing ability to speak of, most often for the purpose of writing an autobiography. Sometimes, established fiction writers hire ghosts to increase their output. They provide the ghostwriter with an outline and have them write the story in the writer's name, preferably copying their style of writing."

"Isn't that cheating?" Ryan asked.

"It's perfectly legal. Many big-name writers use ghosts, but they usually give them credit for the work."

"Are you working on something now?"

"I'm writing an autobiography of a well-known reality star."

"Anyone I'd be familiar with?" Ryan asked.

"Oh yes, but I can't tell you her name. I'd be violating the terms of the contract."

"And how is it progressing?"

"With excruciating slowness. I usually have a good working relationship with my clients, but this woman could probably make the Dalai Lama lose his cool. It's nearly impossible to get her to concentrate for longer than a minute. She's constantly on her phone, checking the number of her Twitter followers and posting selfies. She thinks I can write the book without her input."

"Have you ever tried writing under your own name?" he asked, watching her with interest.

"Yes, but I haven't written anything new since… I'm sorry, I can't…" Lauren looked away as tears threatened to fall. She didn't want to talk about Zack or her reasons for leaving Boston. She was shocked to realize that until Ryan had brought up the past, she'd gone a whole half hour without thinking about Zack, something that hadn't happened since he'd left on his first tour. Lauren angrily wiped away the tear that slid down her cheek and fumbled in her bag for a tissue.

"I'm sorry if I've upset you," Ryan said, his expression somber. "I didn't mean to pry."

Lauren made a dismissive gesture with her hand. "It's not your fault. You couldn't have known. Look, I'm sorry, but I should get going. Thank you for the drink." She stood, and Ryan instantly sprang to his feet.

"Are you sure you won't stay for another drink?"

"Thanks, but no. Have a good night."

Lauren grabbed her purse and headed for the door, hurrying to her car as if someone were giving chase. Once safely inside, she drove back to the house and let herself in, tears spilling down her cheeks as she scooped a sleepy Billy out of his crate and carried him upstairs to her bedroom. She wasn't even sure why she was crying. She'd been having a nice time. Perhaps she simply wasn't ready. After Billy used the wee wee pad in the upstairs bathroom, she deposited him on the bed, changed into her favorite pajamas, turned off the light, and climbed into bed.

As Billy settled himself against her hip, her gaze slid to the moonlight-painted desk beneath the window. Her laptop and notepad covered most of the surface, her modern pens and highlighters occupying the very place where the inkwell had stood. As Lauren lay sleepless, she couldn't help but wonder if the mysterious woman would come to her again. Who was she, and what kept her tethered to this world?

Chapter 5

Sophie
Boston, Massachusetts
April 1726

Sophie pressed her nose to the window, her heart hammering with anticipation. The night before, she'd seen the proud shape of the *Sea Falcon* on the horizon, the three-masted frigate as familiar to her as the storefront of her father's printshop. The ship would dock in the morning and then the offloading would begin, the crates and casks newly arrived from England and the Caribbean deposited onto the dock and sent to the warehouses that fronted the wharf. Sophie had no interest in the cargo, but in the crew, which would come ashore once the ship had been fully unloaded and inspected. With luck, she would see Teddy tomorrow, but she couldn't pass up the opportunity to get a glimpse of him as he made his way from the docks toward his mother's house, just a few doors down from the printshop.

Teddy's homecoming always followed the same pattern. He ate his fill of whatever Mrs. Mercer served up, asking for seconds and even thirds, and wiping his plate with a piece of bread until the dish was so clean it looked as if it needed no washing. After weeks aboard the ship, subsisting on a meager diet of salt pork, hardtack, and ale, he was starved for homecooked food and bread that didn't threaten to break his teeth when he bit into it. Finally sated, Teddy would take a bath to wash off the sweat and grime of the voyage, and then, after a good night's sleep, he'd come to see Sophie, or more accurately, send her a signal to meet him at their secret place since her father would never allow Teddy to call on her openly.

Sophie had known Teddy her whole life, but it was only recently that their friendship had evolved into something that was best kept hidden from her father's watchful gaze. Teddy had been a steady presence in her life, treating her like one of his sisters after her mother died in childbirth when she was eight. Teddy had been ten, a lanky lad who'd always had a smile for her and a little treat when she was feeling sad or neglected. He'd taken her for walks along the docks and showed her the different types of ships and told her of his dreams for the future. Sophie would have listened to him even if he'd chosen to recite the alphabet or quote passages from the scripture. She liked being with him and enjoyed the sense of belonging she felt when she was with Teddy and his siblings. It was as if she were a part of the Mercer family, that loud gaggle of kids who appeared so happy to her young eyes and had a loving, gregarious mother to come home to—unlike Sophie, who returned to the silent rooms above the shop where she lived with her father. As soon as she walked through the door, the melancholy settled like a heavy mantle on her shoulders, crushing her spirit and reminding her just how alone she'd felt since the death of her own mother.

Her father loved her; she was in no doubt of that, but he'd always been a quiet, undemonstrative man, who spent most of his waking hours in the shop, talking softly to his printing press as if she were his one true love. Agnes, their servant, had been meant to keep an eye on Sophie during the day, but the girl, who'd been only fifteen to Sophie's eight, was run off her feet and neglected her duty where her young mistress was concerned, leaving Sophie to her own devices much of the time. In the evenings, Sophie had supper with her father and then they sat by the fire, most often in companionable silence. Mr. Brewster, still grieving for his wife and stillborn son, had no notion of how a little girl might be feeling, so made no effort to comfort her in ways that would have made Sophie's isolation easier to bear.

That was Teddy's job. He'd made a dolly for her ninth birthday, complete with black yarn for hair and two tiny buttons for eyes, and said it reminded him of her. That was when he'd started calling her his 'Poppet.' She loved the pet name he'd given her and secretly tingled with pleasure every time he used it, feeling a sense of kinship with Teddy that she felt with no one else. As the years passed, Teddy's sisters had become wary of Sophie, leaving her out of their games and treating her as an outsider, but never

Teddy. He was her best friend, her honorary brother, and her champion.

They'd spent many happy hours together until tragedy struck the Mercer household. Teddy's father, Robin, had been knifed while trying to break up a fight in his tavern, the stomach wound he received too grievous to allow the Mercers to hope for a recovery. Half the street heard the pitiful moans that came from the upstairs window where Mrs. Mercer spent her nights nursing her delirious husband. As soon as the church clock chimed eight in the morning, Mrs. Mercer left Teddy in charge of his father and younger siblings and went to the tavern, where she remained until nearly midnight, cooking, baking, and serving customers with the help of her two eldest daughters. Robin died of his injuries a week after the stabbing, his death drawn out and painful. A few days after Mr. Mercer died, Teddy's youngest sister, Gladys, took ill, leaving Mrs. Mercer unable to tend the tavern. She sat by Gladys's side day and night, but Gladys died all the same and was buried next to her father a week to the day after his funeral.

Mrs. Mercer returned home from the cemetery a broken and desperate woman. She couldn't manage the tavern on her own, not long term. It was a rough crowd that patronized the Rusty Anchor, and she wasn't safe among men who'd respected her husband but had not a whit of restraint when it came to his wife and daughters. Teddy, being only twelve at the time, was too young to take up the reins of the business or keep his mother and sisters safe from the drunken sailors who'd caused the death of his father, so Mrs. Mercer sold the tavern, asking for a fraction of its worth for lack of having a man of business to guide her. She did, however, negotiate that she and her children would remain in the rooms above the tavern for the duration of her lifetime and work the evening shift at the tavern to make ends meet. The new owner, very pleased with himself for swooping in quickly and securing such a bargain, readily agreed to her terms, glad to have someone who already knew the business and was willing to work for less than he'd have to pay a man.

It was then that Teddy had gone to sea to help his mother support the family. He started out as a cabin boy, then became a sailor, and by the age of nineteen gained the rank of petty officer. He dreamed of being elevated to the rank of midshipman, but given his lowly background, that wasn't likely to happen; rank was reserved for the sons of the wealthy and influential. Teddy was happy, though. He liked being out on the open sea a lot better than being stuck behind the bar in a dingy tavern, surrounded by the dregs of society, who were more likely to piss themselves where they sat than settle their bill. He spent months away from home, but when he returned, it was as if no time had passed and Sophie's life was suddenly transformed overnight, her spirits buoyed by Teddy's good humor and endless affection.

Mr. Brewster hadn't strenuously objected to Sophie's friendship with Teddy when she was younger, but once she turned sixteen, his tolerance had seemed to vanish practically overnight.

"I don't want you spending time with Ted Mercer," her father had said, his gaze leveled on her over the gently smoking bowl of his pipe.

"Whyever not, Father?" Sophie had asked, taken utterly by surprise by her father's stern pronouncement.

"Because your association with that boy strains the bounds of propriety, Sophie," Mr. Brewster replied.

"In what way? You've never said aught before," Sophie argued.

"Sophie, after your mother died, you were in need of companionship, so I didn't object when Mrs. Mercer took you under her wing and encouraged your friendship with her children, but you're no longer a child, and neither is he. Ted Mercer is a grown man, and you spending time with him can be misconstrued."

"Are you saying he'll ruin my marriage prospects?" Sophie asked, gaping at her father, her embroidery forgotten in her lap.

Mr. Brewster nodded, clearly relieved he didn't need to explain his decree. "I'm glad you understand, Sophie. Let's not speak of it again. You may, of course, still call on the Mercer girls when Ted is away at sea."

Sophie had chosen not to argue with her father, returning to her needlework as if they'd been speaking of the weather or the running of the household, but she had no intention of obeying. It didn't matter if Teddy scared off potential suitors; he was the only suitor she was interested in. She knew her father wanted what was best for her and had his own notion of the type of man who'd make her a good husband, preferably someone from an old Boston family who was already a partner in a thriving concern. The son of a dockside tavern-keeper who spent his days surrounded by rough seafaring men was not what her father had in mind, especially when the man in question had a mother and several siblings to support for years to come. Had Teddy been an officer in the Royal Navy, an institution her father had great admiration for, he might have been more flexible on the subject, but as Teddy served on a merchant ship, he saw him as nothing more than a glorified sailor.

It was then that their clandestine meetings had begun. Sophie had no hope of meeting Teddy in the evenings, since her father came upstairs as soon as he closed the shop for the night and adjourned to the parlor directly after supper, where he remained until bedtime, so they snatched a few hours together while Sophie went out during the day under the pretense of going to the shops or taking a walk. She was meant to take Agnes with her, but Agnes, who was bone-tired most days, was only too happy to have an hour or two to rest and made no mention to her master that Sophie had ventured out on her own. Sophie never told Agnes she was meeting Teddy, so that Agnes would never have to tell an outward lie if her employer asked where Sophie had gone, and Agnes never asked. She didn't need to. She knew how Sophie felt and saw no reason to be yet another obstacle in her path. Besides, Sophie was beginning to suspect Agnes had a suitor of her own and had hopes of leaving Mr. Brewster's employ at some point.

Sophie's heart leapt with joy when she finally saw Teddy coming down the street. He had his leather kitbag slung over one shoulder and his long strides were those of a man eager to get home, but he slowed his step as he approached the printshop, glancing up at the window where he knew Sophie would be waiting, concealed behind a lace curtain, and tipped his hat. Sophie couldn't see his expression beneath the brim of his tricorn, but she saw his smile, meant only for her, and lifted her hand in greeting. She knew Teddy couldn't see her clearly, but as long as he could see her outline, he'd know she'd been waiting for him and they'd see each other soon. Teddy turned away and continued walking, mindful of the fact that Mr. Brewster might be in the front helping a customer and would see him loitering outside. Once Teddy disappeared into his own house, Sophie left her post by the window and went to the kitchen to check on supper.

"Will you be going to the shops tomorrow, Miss Brewster?" Agnes asked, smiling coyly.

"I think I might. It promises to be a fine day," Sophie replied, grinning at Agnes conspiratorially.

"Yes, I think you might be right. Abundant sunshine," Agnes confirmed as she removed a pot of boiled potatoes from the fire and went about mashing them with unbridled enthusiasm.

Sophie took down several plates from the dresser and went about setting the table for supper. Her father would be up shortly, hungry and tired after a long day in the shop. Sophie was glad Agnes supped with them, providing a much-needed buffer between father and daughter, especially on a day when Sophie could barely hide her glee. She rearranged her features into a mask of dignified composure as soon as she heard her father's heavy tread on the stairs. He nodded to her when he came in and went to wash his hands before taking his place at the table.

"Did you have a good day, Father?" Sophie asked as Agnes brought out the soup tureen and set it on the table.

Mr. Brewster gave Sophie a tired smile. "I did indeed."

"Oh?" Sophie set down her soup spoon, eager to hear the good news.

"I received a large order today," he replied, his gaze meeting Sophie's across the table. "A young gentleman who fancies himself a poet ordered three hundred volumes of his collected works," Mr. Brewster said, grinning. "He is prepared to pay nearly double the going rate if I finish the order within a fortnight."

"How will you manage?" Sophie asked. Her father needed an assistant, but he refused to engage one and declined her offer of help, seeing to both the printing and the running of the shop on his own.

"I will work around the clock if I have to," Mr. Brewster replied. "He happened to mention that he has several friends with literary aspirations. They are not averse to paying to get their efforts printed so they can distribute them to bookshops and give them out as gifts to friends and family. Securing their custom would be quite a coup."

"It certainly would," Sophie replied, genuinely pleased. "I'd be happy to help."

"No need, my dear. No need. I think we're ready for the second course, Agnes," Mr. Brewster said as he pushed his soup bowl away. "Is that boiled beef I smell?"

"It is, sir," Agnes replied, and bolted from the table.

Sophie smiled at her father, free to show her joy without arousing suspicion. Her father thought she was pleased about the order, but her mind wasn't on some young buck's atrocious poetry; it was on Teddy and their long-awaited reunion tomorrow.

Chapter 6

Sophie's heart fluttered with excitement as she dressed for her meeting with Teddy. She couldn't be too obvious in her efforts for fear that her father would notice and grow suspicious, but she did curl the hair around her face with hot tongs and dabbed a tiny bit of rouge on her cheeks. She was as pale as curdled milk after the winter months and didn't want Teddy to find her looking sallow. She kept the rouge well hidden beneath her shifts and stockings since her father would be angry if he ever discovered its existence and would throw it away. He was hopelessly old-fashioned and didn't believe a young girl should resort to artificial enhancement, like the type of women he didn't care to mention in her presence. Sophie examined the effect in her hand mirror, then put on her favorite gown. Its dusty rose hue and cream lace trim set off her dark hair and gray eyes and brightened her complexion.

"How do I look?" Sophie asked Agnes once she was ready to leave.

"Like a peach," Agnes replied, smiling at her. "Don't forget to purchase new needles," she reminded her. Agnes had broken one needle and lost another, so they were down to only two, which were safely stowed in Sophie's workbox.

"I won't," Sophie promised. She donned her cloak and carefully fitted her straw bonnet over her cap, so as not to disturb the curls that artfully framed her face.

"Go on, then," Agnes said as she walked her to the door. "Be sure to be back by dinnertime. I won't lie to the master if he asks where you are."

"Don't worry, I'll be back in time."

Sophie left by the back stairs and walked along Belcher's Lane, then turned left and continued toward Oliver Street, where she and Teddy usually met. There were several shops that she frequented along the street, so if she came across an acquaintance, her presence could be easily explained. It was a fine day and she enjoyed the fresh breeze that caressed her face as she strolled along. She wished she could take off her bonnet and turn her face up to the sun but resisted the urge and hurried along. She couldn't afford to dawdle if she were to be back by noon.

Slowing her steps, Sophie paused in front of Holland's Book Shoppe and looked around. Several people walked down the street, and a blue-bodied carriage rolled past, the matching chestnuts pulling it beautiful beasts, but there was no sign of Teddy. Sophie made a great show of examining the books in the shop window, then moved on to the shop that sold sewing notions. She bought three steel needles and several skeins of thread, then came back out into the street, her eyes scanning the passersby anxiously. Walking along, she bowed her head in dejection. Had Teddy forgotten to come and meet her? Perhaps he was still abed, tired after several months of rising before dawn and long days of hard work.

A strong hand suddenly pulled Sophie into a dim alleyway and pushed her up against the wall. Her assailant blocked the mouth of the alley, shielding her from view should someone take an interest in what was happening. Sophie stifled a scream, her heart beating wildly, first from terror, then from sheer joy. Teddy took her face in his hands and kissed her gently, his blue eyes crinkling at the corners as he gazed down at her. His greatcoat smelled of the sea, and his face was tanned to a deep brown, a testament to months spent in tropical climes.

Teddy stroked her cheek and smiled into her eyes. "You silly goose. Did you think I wouldn't come? I've been counting the minutes till I could finally clap my eyes on you. I just had a small errand to run, and it took longer than I expected."

Teddy reached into his pocket and extracted a small leather pouch. He held it out to her, his eyes suddenly anxious. "I hope you like it. I had it put on a chain for you."

Sophie pulled open the pouch and extracted a silver chain with a smooth round pendant. She held the stone up to the light, mesmerized by the brilliant colors that sparkled in its depths. It wasn't enough to say that the stone was blue; such a simple description wouldn't do it justice. It was a kaleidoscope of color, the flecks ranging from a deep azure to the pale aquamarine of a winter sky and the lush green of spring foliage.

"Oh, Teddy, it's beautiful," Sophie gushed. "I've never seen anything like it."

"It's a Caribbean opal from Jamaica. The chain is long enough that you can keep it hidden from your father's keen eyes," Teddy joked, knowing Mr. Brewster would not approve of a gift from him. "Shall I help you put it on?"

Sophie handed the necklace to Teddy and turned her back to him so he could fasten the clasp. His fingers felt warm and gentle on her neck, and then his lips followed their path, kissing her until she shivered.

"We mustn't," she admonished him, but in truth, she wished they could remain hidden in that alley forever, safe from prying eyes. "I missed you so," Sophie said, turning to face him. "I wish you never had to leave."

"Me too, Poppet, but these separations won't last forever. Two more years at most, till Janet turns fourteen. Then I can see to my own life."

Sophie nodded. Janet was only twelve, and the youngest of Teddy's sisters. Stella had married last year, and Barbara had found employment as a maid at the home of a British captain. Mrs. Mercer would have a much easier time of it once the remaining two girls either wed or found suitable employment.

"Sometimes I wish my ma would remarry," Teddy said. "There have been one or two interested parties, but Ma saw them off right quick."

"She loved your father, Teddy. She doesn't want to be disloyal to him."

"You can't be disloyal to someone who's dead. My da, God rest his soul, brought it all on himself. Should have let those thugs kill each other, but no, he had to get in the middle, break up the fight. Well, you know where that got him. He left my ma with nothing, not even enough money in the till to bury him properly. Mr. Smithson robbed her blind when he negotiated the purchase of the tavern, gave her a fraction of its worth, and she accepted his offer and said, 'Thank ye kindly, good sir.' The woman doesn't have the brains she was born with. Just gave it all away for a roof over our heads. Not even a bit extra to see us right in the world."

"Teddy, don't judge her so harshly. She was grieving for your father and frightened for the future. She did what she thought was best."

"Which is why she should have had the wisdom to seek counsel. Should have had a man negotiate for her, not go in on her own, tears still not dry on her face. That scoundrel took her for all she was worth. I'm sorry, sweetheart," Teddy said, shaking his head in dismay. "I do go on and on, don't I? It's just that I'm still in a rage about the whole sorry business. I have my ma and my sisters to support when I'd rather be supporting my wife. You are the only reason I come back, Sophie. You are the shining light on the water, the beacon that guides me to shore," Teddy said, his eyes glowing with love. "Come, let's go take a walk."

Sophie threaded her arm through his and they walked out of the alley, heading toward South Battery.

Sophie kept her head bowed, as if she were listening to what Teddy was saying with great interest, but in reality, it was to hide her face from anyone who might recognize her and feel it their duty to report to her father that she'd been seen in the company of a young man. Once they neared the harbor, there was less chance of being recognized since Horace Brewster's acquaintances did not frequent the area.

"When are you shipping out again?" Sophie asked, lifting her eyes to gaze upon Teddy. She hated that she worried about parting from him as soon as they were reunited, but such was the lot of a sailor's sweetheart. Shakespeare had known nothing when he'd said that parting was such sweet sorrow. There was nothing sweet about it, only bitter hurt and lonely tears.

"Not for another few weeks," Teddy replied. "The ship needs repairs. She sustained some damage to the hull during the last storm."

"Was it bad?" Sophie asked, her heart thudding. The *Sea Falcon* going down in a storm was her worst fear, but Teddy shrugged it off as if it were nothing more than a spell of wet weather.

"Nothing she couldn't handle. She's a tough old girl," Teddy said affectionately. "And Captain Barker knows what he's about. Don't you worry about me, Poppet. I'll always come back to you," Teddy said, lowering his head to kiss her.

Sophie melted into him, relishing the comforting strength of his body and his warm lips on hers. The kiss left her breathless.

Teddy wrapped his arms around her and held her close. "Can you get away for a few hours in the evening?" he asked, his voice soft and cajoling. "There's something I want to show you."

"What?" Sophie asked, wondering where he might want to take her in the evening. Teddy often went to a chophouse for supper or to a tavern for a jar of ale with members of his crew, but she could hardly go with him. A woman was only welcome in a tavern if she were dining in the company of her husband, and even then, the married couples were usually seated in a separate parlor. Sophie could never go where Teddy went, not if she wished to keep her reputation intact.

Teddy leaned closer to her, his warm breath caressing her temple. "The *Sea Falcon* is empty in the evenings while it's being repaired, save for a nighttime watchman, who's a friend of mine. I can show you the ship," he whispered.

Sophie's heart leapt with nervous excitement. The few minutes they'd spent in the alley was all the privacy they were likely to get. They hadn't been alone since they were children and hid in the cellar of the tavern while playing a game of hide-and-seek. The thought of meeting Teddy frightened and excited her at the same time. What would it be like to be away from prying eyes, to feel safe in his arms and enjoy his kisses without fear of discovery? Sophie felt a fluttering in her belly, as if dozens of anxious butterflies beat their wings in unison.

"My father plans to stay late in the shop this week," Sophie said, her voice catching with nervousness. Her father would be furious if she were caught, but she could conceivably sneak out and be back in her bed by the time he returned.

"Why's that?"

"He's taken on an urgent commission. With business being slow, he could hardly turn it down," Sophie explained.

Teddy lifted an eyebrow in surprise. "Why is business slow?"

Sophie shrugged. The last thing she wanted was to talk about the printshop, but Teddy seemed genuinely interested. "Father's been turning business away," she explained. "He refuses to print any seditious material for fear that he'll be implicated should their literature be seized by the authorities. Once he turned the rabble-rousers away several times, they stopped coming. I suppose they found someone else to do their bidding."

"Hm, I see," Teddy said. "Too bad, that. There are those who have coin to spare and are willing to pay to spread their discontent. Your father is a fool to let them take their business elsewhere."

"Father would never do anything illegal. It's not in his nature."

"A printer doesn't need to agree with the sentiments he prints. It's a job, no more, no less."

"Yes, but the printshop is our livelihood, and should it be shut down, we'll be destitute," Sophie replied.

"Of course. I understand," Teddy said, the thoughtful look in his eyes replaced by a merry twinkle. "So, will you meet me, then?"

"What time?"

"At dusk, by Gray's Wharf."

"I'll be there," Sophie promised. They were near the printshop now and it was time for her to go in since it was almost noon and her father would expect to see her at the dinner table.

"I'll be waiting," Teddy said. He lifted her hand to his lips and kissed it formally before walking away, his stride purposeful and his greatcoat billowing in the breeze like the sail of a ship.

"I'll be there," Sophie whispered, and hurried home.

Chapter 7

Gray's Wharf was deserted, the only sounds the lapping of water against wooden hulls and the creaking of masts as they swayed in the wind. A three-quarter moon glowed sullenly from behind passing clouds, casting an eerie light on the black masts silhouetted against the dusky sky, the crossbars like ghostly limbs reaching outwards from skeletal bodies. A single lantern on the deck of the *Sea Falcon* cast a pitiful orb of light that beckoned Sophie forward. She huddled deeper into her cloak and peered into the gathering darkness, relieved to see Teddy striding toward her. Even in the dark, she could see the smile on his face and allowed herself to relax. With Teddy there, there was nothing to fear.

Teddy wrapped his arm around her and pulled her close, brushing his lips against her temple. "I'm sorry. Had to stop for this." He showed her a dark-colored bottle that had a wide bottom and a narrow neck.

"What is it?"

"A bribe."

Teddy took her by the hand and pulled her up the narrow gangplank and onto the deck of the *Sea Falcon*. The deck rolled gently beneath her feet and she grabbed onto Teddy's arm for fear of losing her balance. He chuckled and guided her toward the bridge, where a burly sailor sat on a barrel, watching their approach with interest. He was armed with a musket and had a pistol tucked into the waistband of his breeches. Teddy held out the bottle, and the man snatched it eagerly.

"Madeira?" he asked, licking his lips in anticipation.

"From Portugal," Teddy replied. "Only the best for you, Roy."

He took a healthy swig and rolled his eyes heavenward. "Thank you, my friend. This will get me through the next few nights."

"Enjoy."

"And who is this lovely lady?" Roy asked, his tone implying that Sophie was anything but.

"You just mind your own business and we'll get on just fine," Teddy replied archly.

"All right, all right, don't get yourself upset, Ted. I was only being friendly-like."

"No need to be friendly. Just turn a blind eye, friend," Teddy replied, giving Roy a conspiratorial smile. "My lady wants to see where I spend my days when I'm away from her."

"Nothin' wrong with that," Roy said. "Wish I had me a lady who's so interested."

"Clean yourself up a bit and you just might find one," Teddy teased.

"Not all of us can be as pretty as you are, lad. Go on, then. I'll be right here, with my other love." He raised the bottle in a silent toast and took a swig.

"Come, Sophie, let me show you around," Teddy said, placing his hand on the small of her back as he guided her toward the prow of the ship. He stood behind her, arms wrapped around her waist as she looked out over the harbor. A chill wind pulled at her cloak and hair and nipped at her cheeks. Sophie turned her face into its breath, wondering if that was how it felt to be out at sea. She was more comfortable with the rolling of the deck now, but the creaking of the wood sounded ominous to her ears. It was as if the ship were a living thing, a crotchety old woman who wasn't pleased with their presence.

"Let's go down," Teddy said. "It's cold out here."

Teddy lifted an unlit lantern from one of the hooks and coaxed a flame into life before leading her down narrow steps into the bowels of the ship. The light of the lantern did little to penetrate the pitch-black of the hold. The light shifted from side to side as the lantern swayed in Teddy's hand, casting odd shadows onto the thick walls and the empty hammocks that swung gently, as if cradling ghostly occupants. There was very little space between the hammocks, and despite being empty, the hold smelled of stale sweat, human waste, and loneliness.

"Is this where you sleep?" Sophie asked, looking at the neat rows of hammocks and shivering inwardly. She couldn't imagine spending months on end in such close proximity to other people, not only during the day, but even at night.

"Yes. It's quite comfortable, really," Teddy assured her, but she didn't quite believe him. He was the type of person who always made the best of any situation and didn't dwell on the things that upset him; instead he worked to resolve them to the best of his ability. Teddy was a fighter, a survivor, someone who didn't allow hardship to define him. She supposed it was those qualities that had endeared him to her when she was a child. He always made her feel as if nothing was too difficult to overcome.

They left the sleeping quarters and made their way to the cargo hold, which was empty and dark, like the yawning mouth of a cave. A narrow cell was situated behind the stairs, the door fitted with a metal grille and an iron latch.

"What's that for?" Sophie asked, shuddering involuntarily.

"It's the brig," Teddy explained. "It's not as bad as all that," he said, sensing her unease. "I'd take incarceration over a flogging any day," he joked.

"Teddy, can we go up?" Sophie pleaded, her voice swallowed by the ominous creaking of the ship. "I'm frightened."

"Of course. I'm sorry, Poppet. I thought you'd want to see where I spend my days and nights."

"I do, but I'm sure it's a lot more cheerful when the sun is out and when there are other people aboard."

The walls of the hold seemed to be closing in on her, stoking her anxiety. She longed to be outside in the cold air with the meager light of the moon lighting the harbor.

"Come." Teddy took her hand and led her back toward the ladder. "Up you go."

Sophie inhaled deeply the moment she was back on deck, thankful to be outside. She looked toward the main mast, where Roy was nursing his Madeira, his gaze fixed on the spiderweb of rigging above his head. Sophie turned toward the gangplank, but Teddy pulled her back.

"Wait, there's something else I want to show you," he said softly. He led the way toward the back of the ship.

"This is called the stern, and this is where the cabins are. These two are for the quartermaster and the doctor. It doubles as his surgery. And this one is the captain's cabin." He opened the door and invited her to follow him inside.

The captain's quarters were a surprise. The cabin was roomy, and the back wall had a row of windows that would make it light and airy during the day. There was a good-sized bed hung with heavy maroon hangings, a massive desk, a high-back chair, and a bookshelf filled with well-read volumes. There was even a rug on the floor and several potted plants on the windowsill. Unlike the dark, cramped quarters of the crew, the cabin was cozy and comfortable, a pleasant refuge from the daily chaos of life aboard a ship.

Teddy shut the door and set the lantern on the desk, then removed his hat and shrugged off his coat. He approached Sophie slowly, his fingers nimble as he untied her cloak and tossed it onto the bed. His lips were warm and soft on hers and he pulled her close, crushing her breasts against his chest.

"Teddy, I…"

"Shh," Teddy whispered against her lips. "No one will bother us here."

"I don't think…"

Teddy took a small flask out of his waistcoat pocket and unscrewed it. "Here, have a nip."

"What is that?"

"Portuguese Madeira. I siphoned some off for us," he added with a grin. "Drink."

Sophie took a sip of the wine. It was thicker and sweeter than the wine she was accustomed to, but she could taste its potency. A small glass of this would be enough to make her quite drunk. She took one more sip and handed the flask back to Teddy. "I don't like it."

He laughed softly and took a few sips. "I do."

Teddy set the flask aside and pulled her to him again, his lips finding hers. This kiss was different from the tender kisses they'd shared over the past few years. It was urgent, demanding, and a little frightening. Teddy's hand crept up to cup her breast, his thumb massaging her nipple through the layers of fabric. She knew she should put a stop to this, ask Teddy to walk her home, but the desires he was stirring within her were new and exciting, and she gave herself up to the kiss, convinced there could be no harm in a few moments of innocent passion.

Teddy walked her backward toward the bed and pushed her down, his mouth never leaving hers as he continued to caress her. She hardly noticed when he pulled out her tucker and slid his hand inside her bodice, cupping her breast and freeing it from its constraints. Sophie gasped as Teddy flicked his tongue over the tip of her nipple, then closed his lips over it and sucked it into his mouth like a hungry babe.

"Oh Teddy," she moaned as he continued his tender exploration, his hand sliding beneath her skirts and moving up her stockinged leg and beyond. Teddy's fingers brushed the bare skin of her inner thighs, then crept further, sliding between her legs. Sophie cried out in alarm, but Teddy silenced her with a kiss, his fingers sliding into her moist center and probing her in a way that was shockingly intimate. Sophie knew this was her cue to stop, to demand that he respect her wishes and take her home, but she couldn't find the strength to ask him to stop. The feelings surging through her were like nothing she'd ever experienced. They were urgent and surprisingly pleasurable. She didn't want him to stop; she wanted him to continue.

Sophie had always wondered what it would be like to be married, to share a bed with a man and be expected to perform her wifely duty. She didn't know precisely what the act entailed, but she understood the basic principle and had found it shocking in the extreme—unpleasant at best, horribly embarrassing and painful at worst. But over the past year, the idea of Teddy touching her intimately hadn't seemed as mortifying, and the prospect of bringing him pleasure filled her with joy. She'd do whatever it took to keep him happy, to be a good and loving wife, and if loving him meant allowing him access to her body, then she was more than willing. If what he was doing to her was a taste of married life, then she was ready.

"Oh, dear God," Sophie moaned, arching her back.

"Don't take the Lord's name in vain, darlin'," Teddy said with a soft chuckle. He continued to caress her, his fingers sliding in and out until her insides quivered with unbearable pleasure that seemed to radiate from her very core to the rest of her body, making her feel drowsy and limp. Teddy leaned down and gave her a soft kiss. "There now. Wasn't that nice?"

"Yes," Sophie whispered. She didn't care to imagine how Teddy saw her at that moment, lying there with her legs spread and her breasts spilling over her bodice, but the look in his eyes assured her he didn't think any less of her. In fact, the desire in his eyes took her breath away. His gaze never left her face as he withdrew his hand and licked his fingers, one by one, smiling like a cat that got at the cream. Sophie's cheeks flamed with embarrassment and she turned her head away, suddenly ashamed of what she'd let him do.

"Don't look away."

"I'm s-sorry," she stammered.

"And don't be sorry, either. I've spent many a night lying in my hammock, dreaming of touching you like I just did. I imagined you moaning with pleasure and begging me to take you, your gaze clouded with desire, your legs spread in anticipation."

"But you didn't," Sophie said, confused. "You didn't take any pleasure for yourself."

"Tonight was all about you. I wanted to see your face as you experienced pleasure for the first time. I wanted to make you happy," he added shyly.

"I want to make you happy as well," Sophie said as she sat up and looked up into Teddy's blue gaze. "I want to please you."

Teddy got out of bed and held out his hand, pulling her to her feet. "Fix your clothes and I'll walk you home. I wouldn't want your father to find you gone when he returns."

Sophie shook out her skirts, tucked her hair into her cap, and made sure the lace tucker covered her breasts before donning her cloak and fastening the ties. Teddy reached for his coat and hat, and within a few moments they were back on deck. Roy raised a hand in farewell, his gaze glazed with wine.

"What would happen if someone found out we came here tonight?" Sophie asked as they descended the gangplank.

"Roy and I would get flogged within an inch of our lives," Teddy answered, his tone nonchalant.

"Does Roy know that?" Sophie demanded, wondering if Roy had unwittingly made himself an accomplice.

"Of course, he does," Teddy replied. "Roy would risk the noose for a few hours of oblivion. Don't worry, Soph; no one will find out. Tonight will forever remain our secret." He tucked her arm through his, and they set off for home.

A strange halo surrounded the moon, distorting its shape and dulling its cold light as it glowed from behind ominous-looking clouds. The wind tore at Sophie's cap, and the thick mist that permeated the air made her skin feel damp and cold. They walked briskly along the docks, eager to get home. Teddy escorted Sophie as far as the back door, which she had left unlatched before slipping out, and pressed her to the wall, his tricorn blocking out all light. He tipped her face up and kissed her gently.

"Goodnight, my beautiful Sophie."

"When will I see you?" Sophie whispered, her voice catching with anxiety. She sounded desperate but couldn't bear to leave things unsaid. She needed to understand how what had happened on the ship had changed their relationship and what she was to expect in the future.

"Why, tomorrow, of course," Teddy replied, smiling down at her. "And the day after that. And the day after that." He kissed the tip of her nose and walked away, leaving her leaning against the side of the house, her knees weak with longing.

Sophie slipped inside and crept upstairs to her bedroom. The house was quiet, other than the faint clicking of the printing press on the ground floor. Her father was still working. She climbed into bed and blew out the candle, her virginal nightdress covering the skin Teddy had touched only minutes before. She'd been so ignorant, so naïve of what it meant to be a woman. Never had she imagined that the pressure of warm lips, the flick of a tongue, or the touch of a gentle hand could bring such pleasure, and such surprising awareness. Her body thrummed with newly awakened desire, and her mind grappled with what it all meant. Meeting Teddy for a walk or stealing a kiss had been the extent of her fantasies until tonight, but suddenly, it was as if a hidden door had opened, revealing a room full of forbidden desires and untold pleasures, and suddenly Sophie felt as if she couldn't wait another day. She wanted to be with Teddy, to be his wife, his companion. He'd said it might take two more years, but that seemed like an eternity. She was eighteen years old, ripe for marriage. Sophie's bubble of happiness burst as she contemplated the hardships that lay ahead.

Chapter 8

Teddy was true to his word, and they saw each other nearly every day, going for walks along the docks, eating meat pies Teddy bought from a stall by the wharf, and traipsing through the fields that surrounded Boston proper. They never returned to the *Sea Falcon* for fear of getting caught but found creative new ways of snatching a few minutes of privacy. On his last day, Teddy borrowed a friend's trap and took her for a drive in the country, desperate to spend his last few hours alone with her. The sky was the exact color of his eyes, and the spring air was filled with birdsong as Teddy finally made love to her beneath a canopy of newly greening leaves in a forest on the outskirts of Boston.

Sophie cried out when Teddy breached her maidenhead and tried to wriggle away from him, her body rebelling against the intrusion, but once the pain subsided, discomfort turned into pleasure and she marveled at the way Teddy filled her, stretching her to accommodate his need, their bodies fitting as if they'd always been meant to come together as one. Never had she felt as connected to another human being as she did that day, but their newfound intimacy made it that much more difficult to say goodbye when Teddy walked her home that afternoon after returning the trap.

"I don't want you to go," Sophie said, tearful despite her best efforts not to allow herself to cry.

"I'll be back before you know it. Look after yourself and try to enjoy the summer. Spend more time outdoors. You're so pale, so thin," he said, cupping her damp cheek. "I want to see you looking plump as a partridge when I return," he joked, making her smile. "I love you," he whispered, his eyes warm on hers.

"I love you too," she whispered back. She was crying in earnest now, knowing she'd have to suffer months of acute loneliness before he returned.

"Once we're married, I won't go to sea anymore," Teddy promised. "I'll become a respectable business owner, and we'll get us a sweet little house and make it a home."

"And we'll have lots of children," Sophie said dreamily.

"Well, maybe not lots, but two or three would be nice," Teddy replied, brushing his lips tenderly against hers.

"Teddy, when will we be able to marry?" Sophie asked, hoping his answer might have changed now that they'd lain together.

"As soon as I'm able to afford it, Poppet. I will make it happen; you have my word. Give me a year. Can you do that?" he asked, his tone cajoling as he lifted her face with his finger and smiled into her eyes.

Sophie nodded miserably. A year wasn't a long time, but it felt like an age since she was at the very start of it.

"I will speak to my mother before I leave today and tell her of our intention to marry. I'll explain to her that she must find a way to fend for herself and the girls, now they're old enough to earn a wage. I will still help out, of course, but I must see to my own life now."

"She won't be best pleased," Sophie replied.

"Nor will your father be when he learns of our plans, but their disapproval can't keep us apart, and I'm certain they'll come around to the idea in time. Now, give me a proper kiss and send me off a happy man."

Sophie kissed him ardently, her arms around his neck as he held her close. When they drew apart, Teddy took her hand and kissed it formally, and then he was gone, torn from her once again.

Chapter 9

Sophie spent the day after the *Sea Falcon*'s departure going from one task to another, feeling listless and melancholy. She couldn't settle to anything and found herself drawn to the wharf, staring miserably at the quay where the *Sea Falcon* had been docked only the day before. The spot had been taken by another ship, a British man-of-war, and the docks were a beehive of activity. A young officer politely asked her to move on, for her own safety. She apologized and walked away, her vision clouded with unshed tears. She missed Teddy so much it hurt, and she couldn't help wondering if he missed her as desperately or if he was too busy with his duties to pay her much mind.

That night, her father joined her for a glass of sherry before supper. His fingers were stained with ink, but he'd bathed and changed into a fresh shirt. Horace Brewster sank into an armchair and reached for his pipe, sucking on it greedily for a few seconds before blowing out a whiff of bluish smoke.

"Are you finished with the print order, Father?" Sophie asked, silently thanking her lucky stars for the reprieve she'd been afforded while Teddy was at home.

"The young gentleman collected the volumes today, and he's hoping for a second printing."

"That's good news, isn't it?"

Horace scoffed. "I won't turn a profitable commission away, not with the way things currently stand, but I must admit that I wouldn't mind seeing the back of him."

"Why is that?" Sophie asked. Her father rarely expressed a personal opinion when it came to clients, treating them all with courtesy and respect, but couldn't help passing judgement on the content they paid him to print.

"His poems were—"

Sophie was amused to see her father blush and looked at him innocently as he searched for the right word to describe the young man's endeavors.

"Risqué, I suppose you'd call them," Horace concluded lamely.

"Which means they'll sell out quickly and you'll have to print more," Sophie joked.

"You're probably right. There's an appetite for such a thing, and literature of a scandalous nature certainly sells better than religious tracts or political ramblings."

Sophie was curious to read these poems but knew her father would never permit it, so she didn't bother to ask.

"The *Sea Falcon* has set sail," Horace said conversationally, his gaze fixed on Sophie over the bowl of his pipe.

"Yes," Sophie replied.

"Good. I know the Mercer boy came to see you more than once, Sophie," he said, his brows knitting in disapproval as he held her gaze.

Agnes must have ratted us out, Sophie thought angrily. Agnes was her friend, but it was Horace Brewster who paid her wages, and she knew where her loyalty lay.

"He's my friend. He always has been."

Horace shook his head, his expression one of patient exasperation. "Sophie, Teddy was a good lad growing up, but life changes people. Life has changed him."

"In what way?" Sophie demanded, surprised by her father's claim. He never said much about the Mercer family, and although he made it clear that he disapproved of her friendship with Teddy, he'd never openly criticized him before.

"His father's death changed everything for him."

"That was hardly Teddy's fault," Sophie snapped, defensive on Teddy's behalf.

"You're right, it wasn't his fault, but he's had to grow up fast, and his father's hand was there in the making of him."

"I don't understand what you mean, Father."

Horace sucked on his pipe, looking thoughtfully at his daughter. He seemed to make up his mind and set the pipe momentarily aside. "Sophie, Robin Mercer was not a good man, and he died for his sins."

"He got stabbed trying to break up a fight," Sophie argued.

"I don't know what pretty story Teddy has told you, but his father started that fight. He pulled a knife on the excisemen who demanded to see his cellar. Robin Mercer had been smuggling in French brandy and other contraband for the better part of twenty years. His crimes finally caught up with him and he paid for them with his life. He would have anyhow, had he been taken into custody."

Sophie gaped at her father. That couldn't be true. Teddy had said his father had saved someone's life that night. "No," Sophie said, shaking her head. "I don't believe it."

"Sophie, Mrs. Mercer had to sell everything they had to pay the customs fine. It was either that or be arrested in her husband's place. She'd always known what he was doing, helped him, in fact. She got off easy, in my estimation. The customs men felt sorry for her, seeing as she had six young children to bring up, and a hefty fine is always more useful than a body at the end of a rope. So she sold the tavern along with everything in it—whatever was left after they confiscated all the illegal goods, at any rate. She's been barely getting by these last few years."

"Teddy's doing his best to support his family," Sophie said hotly.

"Teddy is his father's son, dear heart. He's been supporting his family, but not just on his meager wages. He's up to his neck, that boy."

"No!" Sophie exclaimed. "Teddy is an honest and hardworking man. We're going to be married." She froze, realizing what she'd just admitted to, but her father didn't look overly surprised.

"You will never marry Ted Mercer, my girl. I know you care for him, but he has nothing to offer you, and if my opinion of him is correct, he'll find himself going the way of his father one of these days. It'll be the gallows for him if he gets caught red-handed. I will have your word that you won't see him when he comes back, or I will have to lock you in your room for the duration of his stay."

Horace Brewster studied his daughter, his eyes sympathetic. "Sophie, you are young and naïve. You don't know the ugly underside of life. I've tried to spare you that. I wish Teddy well, really, I do, but I won't have him in this house or near my daughter. You'll wed where I tell you, and you'll be glad of it."

No, I won't, Sophie thought defiantly, but she lowered her head, as if in agreement. Teddy would be back in a few months. She just had to bide her time till then.

Chapter 10

Lauren

By the time Lauren woke, mid-morning light was streaming through the window, bathing the room in a peachy glow. She reached for her phone and checked the time. It was after ten, a real treat since these days she rarely slept past six. She must have fallen into a deep sleep after the visitation she'd experienced in the early hours of the morning. She'd seen the woman again, sitting at the desk, her fingers absentmindedly fingering her necklace as she stared out the window, her writing implements and a blank sheet of paper before her. Her expression had been unbearably sad, silvery marks marring her pale cheeks where her tears had dried. She'd sat perfectly still, lost in thought, until her silhouette dissolved in the shimmering light of a new day.

Lauren's gaze drifted toward the writing desk, some part of her almost expecting to see the strange woman still sitting there, but all she saw was her laptop, exactly where she'd left it yesterday. There was no sign of the inkwell or the writing paper, or her unexpected visitor. Had she even seen anything, or was it her imagination playing tricks on her? She'd been under a terrible strain these past few months, but she didn't want to think about the events that had driven her from Boston and brought her to Holland House.

Lauren laughed as Billy nudged her side, his brown eyes accusing as he stared her down. "All right, all right, I'm getting up," she said. Billy was back to his normal exuberant self. He was hungry and more than ready for a walk.

Lauren dressed hastily, then carried Billy to the kitchen, where she filled his bowls and made herself a cup of coffee and a toasted bagel with cream cheese. At home in Boston, she always ate a power breakfast of either whole grain cereal sprinkled with sliced almonds for extra protein or Greek yogurt with fresh berries, but since coming to Orleans, she wasn't in the mood for either and was enjoying her carb fix.

Having finished her breakfast, she pulled on a warm fleece and clipped the leash to Billy's collar. She'd learned her lesson about letting him run free. She had yet to explore her surroundings and looked forward to a long walk through the copse surrounding the house. Lauren left by the front door, wondering briefly if she even needed to lock it behind her. Holland House was like Sleeping Beauty's castle, hidden by overgrown trees and shrouded in a somnolent silence. Unable to set aside the habits of a lifetime, Lauren locked the door and headed down a narrow path that led through the woods.

Arrows of light shone through the newly greening branches, dappling the blanket of last year's leaves with shimmering sunlight. The air was fresh and cool, filled with the sound of birdsong. Lauren held on tight as Billy strained against the leash, eager to explore his new surroundings and sniff at anything that grabbed his attention. Lauren hoped they wouldn't encounter too many squirrels, or their walk would turn into a test of endurance on her part.

Thankfully, Billy was too overcome with all the new sights and sounds to chase after squirrels, so Lauren strolled along, her mind replaying the events of last night. Now that she'd had some time to compose herself, she felt foolish for the way she'd reacted to Ryan's perfectly innocent question. He must think her an emotional wreck, running out on him like that. She wished she could have executed a more graceful exit, but there was nothing she could do about it now, except maybe apologize. She'd try him later, after lunch. Instead, she pulled Billy toward the steep edge of the hill, gazing out over the sunlit waves toward the islands dotting the bay.

She wondered which one was Hog Island. Her brother would love the story of Captain Kidd. Xavier worked in IT, but his dream job would have been to be a treasure hunter. He was fond of saying that the ocean floor was littered with untold treasure, cargo from long-lost ships just waiting to be discovered. He emailed her every news article that mentioned some great find, wishing it had been he who'd gone diving for Spanish gold or Chinese jade. Lauren shook her head in wonder. Men only ever pretended to grow up, but deep inside they were little boys who longed for adventure and excitement. That was why Zack had joined the army straight out of high school; he'd told her as much. He wanted to see the world, fight for democracy, and become someone's hero. There was nothing heroic about dying at thirty-two. To her, it was a terrible waste.

She yanked on Billy's leash, taking out her anger with Zack on the dog. Zack had made a decision that cost him his life, and their future. He'd left her on her own, not only to cope with her grief but to find a way forward, to start afresh when she'd thought her life had been mapped out. Instead of trying for a baby, she'd been playing hide-and-seek with her pain and spending her days on writing an insipid memoir instead of pursuing her own career. Well, it was time to throw off her mantle of misery and make a few choices of her own, Lauren decided as she strode back toward the house. And she would start by researching the history of Holland House. As a writer, she had a nose for a good story, and given what she'd seen in the half-light of dawn, she was sure there was a riveting story right in front of her, just waiting to be told.

Chapter 11

After their walk, Lauren drove into town to visit the Snow Library on Main Street. The one-story building was as quaint as everything else on Cape Cod, its cozy interior nothing like the massive libraries of Boston that held thousands of volumes on every subject under the sun. Several parents and children occupied the low tables in the children's section, but the rest of the library wasn't too crowded. An elderly librarian sat behind a reference desk, reading something on her computer screen, but looked up and smiled as soon as Lauren approached.

"Good morning," Lauren said. "I wonder if you could help me."

"Of course. What were you looking for?" the woman asked.

"I was hoping to find something pertaining to the history of Holland House."

The librarian shook her head, her expression thoughtful. "I don't believe we have anything like that. You see, Holland House has been a part of the landscape for centuries, but it doesn't have any actual historical significance."

"I see," Lauren said, disappointed. "Thank you."

"Is it the house you're interested in or the family?" the librarian asked just as Lauren was about to walk away.

"The family," Lauren replied.

"Information on the family should be easier to find," the librarian said. "This is probably before your time, but Holland Books used to be a very popular book chain in Massachusetts."

She was right; it was before her time. Lauren had never seen a Holland Books store in Boston. "Did they go out of business?"

"They were bought out by a national chain in the 1980s. Couldn't compete with the likes of Barnes & Noble and the Strand Bookstores. They went way back, though, to before the American

Revolution. I'm sure you can find loads of articles online," the librarian suggested.

"Thank you. I'll have a look."

Lauren walked toward the bank of computers and chose the last cubicle, which seemed the most private. She preferred to do research on a desktop computer rather than on her phone since the screen was bigger and she could email the articles to herself if she found anything relevant. Numerous entries popped up when she Googled Holland Books. She decided to start with Wikipedia. The bulk of the entry was devoted to the buyout, but there was also a section pertaining to the history of the chain.

"The first Holland's Book Shoppe, as it was called prior to its name change in early 19th century, was opened in Boston by Mr. Lionel Holland in March 1720. Besides locally printed books and tracts, the shop carried all five local newspapers and offered a variety of books from Europe, making Holland's Book Shoppe the literary hub of the colony. In a bold move designed to solidify his family's success, Mr. Holland opened a sister shop in Cambridge, Massachusetts, installing his son, George Holland, as the manager. Three more branches were in operation by the end of the 18th century. Holland Books was the first commercial chain in New England."

Lauren scrolled through several more articles, but they reiterated what she'd already learned. Given that Holland House was built in the early eighteenth century, it stood to reason that it had been commissioned by either Lionel or George Holland, which narrowed down the field of research considerably. At least now she had names to work with—a starting point.

Lauren logged out and left the library. It was past noon and she was getting hungry. She wasn't a fan of fast food or sandwiches, so she decided to stop by the grocery store and pick up some meat and produce. She was in the mood for a steak and could use another bag of dog food.

Having picked up a nice ribeye, she added some fresh vegetables for a salad, several cups of yogurt and berries, and a gorgeous blueberry muffin that was still warm from the oven, then made her way to the dog food isle. Just as she turned in, a rambunctious preschooler came running toward her, a toy police car in his hand wailing and flashing red and blue lights. The child was headed straight for her shopping cart. Lauren yanked it out of the way just as the child's father caught him and lifted the boy into his arms. Their eyes met, and Lauren was surprised to find herself looking at Ryan Kelly.

"Hello," he said, smiling in a friendly manner.

"Eh, hi," Lauren replied. She'd meant to call him and apologize for her behavior last night but was no longer sure she had anything to apologize for, given that he'd clearly left out some information about his own situation as well.

"Are you all right? You left so abruptly last night," he said. He turned off the siren and handed the car back to the little boy, who seemed disappointed either by the ensuing quiet or by his failed escape attempt. He had a mop of dark curly hair and bright green eyes that sparkled with mischief.

"Yes, thank you. I was just tired," Lauren replied. She wished Ryan would move on, but he seemed eager to talk.

"How's Billy?"

"Oh, he's fine. I took him for a long walk this morning, and he was full of energy and curiosity."

"Glad to hear it. Call me if you have any concerns."

"Thank you. I will."

"Let's go," the child whined.

Ryan smiled apologetically. "Tyler doesn't enjoy food shopping. I would have left him with Merielle, but she had plans," he explained as he sat Tyler in the cart.

"Well, don't let me detain you," Lauren said breezily. "Have a good weekend."

"Yeah, you too."

"Bye," Tyler called out as they walked away.

Lauren picked up two bags of puppy chow and headed toward the cash register, walking slowly to avoid bumping into Ryan Kelly again. Her earlier resolve had been replaced with bitter disappointment. She'd liked the man and had enjoyed his company, but whatever his domestic situation was, he'd clearly played her for a fool. Perhaps he made passes at out-of-towners in the hope that he could have a discreet affair without his wife ever finding out. Well, she wasn't in the market for an affair with a married man.

Once the coast was clear, Lauren paid for her groceries and headed for home. She'd been dragging her feet on the Ashley Mann autobiography for weeks, but now she was eager to finish the project. She felt the familiar buzz of excitement as ideas for a new book took shape, the long-neglected recesses of her mind reminding her that she loved the process of plotting out a story. She'd learn all she could about the eighteenth-century Hollands, but as she was writing fiction, she didn't have to adhere to the facts, merely use them as a guide for her narrative.

Billy was snoozing when Lauren got home, so she put away her groceries and took her yogurt and muffin out onto the patio. It was too nice a day to remain indoors. She broke off a piece of the muffin top and popped it into her mouth before reaching for her phone. Her friend Brooke, who was an estate attorney, subscribed to several sites used by professional genealogists for the purpose of tracking down next of kin for clients who died without leaving a will or didn't have an obvious beneficiary. Maybe Brooke could trace the Hollands for her.

"Hey, stranger," Brooke greeted her when she picked up the call. "I hear you rented a house on the Cape."

"And where did you hear that?" Lauren asked, relaxing into the deck chair. Just hearing Brooke's voice made her feel less lonely.

"From Xavier. Who else? I had lunch with him yesterday."

"Business or pleasure?"

"A bit of both, actually. Didn't he tell you he's been consulting for me? I can't afford a full-time IT person, so he's basically on call whenever I have catastrophic computer issues that threaten to derail my business and drive me insane. My computer crashed yesterday, and I couldn't access the client records. Xavier fixed the problem in under five minutes."

"I'm glad he was able to help."

"He wouldn't hear of me paying him, so I took him out to lunch instead." Brooke sighed dramatically. She'd always had a soft spot for Xavier, but Lauren's brother treated Brooke like an honorary sister. "So, tell me about the house," Brooke invited. "Why did you decide to go now, before the tourist season?"

"I needed a change of scenery. I thought it might help to get away from the apartment and the constant reminders of Zack."

"Look, no offense, but I think you're going about this all wrong," Brooke said gently. "What you need is to get out there, not isolate yourself. Take a class, find a new hobby, take up yoga, or whatever. Do something that involves meeting new people. I know you're still grieving, but you have your whole life ahead of you. You need to live it. That's what Zack would have wanted for you."

"I know, but I'm just not ready. I feel like a turtle that wants to hide in its own shell."

"Even turtles stick their heads out from time to time."

"I met this guy for a drink," Lauren volunteered.

"Really? And?"

"And nothing. I freaked out and walked out on him, and then today, I ran into him at the supermarket—with his son. He sort of forgot to mention he had a family."

"He might be divorced," Brooke suggested.

"He might be, but he never mentioned having a child either."

"And did you tell him about Zack?"

"No. I'm just not ready to talk about him to strangers," Lauren said, feeling the familiar lump in her throat.

"Grieving is a process, Lauren. There are stages."

"Yes, I know. I heard it all from the grief counsellor. Denial, anger, bargaining, depression, and acceptance."

"So, where would you say you're at?" Brooke asked carefully.

"I would say that I have my stages reversed. I'm no longer in denial, nor do I try to bargain with God. I think I'm somewhere between depression and anger."

"Well, the next step has to be acceptance, then."

"I accept that Zack is gone, just as I accept that the life we dreamed of will never be. I feel like someone who's standing on the pavement, watching people having a great time through a window. I know that I can open the door and walk in, but my sadness and fear are holding me back." *And lack of trust*, Lauren added mentally. "It's been a long time since I've been single, Brooke. Putting myself out there is terrifying."

"And do you think it's any less terrifying for the rest of us? I get the shakes and want to cancel at the last minute every time I have a date with a new guy, but you know what? I don't. I get dressed, put on my war paint, and go into battle because I believe—no, I know—that one day, I will meet the one, and then all the heartache and disappointment will have been worth it."

"I've already done all that," Lauren complained.

"Yes, and now you have to do it again. It's either that or living alone for the rest of your life, possibly surrounded by cats."

Lauren laughed. "I promise never to get more than one cat."

"I'll hold you to that. Now, I've got to get going. I have an appointment with a new client in a few minutes."

"Brooke, before you go, there's a small favor I wanted to ask."

"Ask away."

"Can you look up Lionel and George Holland, circa 1728? I'm doing some research and I've hit a dead end."

"Is this for one of your clients or a new book?"

"I'm thinking of writing a historical romance," Lauren replied. If she told Brooke she was contemplating writing a ghost story, she'd never hear the end of it.

"Ooh, a historical romance. Now you're talking," she purred sarcastically. "Why can't you write an edgy thriller? That's what I like to read."

"There's not a romantic bone in your body, you know that?"

"Yeah, so I've been told, but I'm an absolute freak in bed," Brooke announced, making Lauren laugh out loud. "I'll look up your dusty relics and get back to you. *Ciao.*"

"Bye," Lauren said, and ended the call.

Lauren finished her lunch and went back inside. She'd been at Holland House for less than a week, but already the lack of TV and Wi-Fi was making itself known. At home, she often turned on the TV just for the background noise, but here, the silence was absolute. Lauren hooked up her phone to a portable speaker, selected a classical music playlist, and settled on the couch with a notepad. She was itching to jot down some ideas, and since she had no places to be or people to see, she had no excuse for not getting started.

She worked well into the night, stopping often to test her ideas against her scant knowledge of local history. It was difficult to imagine what Orleans, or South Eastham, as it was called then, might have been like three hundred years ago. She supposed the seeds of discontent against the British were already taking root in the bigger cities, but Cape Cod had been sparsely populated, the settlements small and some distance apart from one another. The original owners of the house didn't fish or farm, so how did they survive from day to day? Did they purchase foodstuffs from the local farmers, or did they bring supplies by boat and unload them at the dock? Was this house a summer residence for the wealthy family?

Lauren filled several pages with ideas, and twice as many pages with questions, finally going to bed when her eyes burned with fatigue. The forecast called for rain tomorrow, so she'd have plenty of time to continue, seeing as she'd be stuck indoors all day.

Chapter 12

The rain drummed softly on the roof, its pitter-patter steady and soothing. The room was a study in gray, the corners shrouded in deep gloom. Billy snored softly at the foot of the bed, his little body curled into a shrimplike position. Dawn had come stealthily, the heavy mist and dark clouds obscuring the sky and promising a dreary, wet day.

A movement near the window caught Lauren's eye and she froze, her gaze glued to the chair, which was once again occupied. The woman wore a flowing white garment with ties at the throat— a nightdress, presumably. Thick dark hair cascaded down her back and fell into her eyes as she bent over the desk, intent on what she was doing. She appeared to be writing a letter, the quill flying over the page as she poured out her thoughts. Lauren watched in silent fascination as the woman signed her name with a flourish and lifted the page to give it a final once-over. From her vantage point on the bed, Lauren could see that she had the beautiful penmanship of days gone by, the letters even and rounded. She strained to read the name at the bottom before the woman replaced the letter on the desk, sprinkled something that looked like sand over the page, and folded the missive. Lauren couldn't be sure, but she thought her name might be Sophie.

Her uninvited guest stowed the letter in one of the upper drawers of the desk and stood, arching her back when she placed her hands on her lower back. Her belly stretched against the thin fabric of her nightdress, revealing an advanced pregnancy. The woman came to stand by the window and moved the curtain aside, her hand clutching the heavy fabric. Her hand was almost translucent, with only the dull glint of a wedding band marring the ghostly pallor of her skin. She stood there for several minutes, just looking, searching it seemed like, but then the sky outside began to clear and she grew fainter and fainter, her outline dissolving into the brightening light.

Chapter 13

Sophie
Boston
August 1726

"Sophie, you must come to the garden party. It's going to be the social event of the summer," Amelia Holland gushed as she daintily sipped from her teacup, her fair curls bouncing every time she lifted her head. Her cheeks were flushed, and her wide blue eyes sparkled with excitement. "Father is sparing no expense."

"I'm sure he is looking forward to showing off your new home," Sophie replied, wishing she could muster the enthusiasm Amelia so clearly expected. The Hollands had just built a brand-new house on the shore of Mill Pond, a testament to Mr. Holland's business acumen and eye to the future. He'd recently opened a second bookshop in Cambridge, sending his son to run the business in his stead.

"It's not just that," Amelia said, lowering her voice to a confidential whisper. "No one knows yet, well, no one except the family, but Major Dawson has proposed," Amelia gushed. "Father plans to announce the betrothal at the party. Oh, Sophie, I'm so happy," she exclaimed. "I can't even tell you what a relief it is to have it all settled. I simply cannot wait to be married."

"Congratulations, Amelia. I'm very happy for you, and I look forward to meeting Major Dawson."

"Sophie, he's so handsome and charming," Amelia gushed. "And he will be a baronet once his father kicks the—well, you know…" she added with a merry giggle. "Can you imagine it? Little ol' me, Lady Amelia? Why, I get shivers just saying it out loud."

"Will you go live in England then?" Sophie asked.

"I suppose so, but I don't mind. Really, I don't. It will be great fun. I'm sick and tired of boring old Boston. Jeremy says it's nothing but a colonial outpost, full of provincial merchants who aspire to have the freedoms of the ruling class. I suppose he's referring to Father, but I don't care, not if I get to marry into the ruling class." She giggled again. "Say you'll come, Sophie. You really should, you know, and not just for me," Amelia added, her demeanor changing to one of cool practicality. "There will be a number of eligible young men at the party, Jeremy's army friends and such. It would be a wonderful opportunity for you to meet someone. Oh, I know you have your heart set on Teddy what's-his-name, but think of it, Sophie. You could marry an officer, not some grubby sailor who doesn't have a pot to piss in, pardon my saying so. You have prospects, my dear. Don't throw them away on some childish infatuation."

Sophie didn't bother to reply. How could she ever explain to Amelia how she felt about Teddy? She was happy for her friend and wished her joy in her marriage, but Amelia didn't need her good wishes. She'd be happy regardless. Amelia, for all her outward frivolity, was a shrewd and practical young woman who was determined to better her lot in life through marriage. She wasn't looking for love; she was looking for a golden opportunity, and she'd clearly found one. Sophie was in no doubt that Major Dawson believed himself to be the object of Amelia's maidenly affections, but it was his prospects Amelia was after. The fact that the young man happened to be handsome and charming was a bonus, one Amelia was very pleased with, but Major Dawson, or his future title and fortune, would have been just as attractive had he been short and stout with a receding hairline. Amelia would have surely advised him to keep it hidden beneath a powdered wig, at least in public, and encouraged him to order a male corset to improve his posture and smooth out his paunch. Before he knew it, her husband would cut a dashing figure in Boston society and make Amelia, and her father, proud.

Amelia could never begin to understand Sophie's feelings for Teddy, and Sophie was sorry she'd shared her secret in a moment of weakness. Amelia had never betrayed Sophie's confidence, but she also never missed an opportunity to belittle

Teddy and remind Sophie that she could do so much better than the son of a tavern keeper, conveniently ignoring the fact that she was nothing more than a daughter of a bookseller herself. The only difference was that Lionel Holland was a better businessman than Robin Mercer had been and probably kept his nose clean when it came to paying his taxes.

"We are going to serve strawberry ice," Amelia gleefully revealed. "Can you imagine, serving ice in the middle of summer? Father ordered extra ice during the winter just for such an occasion. We will keep the sweet in the icehouse until it's time, then serve it in little silver cups. Oh, it will be wonderful," she said, clapping her hands. "I can't wait. Jeremy will be so impressed. We might be provincial, but we know how to entertain in style."

The promise of strawberry ice made Sophie's mouth water. Something cool and sweet was just what she needed to make her feel better. The nausea she'd been experiencing for the past few months was finally beginning to abate, but she still couldn't abide the smell of bacon or the boiled beef her father was so fond of. She craved sweets, but Agnes rarely baked in the summer, not wishing to spend any more time than necessary in the sweltering kitchen.

"Of course, I'll come," Sophie said, smiling at Amelia, who was munching on a cucumber sandwich. "I wouldn't miss it for the world."

"It's settled, then. I hope you have something pretty to wear. I'm having a new gown made. It's in the latest style, and I will have a bonnet with a matching ribbon to go with it, and new slippers. I wanted the gown to be blue, to match my eyes, you know, but Mama said a pale yellow will look more fetching. More virginal is what she really means," Amelia said with a knowing chuckle. "As if the color of my gown had any bearing on my purity. I'd never be foolish enough to risk disgrace, not ever. On my wedding night, I'll be as pure as the driven snow, and make no mistake about that. Jeremy will be pleased," she concluded as she set down her cup. "Well, I must get going. I have a fitting in half an hour and Mama will be cross if I'm late. I'll see you soon."

Amelia planted a light kiss on Sophie's cheek and breezed out of the parlor, calling for her maid as she went. Her father wouldn't allow her to brave the streets of Boston without a chaperone, and Sissy, Amelia's Negro maid, was only too happy to visit with Agnes while the young ladies took their tea. Agnes, who'd been born and bred in Boston, felt a deep sympathy for Sissy, who'd never known her family. She'd been brought to Massachusetts from Barbados at the age of ten and sold to Judge Harold Thomas, who in turn had sold her to Mr. Holland two years ago when he no longer had need of her. To date, Mr. Holland owned Sissy and two young men, who looked after his horses and carriage but doubled as footmen when Mr. Holland entertained.

Sophie breathed a sigh of relief once Amelia left. It was exhausting to keep up the pretense of normalcy when her mind was in such turmoil. Sophie's hand went to her swelling belly. She was four months gone with child, but the *Sea Falcon* still had not come into port, leaving her in a constant state of anxiety. Until Teddy returned, she was alone in her predicament, and this wasn't the type of situation that would remain a secret for long. They had to get married as soon as possible, before her father learned of her condition. She'd done everything in her power to keep her secret, even going as far as buying chicken blood at the market to smear on her menstrual rags to keep Agnes off the scent, but as the child grew, no amount of subterfuge would suffice. Only marriage could save her from utter ruin.

Sophie collected the empty cups and saucers and carried the tray into the kitchen, where Agnes was already busy preparing supper. The sight of raw meat nearly made Sophie retch, but she took a deep breath and averted her eyes, hurrying to the slop sink by the window. She quickly washed the dirty crockery and put the clean china back on the shelf before retiring to her room for a brief rest. She hadn't done much since getting up that morning, but she felt mentally drained and physically exhausted. As she lay on her bed, she considered which gown she might wear to the garden party. It was more than two weeks away, and at the rate she was expanding, she'd have to lace her corset very tightly indeed to fit into her best frock, so Agnes's help would be required.

"Oh Teddy, please come back soon," Sophie whispered into the shimmering heat of the August afternoon. "I need you." She wished more than anything that she could hear Teddy's voice through the open window as he greeted his mother and sisters, but all she heard was the low hum of the printing press and the buzzing of a fly trapped in the folds of the muslin curtain. Another day had passed without word.

Chapter 14

"Surely it can't be as bad as all that." The voice belonged to a young man with wavy fair hair pulled back and secured with a black bow, and light blue eyes that gazed at Sophie with concern. His round face was pink from the heat of the afternoon and his stocky form was ensconced in a beautifully made suit of blue-gray silk, his waistcoat embroidered with flowers and butterflies.

"I beg your pardon?" Sophie said haughtily, embarrassed at being caught scowling.

The garden party was a huge success, and Major Dawson was just as handsome and charming as Amelia had promised he would be, but it was an inordinately hot day and after several hours spent outdoors, Sophie was tired and overheated.

"You looked very unhappy, so I thought I might offer my services," the man said apologetically. "Forgive me if I misread your expression."

"You didn't," Sophie admitted. "The truth is that my shoes pinch and I'm rather warm, but there are no seats left in the shade." Presented like that, her predicament didn't sound too daunting, but the young man immediately sprang into action.

"Allow me," he said, taking her by the arm and heading toward a table situated beneath a shady oak where several officers, friends of Major Dawson, no doubt, were enjoying their wine.

"Pardon me, gentlemen, but the lady is a tad overheated and needs a moment to sit in the shade."

Sophie went crimson with embarrassment, her cheeks probably as scarlet as the tunics the men wore, but they all jumped to their feet and offered her and her companion the use of the table. They bowed in unison and left them to enjoy the shade.

Sophie sank into a wrought-iron chair and exhaled with relief. Her shoes weren't new, but her feet were swollen, probably due to the pregnancy that threw some new and hitherto unknown discomforts at her every day. It was marginally cooler in the shade and pleasantly peaceful since most of the guests were congregated in an area closer to the French doors that led into the house.

"May I know your name?" Sophie said to the man, who settled across from her as if he were her escort.

"How rude of me not to introduce myself. I do apologize," he said, looking shamefaced. "I'm George Holland, Amelia's brother." Of course, now that Sophie knew who he was, she spotted the resemblance. She'd heard about George but had never met him.

"Sophie Brewster."

"A pleasure to make your acquaintance, Miss Brewster. I've heard much about you."

"Have you?" Sophie asked in some surprise.

"Naturally. Amelia said you are her dearest friend. I take it she never mentioned me," he said with an amused smile.

"Of course, she has. I just didn't immediately make the connection," Sophie replied, flustered.

"I'm sure we would have met sooner had I not been packed off to Cambridge," he replied, a small smile tugging at the corner of his mouth. "May I fetch you a glass of lemonade? You still look a bit flushed."

"Yes, that would be very kind."

George Holland sprang to his feet and strode purposefully toward the open French doors, giving Sophie an opportunity to kick off her shoes and wiggle her toes. Her feet throbbed from being confined for so long and she wished she could go home, but her father was nowhere to be seen, and she was too tired to go searching for him among the throng of guests, particularly since sitting in the shade of the great oak was so quiet and pleasant.

She watched as Amelia strolled from one knot of guests to another, beautiful in her primrose gown and matching straw bonnet, her arm threaded through that of her intended, who glowed with pride as he accompanied her on her rounds. A dull ache pierced Sophie's heart. When she married Teddy, there'd be no party, no joy, and certainly no parental approval to bask in. They'd have to marry on the sly and then present the *fait accompli* to her father and his mother, who'd probably relent a little once they discovered the reason for their haste. Sophie's hand unconsciously went to her belly, which seemed to have grown since last week.

"Here we are," George said as he set a tall glass of lemonade in front of her. He had two cups of strawberry ice in his other hand and presented the sweet to her with a flourish. "I thought you might enjoy the ice. It's sure to help you cool down, and it is delicious. I was looking forward to it all afternoon," he confessed as he used the dainty spoon to taste the ice. "Mm," he moaned theatrically. "Delightful."

Sophie drank some lemonade before attending to her own ice. It was heavenly, and she was grateful to George for being so thoughtful. "You're a very considerate man," she said as she licked her spoon.

"Not at all. I'm just a man who likes his sweets," he replied. "I could eat this every day. Well, maybe not in the dead of winter," he amended.

"Do you like Cambridge?" Sophie asked as she continued to savor her ice.

"It's not so very different from Boston, in my opinion. There's no harbor, of course, but that makes for less riffraff on the streets, what with the sailors not surging into town every time a ship comes into port."

Sophie ignored the rude reference to sailors and attempted to steer the conversation in a different direction. "Do you enjoy reading, seeing as you have unlimited access to new books?"

George shrugged. "Not really. I find it dull, and I can't abide the scholarly types who frequent the shop. They're always arguing about some minor intellectual point, trying to convince each other of the validity of their arguments, but it's all hogwash to me." He smiled apologetically and set his empty cup on the table. "Are you here with an escort, Miss Brewster? Have I unwittingly stolen you away from some ill-mannered young man?"

"No, I'm here with my father, who's probably talking to one of his many acquaintances. He knows I wouldn't like it if he hovered at my elbow all afternoon."

"Very wise of him, I'm sure," George said. "He'd probably scare off potential suitors, and what young lady would want that, especially at a gathering that's chockfull of dashing men in uniform?"

"I'm not here to find a suitor," Sophie retorted, annoyed by his implication that she was desperate to find a husband.

"I'm sorry," George exclaimed. "I certainly meant no offense. It's just that Amelia…" He allowed the sentence to trail off, probably realizing that what he was about to say would be even more unflattering.

"It's just that Amelia said I was still unspoken for and thought she was doing me a great favor by inviting me?" Sophie said, pinning George with her gaze.

"She said nothing of the sort. Amelia is very fond of you," George replied lamely, looking mortified.

Sophie took pity on him and smiled. "Please, don't worry, Mr. Holland. You haven't offended me in the least. Husband-hunting is the only sport young women are encouraged to partake in, so your conclusion was very astute."

"I didn't mean to make assumptions."

"You didn't."

"That's a unique necklace," George said, his gaze caressing the creamy swell of her breasts above her bodice with barely hidden admiration.

"It was my mother's," Sophie lied. This was the second time she'd fibbed about the origin of the necklace. When asked, she'd told her father that she had bought the necklace for herself with the money she'd saved from the weekly allowance he gave her. Thankfully, he'd accepted her explanation and hadn't mentioned the necklace again.

"I've never seen the like. It must be very special to you."

"It is. I never take it off. Now, if you'll excuse me, I think I'll go find my father. It's getting late, and I'm rather tired."

George stood the moment Sophie rose from her seat. "May I see you again?" he asked, his face coloring in a manner that was endearing. "I'll be in Boston for another week, at least, and it would be my honor to call upon you."

"Thank you, Mr. Holland, but I don't think that would be possible. It was a pleasure to meet you. And thank you for the ice."

Walking away, Sophie could feel George Holland's gaze upon her, trailing her progress. He was a nice man, but she had no need of him. What she needed was Teddy.

Chapter 15

As a blisteringly hot August dragged on, Sophie's anxiety mounted, her desperation taking a toll on her already frayed nerves and weakened body. She was nearly five months gone, and although the initial sickness had passed, she felt unwell most of the time, a condition that was becoming increasingly difficult to hide from Agnes. Her face was permanently flushed from the excessive heat, her hands and feet were swollen by midafternoon, and her breasts spilled over the bodice of her gown in a way that was becoming unseemly. Despite the tight lacing, her belly was clearly visible, and the only thing that kept her condition from being discovered was the bum roll that kept the fabric from clinging too tightly to her waist.

Desperate for something to do to ease her suffering, she took daily walks to the harbor, her eyes searching the horizon for any sign of Teddy's ship, but although she'd spotted a few vessels, none of them proved to be the *Sea Falcon*. When not out walking, she gazed out the window for hours on end, hoping for a glimpse of Teddy's beloved face, but she never caught sight of him. She felt even more dejected when an invitation to Amelia's wedding arrived at the end of August. It was printed on thick, creamy paper and decorated with a tasteful border of silver and peach. The wedding was to be on the fifteenth of October at Old North Church, followed by a reception hosted by Mr. and Mrs. Holland.

Sophie allowed the invitation to flutter to the floor as tears of despair blinded her. She'd be nearly seven months gone by then and wouldn't be able to hide her pregnancy any longer. Even if she and Teddy were married by that time, everyone would know she'd gotten with child long before the wedding; people would make snide comments and her father would be forced to deal with the shame of having a wanton daughter, the proof of her disgrace right there for everyone to see. She would have to decline the invitation, but then Amelia would demand to know why she wasn't coming to her wedding, as would her father, who was on friendly terms with Mr. Holland due to their business association.

No, they would have to accept, and then Sophie would feign illness to get out of attending. That was the only logical solution. She reached down and picked up the lovely invitation, wishing it were an invitation to her own wedding. She dreamed of walking down the aisle toward Teddy on her father's arm—pure and innocent of any wrongdoing, not with an unborn child kicking her ribs as she made her vows.

Sophie angrily wiped away the tears that slid down her cheeks. She'd been weepy for months, the slightest upset bringing her to tears. She knew her melancholy had nothing to do with burnt porridge or spilled milk, or the invitation to Amelia's wedding. She was frightened and ashamed, and a cold sense of dread was becoming her constant companion as the days wore on with no word from Teddy.

It was just as the first days of autumn brought some much-needed relief from the relentless heat that the *Sea Falcon* finally limped into port, its middle mast cracked, its hull marred with ugly patches of tar, and its rigging torn and sagging in places. Sophie breathed a sigh of relief as she watched the great ship drop anchor in the harbor, its journey finally at an end. Teddy was home, and she'd see him in a matter of hours, tomorrow at the latest. He'd make everything all right. She'd no longer have to carry the burden of her pregnancy alone. Teddy would be there to support her and to make the necessary arrangements for their future. She returned home and settled in to wait, but her excitement was too great to permit her to sit quietly. She paced the parlor like a caged animal, her head swiveling toward the window every few seconds to make sure she hadn't missed Teddy walking past.

As the flat light of the afternoon began to fade and the shadows lengthened in prelude to evening, she tried to placate herself with the usual excuses. There was much to do before the crew could come ashore. Teddy had walked by without her noticing. He'd needed to reassure his mother and sisters he was well before coming to see her. He feared her father was already at home and didn't want to risk exposing their courtship.

He'll come tomorrow, Sophie told herself over and over as she prepared for bed, her nervous energy replaced by bone-deep fatigue. Divested of her stays, her belly popped out and she felt the child move deep within her, the ripples it made stronger and broader than those of the week before. She stroked her stomach affectionately. At first, she hadn't been able to think of the child as anything but an 'it,' but now that she could feel signs of life, she was beginning to feel great affection for the little person incubating within. She tried to imagine whom the child would look like once it was born and what sort of personality it might have once it grew out of babyhood.

Sophie climbed into bed, blew out the candle, and stared at the darkened ceiling above. To calm herself down, she began thinking of baby names, trying each one on for size and discarding it immediately. It was strange how the names just didn't seem to fit, as if the child already had a personality that needed to be considered. Would Teddy want their son to be named Theodore, after himself? Would he prefer something traditional for a girl, or maybe something a bit more modern, like Georgina or Araminta? No, she hated that name, Sophie decided. She wouldn't even mention it to him. Perhaps Hannah, or Constance. She'd always liked Constance, for the sheer steadfastness of it. Or perhaps Andrew for a boy. Andrew Mercer had a nice ring to it.

The diversion worked and Sophie drifted, her mind and body exhausted after a day of fruitless waiting. *Tomorrow*, she thought drowsily as she finally succumbed to sleep. *Tomorrow*.

Chapter 16

The following morning dawned gloomy and wet, with steady rain falling from a leaden sky as gusty winds tore at the branches of the tree outside Sophie's bedroom window, the glistening leaves fluttering like agitated butterflies. Gone were the dazzling sunlight and heat of summer, replaced by a sudden chill that seemed to creep right into her bones. Sophie washed and dressed, and arranged her hair into a neat bun, but left a few curls to frame her face to soften the effect. Thankfully, her father had risen early and gone down to the printshop, leaving Sophie alone with Agnes, who, having already baked several loaves of fresh bread, was plucking a chicken by the hearth, the feathers landing in her apron.

Sophie tried to eat, but her stomach was in knots and a nagging melancholy yanked at her heartstrings, making her feel frustrated and irritable for no good reason. She knew she wouldn't be able to settle to any task this morning, so she marched into the parlor and sat by the window, determined to watch for Teddy until she finally spotted him. Even if he didn't come right away, knowing he was well was all that mattered. Hours later, she was still at her post, her eyes gritty with the strain of her vigil and her patience worn so thin it was torn in places. She finally gave up and went upstairs to fetch her cloak. She hadn't seen her future mother-in-law in months and hoped Mrs. Mercer wouldn't find her unexpected visitor sadly lacking in manners, but she simply couldn't bear the strain any longer.

As Sophie braved the elements, she wondered if Mrs. Mercer knew of Teddy's promise to marry her. Had he informed his mother of their intentions, as he'd said he would, or had he decided to wait until he returned in order to avoid any unpleasantness for Sophie should Anne Mercer reveal their plans to Sophie's father?

Sophie skirted the building to reach the back door that led to the apartment above the tavern. When no one answered, she pushed the door open, stepped inside the dank hallway, and peered up the darkened stairs. She heard several female voices, but no hint of Teddy's rich baritone. Sophie pushed back her hood, patted her damp curls, and walked up the stairs, hoping Mrs. Mercer wouldn't be too put out with her for simply showing up. The door at the top of the stairs was open, revealing the tiny parlor where the Mercer girls spent most of their time.

Sophie rapped on the door, hesitant to just walk in. A moment later, Lydia emerged from the bedroom and came to the door. She was the prettiest of Teddy's sisters, with blue eyes and chestnut curls that framed a heart-shaped face. She was also the one who resembled Teddy the most.

"Good afternoon, Miss Brewster," Lydia said, her eyes widening in surprise at finding Sophie loitering outside the door.

"Hello, Lydia. May I speak to Teddy?" Sophie asked, her cheeks heating with embarrassment. "It's rather urgent," she added when Lydia failed to reply.

"You'd best speak to Ma," Lydia said, and stepped aside to let Sophie in.

Sophie hadn't been to Teddy's house since she was much younger and came to play with his sisters, but she instantly noticed the drastic changes the intervening years had brought. The settee was worn and sagged in the middle, and the rug on the floor looked faded and threadbare. The drapes were frayed, and there was an empty space on the mantel where a carriage clock had once stood. Mrs. Mercer must have sold it in her hour of need. No wonder Teddy couldn't rush into marriage. His family was on the brink of poverty, their living conditions sadly reduced since the death of Mr. Mercer.

Anne Mercer was in the kitchen, peeling potatoes. A pot bubbled behind her, the fragrant steam filling the small kitchen. She looked up, her graying eyebrows knitting in displeasure, set down her knife, and wiped her hands on her apron before addressing Sophie.

"To what do we owe the pleasure, Miss Brewster?"

"Good afternoon, Mrs. Mercer. I was hoping to speak to Teddy."

"You and everyone else, it seems," she replied.

"I saw the *Sea Falcon* come into the harbor yesterday afternoon. Is he not at home?"

Anne Mercer looked at Sophie with something akin to pity and shook her head. She tried to retain her composure, but Sophie noticed the shaking of her hands, which she tried to hide by picking up the knife again and resuming her task. "Teddy wasn't on board. One of the officers came by last night to give me the news."

Sophie felt sick with apprehension, but there had to be an explanation for Teddy's absence. "I d-don't understand," she stammered. "Where is he?"

"I wish I knew. Mr. Lester said Teddy came ashore in Port Royale, Jamaica. He was in the company of several other sailors but became separated from the group shortly after. He didn't turn up by the time the ship was ready to cast off. Captain Barker sent out a search party, but they found no trace of him. Mr. Lester believes Teddy jumped ship," Mrs. Mercer said. Angry red spots appeared on her cheeks, but Sophie wasn't sure if she was upset with Teddy for leaving his companions or with Mr. Lester for jumping to such a harsh conclusion.

"But why would he do such a thing?" Sophie exclaimed. "Where would he have gone?"

"I can't answer that, can I?" Mrs. Mercer retorted. "That man carried on like my son was a criminal, a deserter. Teddy might have been hurt, or worse," she went on, her knife coming dangerously close to her fingers. "He might be lying dead in a ditch, for all I know, and all they want to do is punish him for abandoning his post. He hadn't even received his wages," she said tearfully. "He'd never have gone off without collecting his pay."

"Will you be able to manage?" Sophie asked, hoping she wasn't being tactless.

"Mr. Lester was good enough to bring me Teddy's pay. He knows the girls and I depend on it, but make no mistake, Miss

Brewster, if Teddy turns up, he'll have to face the consequences of his actions."

"So, you believe he left intentionally?" Sophie asked, wondering if Mrs. Mercer knew more than she was saying.

"I don't know what I believe. Teddy can be unpredictable, moody."

That didn't sound like the Teddy Sophie knew but given that he had been the man of the house for nearly a decade, it was understandable that he should feel the pressure and take it out on those closest to him.

"Teddy would never do anything dishonorable," Sophie said. "It's not in his nature."

"Shows how well you know him," Mrs. Mercer scoffed. She turned and dropped the potatoes into the pot, then sank into a rickety chair with a sigh. "Teddy always talked of striking out on his own, of grabbing something for himself. Perhaps he saw an opportunity and took it. I wouldn't blame him if he did. I just need to know he's alive and well."

"No!" Sophie exclaimed. "He said we'd be married. He said he loves me. He wouldn't simply leave me behind."

"And you honestly believe you're the only girl he's made promises to? I love my son, Miss Brewster, but I know him through and through. Just like his feckless da, he is. Can't help reaching for what he wants, and damn the consequences, and Teddy does have a weakness for a pretty face."

"But I'm with child," Sophie exclaimed. "What am I to do?" Her knees felt weak and she leaned against the wall for support. Her mind was refusing to accept what she was hearing, but her body was already reacting to the shock. She was trembling and thought she might be sick.

"Here, have a drink of water," Mrs. Mercer said, not unkindly. She heaved herself to her feet and poured Sophie water from a chipped pitcher.

Sophie took a sip, then another, and another. After a few moments, the nausea subsided, and she felt a bit stronger.

"Sit yourself down," Mrs. Mercer said as she pushed the chair toward her. "How far gone are you?"

"Nearly five months."

"Well, I'm sorry for you, lass, but I can't help. We're barely surviving ourselves. With Teddy gone, I'll have to find a way to put food on the table. My youngest girls will have to go to work, and it won't be at anything genteel, I promise you that. I'll be lucky if we manage to keep a roof over our heads. Go home, Miss Brewster. There's nothing for you here."

"But what am I to do?" Sophie wailed.

"Throw yourself on the mercy of your father. He's a good man. He won't turn you out. You're not the first or the last girl to fall for the sweet promises of a handsome young man. If you're lucky, the babe will die, and you'll be free of the shame. You'll still have a chance for a good marriage. If not, well, then your day is done," Mrs. Mercer said, her soft gaze diluting the harsh words. "I'm sorry my son let you down. He's let us all down."

A quaking sob escaped Sophie's mouth. It seemed to come directly from her chest, from the vicinity of her heart. She didn't want to believe Mrs. Mercer. Something awful must have happened to Teddy. He had to be seriously hurt, or dead, but he would never have simply walked away from them all. Teddy wouldn't. Perhaps his mother had chosen to believe Teddy had run off since it was easier than thinking he might be dead, and she'd never find out what had happened to him or even get a body to bury.

But the Teddy Mrs. Mercer described was different from the charming boy Sophie had fallen in love with. Mrs. Mercer loved Teddy the most of all her children. He was her eldest, her boy. A mother knew her son better than his sweetheart, and she'd insinuated that Teddy's promises were not to be taken seriously. Could Sophie really have been just another willing partner in a string of sordid dalliances? Now that she thought about it, Teddy hadn't touched her as an inexperienced young man would. He knew what he was about and had seemed intimately familiar with the female anatomy.

He'd had women before her, Sophie realized as she bowed her head to hide her tears. She hadn't been his first, as she had naively believed. How many others had Teddy lain with while he was away at sea, putting in at different ports and possibly joining the other sailors when they went ashore to visit dockside brothels? It wasn't as if he had a wife waiting for him at home, and even if he had, would that have made a difference? How many others might have fallen pregnant with his child? Did he know? Did he care? Had he ever meant to marry her, or was he just having a bit of fun while he was at home?

Her heart stubbornly held on to her faith in him, but her mind was more rational and was already searching for tangible proof of Teddy's intentions. Mrs. Mercer had no reason to lie. She looked too tired and defeated to bother with making up stories. She had bigger problems than Sophie's swelling belly. She still had two daughters to clothe and feed, and she could hardly do that by taking in laundry or hiring herself out as a char woman.

Sophie got to her feet and stumbled from the too-warm kitchen. Mrs. Mercer didn't say anything, just returned to her pot, as if Sophie had been nothing more than a figment of her imagination. Sophie glanced at Lydia as she passed her on the way to the door. Janet was only twelve, but Lydia was fifteen, old enough for some men, who'd pay handsomely for her innocence. Sophie hoped it never came to that, but the dingy apartment and Mrs. Mercer's matter-of-fact attitude spoke of a quiet desperation that could lead to all manner of sins.

Sophie ambled home but didn't go upstairs. Instead she entered through the shop and let herself into the back, where her father was busy setting type for a new order. He looked up in surprise, her damp face and droopy curls not lost on him.

"Sophie, what on earth is the matter? You look a fright. Are you ill?" Horace asked as he wiped his hands on a cloth and came toward her.

Sophie nodded miserably. She did feel ill, but this wasn't the kind of ailment that would either pass or kill her. This was the type of illness that would gnaw away at her heart until there was nothing left and she was just a hollow shell of her former self. What she was about to do was the first step toward an uncertain future, but she no longer had a choice; she was too far gone to hope time would bring forth a solution.

"Father, I'm with child," she blurted out, praying that her father wouldn't cast her out on the spot.

Horace blanched, his ink-stained hand flying to his mouth. "Merciful heavens. Who's the father?" he demanded. "Who's done this to you?" He took one look at her face and the angst in his eyes turned to fury. "Ted Mercer, is it? I told you to stay away from that blackguard. What now? He refuses to marry you, I suppose. Can't say I'm surprised. He probably has a brainless harlot like you in every port."

Sophie cringed at his words, but he was angry and disappointed, so she chose to ignore the vicious barb. "Teddy left his ship in Jamaica and never returned. He's gone."

"Why am I not surprised?" Horace cried. "I never trusted that whoreson."

Sophie gasped. She'd never heard her father use such language before, but then, she'd never put him in such a position before either. He was livid, all traces of sympathy erased from his usually kind face. His eyes were narrowed, and his mouth pressed into a thin line as his gaze bore into her middle.

"How long?"

"Close to five months. What will happen to me, Father?" Sophie asked, her voice trembling with uncertainty. "To us?" Her hand went to her belly, cradling it gently.

"You will remain in this house until the child is born. You will not go out or speak to anyone. I will swear Agnes to silence, and she'll keep her mouth shut if she wants to retain her position or get a good character reference in the future. I will engage a midwife that's not local to these parts. Afterward, we'll tell people you have been ill."

"What of my child?" Sophie cried.

"I need time to think. Leave me. I can't bear to look at you, Sophie. Thank the good Lord your mother is already in her grave, or this would have killed her all over again. To think that a daughter of mine would lie with a lowlife like Ted Mercer, like some street doxy, and bring shame on my house. My imagination never stretched far enough to envision such a future for you. Get out!" he cried, his eyes blazing with anger. "I don't want to see you."

Sophie stumbled from the shop and retired to her room, where she wept until daylight faded and night descended, cloaking her in darkness. She wiped her streaming eyes and sat up, unable to bear her grief any longer. She always tried to find the good in any situation, and this was no different. Her father was understandably angry, but he'd look after her. He wouldn't disown her, not if he was already making plans for the child's birth. Perhaps they'd move after the baby was born. She could pass herself off as a widow and bring up her baby with some claim to dignity. A bitter bark of laughter escaped her. Dignity. She had no dignity left. She'd thrown it away the moment she allowed Teddy to slide his hands beneath her skirts. She'd thought what they'd shared was love, but to her father and Anne Mercer, it had been nothing more than the dirty, sinful coupling of two people who had no morals and no respect for God or the rules of society.

Sophie sighed miserably. As a man, Teddy was always free to move on, to live his life on his own terms, but as a woman, she was left to nurture his seed, growing large with child until she couldn't hide her shame, then bring their child into the world, knowing it would be forever tainted by illegitimacy. Fresh tears began to fall, and Sophie buried her face in her damp pillow, wishing she could turn back the clock and prevent the catastrophe that had befallen her. Her father needn't bother to lock her in her room—she never wanted to leave.

Chapter 17

Sophie spent the remainder of the pregnancy in her room, only going down to the parlor when her father was in the shop. She didn't dare set foot outside for fear of running into an acquaintance, someone who'd quickly conclude that the added girth around her middle, combined with the rounding of her cheeks and the desperation in her eyes, could mean only one thing. Even Agnes, who'd been a steadfast companion since Sophie's mother died, often looked at her with disapproval, particularly when she'd been forced to let out some of Sophie's shifts and waistbands. She saw to Sophie's physical well-being, but quickly changed the subject whenever Teddy's name came up, the resentment right there in her eyes. She didn't blame Sophie for her fall from grace; she laid all the responsibility at Teddy's door, which meant that Sophie could never share her pain or discuss her hope for Teddy's return, which was dwindling with every passing day.

Sophie longed to ask Mrs. Mercer if she'd heard anything, but she hadn't seen her or any of Teddy's sisters since the day she'd learned of his disappearance, and didn't expect to. They didn't care what happened to her; they had their own problems now that Teddy was gone, and she didn't dare try to call on them for fear of being turned away.

At first, Sophie refused to believe the things Mrs. Mercer had said to her about Teddy. She secretly hoped there was a logical explanation for Teddy's actions and that he would come sauntering down the street, whistling a merry tune in the hope that she heard him and came out to meet him at their secret place, but as the days went by, Sophie had to accept that there were only two possible explanations. Either Teddy was dead, set upon by thugs and killed for the few coins he had in his pockets, or he'd simply left them all behind for reasons known only to him. In either case, there wasn't much use in hoping or waiting. Teddy was gone from her, and she had to deal with the situation as best she could for herself and their child.

Every day she went over her limited options, desperate to come up with a solution that would allow her to keep her baby. She still hoped her father would permit her to keep the child, but if he didn't, no one would offer employment to an unwed mother. Even if she were to lie about her circumstances and find a position in someone's household as a servant or nursemaid, how would she care for her own baby, especially in the first months of its life when it'd need to be fed every few hours and she'd be the only source of its nourishment? She might be able to pay someone to look after it while she worked, but such an arrangement would have to wait till after the baby was weaned.

One thing she knew for certain: her father had not forgiven her. He hadn't said a word to her since their conversation in the printshop and chose to take his meals alone. Sophie tried to approach him, but he simply ignored her, looking through her as if she weren't even there. As she sat alone hour after hour, she was beginning to come to the painful realization that she hadn't known either Teddy or her father nearly as well as she'd thought. The two men she'd trusted and counted on had both betrayed her, each in his own way. Teddy might not have had a choice in what happened to him, but her father knew what he was doing, and his attitude toward her made it clear that the estrangement between them was going to be permanent.

His one concession to her well-being was to engage a midwife, who appeared on their doorstep in the middle of December. Mrs. Meeks was short and plump and had a florid complexion that accentuated her bright blue eyes. Her hair must have been carrot-red before streaks of gray toned it down to a pale ginger. She wore a lace-trimmed mobcap that was her only attempt at vanity. The rest of her clothes were drab and serviceable.

"Everything seems normal, Miss Brewster. It won't be long now," she said as she washed her hands in the basin after examining her and dried them on a clean towel.

"Where should I send Agnes when my time comes?" Sophie asked as she pulled down her shift to cover her nakedness and sat up on the bed.

"No need to send anyone anywhere. I'm to stay here until your pains come. Your father paid me quite generously for my time. Should anyone ask, I'm your father's cousin, come to stay for a few weeks," she added.

"Are you a native of Boston?" Sophie asked, her suspicion growing.

"No," Mrs. Meeks replied curtly.

"Where are you from?"

"Oh, here and there."

"I see," Sophie said, and she did. Mrs. Meeks wasn't a local midwife, who might gossip and give Sophie's secret away, which was why she needed a place to stay until the child was born. Outwardly, Mrs. Meeks hadn't done or said anything to upset Sophie, but there was something in her manner that put Sophie on her guard, and she resolved to keep her distance from the older woman. Lonely as she was, she didn't think cozy chats by the fire were in order.

As the weeks passed, Sophie began to resent the midwife's presence in earnest. She seemed to be everywhere at once: preparing a tonic in the kitchen, writing letters at the small desk in the parlor, checking on Sophie in her bedroom. Perhaps Sophie was just irritable because she was becoming increasingly uncomfortable and even more frightened of what was to come, but despite being of an age to be Sophie's mother, Mrs. Meeks was anything but motherly.

"Oh, Mama, I wish you were here," Sophie whispered into the dark as she lay on her side, her hand on her heaving belly. "I feel so alone, and so scared. Is Teddy with you, Mama?" she asked. Would it make her feel more at peace to know Teddy was dead? No, she decided. As long as she didn't know for certain, she could nurture the flame of hope, no matter how tiny it was. Perhaps Teddy would return in the spring. He'd find a ship to carry him home and come back to her. If only she could hold out until then, she prayed as she fell into an uneasy doze. She never slept well these days.

The pains finally came on a dreary January afternoon. A bitter wind was howling outside, and silent snow fell beyond the window, the thick flakes settling on every surface and bleaching the world of color. In the late morning and afternoon, several people walked past the house, their steps hurried, their shoulders hunched, and their heads bent into the wind, but by the time the lilac shadows of twilight tinted the snow, the street became deserted and a strange silence settled over the house. The pain had been dull and came at evenly spaced intervals at first, but by suppertime, it came in relentless waves, each more excruciating than the last.

"Let's get you to bed," Mrs. Meeks said after taking her supper in the kitchen. She didn't seem affected by Sophie's suffering and kept an eye on her as she would on browning loaves of bread to make sure they didn't get scorched if left in the oven too long.

Sophie allowed herself to be helped upstairs by Agnes, who undressed her down to her shift and helped her into bed. Mrs. Meeks arrived a few minutes later, bringing a pitcher of hot water and a stack of towels, which she set on the trunk at the foot of the bed.

"Get your mistress some water," she ordered Agnes.

Sophie gratefully drained the cup and held it out to Agnes. She hadn't realized how thirsty she was. Agnes was just about to say something when Mrs. Meeks ordered her from the room.

"If I have need of you, I'll call you," she said, her tone brooking no argument.

"I'd like Agnes to remain," Sophie protested, but Mrs. Meeks behaved as though she hadn't heard her.

"We have work to do, you and I. It shouldn't be long now," she said matter-of-factly. "Good thing there's a strong wind outside. It'll carry off your hollering, so no one will be the wiser," she said as she drew the curtains against the wintry night.

Sophie wished Mrs. Meeks would be a little more sympathetic, but the woman was like a general heading into battle, all bristle and determination, ignoring Sophie's cries as if they were nothing more than the barking of a dog in the street. The night wore on, Sophie's body refusing to relinquish the child. Never had she known such agony. Sophie was drenched in sweat, her thighs slick with blood, her head pounding after what felt like hours of pushing. She couldn't take another minute of the torture, but the baby had yet to be born. Somewhere in the distance, a church clock struck midnight. Sophie briefly wondered if her father was in the next room, listening to her desperate screams. Was he worried about her, his ears straining to hear her voice and the cry of a newborn child, or did he wish they'd both die and wash away the shame they'd inflicted on him?

"The babe's crowning," Mrs. Meeks said, nodding to Sophie with an air of grim satisfaction. "Push hard."

It was probably no more than a few minutes, but they felt like an eternity, the pressure building up in Sophie until she thought her eyes would pop out of her head and her entrails would explode out of her body. Just as the child's head was finally out, Mrs. Meeks held a cup to Sophie's lips.

"Here, take a sip. You must be parched."

Sophie took a gulp of water. It tasted strange and had a sickly-sweet odor, but she didn't care. Her mouth was dry, and a feverish heat seemed to radiate from her flushed skin. A short while later, a strange heaviness settled in her limbs. Her arms felt like lead, and her thoughts seemed to slow down to a crawl, Mrs. Meeks' words no longer making sense. Sophie tried to raise her head off the pillow, but she couldn't find the strength to move, not even when Mrs. Meeks pulled the baby from between her thighs and quickly cut the cord. An impenetrable darkness seemed to press in on all sides, and she finally succumbed to it, falling into a deep sleep just as her baby let out a weak cry.

Chapter 18

When Sophie woke, the room was bathed in sunshine, the heavy clouds of the day before a distant memory. She was dressed in a clean nightdress and the bedlinens had been changed. A thick wad of rags was stuffed between her legs to keep the blood from soiling the clean sheets, and her breasts were tightly bound with strips of linen. The room bore no signs of her struggle. Sophie turned her head, searching for the baby, but there was no sign of it. The house was quiet.

"Agnes," she called. Then louder, "Agnes!"

She heard Agnes's footsteps on the stairs. "You're awake, mistress," she said, looking at her with ill-disguised apprehension.

"Where's my baby?"

Agnes's gaze slid away from Sophie as her fingers nervously plucked at her apron. "You'd best speak to your father, miss."

She left the room before Sophie had a chance to ask any more questions, and several minutes later, Sophie heard her father's heavy tread on the stairs. He came into the room but didn't advance past the door, as if he needed to ensure a quick exit.

"Are you quite recovered from the birth?" Horace asked, his gaze sliding past Sophie toward the window.

Sophie's body felt battered and bruised. Milk seeped through the bandage, soiling her nightdress, but she had no pity to spare for herself. "Father, where's my baby?" she pleaded when she saw her father's closed expression.

"The child was stillborn. Mrs. Meeks took it away. She'll see that it's properly disposed of."

"Disposed of?" Sophie echoed, the full meaning of the words not quite penetrating her brain. She felt unusually dull-witted this morning, unable to organize her thoughts properly despite trying with all her might to concentrate.

"It cannot be buried at the parish cemetery. Mrs. Meeks knows how to deal with such matters."

"No!" Sophie cried. "No! Please, I want to see it. I need to hold it."

"Mrs. Meeks is long gone. You've been asleep for nearly fourteen hours."

"What?" Sophie had been exhausted by the labor, but she'd never in her life slept this long or this deep. "No." She shook her head. "She gave me something to make me sleep. I heard the baby cry," she exclaimed. "I heard it."

"You only imagined it. You were worn out, not quite yourself."

"I heard it," Sophie cried. "I know I did."

"Sophie, I'm sorry, but your child is gone, and it's for the best. For all involved. You must look to the future."

"No," Sophie cried again, but with less conviction. Had she dreamed the whole thing? Had she been so exhausted by the labor that she'd imagined hearing her baby cry? "What was it?" she asked, her voice catching as the pain of her loss finally began to penetrate her befuddled brain. "Was it a boy?" she whispered.

"Yes."

"I must know where he's buried," Sophie pleaded. "Please, I must go to his grave."

"No, you must not," Horace exclaimed, his cheeks mottled with anger. "You will forget the child and its hapless father. The sooner you accept that they're both gone, the happier you will be."

"Happier? Is that what you expect me to be?" she demanded, shocked that her father would be so callous as to expect her to simply forget Teddy and their son. Had it been so easy for him to accept the death of his wife? Sophie pinned him with a murderous stare. Had he no heart?

Horace Brewster's face twisted with irritation. "You can choose to weep and mourn, but it'll do you no good. Ted is gone. I sincerely hope he's resting at the bottom of the sea, and your son is lost to you forever. Happily, there's hope for a new beginning."

"What hope could there be?" Sophie asked. She was exhausted and wished her father would just leave her to grieve.

"George Holland was quite taken with you when he met you at the garden party. He's written to me, asking if he might call on you when he visits Boston in the spring. I have given my consent."

"I have no interest in George Holland," Sophie protested.

"Lucky for you, you have two months in which to develop an interest. He's a fine man with good prospects and a thriving concern in Cambridge, which will one day be his, as will the rest of the Holland estate."

"You'd marry me off to George Holland without a second thought?" Sophie asked, surprised that her father, who'd proclaimed to love her, seemed to want nothing more than to be rid of her.

"Given recent events, it's clear to me that your only salvation lies in a respectable marriage."

"Teddy would have married me, had he returned in time," Sophie protested meekly. "I love him."

"Love is no excuse for demeaning yourself, Sophie. Had Ted Mercer had honorable intentions toward you, he'd have come to me and asked for your hand, as a respectable man should, instead of tumbling you in some dark corner like a two-bit trollop."

"And would you have given us permission to marry if he had?" Sophie demanded.

"I would not have, and for good reason. I wanted better for you, a man of honor who would look after you and guide you."

"And George Holland is that man?" Sophie asked archly.

"George Holland has given me no reason to believe otherwise. He's behaved with the utmost propriety and solicited his father's guidance on the matter before approaching me directly, which speaks highly of both his character and his intentions. You will receive him when he comes to call, and you will be gracious."

"And if I refuse?"

"You won't," Horace replied coldly. "Not if you wish to remain in this house and consider yourself my daughter."

"Father, please," Sophie pleaded. "Surely I deserve some say in my future."

"I have always trusted your judgement and given you free rein, but you have forfeited my good opinion of you. From now on, you will not leave the house without Agnes, and if I discover that you have done anything to compromise your reputation further, you will be confined to your room until a marriage can be arranged. You might think this is harsh, but you've left me no choice. Now, I wish you a speedy recovery and I hope you take my advice to heart and turn your mind to the future. Good day."

With that, Horace turned on his heel and left the room, closing the door behind him with an angry bang. Sophie turned her face away from the bright light streaming through the window, wishing only for darkness. Never before had she wished for death, but at that moment, she felt as if a great chasm had opened before her, its bottomless maw calling to her with its promise of oblivion. Losing Teddy had reintroduced her to the sharp-edged pain of bereavement, but the loss of her baby pushed her that much closer to the edge of reason. How was she to go on, to live from day to day, completing mindless tasks and seeing to the needs of her physical body when her heart was shattered beyond repair? She'd never even seen her son's face or held him in her arms. She'd been denied the chance to say goodbye. One moment, the baby had been alive, writhing inside her like a hooked fish, and now he was gone, his tiny body nothing more than a bit of rubbish to be disposed of. How could God allow an innocent child to be buried in some unmarked hole because its parents weren't legally married? Her baby would be denied salvation, its orphaned soul floating for eternity through a dark mist with no hope of redemption.

Sophie stuffed a fist into her mouth to stifle her cries. She didn't want her father to hear her suffering, nor did she wish for

Agnes's sympathy. She wanted only to grieve in peace, allowed time to come to terms with her loss. How could she think of marrying when she had nothing to give, no love left for anyone but those who were lost to her? What was she to do? How was she to live without them? She longed for the oblivion of sleep, but the door opened, and Agnes came in, her eyes soft with sympathy.

"Are you all right, mistress?"

Sophie didn't bother to reply. She was alive, but she was far from all right.

Agnes stepped forward, undeterred by Sophie's lack of response. "Mrs. Meeks left instructions for you."

"On how to find my baby?" Sophie sat up, hope welling in her chest. At this stage, even a gravesite to visit would be better than the black hole of emptiness and uncertainty she'd been left with in the wake of her son's death.

"No, on how to stop the milk from coming," Agnes replied apologetically. "She said the flow should taper off in a few days if you keep your breasts tightly bound. And there will be bleeding, for a week at least. Just use the rags, like you do while you have your courses. You should be right as rain in a fortnight or so."

"Agnes, did you see my baby?" Sophie pleaded. "Was it alive at birth?"

"I know nothing, miss. I wasn't permitted in the room."

"Where were you, then?" Sophie demanded.

"I was in the kitchen, minding my own business, as I was told to do."

"Did you hear my baby cry?" Sophie asked, pinning Agnes with her gaze. The kitchen was just below Sophie's room. Surely, she'd have heard something. "Please, Agnes."

Agnes shook her head, but not before Sophie saw the furtive look in her eyes. Sophie reached for the nightstand and extracted a coin. She held it up, allowing the sunlight to glint off the silver surface. Agnes would have to work nearly six months to earn the bribe Sophie was offering.

"Did you hear my baby cry?" she asked slowly, enunciating every word.

Agnes nodded but wouldn't meet Sophie's gaze.

"Are you sure?" Sophie demanded.

All the fight seemed to go out of Agnes, and she let out her breath with a *whoosh*. "It was alive when Mrs. Meeks left. I saw its face. Screwed up with displeasure it was, its mouth opening and closing, like it was rooting for a nipple. I couldn't believe she was taking a newborn out into a raging storm, but she had it swaddled good and proper against the cold."

"Where did she take him?"

"I don't know. Honest, I don't," Agnes replied, her face anxious.

"Did my father give her money?" Sophie asked. There was a crushing tightness in her chest, not from the binding that prevented her from taking a deep breath, but from the sense of betrayal seeping into her soul. Her father must have engineered the whole thing, making sure her child was taken from her before she woke.

Agnes looked as if she were about to cry. She felt loyal to Sophie, but it was Horace Brewster who paid her wages and would sack her without a second thought if she betrayed his trust. She finally nodded, unable to lie in the face of Sophie's grief.

"He gave her a fat purse and told her to make sure the child was well looked after." Sophie held out the coin, but Agnes shook her head. "I don't want your money, mistress. I'm just sorry I could do nothing to help."

"You've helped me by telling me the truth."

"Let him go, mistress," Agnes said, her work-reddened hands kneading her apron. "It's as the master said; it's for the best. Now, is there anything I can get you? Some broth? Or maybe tea and buttered bread?" she asked, fussing as if Sophie were ill rather than recovering from childbirth.

Sophie shook her head, wishing Agnes would just leave. She wouldn't have expected her to prevent Mrs. Meeks from leaving with her baby or lay her livelihood on the line by challenging her employer, but Sophie didn't feel kindly disposed toward Agnes at the moment and wanted only to be left alone with her own thoughts, her introspection edging toward an inevitable conclusion that left her feeling even more deeply wounded than Teddy's vanishing act. Her father had brought in a midwife no one knew, who had drugged Sophie in the final stages of birth, taken her child, and disappeared. Mrs. Meeks had seemed respectable enough, but that didn't mean she'd care for the child or place him with someone who'd give him a loving home. She could have smothered him, or drowned him as soon as she left Boston, keeping the money Horace Brewster had given her for the child's upkeep. Perhaps her father had paid her to do just that, to rid himself of any evidence of his daughter's shame.

The agony of childbirth suddenly seemed minor compared to the visceral pain her own father had inflicted on her. Sophie could understand his reasons, but she would never forgive him for the callous way he'd separated her from her newborn son. Teddy was gone. Her baby was lost to her, and her only choice was to pledge herself to a virtual stranger who'd be her lord and master for the rest of her days. Either that or leave her father's house as soon as she was able and try to fend for herself.

She had no illusions; she wouldn't get very far. She didn't have the skills to hire herself out as a maid, and the only places that would have her would be taverns or farms that were looking for cheap labor. Neither option appealed, and she refused to consider the third, one that took young women and spit out used-up, diseased, broken hags who rarely lived to see middle age. She was eighteen years old. She wasn't ready to commit herself to such a life. Truth be told, she was too frightened of a life in which she'd be adrift on a sea of hardship and loneliness without a home port to return to. With Teddy gone, her father was the only family she had left, and no matter how angry she was with him, she couldn't see severing ties with him forever.

Chapter 19

Lauren

Lauren spent most of the week indoors, partly due to the rain that refused to leave until Friday afternoon, and partly because she was committed to completing the first draft of Ashley Mann's autobiography. Having finally finished, she saved the document and leaned back in her chair with a sigh of relief. She'd go into town tomorrow morning and email it to Ashley, then wait for her comments and revisions. If she knew anything about Ashley, who made a career of being a total flake, she'd approve the first draft and send it to her agent. She was too preoccupied with promoting her brand to take the time to read this version of her own story and make revisions. Lauren hoped she'd finally receive the balance of her fee and be officially done with the project. She was ready to move on.

On Saturday morning, after taking Billy for a walk, Lauren grabbed her laptop and headed to Best Beans in Orleans, intent on killing two birds with one stone. She'd get a latte and a breakfast sandwich and take advantage of the free Wi-Fi the café offered. She got her breakfast and settled at a table near the window, ready to email Ashley and plow through several dozen emails she'd received since her visit to the library. The cellular signal at the house wasn't great, so she put off doing anything that wasn't necessary until she had a strong connection. Having taken care of her emails, Lauren checked her Facebook page, caught up on the latest news, and purchased several new books. She'd worked her way through most of the books on her Kindle and was ready for some new reading material. She also downloaded several audiobooks. Putting the books on speaker would fill the house with the sound of someone else's voice, a comfort she craved in her solitude.

The café was filling up, but she was reluctant to pack up and leave, so she decided to do some more research on the

Hollands. She'd spoken to Brooke last night, and although Brooke had gotten significantly further than Lauren had, there was still too little information to go on.

"Have you been able to find anything?" Lauren had asked, eager to learn anything she could about the elusive Hollands.

"Yes, I have," Brooke had replied proudly. "Lionel Holland married Elizabeth Lowell in 1698. They had three children: Lionel, who died in infancy, George, and Amelia. Amelia married Jeremy Dawson in 1726 and had three children. Their son James was born in Boston, but their two daughters were born in Somerset, England. George Holland married Sophie Brewster in 1727. They also had three children, two boys and a girl."

"Is that it?"

"What were you expecting? That's what genealogy sites give you—names and dates. Did you want to know when they died?"

"No, that's not necessary. Thank you. At least now I have some more information to work with."

"No problem. Happy to help," Brooke had replied before ending the call. She had a date and she sounded very mysterious about it, so Lauren didn't grill her.

She opened a new browser and began a fresh search, but the results were disappointing. There were numerous mentions of the Hollands in later years, and several references to Edward Holland, who'd been active during the War of Independence, but nothing at all pertaining to his ancestors. Lauren did discover that Jeremy Dawson became a baronet upon the death of his father, passing on the title to his son, James.

Lauren gave up and leaned back in her chair. She wasn't sure why, but she was convinced that the woman she'd seen was Sophie Holland. Lauren plugged Sophie's maiden name into the search bar, but unsurprisingly nothing came up. If Sophie had led an uneventful life, there'd be no reason for her name to have survived the centuries. Lauren typed in George Holland's name.

"Good morning," a familiar voice addressed her. Lauren glanced up to see Ryan approaching her table, cup of coffee in hand.

"Hello," Lauren replied, feeling awkward. Having lived in a big city all her life, she wasn't used to small-town life, where people ran into each other as a matter of course. This was the second time she'd come face to face with Ryan Kelly in the space of a week.

"Are you still researching the Hollands?" Ryan asked, clearly surprised.

"Yes, but I haven't found anything of interest," Lauren complained.

"Could be you're not asking the right questions," Ryan replied unhelpfully.

"And you know the right questions to ask?" she snapped. He was making her feel like a fool.

"I might."

"Care to enlighten me?"

"No."

Lauren stared at him in disbelief, but immediately realized he was teasing her. His eyes sparkled with mischief.

"Come to dinner tonight and I'll help you look."

"Is this another false promise?" Lauren asked, smiling despite her annoyance.

"Not at all. I happen to be a decent cook, and I *will* help you look."

"What about Tyler?" Lauren asked, hoping Ryan would take the hint and allude to the whereabouts of his son's mother. He had to be divorced if he was inviting her to his house.

"Tyler usually spends Saturday nights with his grandparents. They love having him, and it gives me a night off."

So, he was a single dad, Lauren concluded. Some stubborn part of her wanted to refuse the invitation, but a need for human contact won out. What was the harm in having dinner with him, especially if he was able to help her with her research?

"All right."

"Do you like Italian food?" he asked.

"Who doesn't? What can I bring?"

"Just yourself," Ryan replied. "Seven?"

"Sure."

"I'll text you the address. Sorry, gotta run. I have office hours this morning. See you later." He smiled beatifically and was gone, the subtle scent of his aftershave lingering for just a moment before dissipating into the coffee-scented air of the café.

Lauren gave up on her search and shut down the computer. She'd pick up a bottle of wine on her way home so she wouldn't come to Ryan's house empty handed, she decided.

**

After changing her outfit three times, putting up her hair, then taking it down, Lauren finally left the house, ready for what she was now sure was a date. She arrived at Ryan's house bearing a bottle of Pinot Noir and hoping she'd make it through the night without having a meltdown. When Ryan opened the door, a wonderful smell assailed her.

"Wow, something smells amazing."

"That's just a tease," Ryan said, grinning. He kissed her cheek and invited her in. He lived in a charming cape-style house with green shutters and a matching front door. The living room was painted a dusky blue, and several table lamps cast a warm glow onto the charcoal gray sofa and chairs and the abstract rug in shades of gray, blue, and beige. A flat-screen TV hung above the fireplace, and several family photographs dotted the mantel. It was a lovely room, trendy but comfortable.

"Where's your dog?" Lauren asked, looking around.

"Tyler won't be parted from him, so Jack gets a sleepover as well," Ryan replied with a smile. He opened the bottle she'd brought but stopped short of pouring her a glass. "I have a bottle of Prosecco in the fridge," he said. "I know you like it..."

Lauren smiled, touched that he'd remembered what she drank. "That's all right. I'll have a glass of red."

He poured them each a glass of wine before disappearing into the kitchen to check on dinner. Taking a sip, Lauren walked toward the mantel to examine the pictures up close. There was a wedding photo of Ryan and an attractive auburn-haired woman. *They look so young and happy*, Lauren thought as she recalled a similar photo of her and Zack from their own wedding. It was a blessing no one knew what awaited them down the line, or they wouldn't bother to get married, she mused bitterly, because here they were, two people who'd found their soulmates and made a lifelong commitment only to find themselves single again before long. Or perhaps Ryan's wife had never been his soulmate and the marriage had ended in disappointment and divorce. He still displayed their wedding picture, so perhaps the decision to leave had been hers, and Ryan was still coming to terms with the breakup.

Tearing her gaze away from the wedding photo, Lauren examined the rest of the portraits. There was a picture of Ryan's parents—she couldn't help noticing that he looked just like his dad—one of Merielle's graduation, and a studio portrait of Ryan, his wife, and Tyler, aged only a few months. At first glance, they looked like any young family, but upon closer inspection, Lauren noticed Ryan's anxious gaze and the dark shadows beneath his wife's lashless eyes. Lauren thought she was wearing a wig.

"Alicia died when Ty was six months old," Ryan said, coming up behind her. "Breast cancer. She might have had a chance had she started chemo and radiation sooner, but she was already pregnant with Ty and refused to terminate the pregnancy in order to start treatment. By the time Ty was born, the tumor had grown, and the cancer had spread to her lungs. She hung on for as long as she could, desperate to be there for Ty, but eventually she lost the battle."

"I'm so sorry," Lauren said, her eyes brimming with tears. What a horrible tragedy for them all. Had Alicia's cancer been caught before her pregnancy, she might have beaten it and lived a long and healthy life with Ryan and their children. She'd given her life to save Tyler's, and now Ryan was a widower and Tyler had no mom.

"She wouldn't have had it any other way. She got to be with Tyler for six months. She considered it a gift."

Lauren wanted to tell him about Zack, but the words died in her throat. Ryan and Alicia had had no choice in what happened to them, but Zack had had choices and he'd made all the wrong ones, leaving her to pick up the pieces of their shattered life.

"You've lost someone too, haven't you?" Ryan asked softly, sensing her grief.

She nodded miserably. "A year ago. Afghanistan."

"I'm sorry," he said. "At first, it feels like life can't possibly go on and you will never recover from the loss, but then, day by day, you learn to live again and even to smile. You learn to go on."

"I'm trying," Lauren whispered. "I'm trying so hard, but it's as if I have to learn everything all over again. I have to rediscover joy and love and the art of getting through the day without wanting to burst into tears. I'm getting there, but it's taking every bit of strength I have," she confessed. "I can't imagine how difficult it must have been for you."

"Alicia left me Ty," Ryan said. "Loving him made it easier. He gave me a reason to go on."

"Have you been able to get out there?" Lauren asked, referring to dating.

"Not yet," he replied, smiling into her eyes. "Maybe we can do it together."

"Maybe," Lauren echoed, returning his warm gaze.

"Come on. Dinner is ready," he said, his smile artificially bright.

Lauren wondered if any date either of them went on would ever be just about them and the other person or whether Zack and Alicia would always be in the room, looking over their shoulders, judging their potential partners, and unintentionally holding them back from moving on.

She followed Ryan into the dining room, where a table was set for two. "Can I help?"

"No. You are my guest. Sit down, relax, and hopefully, enjoy."

Ryan brought out a bowl of Caesar salad and a platter of chicken parmesan over penne pasta. There was also homemade garlic bread, the loaf singlehandedly responsible for the appetizing smell.

"*Mangia*," Ryan invited as he took a seat across from her and passed her the bowl of salad.

"Is it okay if we don't talk about them?" Lauren asked. "I won't be able to get through the meal if we do."

"Let's talk about all the things people talk about when they first meet," Ryan suggested. "I know virtually nothing about you except that you are Lauren Masters, bestselling romance author. I had no idea, by the way; Merielle enlightened me. I'm sorry I didn't recognize the name."

"No reason you should, unless you like chick-lit. What kind of books do you enjoy?"

"I love history, so anything historical, even romance," he joked.

"Is *Treasure Island* a favorite?" Lauren asked, smiling at him.

"Oh yes. I have a tattered copy upstairs. I must have read it a dozen times when I was a kid. I also love thrillers, mysteries, historical and otherwise, and science fiction. What about you?"

"Same, except for science fiction. I love a good romance too, but I haven't been reading too many of those recently. Just not in the mood. I'm thinking of writing a ghost story," Lauren said, smiling shyly.

"Is that why you're so interested in the history of the house?"

"Yes. It's always more authentic when you incorporate real details into the narrative rather than making everything up. And that house has a story to tell."

"I'm sure it does. It's been trying to tell it for years. People have claimed to have seen a woman, but she doesn't appear to just anyone. They say she appears only to widows." Ryan's eyes opened wide as he realized what he'd just said. "Have you seen her?"

"Yes," Lauren admitted. "I've seen her twice. Based on the style of her clothing, I believe she was the first mistress of the house. I think her name was Sophie."

"So, you have been able to find something," Ryan said, nodding in approval, his food forgotten.

"I have a friend who dabbles in genealogy. She was able to trace the Hollands as far back as the end of the seventeenth century, but since the house wasn't built until the 1700s, it stands to reason that the woman I saw was the wife of George Holland, son of Lionel Holland, who started the Holland bookstore chain."

"What would she be doing here in Orleans? And why does she linger?"

"That's what I hope to find out."

"I'd like to help, if you'll let me."

"I'll take all the help I can get," Lauren said. "The history of these people is proving difficult to unearth. This is delicious, by the way," she said as she tasted the chicken. "Do you cook often?"

"I used to, but these days it's all grilled cheese and chicken fingers. I don't like to cook for just myself."

"I know what you mean. Since Zack died, I haven't been doing much cooking either. It's either takeout or a quick omelet or salad."

"Sometimes my mom takes pity on me and brings over a casserole," Ryan said. "I stick it in the freezer and forget about it until she brings the next one."

Lauren nodded in understanding. She hadn't had much of an appetite since losing Zack. Seemed Ryan felt much the same. Regardless of their agreement not to talk about their loved ones, there were four people at that table, not just two.

"So, how do you plan to go about finding the Hollands?" Lauren asked, eager to change the subject.

Ryan took a sip of wine, his expression thoughtful as he considered her question. "In recent years, the government has been the keeper of information, but in the past, it was the church. It was the heart and soul of a community, but also a testament to the lives of its parishioners. The parish registers used to be the only legal form of recordkeeping. So, I did a little poking around this afternoon. There were two churches in this area at the beginning of the eighteenth century, a Protestant church and a Puritan church."

"I don't think the Hollands were Puritan," Lauren said, recalling that the woman she'd seen wore a gown that was not exactly—for lack of a better word—puritanical.

"No, I don't think they were either. However, Josiah Martins, the spiritual leader of the Puritan community, was quite the writer, unlike William Middleworth, the vicar of the Protestant church. Martins not only wrote down all his sermons, but also kept up an ongoing correspondence with other local Puritan ministers and kept a journal."

"I'm sorry, but I don't see how that helps us."

"Any mention of the Hollands can be useful. One clue usually leads to another."

"That's a longshot," Lauren replied, disappointed.

"Yes, it is," Ryan agreed. "We can also try to track down the parish records from the Protestant church, which they must have attended."

"I guess."

"Come on, it's a good idea," Ryan said, clearly discouraged by her lack of enthusiasm.

"It is," Lauren conceded, "but I was hoping for something more concrete."

"Like what? Like a journal written by your ghost?" Ryan joked.

"You must admit, that would be ideal, but I doubt such a document exists," Lauren said.

"Why?"

"Journal-keeping was very popular with the ladies of the Victorian era, but a woman living on Cape Cod in the early eighteenth century wasn't likely to have the resources or the time for such an undertaking."

"The Hollands were a wealthy family. Sophie Holland would have had both the resources and the time, since she'd probably have a houseful of servants."

Lauren shook her head. She couldn't explain the reason for her conviction, but she got the impression that Sophie felt quite isolated in her house on the hill. "Nowadays, having a house that's set apart is usually a sign of prosperity, but at the time the house was built, it was more desirable to be in a town or a village. People needed each other to survive, and they had a better chance of prospering when settling in groups. That house wasn't a refuge, it was a bolt-hole," Lauren said, verbalizing something she hadn't realized she'd been thinking.

Ryan nodded. "That's a very valid point. I hadn't thought of that."

"Let me ask you a practical question," Lauren said, pushing away her empty plate. "How would someone go about sending a letter from here in the eighteenth century?"

"Either with someone traveling in the direction of the recipient or possibly by boat. There was no postal service, as such," Ryan replied, his head tilted to the side as he considered the question. "Why do you ask?"

"Just curious. When I saw Sophie, if that's who she is, she appeared to be writing a letter, possibly to her husband, who must have been in Cambridge."

"Well, let's see what we can find out," Ryan said, pushing his chair away from the table.

Lauren followed him back into the living room and took a seat on the couch. Ryan sat down next to her and opened his laptop, which had been left on the coffee table. Ryan Googled the Reverend Josiah Martins and added Holland into the search. Several entries popped up.

"Take a look," Ryan said, turning the screen toward her.

November 1728

A grand house is being built on a hill overlooking the bay. The ostentatious structure requires much labor and materials. I have made it a point to visit the site, intent on meeting the owner, but found only several laborers who were hard at work. I asked them who is building this affront to modesty, and they said they cannot reveal the name of their patron. I do, however, recall a couple by the name of Holland passing through our settlement. I think they might be behind this.

Lauren looked up, her lips curling into a smug smile. "Sounds like the Reverend Martins had some strong opinions about the business of others," she said, scrolling down and skimming over several paragraphs until she found the next reference.

February 1729

Mistress Holland and her child have been installed in the newly built house along with a young male servant. The woman keeps to herself and only leaves her home to attend the Protestant church, and even that she does not do regularly. I have yet to determine if she's a widow, but my sister, who has an eye for such things, tells me the woman is with child. There's no master in residence, but there's no reason to suspect her husband is dead. Simply gone.

"Why would George Holland build a house so far away from either Cambridge or Boston and leave his pregnant wife there alone with a child and a servant?" Lauren asked.

"Perhaps he wanted to be rid of her," Ryan suggested. "Maybe he had a mistress whom he preferred and had moved her into his house in Cambridge."

"Would this not tarnish his reputation among his customers, given that many of them would have been students of theology at the College of Cambridge?"

Ryan shrugged. "It's hard to say. This website is devoted to the writings of well-known Puritan ministers of the time. Let's see if we can find any other references to the Hollands."

He continued scrolling until he came upon another entry, the last to mention the Hollands.

April 1729

I have instructed all parishioners to shun Mistress Holland and her servant should they come into our settlement for any reason. Riches tainted by the blood of innocents were used to build the witch's house, which is what I now believe her to be, and the man who wore the guise of an honest citizen is in actuality a criminal and a privateer known to colonial authorities. The Devil has installed this sinful family in our midst to test our faith, but we will not succumb to his wiles, which are disguised as easily made coin.

"So, George Holland was a privateer?" Lauren asked, surprised by the implication.

"It's possible, I suppose, but I've never heard any mention of it," Ryan replied.

"Nothing to support Martins' claim came up in my earlier search of the family," Lauren said. "Sounds like he was the type who saw sin behind every bush anyway."

"Preaching about the sinners in their midst might have been a way to isolate the Puritan community and retain his grip on power. In any case, there don't seem to be any further entries pertaining to the Hollands."

Lauren glanced at her watch. It was getting late, and she was tired. "I think I'd better go. Thank you for dinner and for helping me with my research."

"I'll forward you a link if I find anything else," Ryan said as he shut the laptop.

"There's no Wi-Fi at the house, so I can only access the site on my phone, but the signal is spotty."

"You can always do your research here," Ryan suggested, coloring slightly. "I'd welcome the company."

"Thank you. I just might take you up on that. I really am curious about this family."

"I'm not sure I understand why you need this information to write a book. You're a fiction author. You can tell any story you want."

"Yes, that's true, but I find that a story based on real events usually makes for more compelling reading. I can create a plot to fit the few facts I've been able to find, but I'd like to know if I'm on the right track."

"I'm afraid we'll never know the real story."

"Probably not."

"Would you like some coffee before you go?" Ryan asked. Lauren was about to refuse, but the expression in his eyes quickly changed her mind. He didn't want her to leave; that was obvious, and she wasn't sure she wanted to go.

"Yes, please," she said and watched his eyes light up. She didn't really want any coffee, and the caffeine would probably keep her up half the night, but she had no desire to return to her silent house when she could spend some more time with Ryan, whose company, she was surprised to admit, she was enjoying.

Chapter 20

Moonlight streamed through the window, casting a silvery path on the floor beneath. Oblivious to Lauren's incredulous gaze and bated breath, the woman paced the room, an infant in a trailing white gown on her shoulder. The baby whimpered and fussed, its breathing rapid and shallow. It was obviously ill, its mother fretful and tired. Lauren watched as the woman sat on a low stool by the glowing hearth, pulled down her nightdress, and put the baby to her breast. The child rested its head against her smooth breast but didn't begin to nurse. Squeezing the nipple with her fingers, she dribbled milk into the baby's mouth, urging it to drink.

"Please, sweetheart," she whispered to the cranky child. "You're in need of nourishment." She sounded desperate and terrified of losing her baby.

Lauren's heart went out to her. The woman had been dead for centuries, but her anguish resonated through the years and her isolation was palpable, its echo filling the room and making Lauren inexplicably anxious. How frightening it must have been to have no doctor or hospital nearby, the only resources hope and prayer. Infant mortality had been shockingly high, and every family had occupied their own section of a graveyard, many of the stones sad and tiny, like the babies who slumbered beneath them.

The woman rocked the baby, singing quietly until it calmed and went to sleep, leaving her with her own thoughts. She leaned her head back against the tall back of the chair and closed her eyes, but Lauren could tell she wasn't sleeping. Her lips moved in silent prayer and her hand never moved from the baby's chest, as if she were making sure its heart continued to beat as it slept. Translucent tears fell, sliding down her pale cheeks and dripping into her mouth.

"Why aren't you here?" she asked scornfully. "I need you. Why aren't you here?"

Lauren watched the scene, mesmerized, until the shimmering light of dawn left the corner empty and the hearth stone cold. As before, when she'd seen Sophie, Billy hadn't barked, unable to sense her presence. Was she going mad, her mind conjuring up images that weren't there?

Getting out of bed, Lauren strode to the desk and yanked open the drawer where Sophie had hidden her letters. She had no idea what she'd expected to find, but the drawer held some blank envelopes and several outdated stamps someone had left behind. There was nothing there that might have belonged to Sophie Holland—not anymore.

Chapter 21

Boston

May 1727

Sophie lowered herself into a chair and folded her hands in her lap, unsure what to do. The wedding had been a splendid affair, paid for almost entirely by Lionel Holland. As he'd pointed out repeatedly, it wasn't every day one's son got married. Sophie wished Amelia had been there, but she was indisposed due to her advanced pregnancy and couldn't attend the nuptials. The whole day—in fact, the past two months—had felt like a dream, or more accurately a nightmare Sophie hadn't been able to wake up from. She could barely recall George's initial visit or their conversation, having channeled all her energy into keeping a pleasant smile on her face and not bursting into tears. He'd been kind, considerate, and very nervous, his fingers plucking at a loose thread on his waistcoat and his cheeks stained pink despite the chill of the room.

Perhaps it was his distress that had endeared him to Sophie; she could understand just how he felt. For some unfathomable reason, he'd fallen in love with her, and his yearning shone from his eyes like a beacon, signaling to her battered soul and guiding it to shore. She no longer held out any hope for Teddy's return, nor had she been able to find out anything about the whereabouts of her baby. It didn't matter what happened to her now. All that was left was to put one foot in front of the other and hope that, in time, she'd have put enough distance between herself and the tragedy that had shattered her world. And here she was, married to George Holland, about to embark on a future she'd never imagined for herself.

Sophie took in the room. It was one of the guest rooms at Mr. Holland's house, a pretty chamber decorated in shades of pink and cream. Her nightdress had been laid out on the bed by one of the maids, and George's dressing gown lay folded on a chair, his slippers carefully placed beneath the chair. For some reason, it was the sight of the dressing gown that really distressed her. There was something terribly intimate about its velveteen folds that suggested a physical closeness with her new husband she wasn't ready to embrace.

"Shall I help you, miss?" a maid who'd come into the room without knocking inquired of Sophie.

"Yes, please," Sophie replied, unsure her own trembling hands were up to the task.

The maid unlaced the bodice, helped Sophie out of her skirt, petticoats, and stays, and carefully rolled down her stockings before pulling the nightdress over her head. Sophie should have been embarrassed to have a stranger see her in a state of undress, but she felt numb with apprehension and too tired after putting on a show of bridal happiness for the dozens of guests Mr. Holland had invited. All the prominent citizens of Boston had gathered at the church and then returned to the house for the feast that followed. Sophie's father had beamed at his acquaintances and accepted their congratulations, but his show of paternal pride had been nothing more than relief at having Sophie finally wed after the disgrace she'd brought on his head.

Sophie turned toward the door, forcing a smile to her face as George entered their bridal chamber.

"Goodnight, sir," the maid said, and scurried from the room.

"Goodnight," George mumbled.

He shut the door behind her and turned the key in the lock, sending a flurry of nervous tingles down Sophie's back. She was sure the gesture didn't mean anything sinister, but she didn't like the idea of being locked in.

"You made a beautiful bride," George said as he came toward her, holding out his hands. Sophie had no choice but to place her hands in his and rise to stand before him. "I couldn't wait for the party to end."

"Yes, it went on for rather a long time," Sophie agreed.

George smiled, presumably at her naivete at misinterpreting his comment. "Shall we go to bed?" he asked, his voice low and husky.

"If you wish it."

"I wish it," George replied, and having let go of her hands, he unbuttoned his coat. His movements were hurried, as if he couldn't bear to waste any more time.

George tossed his coat atop his dressing gown, then kicked off his shoes, pulled his shirt over his head, and quickly removed his britches, garters, and stockings. His body was doughy and white, the physique of a man who rarely did more than take a stroll down the street. His chest and stomach were sprinkled with coarse brown hair, and his surprisingly large member rose proudly from a thicket of darker curls. Sophie lowered her gaze, worried George would notice the revulsion in her eyes.

"Take off your nightdress," he instructed gruffly. "You won't be needing it." All his nervousness was gone, replaced by impatience and desire.

Sophie did as she was told, pulling the garment over her head to reveal her nakedness. She hoped George wouldn't notice the faint red lines on her belly caused by the stretching of the skin when she was in the final stages of pregnancy. Would he be able to tell she wasn't a virgin? she asked herself for the umpteenth time since accepting his proposal.

George lifted her up and laid her on the bed, immediately covering her body with his own. His lips found hers and he kissed her hard, pushing his tongue into her mouth in his mounting excitement. She could feel the pressure of his shaft against her thigh and felt a growing sense of panic. She didn't want this, didn't want him. He was a virtual stranger to her, this man who was now her lord and master.

George broke the kiss, his face looming above her, his gaze hazy with drink and his pupils dilated with lust. "You mustn't fear me, Sophie. I only want to make you happy," he said. His breath was warm on her face, his body hot against her cold skin. She wanted to press her legs together, to lock him out of her body, but he was her husband now, and she had to perform her wifely duty whether she wished to or not.

Sophie tried to relax as George slid his fingers inside her, exploring her urgently, willing her to feel desire for him. Sophie moaned, but not from enjoyment. George's probing was too forceful, causing her pain. He took her reaction for pleasure and assumed she was ready for him. He pushed his way into her body, thrusting again and again until his seed spilled inside her, wet and hot. He exhaled loudly and rested his forehead against hers, his lips curling into a smile of contentment.

"I hope I didn't hurt you, my dear," he said softly. "I meant to go slowly, but I simply couldn't rein myself in. I've wanted you for so long," he confessed.

"You didn't hurt me," Sophie lied. It wasn't his fault he wasn't Teddy and the mere thought of him inside her made her want to howl with misery. He'd done what any husband would do, and she had to respond as a dutiful wife. She laid her hand on George's chest and he covered it with his own, smiling into her eyes.

"We're going to be very happy, you and I. Wait till you see the house I've found for us. You're going to like it; I know it."

Until the week before the wedding, George had lived in rooms he rented from a widow of his father's acquaintance, but now that he was a married man, he'd need a household of his own.

"I look forward to seeing my new home," Sophie replied woodenly. Once in Cambridge, she'd be even further away from her baby, unable to make inquiries without the aid of Agnes. Agnes had sworn she'd continue to inquire after the child, but Sophie didn't expect her to try too hard. Agnes hoped to be married soon, but until her wedding she'd have to remain in Sophie's father's employ. She'd confided to Sophie that her future husband didn't earn enough to support a family, so they might have to wait a year or two to wed, leaving Agnes to rely on her wages until her situation changed.

"Why do you look so sad?" George asked as he studied her face.

"I'm just tired," Sophie replied, and she was. All she wanted was to be allowed to close her eyes and go to sleep.

"You can sleep in tomorrow," George said, solicitous once more. "We're in no hurry to leave. We can even stay for an extra day. Mr. Williams, my clerk, will see to the shop, and I've asked Mrs. Quarry—that's our new housekeeper—to prepare the house for our arrival. So, you just rest, my dear," George said and kissed her lightly on the tip of her nose. "I'm so happy," he added, cupping her breast in a way that suggested that rest wasn't on his agenda. "Are you as happy as I am, Sophie?"

"Yes, George," she lied again. "But I'm very tired," she reminded him.

George withdrew his hand and covered her with the counterpane, tucking her in like a child. "Sleep, my love. You look done in."

He blew out the candle, and as darkness swallowed the room, Sophie was finally able to drop the pretense and let her tears silently flow.

Chapter 22

The ride to their new home didn't take long. Cambridge was only four miles from Boston and took about an hour and half to reach by carriage. The weather was fine, and Sophie would have enjoyed the journey had George not talked continuously, telling her all about the college and the outlying areas.

"Harvard College is one of the greatest institutions of learning in Massachusetts. It even had an Indian College, but it ceased to operate some years ago. I suppose they couldn't find enough savages worthy of the honor," George scoffed. "There were a few that graduated. I can't imagine that they passed their exams honorably. Those red-skinned devils would cheat their own mothers if they could get away with it. I must admit that opening a sister bookshop near the college was a stroke of genius on my father's part," he continued. "Not only do the students have an insatiable hunger for reading, but we also offer the texts they require for their coursework, making Holland's Book Shoppe an indispensable asset to the school. I suggested to Father that we buy back used texts from the students and sell them at a reduced price to those who are on a stringent budget. Father was skeptical at first, saying that dealing in used books would tarnish the reputation of the shop, but the profit I've made off this sideline has convinced him otherwise. If business continues to flourish, I intend to expand the shop, making it bigger and better than my father's shop in Boston," George bragged.

"Do you sell any books geared toward women?" Sophie asked, and instantly regretted the question.

George raised an eyebrow, then laughed merrily. "What a curious nature you have, my dear. We don't have a women's section to speak of, but there are certain sermons and tracts that address the role of a woman within the home and her responsibilities to her husband. You can borrow them from the shop and read them at your leisure—not that you've been neglecting your wifely duties," he said with an exaggerated wink.

Sophie blushed, deeply embarrassed by any reminder of their conjugal congress. George took his duties very seriously and had made sure to avail himself of her body several more times before leaving for Cambridge. Sophie supposed she was grateful that he'd never questioned her virginity, but if he meant to go on as he'd begun, she'd have no peace from his advances.

"Perhaps I can help you in the shop," Sophie offered. "It would help me meet some of the townspeople."

George pretended to consider her request, then squeezed her hand in a reassuring manner. "I do have Mr. Williams to help me, but maybe you can come by for an hour or two a day. I doubt you'll meet any suitable candidates for friendship. Most of the shop's customers are students and lecturers, and they're all male, obviously. But don't worry, you won't be at a loose end for long," he assured her. "Most of my acquaintances are married, and their wives will be more than happy to welcome you into their circle. I admit that none of them are very young, but perhaps they will offer the guidance you lacked while growing up, having lost your own dear mama at such a young age."

The thought of spending her time with stodgy matrons of George's acquaintance who would make it a point of schooling her on her duties as a wife made Sophie sigh with impatience. George looked instantly concerned.

"Are you unwell? Should we stop for a rest?"

"Thank you, but I'm quite all right," Sophie replied, having no wish to prolong the journey. She was eager to see her new home and figure out exactly how many hours a day she'd have to herself while George was tending to his growing business. "Tell me about the house," she invited, hoping to distract him.

"It's not as grand as my father's house, of course, but it's sure to suit our needs. There's a kitchen, dining room, and parlor on the ground floor, and three bedrooms upstairs. Enough for a growing family, I should think. Should the shop continue to prosper, I intend to buy some land and build us a permanent residence. What do you think of that, my dear?"

"That sounds wonderful," Sophie replied, not energized by the prospect of being mistress of her own abode in the least. "I do hope Amelia is well.".

"You can write to her," George suggested. "I send a letter to my father weekly. You can add a missive for Amelia, and I will make sure she receives it. It's no trouble for the boy to stop off at Major Dawson's house."

"Thank you, George. That's very kind."

"I know you'll miss my sister. She's vacuous and vain, but she can be very amusing when she chooses to be. I don't suppose motherhood will change that. Amelia will hand over that child to a nursemaid as soon as it draws breath," George said, chuckling. "Amelia is not one for motherly emotions."

Sophie considered his comment. She supposed George was right. Amelia cared only for new gowns, shoes, and trinkets. Motherhood would not come naturally to her, but maybe she was the lucky one. Had Sophie been as devoid of maternal instinct as Amelia, she wouldn't feel as bereft at the loss of her baby and would relish the freedom she'd gained by ridding herself of the unwelcome burden. Her head dipped as she thought of her son, the brim of her hat hiding her expression. Would the sharp edges of pain that were forever sawing at her heart ever dull? Her son would be four months and ten days old. *If he lived*, her mind added cruelly, reminding her once again that she had no way of knowing whether her child had survived.

"Nearly there," George said, patting her hand again. "I think you should have a rest once we arrive. I might even join you," he added playfully, his intentions as clear as the cloudless sky outside the window of the carriage.

"That would be nice," Sophie mumbled miserably.

Chapter 23

Lauren

Lauren woke with a start. She first realized she was terribly cold, and then noticed the patio door was ajar. She sat bolt upright, rubbing sleep from her eyes. She'd been listening to an audiobook, and the soothing tones of the narrator must have lulled her to sleep. She grabbed for her phone, but it had run out of juice while she slept, the screen now black and unresponsive. Lauren glanced toward the door. It had been just past 4:00 p.m. when she began listening, but now it was well past seven, the evening beyond the window having gone from overcast to nearly dark, the broody clouds hovering on the distant horizon like steel wool soaked with dirty dishwater. She'd left the door open a crack to let in some fresh air, but the opening was now about a foot wide.

"Oh no!" Lauren cried, realization dawning. "Billy! Billy, where are you?" she called into the ominous silence. He'd been curled up on her legs while she'd been listening to the book, but now he was gone.

She quickly checked the house, but Billy was nowhere to be found, his crate in the corner empty. Lauren yanked open the door and ran out into the night, calling for the puppy as she ran down the steps to the dock. Her heart was beating wildly, her breath coming fast as one horrible scenario after another assaulted her imagination. What if he was hurt again? What if he'd fallen into the water? Dusk had given way to murky, moonless darkness, making Lauren feel as if it were midnight. She shivered in her thin sweater, wishing she'd had the presence of mind to grab a fleece before running out of the house.

Water lapped softly at the dock, but there was no sign of the dog. Lauren peered into the darkness, trying to determine if he'd come this way, but there was nothing to go on save the fact that if he'd come down, he'd not have been able to make it back up the steep steps on his short legs. Billy either hadn't come this way or had already drowned.

Hysteria welled up in Lauren's chest, her breath coming in short gasps as she raced up the steps and into the copse surrounding the house. It was shady and peaceful during the day, but now the woods were dark and sinister, the thick trunks blocking out the light from the house. Lauren thought she heard something and ran toward the sound, holding out her hands in front of her for fear of running into a tree trunk in the dark.

The sound had seemed to come from somewhere on her left, but when she ran in that direction, she realized it had just been the wind moving through the trees. She turned back, walked a few paces, then realized she could no longer see the house. She had no idea which way she'd come. The wind was picking up, the branches swaying above her head like black ghostly limbs that melted into the impenetrable darkness of the sky.

"Billy!" Lauren yelled, but heard no answering bark. "Billy, where are you, you silly pup?"

Fingers of panic crept up her spine, making the hair on the back of her neck rise. How far did these woods go? The closest house was about half a mile away, and it was empty, the owners not having opened it for the summer season yet. Lauren ambled along in the dark, stumbling on thick roots and scratching her hand on rough bark. The night seemed to grow darker by the minute, the air dense with moisture. And then the mist rolled in, effectively cutting her off from the world. She was lost in a sea of white, her face damp, her clothes clinging to her body. She shivered violently as the damp penetrated her canvas sneakers and cotton socks.

In her panic, Lauren nearly fell over a fallen log. She sank down onto the wet bark and buried her face in her hands. She had no idea which way she'd come from and the mist was growing thicker. A sob escaped her chest as she realized she might have to spend the night in the forest. She was no more than a quarter mile from the house, but she couldn't see a thing. She could wander around for hours without emerging into the clearing on which the house was built.

"Calm down," she told herself in her most sensible tone. "You're very close to the house. You just need to wait for the fog to lift, then you can follow the light."

Her voice sounded hollow in the thick air swirling around her, and she thought she saw a faint glow moving between the trees. Lauren lowered her hands and stared straight ahead, her breath catching in her throat as her mind finally caught up to her eyes and the two agreed on what they were seeing. Sophie Holland stood a few feet away, an old-fashioned lantern glowing in her hand. She wore a dark-blue gown and a thick cape, and her hair was tucked into a cap, a few dark strands escaping to frame her face. She raised the lantern, illuminating her face, and Lauren froze, too afraid to draw breath. Sophie was looking right at her, her gaze earnest and direct. She gestured to Lauren, indicating that she should follow.

Lauren stood, and a strangled gasp escaped from her cold lips. In the glow of the lantern, she could just make out the sheer drop that towered above the bay. Had she continued walking, she'd have fallen headlong into the water. There seemed to be no one around for miles, and no approaching boat's light cut through the choking darkness. She could have died had she hit her head on the way down or collided with rocks that slumbered beneath the surface of the still water.

Sophie beckoned again and Lauren followed, her limbs as stiff as those of a wooden soldier. Her mind seemed to shut down, her body operating on pure instinct. She followed the caped figure, transfixed by the yellow light that seemed to encircle Sophie's head like a halo. Eventually, a second orb of light appeared, the glow of the living room window through the swirling fog. Sophie turned and waited until Lauren grasped the significance of this, then seemed to melt into the fog, the light of her lantern vanishing as suddenly as it had appeared.

Lauren drew a shaky breath, coming out of her trance as the light of the house spurred her on. She moved faster, running toward the open patio door as if something were chasing her. She crashed into the living room and closed the door, locking it with trembling hands. For a moment, she forgot all about Billy, but when he came trotting toward her from the kitchen, his tail wagging in greeting, she fell to her knees and held the puppy to her breast, hugging him so tightly he let out a whimper of protest.

"Oh, thank God," she muttered into his warm fur. "Thank God you're safe."

Billy wiggled free of her damp embrace and retreated to his crate, leaving Lauren on her knees in the middle of the living room. She forced herself to get up, grabbed her phone and plugged it in to charge, then selected Ryan's number. Had she thought it through, she might not have made the call, but she was so shaken she had to hear a human voice, and Ryan was the only person she really knew in Orleans.

"Lauren? Are you okay?" Ryan's voice sounded as if it came from far away, and she realized she was sobbing. "Lauren?" Ryan called through the phone.

"I think so," she mumbled. "I got lost in the fog." Her teeth began to chatter, the cold having seeped into her bones. Her clothes were filthy and wet, and her shoes were soaked through.

"I'm coming over," Ryan exclaimed.

"What about Ty?"

"Merielle is here. She'll stay with him."

Lauren sank onto the couch and pulled a chenille throw over her shoulders, too weak to trek upstairs to change into dry clothes. As her body warmed up, coherent thought returned, but she still could make no sense of what had happened tonight. Fragments of thought swirled around her head like the fog that had trapped her but now seemed to have completely dissipated. She tried to conjure up Sophie's face, but all she could recall were those dark eyes, the gaze so direct and intense.

She sprang to her feet when she heard the crunch of tires on gravel and pulled the door open to Ryan, who sprinted up the drive.

"Lauren, what happened?" She fell into his arms and he held her tight, his body warm and comforting, his arms strong and safe.

"I don't know," she whispered. "I'm not sure."

"Come, have a seat. You are all wet." Ryan led her back to the couch and sat her down, adjusting the throw to cover her. "I will get you some dry clothes, and while you change, I'll make a fire. Do you have any whisky or brandy?"

"I don't think so."

"Okay, never mind." Ryan went upstairs and returned with a pair of velour trackpants and a matching hoodie. He also brought a dry T-shirt and socks. As Lauren accepted the clothes, the part of her mind that was thinking rationally again was grateful he hadn't gone through her underwear drawer. She went to the downstairs bathroom and removed all her garments but the panties that were still dry and put on the fresh clothes. She washed her hands and face with hot water and towel-dried her hair before leaving the bathroom.

By the time she returned, Ryan had a little fire going and seemed to have unearthed a half-full bottle of whisky. He poured Lauren a generous amount and held the glass out to her. "Drink."

She didn't care for whisky, but she accepted the glass and took a few sips. The whisky burned its way down her esophagus and settled in a pool of warmth in her belly. She drained the rest of the glass and held her hand out for more in the hope that the alcohol would revive her. She did feel more human after the second drink and settled on the sofa, folding her legs beneath her as she stared into the leaping flames of the fire.

Ryan came to sit next to her. He didn't say anything, just put his arm around her, and she leaned into him, resting her head on his shoulder as if they'd sat that way many times before. Billy decided to get in on the action, probably jealous that Lauren was paying attention to someone else, and came to stand at Ryan's feet, wagging his tail and looking up imploringly. Ryan lifted him up onto the couch and settled him on the other side, his hand stroking Billy's head. The three of them remained like that until the fire burned down, and Lauren's thoughts stopped spinning long enough for her to tell Ryan what had happened.

"She knowingly came to your aid?" Ryan asked, stroking her hair affectionately.

"She led me away from the edge. She was aware of me, Ryan, not like before when she seemed not to notice my presence."

"That's bizarre," Ryan said, shaking his head.

"It is, but that's what happened."

"Were you afraid of her?"

"No. She clearly wanted to help me," Lauren replied, astonished that they were even having this conversation.

"She seems to have chosen you," Ryan said.

"For what?"

"I don't know. Perhaps she feels some sort of kinship with you."

"Why would she? She lived hundreds of years ago. What could we possibly have in common?"

"Maybe she'll eventually tell you, if you stay long enough," Ryan replied.

Lauren snuggled closer to him, enjoying his solid presence. She was intrigued by the prospect. Was Sophie trying to communicate with her? Then a different sort of thought fought its way to the top. Was Ryan humoring her? Did he think she'd imagined the whole thing, but didn't want to tell her outright she was crazy?

"Ryan, I really did see her," Lauren said, her voice small and wobbly.

"I know you did," he replied, stroking her back as if she were a colicky baby. "I believe you."

"You said you didn't believe in ghosts," she reminded him.

"I lied."

"Why?"

"Because I didn't want you to think I was weird," Ryan replied, smiling down at her. "I've never seen an apparition, but after Alicia died, there were moments when I felt her presence, especially when I was worried or stressed. I was a first-time dad, trying to parent a baby on my own. I was scared and unsure of what I was doing half the time. There were a few instances when I really panicked, and suddenly, I heard Alicia's voice in my head, telling me to calm down and follow my instincts."

"Do you think she was really there?"

"Not in any physical sense, but I think my mind conjured up her response based on my profound knowledge of her. I resurrected her because I needed her."

"Do you think I'm resurrecting Sophie somehow?"

Ryan shrugged. "I really couldn't say, but the fact that she's shown herself to you must mean something."

"I think she's lost someone dear to her and can't accept they're gone."

"Kind of like you?" he asked gently.

Lauren nodded, unable to speak. She had lost someone dear to her, but she'd lost a lot more than that, things she hadn't told anyone about, not even her parents. Perhaps Sophie had sensed her pain and reached out through the centuries, stepping through the veil of time to comfort a kindred spirit.

"I wonder who she lost," Ryan mused.

"I think it was her baby. I saw her trying to comfort it when it was ill. Maybe it died and she never came to terms with her grief."

"That could certainly be the case. Medicine in those days did more harm than good, and children were often the first to be carried off in any epidemic."

"I wonder where Sophie's buried," Lauren said, sitting up straighter now that the whisky and fire had done their bit to dispel the chill. "Is there any way to find out?"

"We can certainly check, but not today. I think it's time you went to bed. You look done in."

"Thank you," Lauren said, looking up at him through a haze of fatigue. "Thank you for coming."

"You don't need to thank me. I'll come whenever you call," Ryan replied. He cupped her face and ran a thumb over her cheek, making her shiver with the intimacy of the gesture. She thought he might kiss her, but he gave her a chaste peck on the forehead before getting to his feet. "Do you think you might want to move to a different bedroom?" he asked, smiling in a way that suggested he already knew what she'd say.

"No, I want to be close to her, especially after what she did for me tonight. It's not her I'm afraid of."

Lauren was relieved when Ryan didn't ask what she'd meant. She'd revealed more than she'd intended to tonight, and she was too tired and emotionally overwrought to explain something she'd never meant to say out loud.

"I'll say goodnight, then," he said, opening the door and stepping out into the moonless night. "Call me if you need anything."

"I'll be all right now," Lauren promised, and for some reason, she was sure she would be.

Chapter 24

Sophie

July 1727

The room was unbearably stuffy, the late afternoon sun shining undimmed through the leaded window. Sophie wished she could shed her gown and lie on the bed in her shift, but that wasn't to be. They were dining with the Reverend and Mrs. Chapman, a middle-aged couple of George's acquaintance who invited them to dine every other Monday, like clockwork. Sophie didn't care for Reverend Chapman, a corpulent man with a florid complexion and a grating voice that he liked to exercise to great excess. His wife was a mouse of a woman, badgered and humiliated into submission by a husband who treated her like a dimwitted child.

"Are you nearly ready?" George called from below.

"Almost."

Sophie pushed the last pin into the bun atop her head and covered it with a lace-trimmed cap before descending the stairs. George nodded in approval and they set off. It had cooled a little outside while she was getting ready, and she enjoyed the brief walk, wishing they could just keep walking right past the reverend's house. But George thought it important to keep up with the neighbors, especially ones who had some influence in the community and could be of use. Reverend Chapman taught theology at the college and instructed his students to buy the necessary texts at Holland's Book Shoppe, a favor George greatly appreciated and made mention of as often as he could without sounding sycophantic.

Casting a last longing look at the dramatic sunset, Sophie followed George into the house, where a servant directed them to the parlor. Mrs. Chapman sat in her usual chair, a small glass of sherry in her hand, while the reverend conversed loudly with two men who stood with their backs to the door. For one brief moment, Sophie froze, her heart thumping painfully as her gaze settled on the younger of the two men. His auburn hair was tied back in a ponytail with a black ribbon, the coppery strands catching the last of the evening light. The set of his shoulders and his relaxed stance were so like Teddy's that Sophie let out an involuntary gasp, earning herself a look of reproach from George.

The reverend stopped mid-sentence and greeted the newcomers, forcing the two men to turn around and do likewise. Sophie trembled with relief. As much as she longed to see Teddy again or learn something of his fate, she had no wish to do so in Reverend Chapman's parlor, in front of George.

"Ah, there you are. Allow me to introduce you," the reverend boomed as George and Sophie approached.

"The Reverend Noah Trevor and his nephew Alexander Trevor, who've only just arrived from England. Our esteemed friends and neighbors, Mr. George Holland and his lovely wife."

Sophie lowered her gaze demurely, afraid her resentment of the reverend would show plainly in her eyes. She didn't even warrant an introduction. She was simply the wife, George's chattel. The men bowed over her hand and assured her what a delight it was to make her acquaintance, and Sophie replied in kind, like a well-trained dog.

"Shall we adjourn to the dining room?" the reverend invited, strolling on ahead and completely ignoring his wife, who brought up the rear.

"What brings you to our humble colony?" George asked as soon as the soup was served.

"I've been invited to take up a teaching post at the college, and Alexander has been enrolled to study mathematics," Reverend Trevor replied. "I confess, I'm relieved to have arrived safely."

"Did you encounter stormy weather, Reverend?" Sophie asked, refusing to eat in silence like poor Mrs. Chapman.

"The weather was pleasant for most of the crossing, but there are other dangers at sea," Alexander replied, his eyes sparkling with amusement. "Uncle was terrified we'd be set upon by pirates."

"Pirates?" Sophie exclaimed.

"Indeed, my dear lady," Reverend Trevor replied. "Travel by sea has become most perilous."

"Is that so?" George asked, putting down his soup spoon and fixing his gaze on the Trevors. "Do tell."

"Many a ship has been attacked," Reverend Trevor said, his cheeks reddening with outrage.

"Most pirate companies are based in the Caribbean islands, but they do not limit themselves to sailing the Caribbean Sea. They are coming further and further afield. No ship traveling from Europe is safe," Alexander said, directing his comment to Sophie.

"What happens when they spot a ship?" Sophie asked, her soup forgotten.

"They pursue the ship for a time, staying well within sight to frighten the passengers and the crew, then come close enough to fire a warning shot and demand to board the vessel. If the captain refuses, they fire on the ship. They are well armed, their cannon outnumbering the cannon on any non-naval vessel by at least two to one. It's not in their interests to sink the ship, since the cargo would be lost, but they do enough damage to make sure the ship is no longer seaworthy, effectively sentencing everyone aboard to death."

"And then?" Sophie asked, her breath catching in her throat.

"They board the vessel, plunder the cargo, relieve the passengers of any valuables they might have, take anything they need for their own voyage, like foodstuffs and drinking water, and more often than not, press members of the crew, mostly young men who are fit and strong, into service."

"Do they kill anyone?" Sophie asked, her eyes never leaving Alexander Trevor's suntanned face. Close up, he didn't look anything like Teddy, but something in his manner reminded her of Teddy all the same.

"Only if they try to resist. The passengers rarely put up a fight, but there are brave and foolish captains who decide to engage in a sea battle, the result being a decimated crew, a ship too damaged to make port, and a reputation in tatters for the idiot captain who risked it all for a few sacks of grain or a shipment of fine china."

"How very frightening," Sophie said, her hand flying to her breast.

"Don't you worry, my dear," Reverend Chapman cut in. "Those scoundrels will all be captured and executed. The Royal Navy is on high alert. They're patrolling the seas and eliminating the pirate ships one by one. In fact, I hear the French have joined the fight, as well as the Dutch and the Spanish. The pirates are attacking all ships, regardless of the colors they sail under, so it's no longer strictly a British problem."

"Well, that's good to know," George said. "Of course, no one can hope to compete with the might of the Royal Navy, but it's nice to know those lesser countries are finally taking action. Why, several of the ships we've had goods on were attacked, but luckily for us, the pirates are not interested in literature. They direct their efforts toward stealing more valuable goods."

"There's no cargo of higher value than the written word," Reverend Trevor chimed in.

"I can't imagine they'd earn much profit from a stack of Bibles," Alexander replied, making Sophie smile into her napkin.

"You cannot put a value on the word of our Lord," Reverend Chapman thundered.

"Nor was I trying to, but you must admit that several bolts of fine silk or casks of brandy are more desirable than *Paradise Lost*."

"Young man, you're impertinent," Reverend Chapman replied, his face mottled with anger.

"I do apologize, Reverend. I meant no offense. I was simply stating the obvious," Alexander replied humbly, but Sophie noticed the gleam of triumph in his eyes. He'd enjoyed riling the reverend. His gaze slid toward her and she smiled at him, acknowledging his small victory against the tyranny of clerics who dominated the faculty of the college and therefore the town itself.

"Shall we move on to the second course?" Mrs. Chapman inquired meekly, her eyes downcast and her cheeks flushed as if she'd just asked if they should all disrobe and dance around the dinner table.

"By all means," her husband replied, glaring at the servant who hadn't dared to begin clearing the plates without word from her mistress.

The rest of the meal passed in lively discussion, mostly because Alexander Trevor made it a point to stir things up, his blue eyes dancing with merriment as he irritated Reverend Chapman and his uncle time and again. Since Sophie had made the acquaintance of Reverend Chapman, this was the most pleasant meal they'd shared together, and she hoped the Trevors would be invited back, but given Reverend Chapman's belligerent demeanor, she highly doubted it.

"I do hope to see you again, Mrs. Holland," Alexander said as they prepared to leave. "You have brought beauty and charm to an otherwise lackluster gathering," he added under his breath.

Sophie's cheeks heated with pleasure, but she didn't reply. Alexander Trevor was the type of young man who enjoyed flouting convention. She was simply a means to an end in his quest to liven up what had promised to be a very dull evening.

The heat outside had abated while they were at dinner, and Sophie inhaled the fragrant evening air, enjoying its caress on her face. It wasn't until they'd nearly reached their own house that she realized George had been unusually quiet on the walk home and made virtually no comment on the Trevors, something Sophie found unusual. George was always full of opinions and liked to share them with her whether she was interested or not.

"How dare you humiliate me like that?" George rounded on her as soon as they were inside.

"What have I done?" Sophie asked, taken completely unawares.

"What have you done? Other than brazenly encourage young Trevor to pay attention to you by asking those insipid questions?"

"I was simply participating in the conversation," Sophie replied, stung by his accusation.

"And what made you think your contribution was welcome? What you have to say is of no interest to anyone. You are there simply as my wife, an ornament, nothing more."

"George, I didn't do anything wrong," Sophie protested. The slap that followed made her teeth rattle, and she stared at George as her hand flew to her stinging cheek.

"Don't you ever disrespect me that way again. Is that clear?"

"And if I do?" Sophie snapped, shocked by the sudden change in him. She'd never seen this side of him in the two months they'd been married and hoped that her defiance would make him see the error of his ways, but George came closer, bringing his face within an inch of hers.

"If you ever embarrass me that way again, you will receive a lot worse than a slap across the face."

"Such as?" Sophie whispered, horrified by his behavior.

"Why don't you keep testing my patience and you'll find out. Now, get upstairs and go to bed. I have nothing more to say to you."

George spun on his heel and walked into the parlor, slamming the door shut behind him and leaving Sophie reeling with the injustice of what had just occurred. For one thing, she hadn't expressed any opinions or asked any questions that might be embarrassing to George, and for another, she'd done nothing to encourage Alexander Trevor. He hadn't needed encouragement.

He's jealous, Sophie thought as she trudged upstairs, her shoulders slumped in misery. *He thought I found Alexander Trevor*

145

appealing. She sighed deeply and began to undress for bed, wondering how she might convince George he had nothing to worry about without making it known to him that she understood the reason for his rage. She didn't think calling attention to his masculine insecurity would win her any favors, not when he was in such a black mood.

Sophie hung up her gown, released her hair from its pins, blew out the candle, and climbed into bed. Her cheek no longer throbbed, but her pride had been wounded by George's outburst. She hoped that having had time to cool off, he'd see that he'd wronged her and apologize.

She was already falling asleep when George entered the bedroom. He made no effort to be quiet as he quickly undressed and got into bed. Pretending to be asleep seemed like the best course of action, so Sophie rolled onto her side, facing away from him, and waited for him to fall asleep, but George had other ideas. He reached for her and rolled her onto her back, pushing her nightdress up and shoving his knee between her legs to pry them apart. Sophie cried out as he pushed into her, thrusting roughly several times before achieving his climax and rolling off.

"George," she said, her voice trembling with pain and shock. "I'm sorry. I never meant to offend you."

She'd thought her apology would soften his stony demeanor, but he simply turned on his side and went to sleep, ignoring her distress.

Chapter 25

When Sophie came down to breakfast the following morning, George greeted her with a warm smile. "Good morning, my dear. Did you sleep well?"

"Eh, yes," Sophie replied, wondering if he'd forgotten the whole incident. He hadn't overindulged in liquor, but perhaps he'd drunk more than his limit.

"Excellent. What is your plan for the day?"

"I was going to go visit Mrs. Littleton. She's been unwell, and I thought she might appreciate the company."

"Very commendable of you," George replied genially. "But I would prefer if you were to wait until she's recovered. She might have something catching, and I wouldn't want you falling ill."

"But—" Sophie began, but let the matter drop when George glared at her from across the table.

"You will remain at home," he said, his tone brooking no argument.

"Yes, George."

"I'll see you at noon." He left the table and went to fetch his coat and hat before leaving for the shop.

Sophie remained at the table, staring at the embroidered cloth as if she were seeing it for the first time. She accepted a cup of tea from Mrs. Quarry and took a sip, hoping the strong brew would refresh her and lift her sagging spirits, but one could only expect so much of a hot drink. Sophie didn't have much of an appetite, so she retreated to the parlor with a book and shut the door, needing some time to herself. Mrs. Quarry tended to get chatty given the opportunity, and Sophie simply couldn't bear to listen to her blather at a time when she felt so emotionally fragile. In fact, she reflected bitterly, she felt much like a soft-boiled egg whose contents had been scooped out, leaving behind a cracked, empty shell.

She and George had been married for just over two months, but they hadn't grown any closer in that time. George reached for her frequently when they retired but made no effort to get to know her beyond the marriage bed. He'd been solicitous and kind, until last evening, but rarely asked her anything about herself or invited comment or opinion. Now she understood why. He'd called her an ornament, and she supposed that was what she was—a comely young woman who looked pretty in the gowns he'd ordered for her and inspired other men to think George a lucky devil.

Horace Brewster had encouraged his daughter to read, to form opinions, and to join him in conversation over the supper table, but George clearly wasn't interested in anything she had to say. She had no more value than pretty china or his new walnut writing desk. Two paths lay before her: the first being one of obedience and silence, and the second of gradually teaching George to accept her as a partner rather than just a possession to be shown off to his contemporaries. Sophie decided on the latter. She'd bide her time, but little by little, she'd show George that her opinions were well informed and worth listening to. Perhaps he'd even be proud of her if she managed to hold forth without arousing his jealousy. She highly doubted she'd see Alexander Trevor again, so that particular hurdle had already been overcome and need not be revisited.

Sophie hid in the parlor until nearly noon, when it was time to bring George his dinner. She cut two pieces of bread and placed a thick slice of ham between them, poured some cool ale into a stoppered bottle, and added a handful of strawberries from the garden. George loved strawberries, so hopefully the unexpected treat would brighten his mood. Sophie put her straw hat on over the cap to protect her complexion from the hot summer sun and set out for the shop, just down the street.

George barely acknowledged her when she came in, being in the middle of a discussion with several young men. Sophie took the basket into the tiny office at the back of the shop, where Mr. Williams was hunched over the sales ledger, then came back out, coming face to face with Alexander Trevor, whose face broke into a delighted smile.

"Mrs. Holland, what an absolute pleasure to see you again," he exclaimed. "I came into the shop this morning hoping to ask your husband's advice on a book I require, but running into you has made my day."

"Good day, Mr. Trevor," Sophie muttered, watching George's reaction from the corner of her eye. He was still speaking to the students, but she noted the tightening of his jaw and the narrowing of his eyes as he watched Alexander Trevor.

"I'm sorry, Mr. Trevor, but I'm afraid I must get home."

"Please, don't leave so soon. I'll be happy to regale you with more pirate stories if it'll keep you from going. I confess, after two months aboard a ship, I'm starved for lively company. I'm sure Mr. Holland won't object if I ask your opinion on this book of poetry I've purchased."

He pulled out a slim volume and held it out to her. "Have you read it? John Dunne. I've never actually read any of his poems, but uncle insisted I acquaint myself with his work. I must admit, they're rather good. I like his notion that no man is an island. What say you, Mrs. Holland? Do you think he's correct?"

"Yes, I think he is," Sophie replied. "We all need companionship, in one form or another, and affection."

"I agree wholeheartedly. What's life without affection?" he said, smiling into her eyes as if affection from her would make him the happiest man alive.

"Mr. Trevor, I really must get on."

"Of course. I'm sorry to have detained you. I do hope we'll see each other again. Soon."

"I'm sure we shall," Sophie mumbled as she inched toward the door, George's gaze branding her back with its intensity. Given what had happened last night, she had no illusions. She'd pay for this flirtatious discourse, even though she'd done nothing to encourage Alexander Trevor. George could hardly punish him, so he'd take his ire out on her. She prayed she was wrong, but her insides shriveled at the thought of meeting George over the supper table that evening.

That night marked a true turning point in Sophie's marriage. Many a husband punished his wife for her transgressions against him, but the punishments were generally limited to a tongue-lashing or a slap. Having enjoyed his supper, George ordered Sophie to come upstairs to their bedroom and told her to undress. He then pushed her over the side of the bed, lifted her shift, and administered ten lashes of his belt across her buttocks and thighs, striping the skin with angry red welts. Sophie had never known such pain or humiliation, and as her tears soaked into the flowery counterpane, she vowed never to forgive George for his harsh treatment of her.

After he finished, he cupped her sore buttock in his hand, caressing the reddened flesh as if he'd never seen anything so beautiful, then his fingers slid inside her, probing her aching privates tenderly and thoroughly. It was at that moment that Sophie realized that the purpose of the punishment had been two-fold. He was genuinely angry with her but belting her had aroused him as he'd never been aroused by her before, his shaft rock-hard as he parted her legs and slid inside her, gasping with pleasure. She wept from both pain and fear because she now knew that this would be the norm in their relationship, and any excuse would do for taking a belt to her if it meant giving George greater sexual pleasure.

Chapter 26

Sophie's prediction had been correct, but what she hadn't expected was George's attitude toward this new phase in their relationship. He was always charming and upbeat the morning after, winking at Sophie over the breakfast table as if they shared a delightful secret. He carried on as if his bouts of violence were a game, often inviting her to count along as he doled out the lashes and taking his time as if he were delaying her pleasure. Ten lashes once a week weren't enough to cause her serious harm, and the pain faded in a day or two, but every beating put a dent in her pride and diminished her self-worth, making her feel like nothing more than a whore, bought and paid for, who had to endure whatever her client demanded.

In time, Sophie came to understand that George truly believed she enjoyed her role in this twisted play. He seemed to think that having her bare bottom displayed for punishment, her tender parts clearly visible to him, aroused her as much as it did him. She often moaned when he caressed her after the beating, trying not to cry out in pain, but George took her reaction as validation that she was relishing his attentions. She begged him not to hit her, but in his mind, her fear was all a part of the plan, a ruse meant to drive him to greater heights once he finally silenced her and got on with the evening's entertainment.

After a few torturous months, Sophie thought she'd seen the worst of her husband, but that was still to come. She was sitting in the parlor, her embroidery on her knees, when George came in, his face tight with anger. He'd gone upstairs after supper but returned a few moments later, a letter in his hand.

"Who is she referring to?" he demanded, waving the letter in Sophie's face.

There was no use pretending. Sophie had received a letter from Agnes only that morning when the messenger from Boston arrived, bearing several parcels and letters from George's parents, Amelia, and George's grandmother.

"I repeat, who is she referring to when she says she still can't find any trace of him? Who is she looking for?"

Sophie clasped her hands in her lap to keep them from trembling. "She's referring to a childhood friend," Sophie replied. In part, that was true. Sophie had asked Agnes to let her know if she heard any news of Teddy, but in this case, the 'him' in question was Sophie's son. She'd foolishly assumed her correspondence was private, but she should have known better. George must have been reading her letters from the start. Perhaps he'd even read the letters Sophie had sent, to make sure she made no mention of his appalling behavior or complained in any way about the marriage.

"And why should you be so interested in the whereabouts of this friend?" George asked.

"We grew up together," Sophie replied, her voice shaky.

"Did you now? And just how close were you?"

"We were just childhood friends," Sophie insisted, hoping nothing of her feelings for Teddy showed in her face.

"You're lying!" George roared, his face puce with anger. "Have you been playing me for a fool?"

"What? No. I simply inquired if Agnes had seen him."

"You faithless whore!" George shouted as he advanced on her. Sophie sprang to her feet and tried to flee, but he grabbed her hair and threw her against the wall. "I'll kill you if you so much as look at another man."

"I haven't," Sophie cried.

"I saw the way you ogled that pup, Alexander Trevor. We all did. Have you lain with him?" George thundered.

"No."

"I don't believe you." George's fist slammed into her face, knocking her head against the wall. She screamed, but he didn't stop. He hit her in the stomach and chest and kicked her once she slid to the floor, blood dripping from her split lip.

"George, please," she begged. "I've done nothing wrong."

"I'll be the judge of that. From now on, you're not to leave this house alone. Mrs. Quarry will accompany you everywhere you go and report back to me should you look at any man a second too long. And you will receive no more letters from anyone other than Amelia. Get up, you heartless bitch."

George grabbed her under the arms and hoisted her to her feet, then dragged her from the room and toward the stairs. Sophie stumbled as he hauled her up, terrified, but George shoved her into the bedroom and locked the door, leaving her in a heap on the floor. This confrontation had not aroused him; it had unhinged him.

Sophie curled into a ball and covered her head with her hands. How was it possible for a man to go from the solicitous, shy young man she'd met at the garden party to this monster? Had he been this way all along, or did she bring this out in him in some way? Was it his jealousy that drove him mad, or some internal rage that needed to be periodically released? How could she endure being married to him for the rest of her life? Sooner or later, he'd kill her.

Chapter 27

Lauren

Spring had finally arrived, bringing warmer weather. Lauren wore a T-shirt and jeans as she followed Ryan down a narrow path between the stones. The ancient cemetery slumbered in the shadow of several large oaks, their newly unfurled leaves a juicy green against the aquamarine of the sky. Birdsong filled the air, the cemetery peaceful and quiet at that hour of the morning.

"Here they are," Ryan said as he parked Tyler's stroller next to a group of gray stones. The little boy was fast asleep, his hand clutching a stuffed monkey that was a favorite. "This is where the eighteenth-century Hollands are buried. I wasn't able to locate any old parish records, but Orleans Cemetery is actually one of the oldest on Cape Cod and the one where anyone from the period we're interested in would have been buried."

It looked it. Many of the stones stood at odd angles, some so sunken, only their tops showed through the thick new grass. Some of the inscriptions had been obliterated by time and the ravages of weather, but Lauren noticed a carving of a winged skull above many a name, the image strangely disturbing.

"What does that mean?" she asked.

"In some instances, the winged skull simply represented death, but in others, it meant to suggest that the person's journey wasn't over, and they had yet to ascend to Heaven."

"Meaning the afterlife wasn't assured?"

"Something like that. They were a grim lot, these early settlers."

Lauren walked along the row of stones. There were several that bore the name Holland, but she recognized only two names: Edward Holland and Sophie Holland. Edward Holland was the revolutionary Ryan had mentioned, and Sophie had to be the woman she'd seen. Lauren squatted next to the stone to examine the inscription. It was very basic, just a name and dates of birth and death. Sophie had died in January 1762, aged fifty-three.

"There's no stone for her husband," Lauren remarked as she got to her feet and peered at the rest of the Holland stones.

"No, there isn't. He must be buried in Cambridge," Ryan replied.

"Strange. You'd think husband and wife would be buried next to each other," Lauren mused.

"I guess, but there could have been a number of situations in which they'd be buried separately."

"Like what?"

"George Holland might have died years before her and been buried where he was living at the time. By the time his wife died, there might not have been any space next to George's grave, or perhaps her children or grandchildren didn't see the point of transporting her body all the way to Cambridge for burial."

"Didn't some of them live in Boston and Cambridge, where their book shops were located?" Lauren asked.

"Yes, but perhaps Sophie never returned to either town, for reasons we will never know," Ryan replied.

"Do you think there's anything in what Reverend Josiah Martins said about the house being built with blood money?"

Ryan shrugged. "The man was a raging Puritan. His idea of blood money could have been somewhat skewed. Perhaps he disapproved of the kind of books the Hollands sold in their shops and saw the profit they earned as a handout from the Devil."

"Yes, I suppose you're right. After all, the Hollands did sell a variety of books, not only religious texts."

"Someone like Martins would have vehemently disapproved of the *Canterbury Tales*, not to mention some of the racier offerings of the time."

Lauren raised her eyebrows in surprise. "What kind of racier offerings?" she asked, amused by Ryan's use of the old-fashioned term. The only person she knew who would have referred to something as 'racy' had been her grandmother.

"There was one book I've recently read about. It was called *The School of Venus* and it had been translated from French in the late seventeenth century. It was basically a sex manual for women, complete with illustrations."

"Do you think Holland's Book Shoppe would have carried something like that?" Lauren asked, genuinely scandalized by the idea. She thought of colonial Bostonians as prim and proper, Puritanical even. She was well aware that her generation hadn't invented sex, but the idea of sex manuals being openly sold in the town's bookshops had taken her by surprise.

"They might not have displayed it publicly, but there's always been a market for such things, and they could have stocked a few copies for their very special customers," Ryan replied, a smile of amusement tugging at the corners of his mouth. "Don't tell me you're shocked," he teased.

"No, I'm not. Not really. We tend to think of pornography as a modern trend, but it's been around for centuries. You're right, Reverend Martins' comments were probably based on nothing more than his suspicions."

"I'm hungry," Tyler whined. He'd just woken up and was rubbing his eyes.

"Okay, let's get some lunch, then," Ryan suggested. "I could really go for a lobster roll."

"I'm sorry, but I can't join you," Lauren replied, wishing more than anything she could spend more time in Ryan's company. "My brother is coming up this afternoon." Ryan looked momentarily crestfallen but didn't complain. "Are you busy tomorrow?" Lauren asked, hoping she'd see him again soon.

"Sorry, I have plans. It's my mom's birthday and we're all getting together at their place for a family lunch. Would you like to come? My parents would love to meet you," Ryan said, but there was a wariness in his tone that wasn't lost on Lauren. They were just getting to know each other, their relationship hovering between friendship and the possibly of something more, yet to be explored. She wasn't ready to meet his family, nor did she think he was ready to deal with the endless questions that would surely follow should he bring her to his mom's party.

"Thank you for the invitation, but I couldn't possibly accept. Enjoy the party," she said, hoping she sounded perky rather than dejected.

"Call me if you change your mind," Ryan said.

"Daaaad!" Tyler cried. "Let's goooo!"

"Sorry, I'd better go," Ryan said. "Tyler gets cranky when he's hungry, and I don't want to keep feeding him snacks."

"Go on," Lauren said. "I'll find my way home."

She watched him push the stroller out of the cemetery, then turned and walked among the rows of stones. With Ryan gone, the cemetery no longer felt peaceful. It was eerie and silent, a city of the dead. Lauren turned on her heel and hurried toward the exit. She'd had enough of death for one day.

Chapter 28

Lauren found Xavier on the patio, sitting in one of the Adirondack chairs and looking out over the horizon. "I can see why you love it here," he said, getting up to envelop her in a brotherly hug. "It's beautiful. I hope I'm invited to come up on weekends once it's warm enough to go to the beach."

"You are welcome anytime," Lauren replied, smiling. Now that he was there, she was thrilled to see him. Being with Xavier was like wrapping herself in a favorite blanket that made her feel warm and safe. "How long have you been here?"

"About ten minutes."

"Are you hungry?"

"Not yet. Why don't you sit down and tell me how you are," Xavier invited.

"Did Mom and Dad send you here on a reconnaissance mission?" Lauren asked as she took the other chair.

"You bet. They're worried about you, Lori."

"Well, tell them there's nothing to worry about," Lauren replied. She gazed out over the bay in order to avoid looking at Xavier.

"Isn't there?" he asked gently. "You seemed to be doing all right, under the circumstances, then you suddenly picked up and left, without so much as a word to anyone. And last week Mom found out you'd put your apartment on the market. What gives?"

"Isn't it obvious?" Lauren replied archly. "I just needed a change of air. Everything in that apartment reminds me of Zack."

"So, then why did you wait almost a year to begin the process?"

"I simply wasn't ready to deal with the hassle of moving."

"And now you are?" Xavier asked. "I would think you'd want to be there when potential buyers come to see the place."

"I'm working with a real estate agent. She'll let me know about any potential offers and I will make a decision."

"It's not like you, Lori," Xavier persisted. "What's changed?"

Lauren shook her head. She wished she could tell him the truth, but telling Xavier would lead to her parents knowing. He'd never be able to keep it from them, nor should he. They'd always had a close relationship, and she didn't want him to lie to them. "Look, I simply needed a change. Now, tell me about you," she said, hoping he'd get the hint and change the subject. She was surprised to see a rosy blush spread across her brother's lean cheeks. "What?" she asked, smiling at him.

"I started seeing someone," he confessed. Lauren didn't say anything, hoping he'd feel compelled to fill the silence. Xavier had had plenty of relationships in the past, but she'd never seen him act sheepish about them. Perhaps this one was special. "I'm a little nervous about it," he confessed.

"Why?"

Xavier exhaled loudly as if he were about to get something off his chest. "Because it's Brooke."

Lauren let out a hoot of delight. "She's been in love with you for ages. It's perfect."

Xavier gave Lauren a pained look. "I really like her, Lori, but we've just started dating, and I don't want to hurt or disappoint her. I can't guarantee that we'll be together forever."

"No one can. But can you see a future with her?"

"I think so," Xavier replied. "I just don't want to rush into anything. You know how Brooke is; she's probably bought a dozen wedding magazines and is looking for the perfect dress even as we speak."

"Look, Xav, just be honest with her. You knew what you were getting into when you asked her out, and so did she. Clearly, there's a strong attraction on both sides, but fantasy and reality are two different things, and Brooke has yet to reconcile the two, having fantasized about you for the past fifteen years. How's it been so far?"

Xavier blushed an even deeper red. "Great. I never realized how sexy she is. I mean, I always knew she was smart and funny, but I guess I never really saw her. I always thought of her as your little friend, you know."

"Yeah, I know," Lauren replied. "Xav, Brooke is a grown woman now, not a teenage girl. She's been hurt before and so have you. She understands about giving things time to develop. Don't underestimate her."

"I just don't want you to hate me if things don't work out between us."

"I won't hate you. Either one of you. What happens between you is private, and I don't need to know the details. I love you both and will still love you both should you break up. I hope you don't, though," she added. "Brooke would be my dream sister-in-law."

"There you go, just like I knew you would," Xavier cried, rolling his eyes in exasperation.

"I'm just teasing you, you idiot. I'm happy for you. Truly. I hope it works out."

"Me too," Xavier replied, smiling. "I will kill you dead if you tell her this, but I can see spending the rest of my life with her. I really can."

Lauren nodded and looked away. She could see Xavier and Brooke together. She'd always thought they'd be good for each other. She only hoped they'd have a better chance at a future than she and Zack had.

"Have you found any good restaurants around here?" Xavier asked. "I'm taking you to dinner."

"There's a nice Asian-fusion place in Chatham," Lauren replied.

Xavier immediately whipped out his phone and went on OpenTable to make them a reservation. "God, that took forever. How do you deal with such slow internet service?"

"I manage," Lauren said with a sigh. "I'm learning to do things the old-fashioned way."

"I bet," Xavier muttered.

Lauren didn't bother to tell him there was no cable or Wi-Fi in the house. He wouldn't stay long enough to be troubled by it. If she knew Xavier, he'd leave right after dinner, so he'd be home to report to their parents over Sunday breakfast.

Chapter 29

Sophie

December 1727

As the golds and crimsons of autumn gave way to the grays and whites of a New England winter, Sophie's mental state noticeably deteriorated, so much so that Reverend Chapman remarked on it when they all dined together on Christmas Day. As much as Sophie didn't enjoy the company of the Chapmans, she was glad not to be alone with George.

"I hope you don't mind me saying so, but you haven't been yourself lately, Mrs. Holland," Reverend Chapman said, studying her over the rim of his glass. "Have you been unwell?"

"I'm quite all right," Sophie remarked, desperately trying to maintain her composure. She wasn't all right, or even passably well. George's rages and moods swung so frequently between loving charm and brutal violence that she lived in terror, never knowing what would set him off. She'd initially feared not being able to love her husband, but she'd never imagined that she'd live day after day in fear for her very life. George, on the other hand, seemed most content, going about his life as if this were the type of marriage he'd hoped for. Perhaps he had.

The reverend's face transformed, as if by sudden understanding, and he smiled broadly at the younger couple, winking playfully at George. "Nothing a few months won't cure, eh?" he said.

Mrs. Chapman seemed to shrink, as if the words had hurt her physically. The Chapmans had no children, a state always blamed on the wife's barrenness rather than a husband's inability to get her with child, but they fostered several orphaned children from the parish who were, in essence, their unpaid servants.

George looked at Sophie with some surprise, as if the idea of a child had never occurred to him, then toasted the reverend and

Mrs. Chapman, wishing them a merry Christmas and a prosperous New Year. Sophie was plied with food and drink, as if her pallor and haunted expression had anything to do with a lack of sustenance, but the Christmas goose stuck in her throat, her stomach sour as she tried not to imagine what George would say once they returned home.

He was quiet on the walk back, supporting her arm in the attentive way of a caring husband. Sophie gulped fresh air like a landed fish, desperate to calm her racing heart.

George started in on her the moment they got in. "Are you ill?" he demanded.

"No."

"Are you with child?"

"No."

"Well, thank the good Lord for that at least," George replied.

Sophie dared to sneak a peek at his face. She'd never imagined George wouldn't want children, so his reaction took her by surprise. "Why?" she asked softly.

"Because I can't abide squalling infants," George snapped. "And I don't like to share my playthings," he added, his eyes narrowing as he scrutinized her pale face.

A plaything, that's what I am to him, Sophie thought bitterly. *He plays with me the way a cat plays with a mouse before it bites its head off.*

"The reverend is right; you don't look well."

Perhaps because I live in terror of being physically hurt and emotionally abused, Sophie thought, but said nothing.

"You need a rest," George announced, shocking her to the core. "Sending you to my parents is out of the question. They'll ask too many questions, but Amelia would be glad to have you for a few weeks. Her husband has been sent away on some military mission or some such, so she's alone with her brat. She'll be glad of the company. I'll write to her tomorrow," George promised. "Go on upstairs. I won't trouble you tonight," he said gruffly.

Sophie's chest swelled with gratitude toward the reverend. If his observation had bought her a reprieve, then she was grateful for his forthrightness. A few nights to sleep without fear of being woken in the night or beaten for George's amusement was a gift she cherished above all others. She only hoped George wouldn't change his mind come morning.

He didn't. Having written to Amelia and received a reply with the messenger, he packed Sophie off to Boston, telling her he'd come for her in two weeks' time. Two weeks seemed like an eternity, an enchanted holiday during which she could spend time with Amelia and rest.

"If you so much as utter a word of complaint to my sister, there'll be hell to pay when you return," George said with a smile as he lowered his head to kiss her goodbye. "I expect to see you rested and ready to resume your wifely duties. Am I making myself clear?"

"Yes, George."

"Off you go, then."

He watched as the trap, driven by John Miller, a middle-aged man who served as George's groom, coachman, and general man-of-all-work, pulled away from the house. Sophie gathered the folds of her cloak closer around her and leaned back against the bench, relief surging through her as the wagon left Cambridge Village and headed toward Boston.

"Pleasant day for a drive," John said.

"Indeed, it is," Sophie replied. And it was. The January morning was cold and crisp, but the sky was blue and the freshly fallen snow sparkled playfully, making the world look clean and fresh. How she wished she could be made clean again. Was her marriage to George a punishment for lying with Teddy and conceiving a child out of wedlock? Was losing her baby not penance enough? She was barely nineteen and all she'd known was loss and pain. She realized with a start that she couldn't recall the last time she'd laughed at anything, or even smiled with genuine joy. All the men in her life had not only let her down, but had crushed her like a bug, leaving nothing but a pulpy mess where a young woman had been. How she wished John would just keep on going and take her far away, somewhere where no one would find her.

As much as she looked forward to seeing Amelia, she knew she'd be watched and evaluated. George's parents would no doubt wish to see her and study her narrow waist as they shook their heads with disappointment. Did they know of their son's proclivities, or did they only see the mask George wore before the world? If only she could confide in someone, ask for help. But there was no one. Even her own father was powerless, and indifferent. He hadn't seen her or written to her since the wedding, having no wish to have any dealings with the daughter who'd disappointed him so bitterly. She couldn't turn to him any more than she could beg assistance of Lionel Holland. She was all alone and would remain so for years to come.

Chapter 30

"Sophie, it's so good to see you," Amelia gushed as she drew Sophie into an affectionate embrace. "How I wish we could see each other more often. Come, you must be tired from the journey." She pulled Sophie toward a well-appointed parlor that overlooked the street. Gentle snow had begun to fall, and a hush seemed to settle over the room once Amelia shut the door.

"It didn't take us long to get here at all," Sophie replied. "Good thing the snow held off until we arrived."

"I can't wait for spring," Amelia said with exasperation. "All this snow is damn inconvenient. I'm going mad with boredom. Come sit and tell me everything. How is dull old Cambridge? Oh, I do hate all those intellectual types. All they do is belabor points that no one with even a hint of a social life could possibly care about."

Sophie accepted a seat on a butter-yellow settee and turned to face Amelia, who settled across from her in a matching wingchair. Amelia looked as elegant as ever, but there was a brittleness in her manner that hadn't been there before, making Sophie wonder what her marriage to Major Dawson was like.

"Where's your boy?" Sophie asked. "I'd love to see him."

"Later, perhaps," Amelia said dismissively. "He can be most trying at times. He cries and cries. I simply can't bear it."

"Is he ill?"

"He's teething. I suppose it is uncomfortable for him, but it's not as if there was anything I could do. Jeremy picks him up and walks with him. He says it soothes the baby." Amelia looked bemused, as if the idea of trying to ease her son's discomfort had never crossed her mind. "He's pleased as punch, of course, to have a son. The future baronet. I do wish Jeremy's father would hurry up and die. I want to be a lady now, not when I'm dreadfully old, like thirty."

Amelia blanched, as if realizing how callous her statement sounded, and instantly changed the subject. "How is dear George?

You'd think he was in Philadelphia or New York from how infrequently he visits."

"He doesn't like to leave the shop."

"Doesn't he have an assistant? That colorless little man, Mr. Watkins or Walters or something?"

"He does have Mr. Williams, but George likes to oversee everything himself. He takes great pride in his work."

Amelia scoffed. "He can be such a bore. Ah, here's tea."

A servant entered the room carrying a tray laden with a teapot, cups, saucers, and a platter of sliced cake. The cake looked fancier than anything Mrs. Quarry ever produced and smelled appetizing.

"I have a new cook," Amelia boasted. "Dumb as dirt, but she's an absolute marvel when it comes to baking. You have to try this cake. I ask her to make it once a week, in case anyone comes to call."

Sophie accepted a cup of tea and a slice of cake. It was light and fluffy and had an unexpected flavor. "What's in it?"

"Grated orange peel. Oranges are hard to come by, but Jeremy manages to procure some on a regular basis. He says they help in preventing scurvy. Imagine that!" Amelia broke off a bite-sized piece of cake and popped it in her mouth. "Say you like it," she invited.

"It's delicious," Sophie replied truthfully. It'd been a while since she'd enjoyed anything, mainly due to her mental state, but her brief taste of freedom was already casting its spell.

"I suppose George is disappointed," Amelia said. She sipped her tea daintily, but her gaze never left Sophie's face.

"Disappointed?" Sophie asked, wondering what Amelia had heard.

"That you're not with child yet. Oh, sorry, are you?" she whispered, as if someone could overhear the indelicate question.

"No, I'm not."

"Well, don't worry, there's time. Motherhood is not all it's rumored to be, you know. No one ever tells you the truth of it. First you go through months of unspeakable discomfort, then, just when you think you can't take it anymore, the pains come and you think you're almost done, but the birth is the most awful, demeaning, excruciating finale to the whole ordeal, until you realize it's not quite over yet."

"How do you mean?" Sophie asked, doing her best to pretend that this was all news to her.

"Well, first, you're lactating like a cow, which is utterly disgusting," Amelia said, scrunching up her face. "I couldn't pass that baby on to a wet nurse fast enough. And then there's the bleeding and the saggy skin on your belly. And of course, as soon as you give birth, it's like you're fair game again, if you know what I mean." She made a face to let Sophie know exactly what she thought of that.

"Does Jeremy want more children?"

"Of course, he does. Don't they all? They think it's all we are good for. Well, not me. I've been taking precautions."

"What kind of precautions?" Sophie asked, hoping Amelia would share and not clam up.

"Vinegar, my dear. It kills their seed."

"How do you apply it?"

"You soak bits of thick fabric, like wool, and push them up there before he comes to you. Works wonders."

"Where have you learned this?" Sophie asked, shocked that Amelia would take such a risk.

"From mother's maid. She was quite the chatterbox, that one, always saying the most inappropriate things. Mother dismissed her, of course, but not before I gleaned some useful things."

"Does the vinegar not smell?" Sophie asked, scandalized.

"It airs out, and Jeremy hardly notices anyway. He's usually half-drunk by the time he joins me in bed," she replied dismissively. "Does George trouble you often?" she asked, blushing prettily. When Sophie didn't immediately reply, she went on to answer herself. "I suppose not. He's such a pussycat, our George. He probably worships the ground you walk on. He always was a one-woman sort of man. There was one maid he was obsessed with when he was younger. Father had to dismiss her because she was frightened of George and refused to be in a room alone with him. Imagine being frightened of George. Why, he's the most harmless man I know. Now, Jeremy, when he's in a temper, look out. It's the soldier in him. His first instinct is always to fight, not sue for peace."

Amelia poured the rest of the tea and reached for another slice of cake. "We shall have such fun while you're here. I'll host a musical evening. What do you think? I shall invite the Eislers to perform."

"Who are they?"

"They are a brother and sister, from Vienna, I think. Hans plays the mandolin, and Stanzi sings. Oh, she has the voice of an angel," Amelia gushed. "They're minor aristocracy, but they're quite impoverished, so they perform like trained bears to earn their bread. All very tragic." Amelia waved a hand in a gesture of dismissal. "Now, you must go up and have a rest. George gave me express instructions not to tire you out."

Normally, Sophie would have protested at being dismissed, but she was more than ready to enjoy an hour of solitude. Amelia's chatter did nothing to dispel her sense of isolation. She could hardly share her fears with her husband's sister, and she wasn't at all sure Amelia wouldn't report back to George, making Sophie's situation even more difficult to bear.

"Yes, a rest is just what I need."

"I've had Mary prepare a room for you. It's rather pretty, if I do say so myself. I think you'll be comfortable. If there's anything you need, anything at all, there's a bell-pull on the right side of the bed. You can summon Mary anytime, even in the middle of the night. And don't worry about waking us. We won't hear the bell upstairs," she added.

"Thank you. I doubt I'll need anything in the middle of the night, and I wouldn't want to disturb Mary."

Amelia smiled indulgently at her. "Sophie, that's what servants are for."

"Yes, of course," Sophie agreed, not bothering to argue. She'd have to be on her best behavior in front of Amelia for fear of betraying her dissatisfaction with her marriage, but she didn't think it'd be too hard. Amelia had prattled on about herself almost the entire time, hardly asking Sophie anything about her own life. She'd never realized how self-absorbed Amelia was, but then, she felt as if she'd aged a decade in the past year, going from a naïve, trusting girl to a wary woman who carried the weight of decades on her teenage shoulders.

Chapter 31

The freshly fallen snow crunched beneath Sophie's boots as she hurried toward the wharf. It was bitterly cold, her nose and cheeks stinging from the biting wind, but the heady taste of freedom more than made up for the discomfort. She hadn't taken a walk alone since George confronted her about Agnes's letter. Mrs. Quarry walked at her side wherever she went, even if it was only to the book shop to bring George his dinner. The older woman reminded her of a guard dog that bared its teeth whenever anyone got too close. Her fealty was to George, and she took her guarding duties seriously.

The thought of returning to Cambridge filled Sophie with dread, but she had a week left and she meant to savor it. Amelia made for undemanding company, for which Sophie was grateful. She left Sophie to her own devices for most of the day, not out of consideration, but because she slept till noon and then often went out to pay calls later in the day. She invited Sophie to come along, but Sophie didn't know Amelia's friends and had no desire to spend countless hours on mindless chatter. However, the musical evening Amelia had hosted yesterday proved to be a delight. Sophie had enjoyed it immensely and had felt more like herself than she had in months.

A gust of wind nearly took her breath away and made her cloak billow behind her like the wings of a raven in flight. Sophie grasped at the folds and wrapped them tighter about her to keep out the arctic breath of the Atlantic. Hunching her shoulders, she hastened her steps, eager to reach her father's shop and get out of the cold, but as she drew closer, she experienced a pang of foreboding. No smoke curled from the brick chimney, and the windows glared back with the blank stare of an abandoned building. Sophie tried the door, but it was locked. She stood on her tippy toes and peered inside, but all she saw was emptiness and signs of neglect. It seemed her father hadn't been in the shop for some time.

Sophie stepped back and craned her neck, hoping to see something through the upper-story windows, but even though the curtains still hung at the windows and the glass was relatively clean, she could tell that the apartment above the shop was no longer occupied. Frightened and confused, she walked away, heading toward South Street, where Agnes's family lived at the edge of Coffins Field. This part of town was poorer, the houses closer together and shabbier. Most of the windows were shuttered against the wind to keep the cost of heating down. Sophie found the address she was looking for and knocked on the green-painted door. It was opened by Agnes herself, who immediately covered up her surprise with practicality.

"Come in, miss. You must be half-frozen. Come into the parlor and I'll fetch you a hot drink. We have no tea, I'm afraid, but a cup of broth will warm you through just as well."

She led Sophie to a tiny parlor, took her cloak, hat, and gloves, and invited her to sit on the threadbare settee, which had been moved so close to the hearth, Sophie feared singeing her skirts.

"I'll be back in a moment," Agnes said, and scurried off to the kitchen. She returned with two tin mugs of broth and handed one to Sophie, who accepted it gratefully and wrapped her hands around its comforting warmth.

"Agnes, where's my father? I went to the shop and it's shut up," Sophie said when the other woman settled in a chair across from her.

"Didn't you get my letter?" Agnes asked, her eyes widening in confusion.

"My husband has been intercepting my mail," Sophie replied, squaring her shoulders to counteract the shame she felt at admitting such a thing to Agnes.

"He's gone, miss. He took ill. In late November, it was. First, he developed a chesty cough and then a raging fever."

"Did you not summon Dr. Simonds?"

"'Course I did, but there wasn't much he could do. Said it was lung fever and the master's lungs had filled with fluid. He gave him willow-bark tea to bring down the fever, but the illness had taken hold and wouldn't let go. Gone in a few days, he was. Never even came 'round that last day. I'm sorry, miss."

"Thank you, Agnes, for looking after him. I know you did your best."

"I did, miss. It grieved me something awful to see him suffer that way."

"Agnes, did he ask for me?" Sophie pleaded, desperation gnawing at her insides.

"He did. He asked for you toward the end."

"Where is he buried?"

Agnes told her, and Sophie decided then and there to ask George to pay for a headstone. Surely he wouldn't deny her such a modest request. She never asked for anything, not even a new gown or a silly trinket.

"Where are his things?" Sophie asked, suddenly realizing that someone must have cleared out the shop and the private rooms above. "Did you take his valuables for safekeeping?"

Agnes shook her head. "I couldn't take his things. I'd have been accused of theft. Since you didn't come for the funeral, Mr. Holland told the vicar he'd see to Mr. Brewster's effects, being your father-in-law and all," Agnes said. "He disposed of the lot."

Sophie's head dipped in misery as she stared into the congealing broth. Lionel Holland had known her father had died. He must have written to George, but no one had thought to tell her. Even Amelia had known, which was why she'd bitten her tongue when speaking of Jeremy's father's demise. They'd taken it upon themselves to get rid of her father's possessions, most likely keeping anything of value for themselves, such as the proceeds from the printing press and whatever money her father had saved. There were also several items of value, such as his pocket watch, her mother's wedding band, and the china tea set her mother had loved.

"Did he say anything about…you know—" Sophie asked softly.

"No, not a word. I'm sorry, miss. I know how desperate you are to find your son, but perhaps you're better off not knowing," Agnes said, her eyes brimming with sympathy. "What can you do if you discover where he is? You can't very well inform your husband and demand to bring the boy to live with you. And if he's gone, you're better off not knowing if he suffered."

"I suppose you're right, but my heart won't listen to reason. I need to know what became of him, Agnes. Even if he's with the Lord, I still need to know. I can at least pray for his soul and visit his grave."

"I'll write if I discover anything," Agnes promised. "Oh, but if my letters aren't getting through to you, how shall I pass on the news?"

"I don't know," Sophie replied, shaking her head. "I don't know."

"You come and see me next time you're in Boston. Even if I'm not here, I'll leave word with Ma."

"Is she here?" Sophie asked, realizing that Agnes seemed to be on her own. She was sure Agnes had a brother named Jack, but he was probably out working.

"She's poorly again. Taken to her bed. But she'll get better come spring. She always does. And Jack's at the tavern. Got employment there this past summer. They don't pay him much, but it's better than nothing."

"And what about you, Agnes? How are you?"

"I'm keeping well," Agnes replied. "Rob and I will be getting married in the spring. We thought to wed when I lost my employment, but Ma needs me, and there's no rush, is there? If the good Lord sees fit to bless us with children, He will, and if He doesn't, we'll be all right on our own."

Agnes's attitude surprised Sophie. She assumed every woman wanted to have children, especially one who was past the first flush of youth and didn't have many years of fertility left, but then she'd assumed a lot of things before she realized that life was not always what one expected it to be.

"Thank you, Agnes," Sophie said as she set down the cup and rose to take her leave. "Thank you for everything."

"God be with you, Sophie," Agnes said, reverting to her Christian name in a moment of intimacy. "He knows you've suffered, and He'll grant you peace."

Sophie nodded. What was there to say? She didn't think God much cared about her pain. Plenty of women suffered at the hands of their husbands, and nearly every woman she knew had lost at least one child at some point in her life. It was the way of things. Sophie gave Agnes a hug and left, knowing in her heart she'd probably never see the woman again.

Chapter 32

Had the wind not been howling like a keening woman, Sophie might have heard the footsteps behind her, but she hadn't. She cried out in shock when strong fingers grasped her upper arm and dragged her into an alleyway between two buildings, the man using his body to block them from view. Sophie struggled, terrified of being robbed or molested, but went limp when a familiar voice came from behind a woolen muffler that covered the lower half of the man's face, nearly bringing her to her knees.

"It's me, Poppet. It's me," Teddy whispered into her temple as he held her close. "It's me."

A desperate sob tore from Sophie's chest as she slumped against him, overwhelmed by the intensity of her feelings. Teddy held her close and she inhaled his familiar scent and felt safe for the first time in months. She pulled down the muffler, touching his face to make sure he was real and not a product of her tortured mind. She wanted to ask him where he'd been, to tell him how happy she was to see him, to thank God he wasn't dead, but all she could do was blubber, tears streaming from her eyes and growing ice-cold on her cheeks. Teddy was crying too, silent tears sliding down his stubbled cheeks as he held on to her as if she might vanish at any moment.

"Oh, Sophie, I've been looking for you for so long," Teddy murmured, his breath warm on her face. "When I came back, the shop was shut up, everyone gone. My mother told me your father had passed in November, but I had no way of finding you. I walked the streets, looking for you, hoping to catch a glimpse of your face, but it was as if you'd vanished. I searched for Agnes too, but she'd left after your father's death, presumably to take up a new position."

He held her away from him and studied her face. "When I saw you from the window, I thought I'd imagined you. I followed you, but you'd gone into that house just before I had a chance to call out. I stood outside, waiting, thinking I must be mad, that I'd followed a woman I'd conjured up in my desperation. But it was really you. It's you," he said caressing her face, his lips brushing against hers. "Now that I've found you, we can be together like we always planned."

Sophie could barely manage to form words, so she shook her head, mumbling, "It's too late, Teddy. It's too late."

"It's never too late," he protested. "I've found you at last."

The tears came harder, her body sagging against him in her misery. She had so much to tell him, so much to ask, but she simply couldn't find the strength, so she clung to him until the storm of weeping passed and she was finally able to gather her thoughts.

Sophie took his face in her hands, studying him intently. He looked the same, yet different. The eyes were still as blue, the skin tanned to a golden brown, but there was a crease between his eyebrows that hadn't been there before, and newly etched lines bracketed his mouth. He looked older and tougher, as if the past year and a half had been a test of endurance.

"Sophie, I'm so sorry," he said, his voice hoarse with feeling. "I can't imagine what you must have thought."

"We had a child, Teddy," Sophie cried, desperate for him to understand what she'd been through, what she'd lost. "A son. He was taken from me."

Teddy's tanned face went a sick shade of gray. He stared at her, his mouth opening in shock. "A son?" he echoed. "We have a son?"

Sophie nodded. "I've tried searching for him, but I found no trace of him. Oh, Teddy, life has been so awful since you left. Too awful for words."

"Everything will be well now. I'm going to look after you. We'll get married."

"Teddy, I'm married already. Hasn't your mother told you?"

Teddy's shock was evident in his eyes. "No," he whispered. "No."

"My father pressured me into marrying. He threatened to disown me. I should have resisted, but I felt so lost, so broken. I didn't have the strength to fight back."

"The marriage can be annulled," Teddy said, his eyes glinting with purpose. "You married against your will."

Sophie shook her head again. "I stood up in church and made my vows. There's no annulling it, and my husband won't let me go so easily. His family is powerful. They have money and connections."

"Does he love you?" Teddy asked. "Is he good to you?"

Sophie's bark of laughter shocked him into silence. "He hurts me for his own pleasure. He torments me and controls everything I do and everyone I see. I didn't even know my father had died. He kept the news from me."

"I'll kill him," Teddy said, his voice dangerously low. "I'll kill him and then you'll be free."

"No!" Sophie cried. "I won't have his blood on your hands. You will stay away from him, Teddy. You will not harm him. If I have to watch you swing, I'll die," Sophie threatened.

"My God, Sophie, what has he done to you?" Teddy looked pale and frightened. "You can't go back to him. Come away with me. Now. Today."

"I can't."

"You can," Teddy argued.

"There's something I need to do first. Then I'll go with you."

"Tomorrow, then. Where are you staying?" Teddy asked. The expression on his face told her that he'd come for her if she didn't show. He'd storm the house and take her away. The thought made Sophie warm all over.

She explained that she was staying with Amelia while George remained in Cambridge. "Wait for me by the tree behind the house tomorrow at nine. I will come. I promise," Sophie said, a tiny spark of hope flaring in her breast. "I will come."

"Sophie, please, let's go today. What can be important enough to make you go back to these people?"

"Please, give me one more day, Teddy."

"I will give you every day, my whole life," Teddy replied. He kissed her urgently and she felt the familiar spark of desire leap in her belly. She'd forgotten what it was like to enjoy a man's touch, the pressure of his lips on her mouth, his arms wrapped around her, not like bands of steel keeping her prisoner, but a circle of love and support, a home she could come back to.

"If you're not there tomorrow night, I will go to Cambridge and confront your husband," Teddy threatened after they broke apart. "I won't lose you again. Not ever."

"You won't have to," Sophie promised. "Just one more day."

Chapter 33

When Sophie returned to Amelia's house, she went straight up to her room, locked the door, buried her head in her pillow, and sobbed until the tempest of her emotions subsided. She'd felt like a pot that was boiling over, desperate to let off some steam before settling into a measured simmer. Discovering that her father was dead and buried had been traumatic enough, but seeing Teddy again and suddenly being handed the keys to her prison had been more than she could take in all at once.

Teddy had walked her as far as he could, then stood back and allowed her to leave, swearing he'd be there tomorrow night to take her away from the nightmare that had become her life. There was so much they needed to say to each other, but this afternoon hadn't been the time. They had plans to make and arrangements to put in place.

Sophie didn't come down for dinner, claiming she was unwell, and spent a restless night, her fevered mind refusing to let her rest. Every time she nodded off, the nightmares came back: George getting wind of her plan and stopping her just in time, Teddy disappearing again, this time for good, Jeremy returning home early and preventing her from leaving with Teddy. So much could go wrong. So much already had. In the morning, an exhausted Sophie dressed for church and joined Amelia for breakfast.

"Are you feeling better?" Amelia asked as she deftly sliced the top off her egg.

"Yes, much," Sophie lied. She had no appetite, but she forced herself to eat a slice of buttered bread and a boiled egg to demonstrate her point.

"We'll be taking luncheon with my parents," Amelia announced. "They long to see you. Too bad George won't be joining us. He might have come, it being Sunday, but the roads are knee-deep in snow. It would take him hours to get here."

"Yes, that's a shame," Sophie agreed.

"We'd best get going or we'll be late," Amelia announced. She drank the last of her tea and patted her mouth delicately with a starched napkin. "Would it be blasphemous to say that I hate going to church?" she asked as she rose from the table and headed for the door. "What could be more torturous than a two-hour sermon as one's bottom goes numb from sitting on a hard bench and one's feet nearly fall off from the cold? I'd much rather go back to bed and stay there until at least noon," Amelia complained.

So would I, Sophie thought. In her state of nervous excitement, sitting through the sermon would be even more difficult than usual.

Sophie accepted her cloak, hat, and gloves from the maid and followed Amelia into the snowy morning. The world was swathed in white, the trees sagging beneath the weight of the heavy wet snow. Thick clouds nearly obscured the colorless sky, promising more snow to come. She offered up a hasty prayer, asking God to hold off on the snow until she and Teddy got away, then stopped in mid-sentence, realizing she was asking God to help her escape from her lawfully wedded husband with a man she'd lain with outside of wedlock and with whom she meant to break her marriage vows. *Pretty brazen,* she thought with a hysterical chuckle as she got into the carriage.

It was slow going, but they made it in time and took their seats just as the service was about to begin. Letting the words wash over her, Sophie tried not to allow her imagination to run away with her and catalogue all the things that could go wrong between now and this evening. As long as no one knew what she was up to, she was safe.

She caught Lionel Holland's gaze and acknowledged him with a civil nod. His wife didn't bother to look at her. It wasn't until after they were wed that Sophie had realized George's parents hadn't approved of the match. They'd wanted someone else for their only son, someone who'd bring wealth and position to the family. Now she wished they'd have forbidden George to marry her, but he'd gotten his way, as he always seemed to in the end. Behind the bland exterior, he was a cruel and conniving man, one who fooled all those who came across him into thinking him charming and kind. She'd certainly been taken in, just as she had been by her in-laws, but they were not the people she'd believed them to be.

Luncheon was a dull affair, with Mrs. Holland complaining about the weather, Mr. Holland lamenting that his shipments weren't getting through, and Amelia whining about young Jeremy's nursemaid, who failed to keep him sufficiently quiet during the night to allow her to sleep, a transgression Lionel Holland felt needed to be severely punished. No one cared that the baby was suffering or that he might need to feel his mother's affection from time to time. Strange, but that most basic of human emotions was difficult to come by in a world where everyone seemed to see their children as either a means to an end or a burden to be dealt with. Would Sophie have grown to feel that way about her baby? Would she think of him as a nuisance, or scheme on how best to position him to benefit her own situation?

Neither Mr. nor Mrs. Holland asked her anything, carrying on as if she weren't even there after the stiff greeting they'd bestowed on her and the pointed stare at her middle. She could almost feel their hostility, as if she'd failed them somehow. And no one mentioned her father's death, either because George had forbidden them to bring it up or because they simply couldn't care less about her loss. Sophie sat patiently through the meal, then asked Mr. Holland if she might have a word in private, catching Amelia's frown as she stared at her.

"I only need a moment, Amelia," she promised. "I'll be ready to leave presently."

"All right," Amelia said, sitting back down and asking for more tea.

Mr. Holland invited her into his study and sat behind the desk, leaving her to stand before him like an errant child. He didn't offer her a seat, nor did she wish to get too comfortable.

"Mr. Holland, it has come to my attention that you were the one to see to my father's estate," Sophie began.

"That's an awfully grand word for what your hapless father left behind."

"Nevertheless, putting aside the fact that no one saw fit to inform me of my father's death or wait for me to come for the funeral, you were the person who disposed of his belongings. Were you not?"

"Yes, I was."

"What became of his things?" Sophie demanded.

"Things?"

"The printing press and all the supplies, his books, his savings, his watch and my mother's wedding ring."

"My dear girl, I used the money to pay for the burial."

"Surely no burial costs that much. The printing press alone had to be worth a great deal."

"It was old and outdated."

"Not so outdated that you couldn't find a buyer. What happened to the money, Mr. Holland?"

Lionel Holland slowly got to his feet, splayed his hands on his desk, and glared at her as if she were a piece of filth he'd scraped off his shoe. "You brought virtually nothing to the marriage. Your dowry was laughable, but my son, stubborn fool that he is, had his heart set on you, so we relented. Any proceeds I made off the sale of your father's worthless clutter have gone to offset the cost of the wedding I'd been forced to pay for and the gowns and shoes George had to provide you with since the attire you brought with you was downright embarrassing."

"My father considered you a friend," Sophie snapped, stung by the cruel words.

"I was his associate, but your father was too obtuse to know the difference. He gave me a reasonable price on my orders, and I, in turn, humored him with the occasional jar of ale at the public house. Now, if you were hoping to get something from me, your hopes are grievously misplaced. Even if I were of a mind to pass on the proceeds, I would give the money to my son, not to you. As a woman, you cannot have money of your own or own property, so I suggest you wipe that angry scowl off your face and apologize for your impertinence. My son takes better care of you than you deserve. Be grateful."

"I see that you won't part with the money, Mr. Holland, but I ask that you return my father's watch and my mother's ring. They're keepsakes, and I'm entitled to them."

Mr. Holland considered her request for a moment, then turned and opened an ornate box that stood on the windowsill. He extracted her father's watch and the thin gold band that had belonged to her mother and tossed them onto the desk. "These won't fetch much anyway."

"Thank you," Sophie said, glaring at him across the expanse of the desk. "And thank you for your condolences," she added sarcastically. "They were much appreciated."

She turned on her heel and walked out the door, hoping that was the last she'd see of her father-in-law.

Amelia poked her head out of the dining room. "Are we ready to leave?"

"I'll wait for you outside," Sophie retorted. She couldn't bear to remain in that house a moment longer.

"You really are in a mood today," Amelia said as she climbed into the carriage. "I felt so angry when I first became pregnant. It wasn't anything specific that upset me; it was just everything. I wanted to either rage or cry. Are you sure you're not—?"

"I'm not," Sophie snapped, suddenly wondering if that were a possibility. Could she be with child? She feverishly counted the days since her last courses. Nineteen. She'd have to wait another week to find out if George's seed had been planted in her belly. "No!" she moaned, startling Amelia.

"No, what?"

"Nothing. I'm sorry, Amelia. I'm not myself today."

"I'll say," Amelia retorted, looking at her archly. "When George said you needed a rest, he clearly wasn't being overly dramatic."

"I think I'll lie down for a while before dinner."

"Excellent notion. You look near collapse," Amelia replied, fluffing out her skirts and picking at an invisible piece of lint with her gloved fingers.

"Did you know my father was dead?" Sophie asked. It really didn't matter at this stage, but some part of her needed to know if Amelia had been in on the conspiracy of silence.

Amelia's cheeks colored slightly, and her eyes grew moist. "Sophie, I'm so sorry. George asked us not to tell you. He said you weren't well, and the news would upset you."

"Is that why you didn't try to stop me when I said I was going to the printshop? You wanted me to discover the truth?"

"Your father was your only remaining family. Surely you had a right to know."

"I appreciate that, Amelia," Sophie said softly.

"Look, Sophie, George can be a bit—for lack of a better word—high-handed, but his intentions are good. He was only trying to protect you."

If only I'd had someone to protect me from George, Sophie thought bitterly. She wondered how much Amelia really knew of George's nature. Probably not much. What would a younger sister know of a man's sexual appetites or perversions? Amelia loved George and looked up to him. She genuinely believed that Sophie had lucked out and should be thankful for the match providence had sent her.

"Yes, George has been very ardent in his devotion," Sophie replied, making Amelia grin.

"He's very romantic, isn't he? I wish Jeremy would be more like that." She giggled. "He can be so uptight sometimes, like he has a great big stick up his arse. Men are an enigma to me," she confessed. "They can be so rowdy and fun with their friends, but so humorless with their wives and children. It's almost as if they don't even like us."

"Maybe they don't," Sophie replied. "After all, how well do any of us really know each other before we wed?"

"And how well do we know each other after?" Amelia replied. "What goes on in Jeremy's head is a mystery to me, which is why I prefer when he's not at home. Makes life easier for all involved. Marriage is certainly not the exciting adventure I thought it would be."

"No, it isn't," Sophie agreed, and huddled deeper into her cloak. She was shivering, and not just because it was bitterly cold outside. She was so tightly wound she had no idea how she was going to get through the rest of the day.

Chapter 34

Lauren

The bedroom was bathed in moonlight, the outlines of the furniture clearly visible in its silvery light. Lauren lay sleepless, her body tense. Now that her parents knew she'd put the apartment on the market, there would be questions. Of course, the obvious answer was that she simply couldn't remain in the home she'd shared with Zack, and that was what she'd tell them, but that wasn't the whole truth. The apartment had felt lonely after Zack died, but Lauren had found solace in its familiarity. It had made her feel closer to Zack. They'd shared so many happy hours in their little home, but now it was all ruined. The memories were tarnished, counterfeit. Even the pictures of the two of them that dotted the apartment seemed fake, like the staged photos dating sites used to entice potential clients. *Look at the happy couple having fun on the beach or dressed up for someone's wedding. You could be half of such a couple, someone who belongs, someone who is loved.* Lauren scoffed audibly. Appearances could be deceiving.

She was distracted from her bitter thoughts by a slight movement at the desk. Sophie was back. Lauren hadn't seen her since the night Sophie had rescued her from the fog and had hoped that wasn't the last she'd see of her reclusive ghost. Lauren held her breath as Sophie settled herself at the desk, a shawl draped over her nightdress, her hair loose. Lauren was surprised to notice that several strands were silvered by the moonlight. She was older than when she'd seen her before, Lauren realized.

Sophie sat still for several minutes, just staring out the window, her back ramrod straight, as if she were tense. Then, she reached into the drawer and withdrew a single sheet of paper, which she placed on the desk before her. She picked up a quill and dipped it in ink but didn't start writing. She sat there, quill suspended above the sheet of paper, her brows knitted in deep thought.

"Sophie," Lauren called softly. "Sophie, can you hear me?"

The woman sat up straighter, her head turning to the side as if she'd heard something coming from the direction of the bed. She listened intently for a few moments, then shook her head, as if it were nothing, and returned to contemplating the blank page.

"Sophie," Lauren called again. "Who are you writing to?"

This time Sophie didn't seem to hear her. She dipped her quill in the inkpot again and began to write, but she stopped after a few moments and set down the quill, her gaze straying toward the moonlit bay.

As Lauren studied Sophie's tense profile, questions swirled in her head, questions she'd need to answer before she could turn Sophie into the main character of her story. What would keep a deceased woman tethered to this world? The obvious answer was love, but most people left behind someone they loved when they died, and they didn't all hang around for hundreds of years, writing ghostly letters by moonlight. The more logical answer would be the loss of love. A tragic loss, the kind someone didn't easily come back from.

Sophie had to be pining for her husband. They had clearly been separated, but why? What would cause a husband and wife to live apart in a time when women were defined by their men? They must have seen each other at some point, since Sophie had been pregnant in one of her visitations and had been holding a baby in the next. Did George come to Cape Cod to visit his wife? Did he see his children? If he needed to remain in Cambridge to look after his business, why would he send his family away? Lauren had looked carefully, but she'd seen no gravestone for George Holland anywhere near the Holland family plots. Where was he buried? When did he die? She should have asked Brooke.

Lauren kept her gaze fixed on Sophie until the woman began to fade, becoming completely translucent before vanishing completely as the night finally gave way to the gray light of a new dawn. Unable to get back to sleep, Lauren rose as soon as the first rays of the sun lit up the window and illuminated the top of the writing desk. Lauren's laptop was there, just as it had been last night, but a single sheet of paper lay on top, Sophie's words as black and fresh as if she'd written them only a few minutes ago. With a shaking hand, Lauren picked up the unfinished letter. There were only two lines.

Dearest Teddy,

Last night I dreamed of you...

Lauren stared at the words on the page. Who the heck was Teddy, and what had been his relationship to Sophie? And more important, had Sophie left the letter to send her a message? If she had, then Lauren was clearly on the wrong track. It wasn't George Sophie was pining for, but Teddy, whoever he was.

Chapter 35

Sophie
January 1728

The snow began to fall again just as dusk painted the world outside a lovely shade of violet. Thick flakes silently fell from the sky, settling on rooftops and branches. Sophie stared out the window, her heart hammering as she counted the chimes of the clock in the parlor. One more hour until she was either set free or her heart was irrevocably broken. She tried not to imagine what would happen if Teddy failed to show up. She'd dreaded going back to George, but after seeing Teddy, seeing the love in his eyes and feeling his arms around her, returning to George was unthinkable.

Sophie took out her spare gown, shift, stockings, and stays from the trunk at the foot of the bed and rolled them up as tightly as she could, tying the bundle with stockings to keep it from unraveling. She couldn't very well leave in just the clothes on her back but coming down with a valise would arouse suspicion if she encountered someone on the stairs.

She waited until a few minutes before nine, then crept downstairs and fetched her cloak and hat. Thankfully, Amelia had retired a half hour before, and Jeremy hadn't returned unexpectedly. The servants had all retreated to their quarters, so the house was quiet and dark, the doors locked for the night. Sophie slipped the cloak over her shoulders, pulled up the hood over her cap, and carefully turned the key in the lock of the back door. It opened soundlessly onto a backyard carpeted in nearly a foot of freshly fallen snow.

Sophie glanced up at Amelia's window. She could see the light of her candle through the thick drapes but didn't think Amelia would hear anything untoward. Peering into the darkness, Sophie searched for Teddy, but all she saw was the ghostly outline of the ancient oak and the houses of Amelia's neighbors.

"Oh, Teddy, where are you?" Sophie moaned under her breath. She stood still, waiting and listening. Only a few minutes had passed, but to her, they felt like hours. She had to either leave the house or return upstairs, but she hesitated, hoping Teddy would still come. The world beyond the backyard was silent and dark, the snow coming down from an overcast sky. There wasn't even moonlight to see by. Amelia blew out her candle and the yard was plunged into darkness, the only light coming from the whiteness of the snow.

And then she heard it, a low whistle coming from the darkness. "Sophie." The whisper was carried on the wind, but to her it sounded like the blare of trumpets. "Sophie, come on."

Sophie stepped outside and shut the door behind her, trudging through the snow in her inadequate boots. Her feet grew cold as snow came over the top of the thin leather and soaked her stockings, but she didn't care. She walked as fast as she could, falling into Teddy's embrace as soon as she finally reached him. Behind him, tethered to the tree, was a black horse, its mane sprinkled with snowflakes. The horse looked mildly curious as Teddy gave Sophie a leg up, then settled in behind her. It'd be a slow ride, but the streets were deserted, and the hoofbeats swallowed up by the cottony softness of the snow. Sophie leaned against Teddy's chest and closed her eyes, the tension of the past few hours turning into crippling fatigue. She wanted only to lie down, curl up against him, and sleep until she finally felt ready to face whatever tomorrow would bring.

"It won't be long, sweetheart," Teddy promised, his breath warm against her temple. "Try to remain calm." She hadn't realized she was clutching his hand or that he could probably feel her grinding her teeth as he pressed his face against hers. "I'll keep you safe, Sophie. I promise. Just trust me."

"I trust you," she managed to answer, but the words were snatched from her mouth by a gust of wind. Her hood was blown off, leaving her exposed to the cold and the prying eyes of anyone who happened to see them trotting past.

They left the town proper and continued past frozen fields and darkened farms. The further they traveled from Boston, the safer and calmer Sophie felt, mentally measuring the distance between them and any possible pursuit. All was quiet, the snow quickly covering their tracks as if they'd never passed that way at all. She shivered, half-frozen after nearly an hour out in the bitter cold.

"Nearly there," Teddy said, wrapping his cloak around them like a tent. "Stay with me."

Sophie nodded, wishing she could protect her face from the wind that was so much stronger out in the open where there were no buildings to shield them from its frigid gusts. At last, they approached an isolated farmhouse. A sliver of light was visible through the crack in the shutters, and thick smoke curled from the chimney, promising warmth and light. Teddy caught her as she slid down and kissed her tenderly on the forehead before escorting her to the door. It opened immediately, a large, bewhiskered man filling the doorway and blocking out what lay beyond.

"Ted, come on in. And this must be Sophie. We've been expecting you."

Sophie was ushered into a warm, cozy room that smelled pleasantly of stewed meat and freshly baked bread.

"Sophie, allow me to present Brock and Molly Langford. We're going to stay with them for a short while," Teddy said. He didn't explain how he knew the Langfords, and Sophie didn't ask. She looked around, taking in her new surroundings. The room was square, with a hearth and table on one side and a bedstead on the other. A baby slept in a cradle, its little face peaceful.

"Good evening, Sophie," Molly Langford said. She was short and plump, and her round face radiated welcome. "I've prepared the loft for you. It's nice and warm up there," she assured them. "Have you eaten?"

Sophie hadn't eaten since luncheon, since she'd claimed to have a headache and had gone up to her room, but was too embarrassed to admit she was hungry. She was grateful to Teddy for not sharing her inhibitions.

"Starved. Hardly had time for a cup of ale today," Teddy replied as he shrugged off his cloak and hung it on a peg. "Come, sweetheart. Let's get those wet boots off," he said gently. He untied her cloak, hung it up next to his own, then led her to a bench and waited until she sat down before getting down on one knee and removing her sodden boots. "Hold your feet out to the fire, so your stockings dry faster," Teddy suggested.

Sophie stuck out her feet and sighed as the cold, wet wool began to steam.

Molly ladled stew into two bowls, cut several slices of brown bread, and poured two cups of ale. "Have some supper and go on up to bed," she said. "You both look ready to drop."

"Thank you," Sophie said, turning to face the table. "You're very kind."

Molly smiled warmly in response, but Brock seemed surprised by the sentiment, making Sophie question whether the Langfords were Teddy's friends or simply people he was paying to put them up for a time.

After their delicious and filling supper, Sophie climbed the ladder to the loft, undressed down to her shift, and settled down on the makeshift bed. Straw poked her in the ribs where the cotton mattress was threadbare, but there were two woolen blankets and an illusion of privacy enhanced by the Langfords blowing out the candles and heading off to bed. Teddy undressed and got in next to her, taking her in his arms and holding her tight. Sophie buried her face in his chest, inhaling his familiar smell and absorbing his warmth. She'd forgotten what it was like to feel safe and loved, and the realization that she was free brought tears to her eyes.

"I know you have questions, but honestly, I'm too tired to answer them tonight. Shall we get some sleep, love?"

Sophie nodded into his shoulder. She did have questions, too many to count, but she was exhausted after her emotional day and needed to rest. The questions would still be there tomorrow, and hopefully, she would finally have a clearer picture of what to expect now that they were together.

Chapter 36

Sophie woke sometime during the night, the unfamiliar sighs and groans of the house combined with the snoring from downstairs leaving her momentarily disoriented. There was no light in the loft, and she experienced a brief spell of panic before recalling the events of last night. She snuggled closer to Teddy as joy surged through her, overcoming her fear of the repercussions and uncertainty about the future. They'd be together now, and everything would be well.

Teddy rolled onto his side and pulled her closer, clearly no longer asleep. His lips found hers in the dark and she gave herself up to his kiss, her body melting into his. Teddy was so warm, so familiar, and so aroused. His gentle hands followed the path of his lips, awakening feelings she'd forgotten she was capable of. By the time they came together, she was ready and willing, eager to please him and to be pleased. Waves of ecstasy washed over her as Teddy moved within her, taking her with him on a journey of rediscovery that left her happy and sated.

"Oh Teddy," she whispered, "don't ever leave me again. Not ever."

"I will never leave you, Sophie. I promise," he said softly.

You left me before. "Where have you been?" she asked, determined to finally get some answers.

Teddy rolled onto his back. A low sigh escaped his lips. Whatever had happened, he clearly had no wish to talk about it. "After years aboard the *Sea Falcon*, I came to know the crew and the officers well enough to gauge who might be open to persuasion," Teddy began.

"Persuasion to do what?" Sophie asked, a cold dread settling in the pit of her stomach.

"I was particularly eager to cultivate the goodwill of Mr. Higgins, the quartermaster," Teddy continued. "He was a calculating fellow, always looking to make a bit of clandestine profit. So, we hatched a plan, Mr. Higgins, myself, and two other members of the crew, Jim Royston and Gregory Mason. I'd go ashore in every port and purchase goods with the money we all invested—rum, sugar, tea, whatever was easily obtained—and Mr. Higgins would turn a blind eye while Royston and Mason smuggled the casks aboard and hid the contraband until it was safe to unload it in Boston. I'd made connections over the years and was able to sell the merchandise easily enough, making enough of a profit to keep Mr. Higgins from turning me and the others in."

"What would have happened had he changed his mind?"

"Best case, I'd get flogged within an inch of my life. Worst case, I'd be hanged," Teddy replied, his voice flat.

"Why did you do it, Teddy? Why did you take such risks?"

"I was desperate, Soph," Teddy replied, his voice trembling with feeling. "My wages weren't enough to keep my ma and sisters fed and clothed, and I couldn't go on that way forever. I wanted us to marry, to have a life of our own. My ma would never have let me go as long as she depended on me for her very livelihood. So, I took a chance, and it paid off. I was able to earn ten times my pay, enough to keep ma happy and put something by for our future."

"Did Mr. Higgins turn on you?" Sophie asked, already hating the man.

"No, he didn't. What happened wasn't his fault. I came ashore in Port Royale and headed to my usual haunts, looking to buy some rum. The first stop was no problem. I bought several casks and handed them over to Royston and Mason before continuing on to the Sea Serpent, a tavern of dubious repute," Teddy added with a bitter chuckle. "While I was there, a fight broke out, a vicious brawl between members of two competing crews. The floor of the tavern was slick with blood, bodies everywhere. It was pandemonium. I should have left the cask of rum and returned to the ship, but I'd already paid for it and knew Mr. Higgins wouldn't be too happy with me if I didn't get something for our coin. I hid behind the bar and waited it out, then got out the back way. I thought I was safe."

Teddy pulled her closer, as if her proximity could undo whatever had happened next. "There were two of them, waiting for me in the alley. They were armed with cutlasses and pistols. They were still riled from the fight. They'd have killed me had I resisted."

"Did they want the rum?" Sophie asked.

"They wanted me. They needed men to make up the numbers since both crews had lost a number of sailors that day and couldn't sail with a skeleton crew. Several others were taken as well. Having settled their differences, the captains were willing to share, so they split the prisoners between them. I had no way of getting word to my ship and knew that if I didn't return, Mr. Higgins wouldn't try too hard to find me since he might be implicated in whatever the search party discovered. I was left for dead, and the *Sea Falcon* sailed without me."

"So, you became part of a different crew?" Sophie asked.

"A pirate crew."

"Oh, Teddy," Sophie gasped. "Was it awful?"

Teddy didn't reply, nor would he tell her anything more no matter how many ways she asked. Sophie knew him well enough to realize that he was sparing her the worst of it. Whatever had happened to him after he was taken must have been harrowing and left its mark.

"Have you killed on their orders?" Sophie asked, her voice trembling with horror.

"I did whatever I had to do to survive. I was caught between the Devil and the deep blue sea, love. After the first few months, I was given my first share of the booty, and I've been receiving my cut ever since. The captain wasn't too bad, a Frenchman by the name of Jean Martel. He was fierce but fair. He treated the crew with honesty and respect, not something you'd expect of a pirate. I worked hard to win his trust."

"And did he come to trust you?" Sophie asked, thinking the man must have set Teddy free.

Teddy laughed quietly. "Captain Martel doesn't trust anyone, but he understands the nature of men and uses it to gain loyalty and respect. After a year on his ship, I worked up the courage to confront the man," Teddy said. "I asked to see him privately and explained that I'd left behind a mother, sisters, and the girl I loved. I asked for leave to see to my family."

"And he granted it?"

"He gave me four months," Teddy replied. "From December till the end of March to sort out my private life. If I don't return, he'll have me killed."

"Dear God," Sophie gasped, realizing that the sands of her future with Teddy had just shifted once again. She needed to understand what this meant for her. "Teddy, what do you mean to do?"

"I planned to provide for my mother, marry you and set you up in a house of our own, and then return to Martel, as promised, but when I finally made it to Boston, I learned that your father was dead, you were gone, and my mother was living with a man she'd met while filling tankards at the tavern. I left her sufficient funds to provide a dowry for my younger sisters and live on for years to come, and I still have enough left to set us up, Sophie. You'll want for nothing while I'm gone."

"And if you don't return?" she croaked.

"That could have happened just as easily had I still been part of the crew of the *Sea Falcon*."

"But we'd have been legally wed then."

"We can be legally wed now," Teddy replied. "Will he grant you a divorce?"

Sophie opened her mouth to reply, then closed it again. George had nearly killed her when she spoke in a friendly manner to Alexander Trevor. What would he do if he discovered she was living with another man? He'd want retribution. "I don't think so."

"Well, then I'll have to get rid of him another way," Teddy replied, his voice steely with purpose.

"I won't marry you if you kill George," Sophie snapped. "I won't build my happiness on the death of the man I promised to honor and obey."

"That's very commendable, but that leaves us in something of a quandary."

"We'll think of something. What of our son, Teddy?" Sophie asked, her voice catching.

Teddy turned to face her and kissed the tip of her nose. "Sophie, you have my word that I will leave no stone unturned to find our boy. I pray he's alive, but even if he's no longer on this earth, I will find his resting place so we can pay our respects."

"And how will you find him?"

"I have an idea," Teddy replied.

"What is it? Tell me."

"Not yet. I don't want you to be disappointed should it prove a dead end. In the meantime, we'll stay here with the Langfords. They're good, hardworking people and will put us up until we're ready to set up a home of our own."

"Teddy, if you leave me on my own, George will get wind of it and come after me," Sophie said, her belly in knots.

"George will never find you, not where we are going."

"And where is that?"

"I hear the Langfords getting up, so our planning will have to wait. I don't want anyone to know where we are going."

"Why?" Sophie asked.

"Because everyone has a price, even men who call themselves a friend."

"Are you paying the Langfords to put us up?" Sophie asked, needing to know where she stood. She didn't want to be a charity case.

"Brock is a friend, but yes, I'm paying him for his help. After all, he's got two more mouths to feed while we're here. People's goodwill only goes so far when they are hungry."

Sophie nodded in understanding. "Tell me what I can do to help."

"You must remain hidden," Teddy replied. "If anyone asks, Molly will say you're her sister, come to visit."

"And you?"

"I have our son to find." Teddy made to rise from the pallet, but Sophie grabbed his arm and pulled him back down.

"No!" she said, surprising them both with her forcefulness. "I have a right to know where you're going and how you mean to find Theo."

"Theo?"

"Yes. I named him Theodore, after you. I'm his mother, and I will not be kept in the dark."

Teddy smiled at her in the half-light of the coming morning. "You're right. I'm sorry. I've become accustomed to keeping things to myself."

"Well, then?"

Teddy sat cross-legged on the pallet, and she sat up to face him. The chill bit into her skin once she left the sanctuary of the blankets, but she didn't care. She needed to see Teddy's face when he told her.

"You said that your father brought in a midwife who wasn't from these parts, a woman who was willing to drug you and take our son from his mother," Teddy began.

"Yes."

"Where would a respectable printer find such a person?" Teddy asked, giving Sophie a few moments to ponder the question.

"I don't know. I never considered that."

"He'd have to ask a woman, a woman he can trust."

"The only woman my father knew and trusted was Agnes," Sophie said, horrified by what Teddy was implying.

Teddy shook his head. "Agnes doesn't have a devious bone in her body. There's someone else," he continued, watching Sophie's face for a hint of understanding.

"Your mother," she whispered.

"My mother," Teddy concurred. "My mother helped my father run the tavern for years. She came into contact with all sorts, and she already knew you were with child, so your father wasn't risking anything by talking to her."

"Why would our parents conspire to hurt us like that?" Sophie wailed.

"My mother didn't want me to wed," Teddy said. "Taking a wife would sever the ties of control she'd bound me with since my father's death. She wanted to tether me to her and keep me at her beck and call, so she tried to put you off me, telling you lies about me. My mother would be all too willing to get rid of any child that would make demands on my wages."

"So, you think your mother knows Mrs. Meeks?"

"I think that's a good possibility."

"Will she tell you where she is, do you think?"

"Probably not without an inducement," Teddy replied with a grimace of disgust.

"What sort of inducement?"

"The only kind there is—money."

"Teddy, that's awful. Theo is her grandson."

"Theo means nothing to her. I will pay whatever it takes to get our baby back, Poppet."

"Can you afford to do that?"

"Piracy pays better than honest work," Teddy replied. "I have enough to see us through."

As Teddy got up and dressed, Sophie wrapped the blanket about her shoulders, her legs too wobbly to get up. For the first time since losing Theo, she felt a spark of hope. She hadn't been able to discover anything on her own, but her mind wasn't devious enough to suspect the people she knew of such treachery. Her father had done what he'd done out of a misguided sense of love for her, but Mrs. Mercer had had darker motives. She'd probably hoped Theo would die so as never to make any claim on his father, not that he'd ever know who his father was. How could any woman, especially a mother, be capable of such cruelty?

"Come, love. Get yourself dressed. I'll be leaving directly after breakfast."

Sophie threw off the blanket and hastily pulled on her stockings before reaching for her stays. She was grateful to Molly for leaving a chamber pot in the loft since going out to the privy would be a frigid business. As soon as Teddy climbed down the ladder, she saw to her personal needs, splashed some water on her face from the pitcher Molly had provided, and dressed in her woolen gown, grateful for its warmth. Her boots had dried overnight, and she pulled them on, glad of their protection against the wooden floorboards. When she came down, Brock was feeding wood into the fire and Molly was nursing her baby. It finished eating and looked around, taking in the newcomers.

"And who is this?" Sophie asked, trying to figure out if the baby was a boy or a girl.

"This is our Libby," Molly replied proudly. "She'll be six months come February first. You mind holding her while I get breakfast on?" she asked, clearly not trusting her husband with the baby.

"Of course." Sophie took the child and settled the little girl on her lap. Libby had dark hair as fine as corn silk, and her eyes were a dark brown like her father's. She reached out, grabbed a fistful of Sophie's hair, and pulled with all her might. Sophie yelped and Molly laughed at her surprise.

"They're mischievous little devils, babies are," she said as she added water to yesterday's porridge and mixed it in to thin the gruel. "A few more months and she'll start walking, and then we'll really be in for it. Won't be able to keep her in one place."

Sophie's gaze flew to Teddy, who was watching her with the baby. She'd longed to hold Theo in her arms, to love him and nurture him, but she knew nothing of babies. She'd never even held him before he was taken from her. How would she know how to care for him, if it came to that? How would she keep him healthy and safe?

"Molly knows a lot about babies. Don't you, Mol?" Brock said, smiling at his wife indulgently. "The oldest of twelve, she is."

Molly gave Sophie a reassuring look, and Sophie realized that they knew where Teddy was headed. He must have explained while she was dressing.

"Will you help me if…" Sophie couldn't finish the sentence due to the lump that welled up in her throat.

"Don't you worry, lamb. I'll give you all the guidance you need," Molly said, and patted her hand. She took Libby from her and settled the child on her hip before returning to stir the porridge.

After they ate, Sophie escorted Teddy to the barn and looked on as he saddled his horse. It'd be slow going in the snow, but life didn't come to a halt because of the weather. Teddy tightened the straps and then held on to the reins as he turned toward Sophie, his expression one of regret.

"I hate to leave you so soon after I found you, but time's not on my side," he said, smiling down at her.

"Godspeed," Sophie said. She willed herself not to cry, but her eyes were swimming with tears.

Teddy reached into his coat and took out a leather purse, which he handed to Sophie. "Don't let Brock or Molly see this. Hide it well. It's in case something should happen to me. There's enough there to see you safe for a while."

Sophie nodded. "Come back to me, Teddy, with or without Theo," she said.

"I should be back in a week or two. Keep the faith, love." He kissed her tenderly and held her close before letting her go. "Now, go back to the house and find something to keep you occupied. And don't fret. I'll be all right."

"I know," Sophie said, not knowing anything of the sort.

Sophie waited until Teddy was gone from view before returning to the house. She was cold and heartsick, but the sight of Libby lifted her spirits. The little girl was sitting on the floor, playing with some pegs and smiling. She had four teeth, which made her look like a chipmunk.

"She's sweet," Sophie said as she watched Libby play. "Is there anything I can do to help, Molly?"

"Ted's not paying us to exploit you," Molly replied.

"I'd be most grateful for something to occupy my time. Otherwise I shall go mad with worry."

"All right, then. You asked for it," Molly said with an amused grin. She fetched a basket from the corner and handed it to Sophie. The basket was full of linens: Brock's shirt and hose, Molly's shift and stockings, and Libby's baby gowns.

"Those all need mending. Haven't gotten around to attacking that pile yet. The linen's so threadbare, it tears easily," Molly warned as she fetched a small tin box that held her sewing implements and several skeins of thread. "Just do your best."

Sophie took out a baby gown and surveyed the damage. Molly was right. The linen was practically see-through. The gown must have been fashioned from an old garment of Molly's or Brock's, the fabric too precious to simply throw away. There was a tear in the sleeve by the inseam. Sophie threaded the needle and went to work, grateful to have something to do to fill the endless hours of the morning. By the time Molly set a plate of sliced pork and bread on the table for their midday meal, Sophie had mended three garments.

"You should have a rest after dinner," Molly said. "You look worn out."

"I didn't sleep well," Sophie admitted.

"Up you go, then."

Sophie didn't argue. She was exhausted, having been up since the small hours. She climbed into the loft and lay down on the pallet, pulling the blanket over her. As her mind drifted, she briefly wondered what the Hollands must be thinking and if anyone was searching for her. Had George been informed she was missing, and if so, would he come to Boston to conduct his own inquiry? Sophie smiled drowsily at the notion of his helpless fury before she fell asleep.

Chapter 37

As the days passed, Sophie grew restive and melancholy. After living in Boston and then in Cambridge, which was like an ever-simmering cauldron of intellectual debate, the Langford farm might as well have been on the moon. The absence of news was difficult to bear, as was the lack of company. Brock was not a man given to idle chatter, and Molly was too accustomed to laboring on her own all day to pay much attention to the emotional needs of her guest. Sophie did her best to keep busy and not get underfoot, but when she climbed to the loft at night, her fears got the better of her and she often found herself weeping into her pillow. She grew more despondent by the day, convincing herself that Teddy would either find no trace of Theo or discover that he had died shortly after being taken from her.

More than a week had passed since Teddy's departure when Brock announced he was going into town to sell the cheese and butter Molly had set aside for their regular customers. The Langfords supplied as many as ten households with their products and relied on the coin they earned to supplement their finances and get them through the winter months.

"You make sure to mention what a harsh winter this is turning out to be," Molly reminded Brock as he loaded the cans of milk and several baskets of muslin-wrapped cheeses into the wagon. "Don't let your pride get the best of you."

"Quit nagging, woman," Brock replied affectionately. "I know what I need to do."

Sophie wasn't sure what the Langfords were talking about, but Molly was quick to explain.

"Sometimes the housekeepers who purchase our goods give Brock the household castoffs, things too worn and shabby even for the servants of Boston's finest families to wear. But we're not so proud, are we, Brock?" she asked with a smile. "Some of those garments still have plenty of wear left in them, and what I can't use for us, I'll cut down for Libby once she's out of gowns."

"That's clever of you," Sophie replied, thinking that George would sooner burn the clothes then allow someone like the Langfords to have them at no cost. She hoped Brock wouldn't return empty-handed.

"Brock, if it's not too much trouble, could you purchase a newspaper in town?" Sophie asked, holding out a coin. She didn't dare ask him to incur the expense of buying her a newspaper. "The *Boston Gazette*," she added. "It's a weekly publication, but perhaps there are some left over from last week's printing."

Brock silently accepted the coin and slipped it into his pocket before mounting the bench of the wagon and driving out of the yard.

"Did I say something wrong?" Sophie asked Molly, who also looked as if she'd just bit on a lemon.

"He can't read," Molly replied without rancor. "I suppose he was too embarrassed to tell you so. Don't worry, he'll get the paper. He'll ask someone if he requires help."

Sophie nodded and went back into the house, where she lifted Libby off the floor and settled the child on her lap. The little girl was the only ray of sunshine in her otherwise colorless days, and she sang softly to her, gratified to see Libby listening intently.

"She likes you," Molly said. "You have a way with children."

"Do I?"

"You're a natural. There'll be others, you know," Molly said as she began to peel carrots and potatoes for the stew she was making.

"Other what?"

"Other children. You concentrate on that. It's always better to look to the future than hanker after the past," Molly advised, her knife flashing in the sunlight that filtered through the window.

"You think my baby is dead?" Sophie asked, nearly choking on the word.

"I think that's a possibility, and I'd be lying to you if I pretended it wasn't. Lie with your man as often as you can before he goes off again. Mayhap by the time he returns, you'll have something to show for it."

Sophie couldn't argue with Molly's logic, but the words still cut her to the quick. Teddy had gone on a fool's errand; Molly and Brock obviously thought so. He was looking for Theo to humor her, to prove to her that the child was gone so she could finally say goodbye and turn her attention to the present. She supposed they were right, but she simply couldn't let go of the dream of Theo. In her mind, he was a sturdy little boy with sky-blue eyes and chestnut hair, like Teddy's, who was good-natured and affectionate. He was real to her, even though she'd never seen him or held him in her arms. In her heart, he was alive.

And, in truth, she couldn't focus too much on the future, since she had no way of knowing what it would hold. What would happen once Teddy returned? Sophie refused to entertain the idea that he wouldn't. Where would they go? Where would she be safe from George and his vengeance? She hoped Teddy had a plan, but given that they'd been reunited purely by chance, Teddy had to be making it up as he went along, and any sense of safety she experienced at the out-of-the-way farm was purely an illusion.

When the wagon rattled into the yard in the late afternoon, Sophie fought the impulse to run out and demand to see the newspaper. Brock would be tired, and he'd have to see to the horse and wagon before paying any mind to her, but he came straight in and handed her the newspaper with a flourish. "Snatched the last one," he announced proudly.

"Thank you, Brock," Sophie said, clutching her treasure to her chest. Some small part of her was afraid of what she'd learn, but the greater part simply needed to know something of what went on outside the farm. The light was fading, but she dared not ask for an extra candle to read by since she had no wish to sit at the table where both Molly and Brock would be watching her.

Sophie settled by the window, where there was still enough light to skim through the paper and see if anything of import caught her eye. She could read the rest tomorrow. Sophie's searching gaze instantly picked out the name Holland, and she brought the paper closer to her face and began to read even as the words became more difficult to make out in the gathering darkness.

"Messrs. Lionel Holland and George Holland of Holland's Book Shoppes have mounted an exhaustive search for Mrs. George Holland, who went missing from Major Dawson's home on January 6th of this year. Despite all their efforts and appeals for information, they were unable to learn anything of the lady's whereabouts. A substantial reward has been offered by Mr. Holland Sr. Anyone who has any pertinent information regarding the disappearance of Mrs. Holland or the vicious attack on his son will be handsomely rewarded."

Sophie looked up at Brock, who'd just come in after stabling the horse. His cheeks were ruddy with cold, and he rubbed his hands in anticipation as Molly heaped stew into a bowl and cut several thick slices of brown bread.

"Brock, it says here that there's been an attack on George Holland but offers no other information. Have you heard anything about it while in town?"

Brock sat down at the table and took a mouthful of stew before replying. "George Holland was set upon near Gray's Wharf. Beaten within an inch of his life, or so I hear."

"I wonder what he was doing there," Sophie mused. No ships from England arrived in January, the Atlantic being too dangerous to cross during the gale season, so George wouldn't have been at the docks to inquire after a shipment.

"Looking for your fine self, presumably," Brock replied. "Town's abuzz with gossip. Everyone is wondering what happened to poor Mrs. Holland and if they should start locking up their women."

Sophie felt a pang of guilt at Brock's words. Poor Amelia had probably gotten the brunt of the blame, from both George and her father, and from Major Dawson, who hadn't been there when Sophie absconded, but would probably be blamed by association and expected to order his regiment to join the search even though this was in no way a military matter.

"Don't fret," Brock said, noting her anxious expression. "The Hollands are no longer your concern."

Oh, but they are, Sophie thought miserably. In the eyes of the law, she still belonged to George Holland, and if he ever got his hands on her, there'd be hell to pay and no one would come to her aid, especially not the authorities, who'd see any abuse as a domestic matter. Sophie folded the paper and set it aside. She'd learned enough for one evening.

"Come, sit, Sophie. Supper's on the table," Molly admonished her.

"I'm sorry. I don't feel well," Sophie replied. "Please excuse me."

She climbed the ladder to the loft and lay down on the pallet, her heart hammering with fear. The Hollands had offered a substantial reward for information, and now Brock probably knew that. Would a man who relied on the cast-offs of others be strong enough to resist the temptation of such a sum? Teddy seemed to think so, or he wouldn't have left her with the Langfords, but Sophie knew only too well that people didn't always reveal their true nature until it was too late.

Chapter 38

February arrived with snow and sleet, the winds so gusty, they rattled the windows and banged the shutters. Having no outdoor chores to attend to, Sophie rarely ventured outside, remaining by the window and peering into the distance as if her desperation could conjure Teddy out of thin air. He'd been gone for nearly three weeks and her worry was quickly turning into dread. Neither Molly nor Brock mentioned Teddy at all, their silence making Sophie even more uneasy.

The only benefit to Sophie's time with the Langfords was Molly's tutelage. Sophie had learned how to bake bread, churn butter, prepare simple meals, and tend to a child. These were valuable skills for a woman who'd managed a household but had never done any of the work herself. In the event Teddy never returned, she could use the money he'd left to travel to Rhode Island or even New York. She had enough to sustain her until she could find live-in employment as a domestic, a situation that would not only give her a place to live but make her more difficult to find as she would simply become part of someone's household. She'd never return to George; she'd rather die.

It was toward the end of the first week of February that weak sunshine finally sliced through the impenetrable gray clouds that had been hovering on the horizon like weeping harbingers of doom. The snow sparkled playfully, and the wind had died down, the winter day pleasant after nearly a week of endless sleet. Putting on her boots and cloak, Sophie ventured outdoors, desperate to get out of the house. She couldn't go too far because of the deep snow, but she could go some way up the road that led away from the farm. She walked slowly, enjoying the mild sunshine and filling her lungs with the frosty air. On a day like today, spring didn't feel so far off, and it was easier to feel hopeful.

Sophie shielded her eyes and fixed her gaze on the lone rider making his way toward the farm. Her heart skipped a beat when she recognized Teddy. His face was obscured by the shadow of his tricorn and his cloak was gathered around him to protect him from the bitter cold. He held the reins with both hands, the simple gesture making it painfully obvious that he was alone.

Sophie stood rooted to the spot, her emotions seesawing wildly. She was giddy with relief that Teddy was back at last, but, although she'd steeled herself for bad news, the bitterness of her disappointment tasted like hemlock on her tongue. Molly had been right, of course. It was too late. Theo was gone forever, and she had to look to the future, but the future was as murky as a muddy pond, its deceptively placid surface hiding what lay beneath.

As he drew closer, Teddy lifted his hand in a wave, and Sophie waved back, forcing a smile she hoped would mask her heartbreak. Teddy looked tired and lean, a coppery beard concealing the hollows in his cheeks and contrasting with the shadows beneath his eyes. She'd never seen him unshaven, and despite the familiar features, for just a moment, he looked like a stranger, feral and dangerous. Finally, he drew alongside her and smiled, dispelling the impression of danger.

"You're a sight for sore eyes, Poppet," he said, looking down at her upturned face.

"As are you," Sophie replied, trying desperately to keep the tremor out of her voice.

"I need a hearty meal, a bath, and a good night's sleep, in that order," Teddy said warily. "Shall we go to the house?" Sophie thought he might dismount and walk alongside her, but Teddy remained where he was, probably too worn out to walk the half mile back to the farm.

Then, very gently, he pulled aside his wool cloak to reveal a little face, the eyes closed in slumber, dark eyelashes fanned against pale skin. Sophie let out a cry and instantly clamped her hand to her mouth so as not to wake the sleeping child. He looked exhausted nestled in the crook of Teddy's arm, and so small. Teddy's grin grew wider as he savored her surprise.

"Come, let's get him indoors," Teddy said quietly. "He'll be hungry when he wakes, and he could use a wash."

Sophie rushed to the farmhouse, her feet barely touching the ground in her haste. She burst into the house, panting with exertion as she shook off her cloak and peeled off her gloves, her heart thumping with excitement.

"What's happened?" Molly cried.

"It's Teddy," Sophie exclaimed, still breathing heavily. "He's back. With Theo."

"God be praised," Molly cried. "Well, this is cause for celebration if there ever was one."

"They're hungry and tired. We'll need hot water and something soft to feed Theo. Is there any porridge left over from breakfast?"

Molly laid a restraining hand on her sleeve. "Sophie, Theo can have a slice of buttered bread and a cup of milk, and I'll heat the leftover stew for Ted. Sit down for a moment and gather your wits," Molly said kindly. "You're in such a state, you'll frighten the child."

Sophie did as she was bid and sank onto the bench, her gaze fixed on the leaping flames in the hearth, her mind only now beginning to absorb what Molly had said. Theo was a year old. He'd have teeth, not the bare gums of a newborn baby. Perhaps he even had some speech. He was no longer the baby that had been taken from her but a little boy, a person in his own right.

When Teddy finally approached the house, Sophie stepped outside and positioned herself on the threshold, anxiously waiting for him to dismount. Teddy carefully lifted the child and handed him to Sophie, who grasped him so tightly he woke up.

The boy looked up at her, his gaze clouded with confusion. His eyes were blue, just as Sophie had imagined, but his hair, curling from beneath a knitted cap, was nearly black, like hers, and his nose was a smaller replica of her own. Looking at him, she had no doubt this was the boy she'd given birth to. However, he was smaller and lighter than she'd expected, not the sturdy boy of her dreams but a frail child about the same size as Libby, who was five months his junior. Beneath the warm blanket he'd been wrapped in, he wore woolen stockings and a smock that must have been white at some point but was now grubby and soiled and smelled like a privy.

"I think one of Libby's gowns will fit him," Molly said as Sophie carried Theo into the house.

Theo scrunched up his face and began to wail, no doubt frightened by the new faces he'd woken to. "Shh, sweetheart," Sophie cooed. "It's all right. There's no reason to be afraid. Would you like something to eat?"

The child instantly stopped crying and nodded, his eyes searching for food. Sophie sat him in her lap at the table and held the cup of milk for him as he drank deeply. She then handed him the bread Molly had buttered. His hands were small, his fingers thin and graceful. He grabbed the bread with both hands and bit into it, chewing quickly, as if someone might take it away if he didn't eat it fast enough. Sophie's gaze flew to Teddy as he entered the house, looking even more tired up close. Beneath the cloak, his clothes were filthy, and he must have lost at least a stone since she'd seen him last.

"Come and sit down," Molly invited, pushing a bowl of stew and two slices of buttered bread toward Teddy. He wolfed down the bread and gulped two cups of milk before turning his attention to the stew, which he ate slower, savoring the flavor. At last, he wiped his mouth and sighed with contentment.

"Thank you, Molly," he said, giving her a tired smile. "I can't remember the last time I had a proper meal, or a good night's sleep," he added. He looked like he would keel over with fatigue.

"Teddy, wherever did you find him?" Sophie asked, stroking Theo's hair with a gentle hand as he ate.

"I'll tell you everything later. I'm too tired to do anything but have a wash and sleep. His name is John, by the way," Teddy added before accepting a jug of hot water and a washrag from Molly. He climbed up to the loft for a bit of privacy, leaving Sophie with the child.

"Throw down your clothes," Molly called up, wrinkling her nose. "I'll wash them."

Teddy's shirt, breeches, hose, and drawers fluttered down from the loft and landed in a heap at the bottom of the ladder. Molly scooped them up and placed them in a basin, before pouring hot water over them and leaving them to soak. She then turned her attention to Theo/John, who was done eating and was looking around fearfully.

"Let's get him cleaned up," Molly said.

She brought one of Libby's clean gowns and helped Sophie undress him. They washed him quickly and efficiently, then rubbed him dry, dressed him, and wrapped him in a blanket to keep him warm. His eyes were already fluttering, so Molly offered to let him sleep on her bed, where they could keep an eye on him.

"He's so small, Molly," Sophie whispered as she sat down next to him to keep watch.

"We'll feed him up," Molly promised. "All he needs is good food and fresh air and he'll be right as rain."

Sophie nodded, unable to speak. She was overcome with tenderness, and silent tears slid down her cheeks as she watched the little boy she'd dreamed of every day since he was taken from her. She couldn't control her emotions, which were swinging wildly from pure happiness to worry to sadness for the life he'd had, then back to happiness at having him back and gratitude to the good Lord for keeping him alive.

"Go on and lie down next to him," Molly suggested. "I know you need to remain close."

"Thank you," Sophie said, and climbed into the bed, wrapping her arm around the sleeping child and pulling a blanket over them both. *John*, she thought drowsily. *My John.*

Chapter 39

By the time Teddy awoke, John was sitting on the floor next to Libby, playing with her wooden pegs. He looked around anxiously from time to time, watching the two women with a wary expression, but didn't cry. Sophie left him in Molly's care and climbed up to the loft, where Teddy had pulled on some clean clothes and was sitting on the pallet. Sophie sat down next to him and he pulled her down, wrapping her in his arms as he kissed her soundly. As much as she'd missed him, this wasn't the time for a romantic reunion, not when her every thought was for their son.

"I need to know where John has been for the past year," she said, gently pushing Teddy away. It felt strange to think of their boy as John, but she supposed she'd have to get used to it.

Teddy rolled onto his back and stared up at the low ceiling, his expression glum. "Getting my mother to admit to knowing Mrs. Meeks didn't take much persuading," he began. "As soon as I threatened to withhold the money, she told me what I wished to know, but finding the woman proved a lot more difficult. I spent the better part of two weeks traipsing from one ale house to another, asking after her. Had I been a woman, I might have elicited sympathy and gotten results, but as a man I posed a possible threat, so no one would talk to me. It was about four days ago that I finally came across someone who had a grudge against Mrs. Meeks and was willing to tell me where she could be found."

"What sort of grudge?" Sophie asked, curious despite herself.

"The child she sold this man died two days after she received payment. She refused to return the money, claiming she wasn't clairvoyant and couldn't be expected to know which children would live and which would die."

"Is there really a market for stolen babies?" Sophie asked, shocked that such a thing went on right under the noses of the authorities.

"There's a market for everything, my love. You only need to find the right sort of customers," Teddy replied matter-of-factly. "There isn't much demand for newborn girls, from what I gathered, but there's a thriving market for boys."

"Why?" Sophie cried. "Why would someone want to purchase a child?"

"Many reasons," Teddy replied. "Boys are valuable, not only as future workers, but also as heirs. There's many a wealthy man who doesn't have an heir and acquiring a baby at birth makes it easier to pass it off as one's own."

"All right, I suppose I can understand it in the case of childlessness, but why seek a newborn if you wish for a worker? There are plenty of orphans who'd be happy of a roof over their heads."

"Because acquiring a baby is cheaper than buying a slave or paying a man or a boy a fair wage, and the child grows up as the son of the house and feels a duty toward its parents. Mrs. Meeks takes something unwanted and makes a healthy profit off its disposal."

"That's diabolical," Sophie said with disgust.

"Yes and no," Teddy argued. "Most of these children would probably not see their first birthday if not for her. She finds them a home, so she's saving them in her own way."

"That's one way of looking at it, but if she took my baby without permission, she must have taken others," Sophie persisted.

"Oh, she had permission," Teddy replied. "Your father paid her handsomely to get rid of his daughter's bastard, which she did."

"So, where did you find her?"

"Concord. She has a house there that she shares with her sister. When I confronted her, she refused to tell me where our boy was, not even after I offered her money."

"Why would she refuse money? Isn't money the only reason she does this? Please don't tell me she does it to save the children."

"Of course not. The children are a commodity, but she has a reputation to protect. Her customers expect anonymity. Should word get out that she's willing to sell the information, not many will come to her."

"So, how did you find out where John went?" Sophie asked.

"I pulled a knife on her," Teddy replied, chuckling when Sophie gasped with shock. "I wasn't going to hurt her, but I needed to frighten her enough to believe that telling me would save her life. A knife against one's throat is very persuasive."

Sophie remained quiet, trying to ignore the fact that the Teddy she'd known before would have never said such a thing. His time among criminals had changed him, but, in this case, she didn't care about the means, only the result. "Where was he?" she asked quietly, bracing herself for whatever Teddy was about to share with her.

"Meeks had sold him to a man named John Fuller, who owns a farm a few miles north of Cambridge."

"He was only a few miles away from me all this time?" Sophie cried. "Oh, if only I had known."

"What would you have done?" Teddy asked. "Bring him home to your husband and announce that you're keeping him? I'm sure that would have gone over well. He'd have beaten you to death, and the child along with you."

"Don't be cruel," Sophie snapped.

"I'm only saying what you already know to be true," Teddy replied, unperturbed by her anger.

"Just tell me what happened."

"The closer I got to the farm, the more nervous I became," Teddy confessed. "A part of me was terrified that I was too late, and another part of me feared that they wouldn't surrender the child. He was theirs, bought and paid for. Even if they didn't care for him, they'd have no reason to simply hand him over to me. When I explained my errand to Mr. Fuller, he reached for his musket," Teddy said. "Told me to get out and never come back. John was his son, and his son he would remain."

"How did you convince him?" Sophie asked, impressed with Teddy's ingenuity. Obviously, he'd found a way.

"Everyone has their price, Poppet. Mrs. Fuller cried and begged her husband to let her keep the baby. She'd had four stillbirths in the past five years, she said, and John was her beloved boy, but her husband couldn't say no to the money. He demanded an exorbitant sum, and I paid it. He cared for the child, I could see that, but the farm is struggling, and the money will go a long way toward restoring their fortunes. No doubt another child will miraculously appear in a year or two. I gave him enough coin to buy half a dozen."

"And John? What did they say about our John?" Sophie asked.

"Mrs. Fuller said he'd been poorly and asked me to keep him warm and dry. She gave me an extra blanket for him. She loves him, and to be truthful, I felt awful taking him away from her. Losing him broke her heart, and it was hard on the child as well. He cried and cried after I left with him, reaching out toward the house and calling for his mother. I almost went back," Teddy confessed, giving Sophie a guilty look. "I couldn't bear his pitiful cries, but then I thought of you, and how you'd feel if I came back emptyhanded, and I hardened my heart to his misery."

"It took you four days to travel here from Concord?" Sophie asked.

Teddy gave her a look of exasperation. "I was traveling with a one-year-old, Sophie, and once I left the farm, I realized I had no notion of how to care for him. He pissed himself a few minutes after we left, then soiled himself before I even made it to the nearest public house. I had no spare clothes for him nor any food."

"I'm sorry, Teddy," Sophie said, putting her hand on his arm. "I should have realized. Having no experience of babies, these things never occurred to me."

"Me either," Teddy said, turning to smile at her. "But I managed."

"How?"

"Where there's a publican, there's a publican's wife or daughter," he replied smugly. "Few women will refuse a plea for help from a recently bereaved husband traveling to his parents' home with his small son. They helped me clean him, feed him, and put him to bed. One even gave me two extra baby gowns left over from her own son and instructed me on how to keep him from soiling them every hour."

"How?" Sophie asked, mystified. Libby still wore clouts, so she knew nothing of teaching a child how to use the pot.

"She told me to stop every hour or so, stand him up against a tree, and tell him to piss. Not an easy feat when traveling during the winter, but I managed. I had to hold him up so his feet wouldn't get wet and hold his gown up with my other hand, but we got the hang of it eventually and had fewer accidents."

"Did he continue to cry?" Sophie asked, her heart going out to the poor baby.

"He cried, but I think he sensed that I meant him no harm and turned to me for comfort. I talked to him as we rode along and sang songs. Mostly, I managed to bore him to sleep, but at least he wasn't as upset. He's young enough to forget the Fullers. He just needs love and care."

"And feeding up. He's so small."

"Mrs. Fuller said he's a sickly child," Teddy said. "I do think she gave him the best of care."

"Should we keep calling him John?" Sophie asked. She felt cheated of the right to name her baby.

"Maybe we should start with John Theo and gradually drop the John, once he's become accustomed to it," Teddy suggested.

"Yes, that sounds like a good idea," Sophie agreed. She snuggled closer to Teddy and pressed her lips to his cheek. "Thank you, Teddy. I know this wasn't easy, and I love you for not giving up."

"I'd do anything for you, Sophie," Teddy replied earnestly. "And he is my son too. We do have a problem, though," he said softly.

"What's wrong?"

"I don't have much money left, not after staying at inns for nearly three weeks and paying off the Fullers. And I must rendezvous with my ship by the end of March."

"What are you saying?" Sophie demanded.

"I'm saying that I must find a way to provide for you and the child while I'm away, and I need to find someone to look after you."

"Are you asking me to stay here?" she asked, her heart sinking with disappointment.

"No. This is too close to Boston. Once spring comes, people will travel more, and someone will let it drop that there's a new woman in the parish fitting the description of the one who vanished without a trace. A reward is a powerful incentive for giving someone up," Teddy said. "I need to know you're safe, and I can't ask Brock to risk his life for you. He's got his own family to look to."

"So, where will we go?" Sophie asked.

Teddy folded his arms behind his head and looked up at the ceiling, his expression thoughtful. "Give me a few days to work that out," he said. "That's not a decision I can make in haste."

Chapter 40

Lauren

Lauren smiled to herself when an incoming call displayed Ryan's name on Saturday afternoon. He had the day off and had planned on taking Tyler to the Heritage Museum and Gardens in Sandwich, but they had agreed to have dinner together later. It was just past two o'clock, so he probably wanted to confirm their plans.

"Hey, are you doing anything in about an hour?" Ryan asked without preamble when she answered the call.

"I am now. What did you have in mind?"

"It's a surprise."

"I don't like surprises," Lauren replied, still smiling.

"You'll like this one. Ty and I will pick you up."

"Okay, see you then."

Lauren closed the document she'd been working on and ran a hand through her hair. To her shame, she was still in her pajamas. She took a quick shower and got dressed. The weather was glorious; summer was well and truly on its way. She put on a linen dress in a pretty shade of periwinkle and strappy sandals, then applied some makeup and wound her hair into a messy bun. She hadn't spent much time on her appearance since Zack died, but since coming to Orleans—or more specifically, since meeting Ryan—she suddenly wanted to look her best, and her desire to hide from the world was beginning to fade away.

I think I'll go shopping next week, she thought as she poured some dog food into Billy's bowl and refreshed his water. *I want to buy something fun and flirty, and colorful*, she decided. Billy wagged his tail, his face turned up to meet her gaze.

"I'm sorry, buddy, but you have to stay behind," Lauren said. "We'll go for a long walk tomorrow. I promise."

Billy gave her a look of pure scorn, but seemed to accept the rejection and walked away, settling in his favorite spot by the sliding doors, where he could watch the outside world. The crunch of wheels on gravel heralded Ryan's arrival and she grabbed her purse and let herself out.

"Hello," Ryan said. He smiled at her and leaned forward to kiss her cheek once she settled in the passenger seat.

"Hello," Lauren replied, blushing. "Hi, Tyler," she said, turning around to greet the little boy. Tyler was strapped into his car seat, a toy in his hand.

"Hi," Tyler replied.

"Do you know where we're going?" Lauren asked him.

"Hey, that's cheating," Ryan said, but not before Tyler said, "Auntie Ann's."

"And who is Auntie Ann?"

"Well, now that you've ruined the surprise, I might as well tell you," Ryan said as he pulled out of the driveway and maneuvered the car down the narrow lane. "Auntie Ann happens to be Ann Oliver, the president of the Heritage Society. I know how much you wanted to talk to them, so I arranged a home visit."

"And how is it that you have such pull with the Heritage Society?" Lauren asked, extremely pleased with Ryan's answer.

"Ann Oliver is also one of my mom's oldest friends. They met in kindergarten."

"Is she very stern?" Lauren asked. She always pictured historians as being dusty old relics who were more interested in the past than the present.

Ryan laughed. "I'll let you judge for yourself."

As they drove onto Main Street, Lauren asked Ryan to stop at a bakery. "I can't show up empty-handed."

"Almond cookies," Ryan said as she prepared to get out of the car.

"What?"

"Her favorite. Almond cookies."

"And what are Tyler's favorite cookies?" she asked softly so Ty wouldn't hear.

"Chocolate chip," he called from the back seat.

"May he have some?" Lauren asked.

"Sure," Ryan replied. "Is that it, then?"

"How do you mean?"

"Don't you want to know what my favorite cookie is?" he teased.

Lauren's cheeks suffused with heat. "Of course. What is it?"

"I don't like cookies," Ryan replied haughtily, making her laugh.

"I don't believe you. Everyone likes cookies."

"Okay, you got me. I like the tri-colored ones."

"All right. Cookies for everyone," Lauren announced, and got out.

She bought a box of cookies for Ann Oliver, several chocolate chip cookies for Tyler, and tri-colored cookies for Ryan. It was the least she could do to repay him for his kind gesture.

"I want my cookie now," Tyler cried as soon as she returned. "Pleeease."

"All right, but only one," Ryan said.

"And then another one," Tyler countered.

Ryan rolled his eyes, his face a mask of paternal suffering. "All right, give him two."

"Three," Tyler exclaimed, sensing victory was close at hand.

"One," Ryan replied.

"Two," Tyler screamed.

"Two it is. I'm glad you saw it my way."

"Interesting negotiation technique," Lauren said, chuckling at the exchange.

"It worked, didn't it?"

"Would you like one too?" she asked.

"Maybe later. We're nearly there."

Ann Oliver lived in a charming house on a tree-lined side street. Her front garden was already in full bloom, azalea bushes lining a white-picket fence that surrounded the property. Ann came out to greet them, smiling broadly when Tyler waved to her from the back seat. Lauren smiled shyly when their eyes met. She had to admit that Ann Oliver was not at all what she'd expected. The woman had to be in her mid-sixties, but she clearly thought sixty was the new thirty. Her gray hair was short and spiky, and she wore skinny jeans and a hot-pink top accessorized with a black and fuchsia silk scarf artfully tied at her throat. She looked young and stylish, and not even a little stern.

"Hello, sweetie," she said as she opened the back door and reached in to unfasten Tyler's seatbelt. "I see you've been eating chocolate." She pulled a tissue out of her pocket and wiped Ty's hands and face before scooping him out of the car seat. "Would you like to go on the swing?"

"Yes!" Tyler cried, and made for the backyard as soon as his feet hit the ground.

"I guess that's my cue," Ryan said, and took off after him without making an introduction.

"Hello, Mrs. Oliver," Lauren said, feeling like the new kid on the first day of school.

"Please call me Ann. Come on in," she invited. "Tea or coffee?"

"Tea would be great," Lauren said, offering her the box of cookies. "Ryan said almond cookies are your favorite."

"They sure are. Thank you. Make yourself comfortable and I'll be right back."

She escorted Lauren into the living room and disappeared into the kitchen. The room was just like its owner: tasteful, colorful, and welcoming. Lauren sank into the chenille sofa and admired the eclectic paintings and the numerous plants that filled the room. The effect was charming.

Ann returned with a tray and set it on the coffee table. "I like real tea, not the stuff that comes in bags," she said as she poured tea from an adorable teapot painted with poppies. "Orange pekoe, one of my favorites. Tastes even better with almond cookies," she joked.

Lauren accepted the tea and added a spoonful of sugar. It did taste better brewed fresh.

Ann leaned against the cushion and studied Lauren over the rim of her cup. "Ryan tells me you're interested in the history of Holland House."

"I am. I don't know if Ryan mentioned it, but I'm a writer, and I'd like to write a story that incorporates the history of the house."

"Why?"

The question took Lauren by surprise. "I just feel—" She allowed the sentence to trail off, unable to say 'a presence' out loud.

"You feel a connection," Ann supplied.

"Yes, a connection," Lauren agreed, and noticed the sparkle of humor in Ann's eyes. Did she know about the ghost, or was Lauren just being overly sensitive?

Ann studied Lauren with interest as she nibbled on her cookie. "There are no actual documents that support any of the stories that have swirled around that house for centuries, but there's local lore."

"I'd love to hear it," Lauren assured her. "My story will be a work of fiction, so I don't need to document my sources. I'm particularly interested in Sophie Holland and her family." Lauren was grateful Ann didn't ask for her reasons.

"As you already know, Holland House was built in the first half of the eighteenth century, but it wasn't called Holland House until some fifty years later, during the Revolutionary War when Edward Holland used the private dock to smuggle in ammunition and ferry rebel spies."

"What was it called before?" Lauren asked.

"Those who profited from the residents of the house called it 'The House on the Hill.'"

"And those who didn't?"

"Those people referred to it as 'The Witch's House.' It's said that the name was first used by Reverend Josiah Martins, the spiritual leader of the Puritan settlement. He called on his parishioners to shun the family for fear of catching their evil."

Lauren set down her teacup and stared at Ann. "Why? Was Sophie Holland a witch?"

"Was any woman?" Ann asked archly. "Sophie Holland lived in a time when a woman who was different or a little too independent was instantly suspected of being an instrument of the Devil. It was only about thirty years after the Salem witch trials, you know. Superstition and fear were alive and well."

"What made them think she was a witch?"

"There were some who suspected her of adultery and thought she might even share her bed with more than one man."

"Why would they think that?"

"There was a young man who lived at the house. He was supposedly in the employ of the family, but he was certainly old enough to have fathered her children, and he was alone with Sophie for long stretches of time."

"What of her husband?" Lauren asked. "Did he not have this house built for her?"

"The husband was rarely seen after the family settled in."

"Is that all?" Lauren asked, amazed that something so trivial would be enough to accuse a woman of witchcraft.

"There was something else. Totally unrelated, I should think, but the events were given credence at the time. Shortly after Sophie arrived, several children died in quick succession at the Puritan settlement. Given the religious zeal that passed for faith in those days, it was immediately assumed the deaths were the result of some spell she cast on the settlement as payback for some minor slight. Of course, most people would not have made that connection had it not been suggested from the pulpit, but Reverend Martins used the tragedy to further his own agenda."

"Which was?"

"To hold the community in the death grip of fear and ignorance. It's hard to manipulate folk who are educated and well informed, but it's a piece of cake when the people's only source of information is the Sunday sermon."

"Was Sophie threatened?" Lauren asked, intrigued by this new angle.

"I don't know if she was threatened, per se, but she certainly wasn't made welcome. And there were other rumors about her as well."

"What kind of rumors?"

"People said the house was built using blood money, and that her husband never showed his face because he was a wanted man."

"Was this based on anything concrete or just more insinuations from the pulpit?"

"Shortly after the family took possession of the house, two men came looking for them. They went up the hill, but never came back down. The most likely explanation was that they simply left the area, having fulfilled their mission, and no one had seen them go, but the Reverend Martins turned their disappearance to his own advantage as well, bidding his parishioners to remain vigilant for the disciples of the Devil in their midst who'd just as soon kill a man as allow him to get away with his soul intact."

"So, there was absolutely no proof that any harm came to the men?"

"None," Ann replied. "It was all conjecture."

"Why did Sophie remain here, I wonder?" Lauren asked, hoping Ann would tell her something of Sophie's marriage. Had she come to Cape Cod to get away from George? Had he banished her to Orleans as some sort of punishment? Or had she run off with Teddy?

"I'm sure she had her reasons. Little is known of the woman. She kept mostly to herself, which is always an invitation for people to speculate."

"And what became of her children?"

"They lived into adulthood, married, and had children of their own."

"Did anything out of the ordinary happen in this area around the time Holland House was built?" Lauren asked, still hoping for something concrete to go on.

Ann laughed, her eyes crinkling at the corners. "Well, that depends on what you consider to be out of the ordinary. The period you're asking about was known as the Golden Age of Piracy. It began around 1650 and continued well into the 1700s. People always associate piracy with well-known figures like Captain Kidd and Edward Teach, who you might know by the name Blackbeard, but there were many others who didn't limit their activities to the Caribbean, as the movies would have you believe. These pirates sailed as far as the West African coast and the Indian Ocean and came as far north as Maine."

"Were any of the pirates American?" Lauren asked, feeling a little foolish for her ignorance.

"Quite a few. The earlier pirates were mostly of Anglo-French origin, but the later surge of piracy is attributed to Anglo-American sailors and privateers who lost their livelihood when the War of the Spanish Succession came to an end after thirteen years of fighting. There was one American-born pirate who was quite notorious," Ann said. "Captain Theodore Mercer."

Lauren's stomach flipped when she heard the name. Theodore. Teddy. Now she was finally getting somewhere. "What made him notorious?" Lauren asked, not sure she was ready to hear Ann's response.

"Mercy. He pillaged and plundered with the best of them, but he never killed anyone after a ship had been taken and left enough provisions on board for the vessel to make the nearest port without any casualties. He was known as Mad Ted or Merciful Mercer."

"Why mad?"

"Because his contemporaries thought it was madness to be so magnanimous. They believed that a captain's strength lay in his ability to inspire terror, not only among his prisoners, but in his crew, but Ted's men genuinely loved him and respected his views on unnecessary loss of life."

"I've never heard of him," Lauren said. "I have heard of Blackbeard, of course, and Ryan told me about Captain Kidd and the treasure he supposedly buried right here on Cape Cod."

"There are all sorts of legends inspired by tales of buried treasure, but Mad Ted shared his booty equally among his crew."

"What became of him?"

"I don't know. Unlike Blackbeard, who was killed by Lieutenant Robert Maynard, and Captain Kidd, who was executed on charges of treason in London, Mad Ted sort of just fell off the radar."

"The Edward Holland you mentioned, the revolutionary, was he Sophie Holland's son?" Lauren asked, wondering if Edward might have been fathered by Ted Mercer.

"He was her grandson. In fact, rumor has it that he funded some of his more colorful activities by nefarious means."

"Meaning?"

"Meaning that no one knew where his money came from. There were those who said he'd found a horde of Spanish gold."

229

Or perhaps he'd inherited it, Lauren thought. She was about to ask for more information about Edward's activities during the war when Tyler burst into the room, a wicked grin on his face. Ryan wasn't far behind.

"Give me that," Ryan demanded, holding out his hand.

"What's he got?" Ann asked, clearly amused.

"A worm," Ryan replied as a gleeful Tyler dove behind the couch.

"As long as he doesn't eat it, he'll be just fine," Ann said, smiling. "Worms taste awful."

"Ewww!" came a voice from behind the couch.

"There you have it," Ann told Ryan triumphantly. "Have some tea, Ryan."

Ryan accepted a cup of tea and sat down on the couch next to Lauren. "So, have you learned anything interesting?"

"Lots of things," Lauren replied happily. "Definitely some good material to work with."

"Where are you two headed now?" Ann asked.

She made them sound like a couple, and Lauren felt an unexpected twinge of pleasure. She hadn't realized how much she longed to be part of a couple again, and also part of the greater world. She'd shut herself away since Zack's death, that was true, but she'd had help. Many of their friends, people she'd known for years and had looked upon as a sort of extended family, had gradually drifted away. While she was with Zack, she'd been part of a couple, an acceptable unit suited to any manner of gatherings, but as a single woman, she was suddenly less socially desirable. Some people were uncomfortable with her grief, while others preferred to avoid the awkwardness associated with inviting a single, bereaved friend.

A few friends had remained loyal, like Brooke, but Brooke had been her friend long before she'd met Zack, and their friendship had always been separate from Lauren's marriage. And Brooke had also been single, although she did tend to change boyfriends quite often. Xavier was always there for Lauren, but the social circle she'd cultivated while with Zack had gradually fallen away. She wondered if the friends who'd turned their backs on her after her loss would come out of the woodwork once she had someone new in her life. Would they be more open to her if she were no longer single, or would she still be someone they left off the guestlist because she was no longer Zack's wife?

"We're going back to my house," Ryan replied. "I feel like grilling tonight."

"Sounds lovely," Ann said. "Enjoy. And don't forget the little rascal who's hiding behind my couch."

They all laughed when Tyler shot out from behind the couch and grabbed a cookie on his way to the front door, his giggles filling the house. Lauren grabbed her bag, thanked Ann Oliver again, and followed Ryan and Tyler outside. For the first time in a long while, she felt completely content. She no longer cared if her old friends would come back or if they'd approve of a new man. It didn't matter, because she no longer wanted them in her life, not after they'd left her alone in her hour of need. There would be new friends, and new experiences, and as she gazed at Ryan, she hoped there'd be new loves as well.

Chapter 41

"Have you ever heard of Mad Ted?" Lauren asked once they pulled out of Ann Oliver's driveway. Having released some of his energy, Tyler was now sitting quietly, staring out the window.

"Yes. Why?" Ryan asked. "What's he got to do with anything?"

Lauren filled Ryan in on what Ann had told her, then pulled out the letter Sophie had left from her purse. She kept it in a Ziploc bag to keep the ink from smudging. "Pull over for a moment," Lauren said. "I'd like to show you something."

Ryan pulled into a parking space and turned off the engine. He looked at Lauren expectantly.

"Sophie left this on the desk."

Ryan took the plastic bag from Lauren and quickly read the short message before turning to face Lauren, his eyes wide with astonishment. "You think this was meant for Ted Mercer?"

"I do. I think Sophie Holland was his mistress."

"That's an interesting theory, but there's precious little to back it up," Ryan said, his expression thoughtful. He was about to say something else when his cellphone rang.

"Excuse me," he said, and took the call. His face grew serious as he listened to the person on the other end.

"I need to go into the office right away. Mrs. Leonard's dog has been hit by a car. Merielle went to Martha's Vineyard with my parents," he said, his expression anxious.

"You can leave Tyler with me. He'll be just fine," Lauren said. She hadn't spent several hours alone with a preschooler since she babysat as a teenager, but she was sure she'd do fine.

"Are you sure? I don't want to put you out."

"You're not putting me out. I'm happy to help."

Ryan breathed a sigh of relief. "I'll take you to my house and head straight to the office. Mrs. Leonard will be there in about fifteen minutes. She says Brutus is badly hurt."

"My house is closer," Lauren pointed out.

"Are you sure you don't mind?"

"Not at all. You do what you need to do and don't worry about us. We'll be fine," Lauren assured Ryan as he pulled up in front of Holland House.

Ryan unstrapped Tyler and carried him inside. Tyler immediately made a beeline for Billy, who wagged his tail happily, boy and dog forging an instant bond.

"I appreciate this more than you know," Ryan said. His gaze was soft and his lips warm as they brushed hers in a tender kiss. Not for the first time, Lauren felt that much remained unsaid, but this was not the time or place to delve into what lay between them. So instead, Lauren cupped his cheek and smiled into his eyes, letting him know that she'd be there when he came back.

Ryan's smile was full of regret, and then he was gone, tires kicking up gravel as he made a U-turn and headed down the hill.

"Daddy!" Tyler cried once he realized Ryan had left.

"Daddy will be back soon," Lauren said, suddenly realizing that she had no idea how to keep Tyler entertained. She had no TV or Wi-Fi, so watching cartoons or a movie wasn't an option. She had no children's books or toys, and Tyler was too active a child to patiently wait for his father. "Would you like to take Billy for a walk?" Lauren asked, hoping Tyler wouldn't refuse.

"Can I hold the leash?" Tyler asked.

"Only if you promise to hold on tight and not let go. Billy fell down those steps outside a few weeks ago. He got badly hurt, but your daddy helped him to feel better."

"I won't let go. I promise," Tyler said, his blue gaze solemn.

"All right, then. Let's go."

After a forty-minute trek through nearby woods, boy and puppy were both exhausted. Billy curled up in his crate and Tyler climbed onto the couch and looked around.

"I want to watch TV," he said, his voice plaintive.

"I don't have a TV."

"Why not?"

"I prefer to read. Would you like me to tell you a story?" Lauren asked, frantically trying to recall a story that might be appropriate for a three-year-old.

"I'm hungry," Tyler whined.

Lauren opened her mouth to reply and promptly shut it again. When she was a kid, peanut butter and jelly had been a staple, but she couldn't be sure that Tyler didn't have a peanut allergy. She'd forgotten to ask Ryan what she should feed him for dinner should he not return in time. "What would you like?" she asked carefully, hoping he wouldn't make some unreasonable demand. Her cooking skills stretched only so far, and she didn't have anything child-appropriate in the fridge. Perhaps she could order a pizza.

"Grilled cheese," Tyler replied.

Lauren breathed a sigh of relief. She made a mean grilled cheese sandwich. "Coming right up."

"Do you have any chips to go with it?" Tyler asked.

"No. How about some carrot sticks?"

Tyler made a face that made her laugh. "I like cherry tomatoes," he said.

"I have cherry tomatoes, so we're in business."

Lauren was about to leave Tyler in the living room with Billy and go to the kitchen but thought better of it. He was too young to be left to his own devices, especially when there was no television to keep him occupied. "Come and help me," she said.

Tyler reluctantly got off the couch and trailed after her. "I don't know how to cook," he whined.

"Do you know how to count?" Lauren asked.

"I can count to twenty," Tyler boasted.

"Excellent. Then you can count the tomatoes."

"Okay."

After taking out the ingredients, Lauren started on the sandwiches while Tyler carefully counted the tomatoes she'd washed and put on a plate.

"How many have we got?"

"Fourteen," Tyler replied proudly.

"Good. Now, divide them in half."

Tyler looked worried for a moment, but then began to divvy up the tomatoes, muttering, "One for you, and one for me," until the tomatoes were equally divided.

"Great job!" Lauren exclaimed. She placed a plate in front of Tyler and poured him a glass of milk. "What do you think?" she asked as the little boy bit into the sandwich.

"Good," Tyler replied through a mouthful of bread and cheese. He wolfed down the sandwich, then reached for what was left of hers. Lauren handed it to him, and he ate that too, popping cherry tomatoes into his mouth after every bite.

"How about I show you my room after we wash your hands?" Lauren suggested when he was finished.

"All right."

Lauren helped Tyler up the steep steps, then led him into her bedroom. He looked at the canopy bed with interest.

"That's a weird bed," he said. "It's like a ship, and that thing is the sail."

"Would you like to sail my ship?" Lauren asked. She lifted Tyler up and set him down on the bed.

He lay down and curled up on his side, his eyelids fluttering with fatigue. "Lie down next to me," he whispered. She did, and he pressed himself close to her and was instantly asleep.

Lauren pulled a throw over them both and wrapped her arm around him. He looked small and vulnerable, and her heart turned over with tenderness for the little boy. How unfair it was that he'd lost his mom before he'd even known her. He'd have no memories of the woman who'd sacrificed her life for him. Lauren gently brushed the dark hair aside and pressed her lips to Tyler's forehead. It was just a fleeting thought, but there was an answering pang in her heart. *I wish you were mine.*

Chapter 42

A full moon hung above the bay, its light shining gently on Tyler's face. He lay on his back now, his lips stretched into a beatific smile. Sophie sat on the side of the bed, her nearly translucent hand stilled in a loving caress over his cheek. Silvery tears slid down her cheeks as she looked down at the little boy, grief etched into the lines of her face. She didn't look up or acknowledge Lauren's gaze. She stood up and was swallowed by the shadows before Lauren was even fully awake. She wondered if it was her waking that had forced Sophie to leave, but as soon as the thought crossed her mind, she heard a car coming up the hill. Ryan was back.

Lauren peered at her watch. It was just after ten. She'd been asleep for nearly two hours. She slid out of bed and crept downstairs to open the door. Billy raised his head, his dark eyes glazed with sleep.

"Go back to sleep," Lauren whispered to him, hoping to keep him from barking and waking Tyler. Billy laid his head back on his paws and closed his eyes, too tired to worry about who dared to come calling at such a late hour.

Lauren opened the door and watched Ryan get out of the car. His movements were sluggish, as if he'd been drinking, his face drawn and shadowed despite the light of the moon. He walked toward her, and she opened her arms to him, sensing that he needed comfort.

Ryan walked into her embrace and rested his chin atop her head. "I couldn't save him," he said quietly. "He was too broken."

"I'm sorry," Lauren whispered into his shoulder. "I'm sure you did your best."

"Sometimes my best isn't enough. Mrs. Leonard is devastated. She's in her eighties, and Brutus has been with her since before her husband died. He was her trusted companion, her best friend. She'll be lost without him."

"Does she have children?" Lauren asked.

"She does, but children often neglect their aging parents and assume they're as self-sufficient and energetic as they used to be. I don't think Mrs. Leonard will last long on her own. She might need to go into a home."

"Come inside," Lauren said softly. "Can I get you a drink?"

"Yes," Ryan said. "I could use one. How's Ty?"

"He's asleep in my bed. We went for a long walk, had grilled cheese sandwiches, and then I put him to bed."

"I hope you had cherry tomatoes," Ryan said with a sad smile. "Ty loves them."

"Not to worry. Cherry tomatoes were enjoyed by all."

She took Ryan by the hand and led him to the living room, where he sat heavily on the couch. He looked exhausted and heartbroken. Lauren went to the kitchen and opened a bottle of red wine. Ryan probably needed something stronger, but she didn't want to offer him the whisky if he were to drive home. She poured two glasses and brought them into the living room. Ryan was exactly where she'd left him, staring out into the night beyond the patio door. He accepted the wine and drank it in three gulps, then set the glass on the coffee table.

Lauren sat next to him and he reached for her hand, enveloping it in his own. "It's the people left behind I always feel sorry for," he said softly. "They're the ones who suffer the most."

Like you and Tyler, Lauren thought miserably. *Like me.* Death was hardest on those left behind.

Lauren rested her head on Ryan's shoulder, and he planted a kiss on the top of her head. "You understand," he said. His voice was barely audible, but she heard him. Yes, she understood.

She lifted her head to tell him as much, but never got the chance. His lips found hers, and she kissed him back with all the desperate longing she'd been trying to suppress since she first met him. She hadn't realized it at first, but she was in love with him, with his gentleness and sensitivity that she had sometimes found missing in Zack. She knew a part of Ryan's heart would always belong to Alicia, but she felt no jealousy or resentment. In fact, she respected him all the more for not rushing to replace the woman he'd loved.

Ryan pulled her closer and her thoughts fragmented. She'd forgotten what it was like to feel that surge of need or the heat pooling in her lower belly as white-hot passion throbbed between her legs. She wrapped her arms around him and pulled him down on top of her, kissing him hard.

Ryan responded instantly, his body pinning her down and his hips grinding against her. Lauren could feel his arousal against her thigh, and suddenly she wanted nothing more than to have him inside her, their bodies finally joined together after weeks of dancing around their obvious attraction. She slipped her hand beneath his shirt, her fingers exploring his taut stomach and the velvety skin of his chest. Ryan's lips traced the curve of her neck, his hand cupping her breast. Lauren arched her back, needing to feel him closer, to become a part of him.

"Daddy!" Tyler called out. He was standing at the top of the stairs, rubbing sleep from his eyes. "Daddy, I want to go home."

Ryan sat bolt upright, his gaze instantly going to his son. "Great timing, buddy," he murmured. "I was hoping he'd sleep a little longer," Ryan said apologetically. "I have to take him home."

"You can both stay here," Lauren suggested, but Ryan shook his head and stood, leaving her alone on the couch.

Lauren watched as he walked out of the room and up the stairs and lifted Tyler into his arms. Tyler instantly rested his head on Ryan's shoulder and closed his eyes, no longer frightened of finding himself alone in a strange bed.

"The bed is like a ship," he muttered. "I was afraid it would take me away."

"Don't you worry, Ty," Ryan replied softly. "You're not going anywhere, not without me. Come, let's get you home."

Lauren followed Ryan to the door, where he stopped to face her, reaching out to caress her face. His eyes were filled with regret. "I'm sorry. There's nothing I'd like more than to stay," he said softly.

"You've nothing to apologize for," Lauren said, but she was sorry too.

Ryan nodded. "I'll call you tomorrow?" Ryan leaned forward and planted a tender kiss on her lips. "Sleep well."

Chapter 43

Lauren locked the door after Ryan and returned to her room. The euphoria she'd felt earlier had fizzled, leaving her feeling alone and unsettled. She'd wanted Ryan, there was no question about that, and she was sure he'd wanted her just as much, but what would the morning have brought had they slept together?

Lauren climbed into bed and gazed toward the desk. She almost wished Sophie were there, gazing out over the moonlit bay, her face filled with longing. Lauren wasn't sure why, but she felt a kinship with the woman, an odd sort of connection. Perhaps it was because both of them had suffered at the hands of love.

Kicking off the blanket, Lauren marched to the window and opened it to let the cool spring air wash over her. She was hot, and frustrated. Ryan's kisses had made her feel like a snowdrop bloom that had pushed through the snow to reach for the sun. For just a few moments, she'd come alive, her body thrumming with the need to give and receive. She'd felt the heat of Ryan's skin and tasted the question on his lips, and her answer had been yes. She was ready. But was he? Circumstances she'd told no one about had diluted her grief and forced her to take a good hard look at her marriage, but Ryan's situation had been different, and he had a small child to think of. She thought he wanted a relationship with her, but how would it work with three rather than two people?

Tyler would always come first, and she'd have to stand aside and allow Ryan to see to his son's needs, both physical and emotional. She was sure she could love Tyler; in fact, she was half in love with him already, but would she feel left out and resentful if her feelings were consistently put on hold? She wasn't sure. She'd never had a child of her own, so she couldn't fully understand the feelings of a parent, but some primal instinct told her she'd be a good mom, a selfless mom, even to a child she hadn't given life to. Tyler needed love, they all did, and sometimes one plus one added up to three. But was Ryan ready for a committed relationship, or was he, too, looking for a way to break through the layers of snow and ice to look at the sun?

Chapter 44

Sophie
February 1728

Sophie was eager for her life with Teddy to truly begin, but she was also scared out of her wits. Teddy would leave her by the end of March. During the intervening weeks, they'd have to find a place to settle and a way for Sophie to manage on her own until Teddy was able to return to her. The threat of George finding her was as great as ever, and Teddy's depleted finances left them in something of a lurch. The money wouldn't last longer than a few months, not after the initial expenses of setting up a home were seen to.

Sophie wrapped the blanket tighter around John Theo and kissed the top of his head as they prepared to leave. After several days of living with his new parents, he seemed less frightened, but he didn't make eye contact with anyone or utter any sounds. His withdrawal terrified Sophie, especially when compared to Libby's animated chatter, her meaningless babble beginning to sound like words.

"Give him time, Sophie," Molly said, her gaze on the silent child. "He's been separated from the only family he's ever known. He was loved and cared for, and he was taken away from them without any warning. He doesn't have the words to express how he feels, but surely he's in great turmoil."

"But Teddy and I are his real parents," Sophie protested.

"But he doesn't know that, nor does he care at this stage. He was taken from people he loved and trusted and thrust into an unfamiliar situation. Have patience."

Sophie nodded, tears gathering at the corners of her eyes. Put like that, what they had done to John Theo sounded positively barbaric.

"I'm your mama, John Theo," Sophie whispered to him once they were seated on the bench of the wagon. "I love you, and I will be the soul of patience. You take as long as you need, my dove."

Teddy reached out and patted her hand in a silent gesture of support. Sophie felt uneasy as she waved goodbye to Molly and Brock, who'd come outside to see them off, but Teddy was eager to leave, his thoughts already on the journey ahead

"How far are we traveling?" Caleb asked from the back of the wagon. He was a stocky youth of about fifteen, with an unruly mane of dark hair and the blue eyes that were so prevalent in Teddy's family. Caleb was the son of Teddy's father's only sister, who'd died recently, leaving Caleb to fend for himself. Having learned of his aunt's death from his mother, Teddy had asked Brock to locate Caleb and bring him back to the farm should he be interested in better-paying employment than working at the docks.

"Why does he have to come with us?" Sophie had asked as they lay entwined on their pallet in the loft the night before.

"I can't leave you on your own, Soph. Surely you understand that. You need a man about the place, someone to chop wood, carry buckets of water, and come to your aid should anything or anyone threaten your safety."

"You mean George."

"I mean anyone, Poppet. A woman is not safe on her own. Caleb is a good lad. He's young and strong, and most importantly, he's resourceful. He'll look after you and John Theo."

"I wish you didn't have to go," Sophie moaned.

"I hate to leave you when I've only just found you again, but I've no choice. Besides, we need my share of the plunder to live on. I'm in no position to seek honest employment. As soon as word gets out that I'm back, I'll be arrested."

"But what happened wasn't your fault," Sophie argued. "You were taken against your will."

Teddy shook his head at her naivete. "Sweetheart, it was my fault, and I'll be charged with smuggling, dereliction of duty, piracy, and quite possibly even treason, since Captain Martel had ordered us to fire on a British man-of-war when it gave chase."

Sophie sighed. Teddy was right. There was no going back. He was an outlaw and she was a runaway wife. Neither one of them would ever be safe again, especially if they remained anywhere near Boston. Teddy hadn't said anything, and she'd been too afraid to ask, but she had her suspicions about the attack on George. Teddy couldn't do anything to repay George for his treatment of her openly or legally, but she couldn't imagine he would let George's cruelty go unpunished. If Teddy had been the one to administer the beating, she could hardly fault him, nor could she deny that she felt a glow of satisfaction at the knowledge that George had suffered not only emotionally but physically. Perhaps now he'd know how it felt to be the helpless victim of someone who meant to cause him pain.

When morning came and they loaded their wagon and set off, Sophie hadn't bothered to ask where they were heading. Caleb might be resourceful, but Teddy was as wily as a fox and he'd see them safe. Despite her initial fear, she trusted him not only with her own life but with the life of their son, and knew Teddy took his responsibilities to his family seriously. He would see them right, but even if something went wrong, she'd rather go down in flames with him than ever be parted from him again.

Chapter 45

September 1728

The house was still shrouded in darkness when Sophie awoke, but she instinctively knew it was close to sunrise. She slid from the bed, tucked the blanket around John Theo, who was still sleeping soundly, and wrapped a shawl around her shoulders before quietly stepping outside. Watching the sunrise had become her ritual during the past few months, the only consolation to her inability to sleep.

Sophie sat down on the bench Caleb had built for her just beneath the window of the cottage and leaned against the shingled wall, her eyes trained on the horizon. The sky was a study in deep blue, but a thin sliver of gray was already visible in the east, the beginning of a new day not far off. Sophie held her breath as first a speck, then a narrow band of shimmering light appeared on the horizon, the sun beginning its ascent into the heavens. It promised to be another fine day, but autumn was in the air, and she hoped the approach of winter would herald Teddy's return. He'd been gone for nearly six months, but she'd been lucky enough to receive two letters during that time, sent from exotic-sounding ports and delivered to her in a state of near disintegration after being handled by so many strange hands along the way. The letters took months to reach her, but she treated Teddy's words as if they had been written only yesterday and heard his voice in her mind as she read them.

Sophie never bothered to reply, since she knew her letters would never reach him, but wrote him a mental letter every night before falling asleep, updating him on the day's activities, giving him a progress report on their boy, and assuring him that they were safe. Teddy had settled them in Sandwich, a rural community on Cape Cod. The house was tiny, only one room, but it was all Teddy could afford, and he'd chosen wisely. Their closest neighbors were Quakers, people who were kind, tolerant of others, and always eager to help. They were also farmers, which gave Sophie access to fresh milk, butter, cheese, and meat, since she kept no animals of her own save the horse Teddy had left behind should they need to get away. She felt safe among them and knew that should anyone come looking for her, her neighbors would never willingly point them in Sophie's direction.

Having found understanding and companionship among the women, Sophie had learned to be patient when it came to her son. At first, John Theo had simply existed. He'd eaten, slept, and soiled himself, but did little else that could be construed as interaction. He'd refused to look at Sophie, and although he'd responded to her voice and gentle commands, he'd made almost no sounds and didn't attempt to speak. Her only maternal comfort had come at night when the child pressed himself against her as he fell asleep, sucking his thumb as was his habit. He often woke with a start when she got up during the night to use the pot and didn't go back to sleep until she lay down next to him again. Sophie had confided to Alice, a Quaker woman she bought milk from, that she thought John Theo might be what others unkindly referred to as dimwitted, but Alice assured her that she saw nothing wrong with the boy. Alice had seven children of her own, six of them boys.

"Don't fall into despair, Friend Sophie," Alice had said in her rich, soothing voice. "People like to think men are the stronger sex, but in truth, they're not nearly as resilient as women. They don't need to be. Give him time and love, and he will surprise thee," she'd said, her eyes warm with sympathy.

"I hope you're right, Alice, for I'm beginning to fear I might never hear his voice," Sophie had confided tearfully.

"Thee will. John Theo will speak when he's ready."

Alice had been right. By the time summer came to Cape Cod, John Theo's toddling gait had become more of a confident walk, and he'd begun to take an interest in Caleb's doings. Perhaps he saw him as a father figure, for lack of a father of his own to look up to, or maybe as an older brother, but he followed Caleb whenever he left the house, hurrying after him on his sturdy little legs. Sophie rejoiced in his improved health but fretted endlessly about his lack of intellectual development. She'd never expected

Caleb to take on the role of teacher, but the young man was resourceful, as Teddy had pointed out, and seemed to have a genuine affection for the child.

One day, Caleb stopped and turned, and, putting his hands on his hips, addressed John Theo, who was trying to keep up with him. "Now, listen here, J.T., if you mean to come with me, you're welcome to do so, but you've got to tell me, otherwise you have to go back to your ma."

John Theo just stared at his feet, confused by this turn of events. Sophie's heart swelled with pity as she watched the two, but she didn't interfere. "That's right," Caleb continued, his blue eyes warm with affection for the boy. "You have to say, 'Come.'"

John Theo remained mute.

"Go back home, then. Your ma will be missing you. I can't take you along unless you tell me you want to come with me."

John Theo returned to the house, hanging his head in dejection, but the following day he tried to follow Caleb again. Caleb repeated his request and would not allow John Theo to come along when the boy refused to say anything.

"I need to hear the words, boy," Caleb said.

"Caleb, please, don't be unkind to him," Sophie pleaded that evening after John Theo had fallen asleep. "He'd say the words if he could."

"You're too soft on him, mistress. You coddle him too much because you are overcome with guilt. Well, I have nothing to feel guilty about, so I will take him in hand. You just give me a chance to prove to you that John Theo is as normal as any other boy."

"And if he isn't?"

"Then no harm done," Caleb replied confidently. "I won't be the first or the last person to tell him I don't desire his company."

Sophie's heart squeezed in protest, but deep down she knew Caleb was right. If John Theo remained silent, people would be cruel to him and treat him as if he were soft in the head. It took nearly two weeks, but one day, when John Theo grew desperate enough, he glared at Caleb and yelled, "Come!"

"Well, well. Look who's talking. Now that I know what you want, I'll be happy to take you along with me. Shall we go fetch some eggs for your ma?"

John Theo nodded, but Caleb wasn't satisfied. "Say it, J.T."

"Yes," John Theo murmured.

"That's my boy," Caleb replied, grinning. "Let's go, then."

The words came slowly and painfully. Just because John Theo said something once didn't mean he'd say it again, but Caleb didn't give up, and Sophie began to demand the same of her son.

"Tell me what you want, John Theo," she said as he held out his hand for an apple.

"Apple," he said shyly, then added, "J.T."

"You'd like me to call you J.T.?" Sophie asked, surprised. He nodded.

"All right. If that's what you wish." Sophie turned away from the child and grinned to herself. She didn't like the sound of J.T., but she liked the fact that John Theo had taken a stand and expressed his feelings. It had to be the start of something new and wonderful between them, and she'd indulge any request as long as he made it verbally.

J.T. began to look at her as well. Shyly, at first, but then with more boldness as he made his wishes known. He seemed happy to have finally found his voice. Over the course of the summer, his vocabulary grew, and by the start of September, he was stringing words together.

"Coming with you," he'd cry when Caleb was ready to set off on one of his errands.

"Well, come on, then," Caleb would reply patiently. "I haven't got all day to wait for you."

One day, when Sophie had put on her shawl and reached for her basket, ready to go visit Alice, J.T. grabbed her hand and looked at her imploringly. "Where you go, Mama?" he asked.

Sophie nearly swooned with joy. That was the first time he'd called her Mama. She was so happy she wanted to shout her joy from the roof, but instead she smiled kindly and said, "I'm going to visit Friend Alice. Would you like to come along?"

"Yes, please."

"Put on your shoes, then. You can hardly go barefoot."

J.T. quickly stuck his bare feet into shoes and joined her by the door, his face eager. Alice's youngest was about his age, and they'd played together several times while Alice and Sophie talked. She held out her hand to J.T. as they left the house and he took it, sliding his own warm little hand inside hers. As they walked along the narrow track toward the Miller farm, she knew that she would always remember this day as one of the happiest of her life.

**

Once the sun finally rose and the darkness had been replaced by the brilliant blue of the autumn sky, Sophie relinquished her seat and returned to the house to start breakfast. Caleb was already awake and in the midst of a hushed conversation with J.T. Caleb did most of the talking, but J.T. listened attentively, hanging on every word. He idolized the older boy.

"Now, J.T.," Caleb said, "why don't you use the pot, get dressed, and come help me fetch some water while your ma makes us breakfast," he suggested.

J.T. scrambled out of bed, pulled the chamber pot from beneath the wooden bedstead, and lifted his nightshirt, sticking his belly out as an arc of pee erupted from his stubby little penis. He finished and tried to pull the shirt over his head but found it too difficult and turned to Sophie for help. She lifted the nightshirt as he held up his arms, handed him his drawers, britches, hose, and shirt, and watched as he began to dress. He still needed assistance, especially with the hose, but Sophie didn't immediately offer to help, allowing him to struggle for a few minutes before stepping in. J.T. became more self-sufficient with every passing day, something they were both proud of.

"Your papa will be so surprised when he comes home," Sophie said as she handed the child his shoes. "He will not even recognize you. He'll say, 'Who's this big boy?'" J.T. glowed with happiness and pride. "Now, you go fetch me some water, and I will boil us some eggs for our breakfast. Would you like that?"

Alice had advised Sophie to give J.T. as many eggs as she could. She said they'd make him strong and keep him full longer than just bread and butter. She seemed to know what she was talking about. Her children were all hale, and as far as Sophie knew, Alice had never lost one to ill health.

Later that day, after Sophie had given J.T. and Caleb their dinner and settled J.T. for a nap, she came outside to take down the laundry she'd done that morning and was surprised to see two men heading in her direction. The house was isolated, not being part of a settlement or a village, so anyone who came that way was either lost or meant to come calling.

"Caleb, get the musket," Sophie called out softly. "We have visitors."

Chapter 46

Caleb reached for the musket, loaded and primed it, then stepped outside and stood next to Sophie, who was numb with fear. She couldn't make out the men's faces, but one of them was stocky and thick around the middle, just like George. She barely glanced at the other man, so desperate was she to confirm if her husband had finally come for her. Sophie's heart thumped and her breath came in shallow gasps. It'd been nine months since she left George, but she still lived in fear every day that he would somehow find her and come for her. And if he came, only a teenage boy with a musket would stand between her and George's need for vengeance.

"Caleb, should anything happen to me, please look after J.T. Don't let any harm come to him," Sophie pleaded, her gaze pinned on the men, who were getting closer.

After peering into the distance for a few tense moments, Caleb set the musket against the wall and reached for her chilled hand. "Do you not recognize Teddy, mistress?" he asked softly. "It's Teddy come home to us."

Sophie's knees nearly buckled with relief and her heart leaped with joy. Now that Caleb had pointed it out, she clearly saw Teddy's face and recognized his walk. Sophie breathed a sigh of relief. Whoever the other man was, the only thing that mattered was that he wasn't George. Had Teddy been alone, Sophie would have hitched up her skirts and run to meet him, but the other man didn't look familiar and she couldn't guess the reason for his visit, so she remained where she was, her heart beating like a drum as the men drew nearer.

As soon as they came into the yard, Teddy swept her off her feet and spun her around, kissing her soundly before setting her on the ground. He then shook Caleb's hand and peered carefully behind the young man, who was being used as a shield by J.T.

"And who do we have here?" Teddy said, bending down, his hands behind his back so as not to frighten the child.

"J.T.," the boy answered shyly.

"J.T.? What a clever name you have. I quite like it."

J.T.'s round cheeks flushed with pleasure. "Thank you, sir."

"May I shake your hand?" Teddy asked, holding out his hand to the boy. J.T. took it solemnly, and Teddy shook his hand as if he were a grown man.

"And may I scoop you up and throw you in the air?" Teddy teased as he lifted the boy and tossed him upward, making him whoop with laughter. "And can I do it again?"

While Teddy was getting reacquainted with his son, the man who'd come with him addressed Sophie. "Roy Smith, at your service, madam," he said, removing his stained hat and bowing from the neck, which was wrapped in a filthy neckcloth. The man had to be in his late twenties, like Teddy, but that was where the resemblance ended. His dark hair hung in greasy sheets, and his pockmarked skin was covered with a sparse beard. The look in his green eyes, which were quite beautiful, was watchful and calculating. Sophie had no obvious reason to be afraid, but she felt threatened by the man's presence and his overly familiar stare.

"Good to meet you, Mr. Smith," Sophie replied. Normally, she would have given her own name, but her legal name was Sophie Holland, and that wouldn't be the wisest thing to reveal. She assumed Teddy had told the man she was his wife.

Smith's mouth stretched into a lazy grin. "We've met before. Don't you remember?"

"I'm s-sorry," Sophie stammered. "You have me at a loss."

"Roy will be staying with us for a few days," Teddy said once he set a giggling J.T. on the ground.

"I hope I'm welcome, mistress," Roy Smith said, his shrewd gaze fixed on Sophie's face.

"Of course, Mr. Smith," Sophie replied stiffly. She wished more than anything the man would just get on his way. "You two must be hungry after your journey," Sophie said as they stepped into the house. She hadn't started on supper yet, so she set out a loaf of bread, a wedge of cheese, and several slices of cold pork.

Caleb placed a jug of ale on the table next to the bread and took out two plates and cups.

"Thank you, my dear," Teddy said. He smiled, but Sophie saw the warning in his eyes and didn't ask any questions. Instead, she sat by the window with her mending, allowing the men to eat in peace. They talked easily, but she knew Teddy well enough to sense his guard was up. Why had he brought this man to their home if he didn't trust him?

Having finished the meal, Teddy turned to Sophie. "What say you to a little stroll?" He walked toward her. "It's been too long since I've been alone with my lady," he said, making her blush furiously.

She set aside her sewing and took the hand Teddy held out to her. They left the cottage and set off at a leisurely pace. "Teddy, what is—?" Sophie began, but Teddy shook his head and put a finger to his lips. Sophie nodded and they continued to walk, his hand warm on hers.

As soon as they were far enough from the house, Teddy pulled her into the trees and kissed her soundly as he backed her up against a thick tree trunk. Sophie gave herself up to his kiss, all her questions forgotten. Teddy slipped his hand beneath her skirt, and she cried out and arched her back as he set about pleasuring her, his gaze never leaving her face.

"I thought I'd die with the wanting of you, Poppet," he whispered as he withdrew his hand and unbuttoned his britches. "And I can't wait much longer."

Teddy lifted her up, and she wrapped her legs around him as he took her right there, up against the tree. She threw her head back and closed her eyes, oblivious to everything but the unbearable pleasure of having him inside her. He moved slowly at first, but then quickened the pace, thrusting deep inside her until she dug her nails into his shoulders and let go, her body going limp in his arms as if she were a rag doll. Teddy set her down gently but didn't let her go. He held her close, and she could feel the heat of his hands through the fabric of her gown.

"I love you so, Poppet," he whispered in her ear.

Sophie should have felt elated, but a shiver of apprehension ran up her spine, making her push Teddy away so she could look him in the face. Instead of meeting her gaze, he looked down while he buttoned his britches, then took a step back.

"Theodore Mercer," Sophie said, her tone commanding. "You will tell me what's going on this minute, and you will leave out nothing."

Few women would speak to their husbands that way, but Teddy wasn't just her partner, he was her friend, her confidant, and the man she'd risked it all for. She had a right to know what he was up to, and she wouldn't be fobbed off with half-truths or sugary reassurances.

Teddy sat down on the ground and pulled her down beside him. "I parted with Captain Martel's crew in North Carolina," Teddy said.

"A pirate ship can just come into port?" Sophie asked, stunned by the brazenness of the captain.

Teddy shook his head. "Not exactly, but there are many secret coves where a ship can remain well hidden for several days. I made my way to Wilmington and then obtained passage to Boston on a merchant vessel traveling up north. I gave a false name, so no one asked any awkward questions," Teddy said. "Upon arriving in Boston, I went to visit my mother. I still haven't forgiven her for what she's done, but she's my mother and I have a duty to her and to my sisters. I also wanted to hear the latest news."

"And?" Sophie asked, breathless with apprehension.

"They're still looking for you, Soph. Lionel Holland hired some man, newly come from New York, a retired major by the name of Elijah Boothe. They say he has a reputation for solving difficult cases."

"You mean he finds people for a price?"

"From what I heard, he doesn't do it solely for the money. Enjoys the challenge, they say. Likes to puzzle things out."

"Well, he hasn't found me yet," Sophie snapped, her irritation fueled by fear.

"No, but all he needs is one solid clue and then he'll be on our trail like a bloodhound after its prey."

"What's this to do with Smith?" Sophie asked. "Why have you brought him here?"

"I stopped into a quayside tavern to have a jar of ale and inquire if anyone might be sailing for the Cape when I ran into Smith."

"How do you know him?"

"He was one of the crew of the *Sea Falcon*. He was on guard duty the night I took you onboard."

"That was him?" Sophie asked, her recollection of the man hazy. "The one you brought a bottle of Madeira?"

Teddy nodded. "He was always a shifty fellow, but I didn't have too many personal dealings with him." He bent his legs and rested his elbows on his knees, his hands hanging down between them. "Smith offered to buy me a drink, for old times' sake. I could hardly refuse. He found us a table in the corner and told me what was on his mind," Teddy said bitterly.

"Which was?"

"He knows about us, Poppet. He recalled me talking about you while I was aboard the *Sea Falcon*. Everyone spoke of their wives and sweethearts, and I mentioned you more than once. Had your name been Elizabeth or Anne, he might not have made the connection, but there aren't that many young women named Sophie, especially ones who run out on their husbands and vanish without a trace."

"But he had no proof, until now," Sophie replied hotly. "Why did you admit to it? You could have said you hadn't seen me since my marriage."

"He knew about my arrangement with the quartermaster and had no trouble figuring out what I've been up to since leaving the *Sea Falcon* in Jamaica. If arrested, I'd swing, Sophie. This man holds my life in his hands."

"So you brought him here?" Sophie exclaimed, her heart pounding with blind panic.

"He blackmailed me."

"What does he want? Money?"

"Yes and no."

"Teddy!" Sophie cried, exasperated. "Just tell me."

Teddy exhaled loudly. "When we served aboard the *Sea Falcon*, I never really got to know the man. Never liked him enough to get too friendly. Well, it turns out Smith hails from London. Arrived in Boston twenty years ago with his parents. His father was employed as a jailer at Newgate Prison for more than two decades before deciding to try his luck in the colonies."

"So?"

"So, he was there when William Kidd was held prisoner. Brought him food and writing implements, and such. The captain wrote a letter to his wife after he was sentenced to hang and paid Smith to send it. I daresay he thought the man was illiterate and wouldn't get too nosy about the contents. As luck would have it, Smith knew his letters and was canny enough to suspect the captain might be telling his wife the coordinates of the treasure he'd hidden, given that he was about to die. Smith opened the letter and read it, finding it to be exactly what he expected, a farewell to his wife and children. At the end of the letter, there was a paragraph written in some sort of code, which he took to be the very information he'd been hoping for. Smith never sent the letter for fear that Mistress Kidd would retrieve the treasure. He held on to it, hoping to find a way to break the cypher. He died two years ago, but before he breathed his last, he passed the letter on to his son, hoping Roy might find means to decipher the code."

"I still don't see what this has to do with you—with us," Sophie cried.

"He's convinced the treasure is buried here on Cape Cod. He just needs to figure out the exact location. He's willing to split the booty with me if I help him."

"And if you don't?"

"He'll report me to the authorities and make sure George Holland knows exactly what happened to his errant wife. He'll destroy us, Sophie."

"And if you help him to find this treasure, he'll just leave us alone?" Sophie asked, her tone more sarcastic than she'd intended. Teddy obviously felt terrible. It was pointless to make him feel worse.

"If he's in possession of that kind of loot, the last thing he'll want is to bring attention to himself or how he came by such wealth. We're a means to an end, not the end itself," Teddy replied.

"And you think you can crack this cypher?"

"No, but I think you can," Teddy replied, giving her a watery smile.

"Me?"

"Sophie, you're the most learned woman I know. You've read so many books. Perhaps you can see something Smith and I can't."

"And if I am unable to help?" Sophie demanded, now even more frightened.

"We'll think of something else. Perhaps we'll come up with a false location, and while he and I are off searching, Caleb will move you and J.T. to a safe place."

"But we'll never be safe, will we?" Sophie asked. "He can still report you to the authorities and offer this Major Boothe a clue to my whereabouts. He has the power to decimate our family."

"Which is why we must tread carefully, Poppet. We'll have one chance to get this right."

"Oh, Teddy," Sophie moaned as she rested her head on his shoulder. "Will we never find peace?"

"We will, but it won't be anytime soon," Teddy replied as he wrapped his arm around her and held her close. "Come, we'd best get back before Roy starts working on Caleb. I wouldn't let him out of my sight if it weren't for the need to spend a few moments privately with you."

Teddy smiled suggestively, but Sophie ignored the implication. "If there's a market for boys, then he can sell John Theo, as well. This could be a win-win situation for him. Get the treasure and grow rich or claim the reward from the Hollands and sell a child to whoever is willing to pay. Lord, Teddy, I never knew there was such evil in the world."

Teddy didn't reply, but Sophie saw the pain in his eyes. He'd seen suffering, and he'd seen death—brutal, senseless death. She wished she could lighten his burden, but Teddy would never saddle her with his fears. He loved her too much to add even a tiny bit of anxiety to her already uncertain situation.

"I love you, Teddy," she said softly.

Teddy pulled her to her feet and kissed her softly. "We'll get through this, Sophie. Just trust me."

"I always have."

When they returned to the house, they found Roy Smith outside, sitting on the bench. He'd been watching for them, likely wondering if they'd made a run for it. If Sophie had disliked the man before, she hated him now. Their very existence rested in his dirty hands, and he knew it and was relishing his position of power.

"You two were gone a good while," Smith said, his slow smile making her flesh crawl. "Must have been some reunion. Nice to see folks in love," he added, leering at Sophie. "Would be a damn shame if anything came between you two." *Like the gallows, or Sophie's legally wedded husband*, his narrowed gaze seemed to be saying.

"We are back now," Teddy replied, his jaw stiffening with anger.

"Did you explain the situation to your…eh, what would you call her exactly?" Smith asked, grinning evilly.

"My wife," Teddy hissed.

"Last I heard, polygamy was a crime," Roy drawled.

"And last I heard, a fool could get himself killed for insulting a man's wife," Teddy replied.

"Now, take it easy, Ted. I was just joking. Shall we get to work?"

"Now?" Sophie asked.

"No time like the present," Roy replied, and pulled a folded letter from his pocket. "Take a look while the light's still good, mistress."

Sophie took the letter and allowed her eyes to scan the page. The ink was faded but still legible. The paragraph at the bottom was a jumble of letters, the words making no sense. Ignoring Roy's questioning gaze, she stepped inside and went to fetch paper and ink. She carefully copied the paragraph onto a clean page and handed the letter back to Roy Smith. "I will think on it and let you know," she said.

"When?" Smith demanded.

"When I have something to impart. In the meantime, please treat me with respect in my own house, or you will find yourself sleeping outside."

"She's a feisty one," Smith said to Teddy, grinning at her as if he were appraising a young filly.

"You heard what she said," Teddy replied.

Roy Smith gave her an exaggerated bow. "I sincerely apologize if anything I said offended you in any way. I'm entirely at your command."

At least until I find your goddamn treasure, Sophie thought. She inclined her head to indicate that she'd heard the apology and accepted it, then put the folded paper in her pocket and went to start on supper. She wouldn't give Roy Smith the satisfaction of doing his bidding. She'd look at the cypher when she was good and ready. As it was, she wished Teddy would make Roy Smith sleep elsewhere. The idea of him lying so close to them, especially when she was in a state of undress, made her extremely uncomfortable, and she resolved not to drink any ale with supper to avoid having to make water during the night. The man frightened her, and she wouldn't put anything past him.

She stole a peek at Teddy as he played on the floor with J.T. He'd brought him a carved wooden boat, complete with three masts and canvas sails. J.T. was in raptures and begged Teddy to let him sail the boat. Teddy found a basin and filled it with water, then let J.T. take the ship on her maiden voyage. Caleb sat next to J.T., but his gaze was fixed on their unwelcome visitor, his lips pressed into a thin line. Sophie breathed a sigh of relief when Roy Smith went outside to smoke a pipe, but the smoke that drifted in through the window reminded her they couldn't speak freely. Teddy's homecoming should have been a joyful time, not this tense standoff that she found herself in the midst of. Roy Smith didn't strike her as someone who would simply go on his way and forget he'd ever seen them. Roy Smith would have his pound of flesh.

Chapter 47

The following day, Teddy and Roy went off together directly after breakfast. Teddy had been less than satisfied with the thin stew, made mostly of root vegetables, that Sophie had served for last night's supper. After months aboard a ship, he wanted fresh meat, and he'd have it. Roy hadn't been in the mood for hunting, but Teddy wasn't about to go off and leave the man with Sophie.

"She needs peace and quiet to think," Teddy said to Roy. "Caleb will take the boy out and Sophie will apply herself to the cypher."

"She'd better," Smith grumbled, but didn't argue. He followed Teddy into the damp morning, his shoulders hunched, and his hat pulled low over his eyes to shield his face from the mist.

"Can you do it, mistress?" Caleb stood behind her, peering over her shoulder at the strange collection of letters on the page.

"I don't know," Sophie replied. The words looked like gibberish to her, but every code had a key, and if she could find a starting point, she just might figure it out. If she couldn't get anywhere, she and Teddy would come up with a location of their own. Anything to get Smith away from her and J.T.

Sophie finished clearing after breakfast, then went outside and sat down on the bench, where she'd have more light. The mist had cleared, and gentle sunlight streamed from a cloudless sky. She took out the paper and unfolded it, staring at the cypher once again.

"Xli gliwx mw fyvmih sr lsk mwperh, xir tegiw rsvxl jvsq xli wtpmx wxsri ex xli xst sj xli lmpp. Ampp mw oiitmrk mx weji jsv csy."

Sophie read the words, then tried reading them backwards, but that didn't work. It would have been far too obvious anyway. The man who'd written the letter had to protect the information at all cost, and probably had a prearranged system by which to tell his wife what she needed to know. Sophie looked at the words again, trying to discern a pattern. The word 'xli' appeared four times. What was the most common word in the English language that had three letters? Man, maybe. She considered this for a moment. Given that the first instance was at the beginning of what had to be a sentence, it was possible that 'xli' was 'the.' Sophie rewrote the words, substituting t for x, h for l, and e for i. What she got was,

"The glewt mw fyvmih sr lsk mwperh, xer tegew rsvth jvsq the wtpmt wtsre et the tst sj the lmpp. Ampp mw oiitmrk mt weji jsv csy."

Sophie considered this new version of the text. It was still garbled and there were no obvious clues, except for maybe 'et.' Could it mean 'at'? If she substituted e with a, then the text would read,

"The glewt mw fyvmeh sr lsk mwparh, xer tagiw rsvxl jvsq the wtpmt wtsre at the tst sj the lmpp. Ampp mw oiitmrk mt waje jsv csy."

Sophie frowned. That didn't help much, but she thought she might be on the right track. Something was niggling at her, but she couldn't quite put her finger on it. She refolded the paper and put it in her pocket. She had to take a walk to clear her head. Something was tugging at the loose thread of a memory, and if she could manage to grasp the thread before it slithered away, maybe she'd figure out what that was.

She walked at a brisk pace, going about a half mile down the lane before turning back again. Her brow was furrowed, and her lips pursed as she tried to recall what she knew of cyphers, if anything at all. The elusive thought swam to the top of her brain like a fish enticed by a worm but vanished just before she could get it on the hook. She turned and retraced her steps, almost trotting in her agitation. She was perspiring freely, her hair damp beneath her cap. And then she stopped suddenly and looked up at the sky, her mouth opening in a wide O as she settled her hands on her hips and arched her back.

"Oh-ho!" she cried, pleased with herself. Of course. She'd read about this very thing years ago in one of her father's books.

Rushing back, Sophie went inside and fetched her pen and ink. She laid the paper flat on the table and counted under her breath, carefully replacing letters with other letters. When done, she reread what she'd written, her brows lifting in amazement. It really had been almost too easy. Would Captain Kidd have resorted to such an obvious method of communicating with his wife? She had no way of knowing, but what she now had before her was the message, and it made perfect sense.

"The chest is buried on hog island, ten paces north from the split stone at the top of the hill. Will is keeping it safe for you."

Sophie whooped with delight. She'd done it. She'd broken a cypher written in 1701 in one morning. Teddy would be so proud of her, she thought as she hid the note beneath her pillow and turned her attention to her chores. Now, all they had to do was find the loot and send Roy Smith on his way.

When Teddy and Roy returned in the late afternoon, Sophie waited patiently while they hung the carcass of a doe they'd killed off a sturdy branch, slit its throat to allow the blood to drain, and buried the entrails to keep the animals away. Teddy carved a chunk of meat from the haunch and handed it to Sophie to use for their supper. The rest would have to wait till tomorrow. Teddy and Roy cleaned themselves up while Sophie added chunks of fresh meat to the broth and vegetables she had simmering over the open flame. As the aroma of cooking meat filled the house, she set the table and invited the men to sit. Everyone tucked into the food, savoring the hearty stew that stuffed their bellies until they were pleasantly drowsy.

"Have you looked at the cypher?" Roy asked, his gaze burning with resentment. "I see you had time to bake bread, wash Teddy's drawers, and make supper. Surely you had time to study the text."

"As a matter of fact, I have looked at it," Sophie replied noncommittally.

"And?"

"And it's a simple Caesar cypher," Sophie replied.

"What's that, then?" Roy demanded.

"Julius Caesar, Roman emperor," she elucidated for Roy's benefit, "used this cypher to send coded messages to his generals and advisors. Basically, he simply shifted the letters by a previously agreed upon number."

"Meaning?" Roy Smith growled, not amused by Sophie's smugness.

"Meaning that if he used the number three, a would become d, b would become e, and so forth. Once you figured out the number, the code was easy to break."

"And have you broken it?" Roy asked, his mouth open in admiration.

"I have. Captain Kidd used four." Sophie took out the note from her pocket, unfolded it, and laid it on the table before Teddy and Roy with a flourish, the message clearly written at the bottom.

"Well, I'll be," Roy said, shaking his head. "That's one brainy woman you've got there, Ted." He smiled broadly. "We should go tomorrow."

"Now hold on a minute," Teddy said, staring thoughtfully at the note. "First of all, it's been thirty years since this letter was written. There's a good chance the captain sent more than one letter to make sure his wife received his final farewell. And second, if we mean to go after the treasure, we need to make preparations."

"There's only one way to find out if the treasure is still there," Roy retorted. "As to preparations, what do we need?"

"A boat, for one," Teddy replied. "We also need shovels, a sturdy rope, a lantern, and a way to dispose of the loot."

"Those things are gotten easily enough if you have coin to spare," Roy replied, his eyes glinting with excitement. "As for the disposal of the loot, don't you concern yourself with that. I'll take care of my share. You may do as you please."

"Who's this Will who's keeping the treasure safe for the captain's wife?" Caleb asked.

Teddy looked like he'd suddenly developed indigestion. He looked away, but Roy wouldn't let the matter drop.

"Spit it out, Ted. Who's Will?"

"Will was most likely a sailor from Captain Kidd's crew who was left buried atop the chest. He might have already been dead, but it's more likely that he was killed on the island, his decaying corpse used to deter anyone who might come digging, and his spirit haunting the spot for eternity."

"Are you frightened, Teddy?" Roy asked in a little girl voice, then broke into hearty laughter. "No thirty-year-old corpse is going to deter me. You have two days to prepare. Then we go to Hog Island."

"As you wish," Teddy replied. He seemed resigned to seeing this through.

"And your woman comes with us," Roy added spitefully.

"I think not," Teddy retorted, his eyes narrowing with anger.

"What kind of fool do you take me for, Mercer? For all I know, your clever little honeypot made the whole thing up and will take the child and vanish the minute you get me away from this place. Oh no, she's coming with us. The boy can stay with Caleb until you return. Once we find the treasure, we'll split it and go our separate ways. And if this whole thing was a ruse, your boy will suddenly find himself orphaned."

"Don't you threaten me," Teddy said, his voice dangerously low. "I've fulfilled my end of the bargain."

"Not yet you haven't. See any gold? Neither do I. Two days, Mercer. Two days."

He got up from the table and walked over to the bed, where he pulled out the chamber pot and unbuttoned his britches, not bothering to turn his back. Sophie watched with disgust as he exposed himself and let forth a stream of urine, sighing with contentment once he finished. He left the pot where it was, not bothering to empty it outside, and returned to the table.

"I think it's time you went to bed," he said to Sophie. "Ted and I have business to discuss."

Sophie collected the dirty plates and placed them in a basin of water, covered the remaining stew, and wrapped up what was left of the bread. She gave Teddy a meaningful look and he went to fetch the chamber pot and took it outside to dispose of Roy's piss.

"Goodnight, then," Sophie said sweetly, and went to lie down next to J. T., who was already asleep in the bed.

Chapter 48

Sophie had hoped that Teddy might persuade Roy to allow her to remain with J.T., but Roy was adamant that she accompany them, and Teddy allowed him to have his way. She spent the days before their departure fretting and peppering Caleb with instructions, but the young man just smiled and assured her that J.T. would be absolutely fine in her absence and she was not to worry. Three days after Teddy and Roy had arrived in Sandwich, they set out for Hog Island, armed with shovels, lanterns, rope, and sacks. Sophie had been in charge of blankets, provisions, and a change of clothes for herself and Teddy.

Roy intended to travel overland directly to Eastham, then hire a boat and row out to Hog Island, but Teddy had other ideas, which he presented to Roy carefully, as if afraid of Roy's reaction.

"I wouldn't recommend doing it that way," Teddy said, surprising Roy into silence.

"I call the shots around here, Mercer," Roy snarled.

"We must exercise caution if we hope to get away with the loot," Teddy replied calmly. "We should travel as far as Chatham and find an inn to stable the horses and wagon. Then, we should find a boat for hire and sail north, approaching Hog Island from the east rather than from the west, and preferably at night."

"Are you mad?" Roy shouted. "That'll add days."

"No, I'm not mad," Teddy replied in a tone he might use to address a rabid dog. "If you arrive with a wagon packed with shovels and lanterns in Eastham, find the nearest inn, hire a boat, and row out to Hog Island, you'll have a dozen men there within the hour. Everyone's heard the legends, so you may as well get up on a table at the inn and make an announcement. Stealth, Roy, is the only way we can ever hope to find the treasure and get it off the island without being relieved of it, either on the island or as soon as we return to Eastham. You've waited this long; a few more days won't make a difference."

"You're stalling," Roy snapped.

"Why would I stall? I want to find it as much as you do, and get back to my son, who's probably crying for his mother."

"I'll kill both you and her if you try to cheat me," Roy threatened. He'd demanded that Teddy leave his weapons at home, so Teddy would have nothing save his bare hands should he give in to the urge to attack Roy. Roy weighed at least two stone more than Teddy and was a head taller. Taking Roy on would be madness, something Teddy was well aware of.

"I'm not trying to cheat you, Roy," Teddy explained patiently. "I'm trying to use the sense God gave me to get that which will benefit me and mine."

"I'm watching you," Roy replied, baring his tobacco-stained teeth in a nasty grin.

Not as carefully as I'm watching you, Sophie thought as she sat quietly in the back of the wagon. Normally, she'd be drowsy from the motion and long for sleep, but she was tense, her back rigid as a plank. Her shoulders were stiff, her neck hurt, and her legs were beginning to cramp. She stretched them out and tried to relax, but her mind wouldn't let her rest, her thoughts going round and round. She understood Teddy's reasons for joining Roy Smith on this mad quest. He was trying to protect them, hoping the gold would be enough to satisfy Roy, but did he really think Roy would simply forget about them? Or was Teddy hoping to distract Roy long enough for them to leave Cape Cod and settle someplace else? Was he simply playing for time? Was he hoping Roy would trust him if they found what they were looking for and consider him his partner in crime?

Sophie didn't believe Roy's greed would ever be satisfied, and she had serious doubts that he would allow Teddy to take half the treasure as they'd agreed. And what would he do if there was nothing to find? Would he blame Teddy for taking him on this wild goose chase? Would he turn him over to the authorities out of spite? Lionel Holland had offered a substantial reward for information on Sophie's whereabouts and hired that New York man to track her down. Would Roy pass up the opportunity to cash in? Teddy seemed convinced that if they found the loot, Roy wouldn't want to draw too much attention to himself, but given his argument with Teddy, Sophie didn't think the man was blessed with much intelligence. His greed would overshadow good sense, and he would go back on his word and see them hunted all the same.

But what alternative did Teddy have? Roy had recognized him and had been quick to blackmail him. Teddy was only looking out for his family. Had Roy not insisted that Sophie come along, she'd be on her way to a new place where she would rendezvous with Teddy once he managed to lose Roy and disappear into the wilderness. Still, they'd never be safe. Not as long as Roy was out there and knew their darkest secrets. He might not be good at strategic thinking, but he knew how to get what he was after and use his knowledge and size to intimidate. With a shiver of fear, Sophie came to the realization that Teddy was scared. She'd never known him to be afraid of anything. He was her fearless Teddy, the one person she could always count on to protect her, but Roy had Teddy up against the wall, his hands around his throat, and Teddy was terrified.

Sophie's heart turned over with love for her man. What right did she have to judge him? He'd been through so much with his father's murder, his capture on Jamaica, and then his mother's betrayal and Sophie's marriage. He was only trying to find a way out of this deadlock, and she'd go along with whatever he decided to do. Perhaps this was the new Teddy, and she'd have to get used to a man who was cautious and fearful.

Chapter 49

Hog Island rose out of the bay like the spiked hump of some sea creature. It looked forbidding during the day, but at night, it was downright sinister. Strange noises came from the thickly wooded slope, and Sophie wondered if there were any wild animals on the island.

Teddy jumped out of the boat and reached for Sophie. He carried her to the rocky shore to keep her skirts and shoes from getting soaked while Roy pulled the boat onto solid ground so it wouldn't wash out to sea with the tide. The men unloaded the shovels, lanterns, and provisions, and distributed them among the three of them before lighting a lantern and starting their trek to the top of the hill, which, on this moonless night, resembled a dormant volcano Sophie had seen in a book once. Vesuvius, it had been called. She trudged after them, carrying a bundle of food.

It was hard going, and they stopped often to rest. The forest was nearly impassable, the ground thick with brambles, pinecones, and bracken. Sophie felt every jagged rock and sharp branch through the soles of her shoes and wished she had sturdy boots like Teddy and Roy.

It was nearly sunrise by the time they reached the top of the hill. The light had changed from tar-black to murky gray, and birds, which had been eerily silent during the night, burst into their morning song, ready to greet the new day. The morning arrived slowly, the overcast sky pressing down on thick woods. Teddy extinguished the lantern and continued to climb, turning periodically to check on Sophie, who was exhausted, dirty, and covered in scratches and brambles.

"We should make a fire to warm ourselves and have some breakfast," Roy suggested once they finally spotted the split rock.

"The plume of smoke will be seen from the shore," Teddy replied.

Roy nodded in agreement, choosing not to argue for once. They found a level spot to sit on, and Sophie took out a stoppered jug of ale and unwrapped the food. They ate in silence. Sophie wished she could wash her hands and face, but there was no water nearby, so she settled for several dew-covered leaves and ran them over her grimy face. It felt pleasant, so she offered some leaves to Teddy, who accepted them wordlessly. He looked grim as he surveyed the area. It'd been thirty years since Captain Kidd had hidden his treasure. The landscape didn't look to have been tampered with, but who knew how many people had been in on the secret. The treasure could be long gone, their efforts about to be wasted.

"Find the spot," Roy ordered Teddy as he handed him the instructions.

Teddy approached the rock, then stood still for a moment before making a half turn. "That's north," he said. He then counted out ten paces. "This should be it."

The ground beneath Teddy's feet looked undisturbed, with several inches of thick vegetation covering the topsoil.

"Come on, then," Roy said. "You keep a lookout," he tossed over his shoulder to Sophie.

The island was uninhabited, but she supposed someone might still take an interest in their activities. From her vantage point, she could see the white-capped gray waves of the Atlantic and the calmer and bluer water of Pleasant Bay. All was quiet and calm.

Roy picked up a shovel and drove it into the ground, cursing eloquently when the shovel failed to penetrate the soil. "This is going to be hard going. The ground is thick with roots and rocks. And we have no idea how deep the chest is buried."

If it's here at all, Sophie thought. She spread a blanket beneath a leafy tree and sat down. This was going to take a long time.

By noon, Teddy and Roy had managed to dig down only about three feet. They had to hack through the thick roots that intertwined beneath the earth and formed an impenetrable web. Both men were now shirtless, their torsos glistening with sweat.

"Keep digging," Roy ordered when Teddy leaned on his shovel to take a break.

"We need a rest," Teddy replied. "And food." He wasn't used to this kind of work, not being a farmer. His hands were red and blistered, and sweat ran freely down his face.

Roy threw aside the shovel and sat down with his back against the rock. He looked angry and disappointed. "I don't think there's anything there," he finally admitted.

"Neither do I," Teddy agreed. "Shall we stop digging?"

"No. We go another foot down, then reassess."

"All right. You're in charge," Teddy agreed amiably.

The men ate a light meal, then continued digging, the silence broken only by their grunts and the sound of iron hacking at stubborn roots. The earth wasn't as rocky down below, and the work went a little faster.

"We're about four or five feet down," Roy said as he stood at the edge and stared down into the pit.

"I need a drink," Teddy said. "Give me a hand."

Roy reached out and helped Teddy out of the hole, then took off his hat and scratched his head in consternation. "We'd have reached it by now," he said.

Having taken a drink, Teddy came up behind him. "Another foot, I think," he said. "Then we call it a day."

Roy stared morosely into the pit, shaking his head. "I don't know if it's worth the bother. There's nothing there."

"There will be," Teddy replied.

He picked up his shovel, raised it, and brought it down on the back of Roy's head with all his remaining strength, sending Roy tumbling headlong into the pit. Roy's roar of shock and pain reverberated through the island, and the birds took to the sky, spooked by the unexpected sound. Roy's hands went to his head, his eyes rolling wildly as he tried to understand what had happened. Teddy jumped in after him and brought the shovel down again, wielding it like an axe and splitting Roy's skull. Sophie screamed, watching in horror as blood soaked into the thirsty earth. Teddy tossed the shovel over the lip of the pit and climbed out. He didn't look at Sophie, but began to shovel dirt over Roy, working quickly and steadily until Roy's corpse was no longer visible.

"Teddy, what have you done?" Sophie whispered as she watched him work. She was trembling with shock, the memory of Teddy's face when he brought the shovel down on Roy's skull forever imprinted on her brain.

"You didn't really think I'd let him go, did you?" Teddy replied conversationally as he continued to fill in the grave.

"Did you intend to kill him all along?" Sophie asked, shocked by Teddy's lack of remorse.

"Of course. I needed to get him to a place where no one would find his body, or if they did, they'd have nothing to connect him to me. I gave a false name when I made the arrangements at the inn and when I hired the boat, and paid in paper notes rather than Spanish dollars, which would raise suspicion."

"Spanish dollars?" Sophie asked, having never considered the question of money.

Teddy finished filling in the grave and leaned on his shovel, breathing heavily. "Plunder comes in many forms, Poppet. The pirates take anything of value from jewelry to foodstuffs to Spanish gold. Most colonies accept the Spanish dollar as currency, but since Massachusetts has its own printed money, I thought it wise to use that while here and made sure to obtain some paper notes while in Boston. There are people who'll happily fence stolen goods and foreign coin and pay in whatever currency the seller is interested in."

"You've thought it all through, haven't you?" Sophie asked as she stared in horror at the fresh grave. She kept expecting Roy Smith to come to and fight his way through five feet of thick earth, but the grave remained undisturbed, the only sounds the chirping of birds, who'd returned to their branches, and the wind in the trees.

Teddy didn't reply. Instead, he walked back toward the rock and faced in a slightly different direction than before.

"What are you doing?" Sophie asked.

"Counting ten paces to the north," Teddy said, and then walked forward, counting to ten.

"But you've already done that," Sophie replied, confused.

"I counted ten paces to the north-east," Teddy replied. "Smith never realized I wasn't facing true north. He wasn't paying attention."

"Are you suggesting there's still the possibility of finding the treasure?"

"There is that possibility, yes," Teddy replied absentmindedly as he drove the shovel into the new spot he'd marked. "Since we're already here—"

Sophie sank back down on the blanket, trembling with shock. She was relieved that Teddy had eliminated the threat that was Roy Smith, but she couldn't quite believe how easily and efficiently Teddy had disposed of him, as if he'd killed a chicken or a rabbit.

Sophie cradled her head in her hands and began to rock back and forth, a low keening sound erupting from somewhere deep within her. Teddy tossed down the shovel and came toward her. He sat down and pulled her close, applying more force than necessary when Sophie refused to be drawn into his embrace. Sophie pummeled his chest with her hands as she hurled abuse at him, but Teddy overpowered her and pushed her down onto the blanket, pinning her wrists and covering her body with his.

"Stop it," he said forcefully. "I did what I had to do to protect our family, and I'd do it again in a heartbeat. That man would have sent me to the gallows, and he'd have sent you right back to your husband. Our son would have been left orphaned and alone." Teddy let go of her wrists and took Sophie's face in his filthy hands, forcing her to look at him. "Should I have let him live?" he asked, his eyes an inch from hers. "Answer me, damn it!"

Sophie looked into Teddy's eyes, and all the fight seeped out of her. "No," she replied truthfully.

"I can't hear you," Teddy taunted.

"No!" she cried. "I'm glad you killed him."

"Good, because no amount of breast-beating can undo what I've done. What we've done. We're sinners, you and I. We've broken the laws of man and the laws of God. You can either spend the rest of your life on your knees, begging for forgiveness, or go forth unrepentant, proud that you've taken charge of your life. Which will it be, Poppet?"

Sophie didn't reply. Instead she kissed him hard, reaching for the buttons of his britches. Teddy bunched up her skirts around her waist and plunged into her, pounding into her with a fury that left her breathless. She matched him thrust for thrust, slamming her hips against his with wild abandon. She'd never done anything like this before, but the need that drove her was as primal as the instinct to kill to protect what one held dear. Teddy was right, they were sinners, but only because life had dealt unfairly with them. They could have made the best of their situation and spent the rest of their days in abject misery, or they could have done what they did and fought for their happiness.

It was too late to turn back now, not that she would. She had her Teddy, and he'd take care of her and John Theo no matter what life hurled at them. Teddy wasn't cautious or afraid; he was cunning and fearless, and that knowledge fueled her passion as she took Teddy deep inside her and gave back as good as she got. When they were finally spent, Teddy rolled off and lay on his back, panting with exertion. Sophie reached out and took his face in her hands, much as he'd done only a few minutes earlier.

"Let's go find that treasure," she said. Sophie got to her feet, adjusted her skirts, and reached for Roy's shovel.

Chapter 50

"We have to stop for tonight," Teddy said.

They'd dug up only about two feet of soil, and Sophie's hands were now as red and blistered as Teddy's. He drove his shovel into the packed earth and looked around, taking in the view for the first time. It had cleared during the afternoon, but thick clouds still blanketed the sky, leaving a wide band of deep blue along the horizon. The crimson rays of the setting sun lit up the clouds from beneath, giving the sky an apocalyptic appearance. Teddy stood very still, looking toward the shoreline bathed in an unearthly red glow.

"It's beautiful here," Teddy whispered, mesmerized. "Really beautiful."

Sophie followed his gaze. He seemed to be looking at a wooded hill across the bay, the top enveloped in a crimson haze. A few of the leaves had already begun to change, the trees dotted with spots of red and orange, and the blue-gray water of the bay lapped against the foot of the hill. The shore appeared deserted, not a house in sight.

"Yes, it is," Sophie agreed. "Very serene."

"I want to build our house up there," Teddy said, pointing to the top of the hill.

"Looks a bit isolated," Sophie replied.

"That's what makes it so perfect. It's not suitable for farming or fishing, but it forms a natural harbor. All it needs is a dock."

"Do you have the funds to build us a house?" Sophie asked, somewhat surprised by Teddy's observation.

"I will if we find this treasure. Do we have any food left?"

They used some of the water they'd brought up to wash their hands and faces and settled down to eat. The sky above them was growing dusky, but they didn't make a fire. Instead, they huddled together, wrapped in blankets to keep out the autumn chill.

As the wind picked up, the sky cleared, and thousands of stars appeared overhead, no longer hidden behind the woolly clouds. A crescent moon hung above the ocean, its points as sharp as those of a sickle. It was about as romantic as it could get when lying a few feet from a fresh grave, but Teddy seemed unconcerned; he had other things on his mind.

"Sophie, when we get home, I want you to write a letter," he said.

"To whom?"

"To Mr. Barron of Boston. He's a lawyer I plan to engage on your behalf," Teddy replied.

"To file a petition of divorce?"

"No."

"Then why do I need a lawyer?"

Teddy shifted next to her and rested his head against hers. "Lionel Holland is a very wealthy man, Poppet, and he has only one son, who will inherit his wealth upon his death. George Holland cannot remarry and sire an heir while he has a living wife and son, who will become his sole heir should anything befall him," Teddy said.

"But George and I never had a child."

"He doesn't know that."

"Teddy, what on earth are you talking about?" Sophie demanded.

"That preacher you told me about thought you were with child just before George sent you off to Boston. Who's to say you weren't? Had you been, your baby would have been born about a month ago. You will write to Mr. Barron telling him of the birth of your son and explaining that you left George because you feared for your life. I will instruct the lawyer to do nothing with the letter, but simply keep it safe. Should George try to have you declared dead so that he can remarry, or should he die himself, then Mr. Barron will produce the letter. It's for your protection, Poppet, should anything ever happen to me."

"But John Theo is nearly two," Sophie said, still trying to make sense of Teddy's unorthodox proposal.

"He is small for his age. Besides, you will provide Mr. Barron with a copy of the baptismal certificate."

"I don't have a baptismal certificate. If John Theo had been baptized, it'd have been by the Fullers."

"I'll get us a certificate," Teddy replied. "All you have to do is play along."

"I won't do it, Teddy. It's wrong."

"Wrongdoing is relative," he replied. "Some would say that what George did to you isn't wrong. He was within his rights as a husband, but I doubt you would agree, so I'd say people's actions are open to interpretation."

"You've changed, Teddy. You used to know right from wrong," Sophie snapped. She'd known Teddy wasn't the boy she'd fallen in love with as soon as he'd returned, but this day had been eye-opening.

"Sophie, life is not as black and white as you'd like to believe. It's mostly shades of gray that vary based on one's circumstances."

"No, I don't believe that. Some things are wrong, regardless of interpretation or circumstances."

Teddy turned to face her, his gaze defiant. "I would never have laid a hand on Roy Smith had he not threatened me. Was it wrong of me to protect myself and my family?"

"No."

"Then you admit that the murder I committed is justified?"

"Yes."

"I would also never dream of defrauding George Holland had he not abused you the way he had. Legally, he's still your husband; therefore, his estate should pass to your son should he die. Is that not so?"

"But John Theo is not his son."

"No, but as long as George is married to you, he cannot beget a son of his own, making our son his only legal heir," Teddy explained. "I'm simply looking out for you both should anything befall me."

Sophie pressed her cheek to Teddy's arm. The thought of losing Teddy was more than she could bear, but she knew he was right. If anything happened to him, she'd be left alone with no means of support. Her only options would be to return to George and face whatever punishment he chose to dole out or find employment, not an easy thing to do with a small child to look after. Perhaps Teddy was only being practical. After all, he had no wish to use the letter while George was still alive.

"Perhaps we should baptize John Theo ourselves," Sophie suggested. "We don't know that he was ever baptized by the Fullers."

"No, we don't, and the certificate doesn't indicate the age of the child, only the date of the baptism. George Holland will not be able to prove the child is not his."

"Thank you for looking out for me, Teddy," Sophie said as she pressed herself closer to him.

"I'd walk through fire for you, my love," Teddy replied, his voice quivering with emotion. "You and John Theo are the only reasons my life is worth living. Knowing you were waiting for me helped me survive capture and the unspeakable brutality I was forced to perpetrate to stay alive so that I could return to you. I will rest easier knowing you'll have legal recourse should I die."

"And what if I die?" Sophie asked.

"It would break my heart," Teddy whispered. "But know this. I will look after our boy and make sure he's provided for should anything happen to me. You never have to worry about that. We'll be all right, Sophie, no matter what."

"No matter what," Sophie echoed.

"Go to sleep now. You're worn out, and so am I. If we don't find the booty tomorrow, we will leave this accursed island and never come back."

"Amen to that," Sophie muttered, already half asleep.

Chapter 51

The following day dawned chilly and bright, the biting wind off the Atlantic making Sophie huddle into her shawl. She was too tired to dig, so Teddy went at it alone, hacking at the hard earth for hours. Sophie wished they could just leave and go back to John Theo and Caleb, but Teddy was determined.

"It's here, Sophie. I can feel it in my bones," he said while taking a break.

"Teddy, it's nothing more than a tall tale, and that letter might have been a fake. Who's to say that Captain Kidd even wrote it? Perhaps Roy Smith's father got it off someone else, and who knows where they got it to begin with?"

"No, I think it's genuine. The man held on to that letter until the day he died, and I suspect he left England and came to Massachusetts hoping he'd find the treasure someday."

"It's nothing more than a poor man's dream."

"But you were the one to crack the cypher, Poppet. You saw the words with your own eyes."

"Yes, I did, but perhaps it was all a clever jest. Maybe the captain only wrote that letter to distract his enemies from the true location. I wager his wife knew where the treasure was buried all along and has been living off that money for decades. Or it might have been divided among the members of his crew. Surely he didn't bury that chest by himself. Someone had to have been there to help him, and that someone would have returned to claim the booty."

"Not if that someone was taken prisoner along with his captain or was already dead," Teddy argued.

"You have till noon," Sophie said, hands on hips. "If you find no trace of anything by then, we're leaving."

"All right," Teddy agreed. "That's reasonable."

He turned his back to her and hacked even harder, leaving Sophie to her own thoughts.

Sophie came awake slowly, her body achy from lying on the hard ground. She didn't sit up straight away, but looked up at the sky, watching a seagull wheeling just above her head, its body gilded by the rays of the sun, which was riding high in the sky. It had to be nearly noon, and she suddenly realized that Teddy had stopped digging. All was quiet and still.

Sophie sat up and looked toward the pit. The shovel was lying on the ground, its angle a testament that it had been tossed aside without care. She looked around, expecting Teddy to come out from behind the rock or a tree where he'd gone to relieve himself, but there was no sign of him. When she'd fallen asleep, the pit had been only about three feet deep, not enough to hide him from sight.

Sophie's heart thumped as she scrambled to her feet and looked downhill toward the boat, half-expecting it to be gone, but it was still there. "Teddy!" she screamed frantically. "Teddy, where are you?"

"In here," came Teddy's muffled voice from the pit.

Sophie approached the pit and looked down. Teddy was squatting, his gaze fixed on a grinning skull peeking out of the earth, the bone gleaming white in the afternoon light, the eye sockets packed with dirt. What Sophie took to be roots at first was in fact the ribcage, the bones surprisingly delicate. She took a step back, frightened.

"Do you know what this means?" Teddy asked as he straightened and faced her.

She nodded. The treasure chest had to be buried beneath the skeleton. "Be respectful, Teddy," Sophie said quietly.

"I will."

Teddy carefully unearthed the rest of the skeleton, doing his best to keep the bones from coming apart. The clothes had rotted away over time, but there were still large chunks of moldy leather clinging to the remains. Tall boots covered his legs nearly up to the knee, and a belt with a large buckle encircled what would have been his waist. What remained of a doublet clung to the shoulder bones, and a beat-up hat was tilted back, exposing the top of his skull. Sophie peered inside and saw the top of a chest, now clearly visible just beneath the remains.

"Do you think they killed him after burying the chest?" she asked, marveling at the cruelty of people who could murder one of their own without a second thought. Presumably, the sailor would have been a part of Captain Kidd's crew, not some random person he'd forced to come along.

"I doubt they brought a dead body with them and carried it all the way up this hill just to bury it atop the treasure, but I really couldn't say. I've never heard it said that Captain Kidd was a heartless man. His crew was devoted to him, so perhaps they did drag a body up here."

Teddy carefully slid the skeleton off the chest, making sure to keep it intact. He didn't say so, but Sophie could tell he was spooked. He didn't like the idea of disturbing someone's resting place. Teddy dug around the chest until all of it lay exposed. The chest wasn't large, about the size of a newborn's cradle, but it was heavy since Teddy couldn't lift it on his own. He picked up the shovel again and struck off the rusted padlock, and the chain slithered into the dirt at his feet. Teddy looked up at Sophie, his face aglow with anticipation.

"Dead man's chest," he said under his breath as he nudged it with his foot, almost as if he expected the lid to fly open and something to pop out. Teddy stood back as much as the pit would allow and used the shovel to slowly lift the lid.

The glint of gold blinded Sophie. The chest was full of coins, with pieces of jewelry thrown haphazardly in. There were pearl chokers, several rings, earrings, and bracelets.

"Dear God in Heaven," Sophie breathed.

"Don't take the Lord's name in vain," Teddy joked. His eyes shone with excitement, his grin huge. "Hand me one of those sacks," he instructed.

Sophie gave him a sack and he began to transfer the coins into it, leaving the jewels for later.

"Fancy trying this on?" he asked as he handed her a lovely pearl necklace.

Sophie shook her head and drew back from the edge of the pit. The idea of putting on something that had belonged to another, someone who might have been killed for their possessions, was abhorrent to her. Teddy was ecstatic, but she was afraid, a cold chill sending shivers down her spine. This had to be bad luck, but nothing she said would stop Teddy from helping himself to the loot. He filled the sack halfway, then asked for another.

"God damn it," he exclaimed.

"What? What is it?"

She peered into the chest. Having scooped out the top layer of the treasure, Teddy had discovered that the chest wasn't full, at least not of coin. Beneath the booty were several thick leather-bound volumes that took up at least half the space inside the chest. Teddy lifted one out and leafed through the pages before tossing it back in disgust.

"What are those?"

"Captain's logs," he replied.

"Why would Captain Kidd bury them with the treasure?"

"Probably to keep the authorities from getting their hands on them. There's enough here to convict him a hundred times over. He probably thought he'd be able to beat the charge, or spend a few years in prison, at worst. I doubt the man thought he'd be executed on some trumped-up charge of treason."

"How do you know it was trumped up?" Sophie asked, curious despite her fear.

"Captain Kidd was liked and respected and left largely in peace as long as his activities benefited those in power. But adversity makes strange bedfellows, as Shakespeare wisely observed, and suddenly, he was locked out of the bedroom."

Teddy hefted the now half-empty chest out of the pit and set it beside the bags. He then began to fill in the pit. "Rest in peace," he said to the skeleton as the earth swallowed him up once again.

"What are you going to do with the logs?"

"I'm going to put them back in the chest, then add some rocks and sink it," Teddy replied. "Should anyone come looking, they'll find nothing more than two men buried at the top of the hill—two nameless men."

"What does it matter if they find the chest and the logs?"

"If the chest is found years from now, it won't matter, but if it's found shortly after we've been here, someone might ask the right questions and track us down, thinking they could still get rich. And what better way to relieve me of the treasure than by accusing me of murder?"

Sophie sighed. Regardless of the reasons, Teddy was a murderer, and she was complicit in the crime. She'd always believed her life would be forever joined with Teddy's; she'd just never imagined they would be bound by lies, theft, and murder. But things could be worse, Sophie mused as she helped Teddy stack the books back in the chest. She could still be with George.

Having packed up their camp, Teddy and Sophie carried everything down the hill and loaded it in the boat. Then Teddy handed Sophie into the boat and pushed it out into the bay before getting in himself. He was cold and wet, but he was also happy.

"This is the start of a new life, Poppet," he said, grinning. "You'll see."

"I just want to get back to John Theo," Sophie said.

"And you will, but there's something we need to do first." As soon as they were far enough from the island, Teddy pushed the trunk overboard and they watched it sink as it filled with water that would destroy the pages that had kept Captain Kidd's secrets for decades.

"What?" Sophie asked.

"First, we will retrieve the wagon and horses from the inn, then go to Eastham."

"Why?"

"Because we no longer need to live like paupers," he replied. "We have coin enough to build a palace, should we want one."

"I've no need of a palace, Teddy," Sophie replied.

"No, but you need a proper home, and so does our son. And I need access to a waterway."

Sophie didn't argue. Teddy was cleverer than she was. Where she only saw what came next, Teddy was always several steps ahead, assessing the consequences and taking appropriate action. As she watched Teddy row the boat toward Chatham, bags of gold and jewels lying in the bottom of the boat between them, she knew that they'd crossed a line they could never uncross. It was small comfort that they'd crossed it together.

Chapter 52

Lauren

Lauren rose early. Her body and mind were still in turmoil after Tyler's untimely interruption, a part of her wondering what might have happened had Tyler slept through the night, so she decided to take Billy for a long walk and try to focus on work instead. She was in possession of several random facts about Sophie Holland's life, but she still had to organize them into a coherent narrative before they could add up to a plot.

She had a light breakfast of yogurt and fruit, waited for Billy to finish his meal, then put him on a leash and headed out the door. Lauren inhaled the wonderful piney smell of the forest and smiled to herself. A city girl through and through, she'd never thought of herself as someone who would enjoy the peaceful embrace of nature, but these past weeks had brought out a different side of her. She was finally in a place where she was ready to accept her new circumstances and move forward.

Everything was beginning to come together. Ashley Mann's book was already with the publisher and Lauren had received the balance of her fee, and according to Della Jackson, her Boston real estate agent there were several parties interested in buying her apartment. And, of course, there was Ryan. There were no guarantees their relationship would progress, or last, but she felt strong enough to take the risk. Ryan was worth it.

Setting Billy free, Lauren trailed after him, her thoughts returning to Sophie. The new information about Ted Mercer had thrown all her previous theories into disarray, but also presented Lauren with a whole new angle. "The plot thickens," she said to herself, grinning. Sophie clearly wasn't the colorless recluse Lauren had first imagined her to be, nor was she a woman who had died with a clear conscience. Things were beginning to fall into place in Lauren's mind, but there were still a number of unanswered questions. What had become of Sophie's husband, George Holland, and had he been aware of her relationship with

Ted Mercer? Given that the house was called Holland House, it stood to reason that Sophie had never married her lover. Her children had borne the name Holland. Was it possible that Sophie and George had reconciled?

Lauren paused to consider this theory. *Dearest Teddy*, *Last night I dreamed of you*, Sophie's letter had read. These were not the words of a woman who loved her husband. This was a lament for a lost love. "Is it Teddy you're waiting for?" Lauren asked out loud, almost wishing Sophie would appear and reply to her. "What happened to him, Sophie?" she continued, safe in the knowledge that no one would hear her talking to herself except possibly the woman she was addressing. "Did he leave you? Did he die?"

A soft breeze ruffled the canopy of trees above her head, the rustling of the leaves whispering secrets she'd never learn. These trees were old enough to have been here when Sophie had walked these paths and dreamed her dreams. "What happened to you?" Lauren asked again, and then stopped walking. Maybe what had happened to Sophie wasn't so different from what had happened to Lauren. Perhaps that was why Sophie came to her, because in Lauren she saw someone who'd suffered, a young woman whose well-ordered life had been destroyed, the fabric of her beliefs shredded by the sharp edges of the truth.

"Did Teddy betray you?" Lauren asked the wind. "Did he break your heart? Is that why you still write letters to him, to work through your pain?"

Suddenly, Lauren didn't feel like walking anymore. The sun had disappeared behind a cloud and the morning turned gray and cold. Lauren clipped the leash to Billy's collar and pulled him back toward the house, eager to be indoors and away from the ominous silence that had settled over the forest. She'd left her cell phone charging in the kitchen and felt vulnerable without it. She knew she was being silly, but she quickened her steps toward home.

Billy gave her an accusing stare when she pulled him back inside the house but didn't bother to protest. He trotted toward his water bowl, then retreated to his crate, laying his head down on his paws as if she'd disappointed him and he needed time to recover.

Lauren squatted next to the pup and laid a hand on his head. "I'm sorry, buddy. I know I promised you a long walk, but I suddenly felt a bit wobbly," she explained. The dog gazed at her as if he understood. "Silly, I know. We'll go into town later. Would you like that? I need to get access to Wi-Fi." Billy turned away from her. "I'll get you a treat," she cajoled. This promise was greeted with a forgiving woof. "You are the sweetest puppy in the world," Lauren said, and kissed him on the nose.

There were several missed calls on her phone. Lauren listened to a message from Della Jackson first. "Good morning, Lauren. Just wanted to touch base. I ran an open house at your apartment last Sunday, and I've received several offers within the past few days, two of which I think you'll be happy with. Please call me to discuss."

Lauren disconnected from voicemail and sighed. This was it. All she had to do was accept one of the offers and her last connection to Zack would be severed. She felt a pang of sadness but shooed it away, annoyed with herself. She'd spent enough time crying into her pillow and nursing the wound Zack had inflicted. The decision had been made, and now she had been presented with an opportunity to follow through on it. It'd be hard to pack up the apartment, especially Zack's stuff. She'd keep a few mementoes but would donate the rest, she decided. It was time, and she hoped someone else would benefit from the things he'd left behind. Lauren took a deep breath and selected Della's number.

Della picked up on the second ring. "Hey, there. You are a hard woman to get hold of," she joked. "I'm glad you called me back."

"I'm sorry I haven't been in touch. I had some things to work through," Lauren replied.

"Selling your home is not easy, especially when that was never the plan," Della said, her tone sympathetic. "I won't pretend I know what you're going through, but I understand how hard it must be."

"Tell me about the offers," Lauren invited, uncomfortable with Della's pity. She was right; she had no idea what Lauren was going through, and she wasn't about to explain.

"As I said in the voicemail, there are two offers. One is from an IT executive who's ready to put down twenty percent. He has a preapproval for a mortgage and a pristine financial background."

"And the second offer?"

"The second offer is from a newly married couple. They're ready to put down ten percent, but they offered five thousand dollars more. They're also preapproved, but their credit history is a little spotty."

Della named the sum they were offering. It was very close to the asking price. Lauren leaned against the fridge and considered her options. She wanted the sale to go smoothly and close as quickly as possible.

"I'll accept the exec's offer," she said.

"Would you like some time to think about it?" Della asked, clearly surprised by Lauren's decisiveness.

"No. He's the one."

"Great. I'll email you the contract. You can sign it electronically and email it back to me."

"Actually, I'd prefer to come into the office," Lauren said. "I don't have a secure connection here, and there are some things I need to attend to at home."

"Suit yourself," Della replied. "What day works for you? Obviously, the sooner the better."

"How about Monday morning? Say eleven o'clock?"

"Sure. See you then. And congratulations. I hope you're pleased."

"I am. Thank you, Della."

Lauren ended the call but remained where she was. This was it. There was no going back. Lauren dialed Xavier.

"Hey, Xav. I'm going to be in Boston on Monday. Want to meet for lunch?"

"Sure. Should I invite Brooke?" he asked carefully.

"Absolutely. I'd love to see you both. Hopefully, we'll have reason to celebrate," Lauren said. "I've found a buyer for the apartment."

"Lori, are you sure you want to do that? I know that place holds a lot of memories, but where will you go? Real estate prices in Brookline are through the roof. You'll end up paying double for an apartment of the same size."

"I don't think I want to stay in Boston," Lauren replied.

"No? Where, then?"

"I think I'd like to settle down here, in Orleans," Lauren said. She hadn't realized she'd made the decision until she said the words.

"Are you sure? I know Cape Cod is pretty in the summer, but what are you going to do there in the off season? It's probably dead."

"I don't mind," Lauren replied. "I like it here."

"Right," Xavier replied. "Can I tell Mom and Dad?"

"I'd rather you didn't. Not yet. I'm not ready to explain."

"Lori, what's going on? Explain what? This isn't like you," Xavier said softly, taking on his big brother persona.

"Look, there are things I'm not ready to talk about. Just trust me on this."

"I will support you, whatever you decide," Xavier said. "See you on Monday?"

"See you," Lauren said, and ended the call. She felt better for having told Xavier. Once she had a closing date, she'd tell her parents. She'd come clean.

Lauren poured herself a glass of orange juice and sat down in her favorite spot in the living room. Butterflies fluttered in her belly as she selected the next message and pressed play. Ryan's rich baritone spoke softly in her ear. "Don't make any plans for Saturday. I'll pick you up around five."

Smiling in anticipation, Lauren laid the phone next to her. Saturday couldn't come fast enough.

Chapter 53

Sophie
September 1728

Sophie looked around with interest as they approached Eastham. She could see the ocean in the distance, shimmering in the flat silver light of autumn. Its vastness was not quite so intimidating when the waters were calm, stretching toward the horizon like a placid lake. The air was crisp and fragrant with the smell of hay. Now that it was nearly October, the days were noticeably shorter, and the trees lining the road were ablaze with color. She should have been happy, but she longed to be at home with John Theo.

"This is the place," Teddy said as he studied his surroundings. He jumped out of the wagon and helped Sophie down before walking up to the top of the hill to look out over the bay, his gaze searching for Hog Island. "Yes, this is it," he said under his breath.

A short while later, they arrived at the nearest settlement, which thankfully wasn't Puritan. The village they'd gone through just before reaching Teddy's hill reminded her of a crow's nest, with both men and women clad in black, their demeanor wary and watchful. She could never live among the Puritans; she wouldn't. The settlement they came across wasn't large, but there was a pretty white church, a smithy, and a tavern—all important in their own way.

"Stay with the wagon," Teddy instructed. He walked into the tavern and returned a few minutes later, looking gratified. "Jacob Hayworth," he said, taking up the reins. "Two miles north."

Sophie nodded. She was tired. They'd slept in the wagon the past few nights, afraid to leave the loot unguarded, but equally wary of bringing it inside an inn for fear of arousing suspicion. Teddy had purchased two large casks of cider and submerged the sacks to hide them from view, but he was still worried. They simply couldn't take the risk of leaving the treasure unattended.

"Lie down for a spell," Teddy said as they reached a fine house situated on rich farmland. The house was the largest in the area, two-storied and solidly built. There were numerous outbuildings, and several horses and cows grazed in a field just beyond the house. Teddy tied the reins to a post in the yard and went to knock on the door while Sophie stretched out in the back of the wagon, her body weary from days on the road. She must have fallen asleep because it was only when Teddy stroked her cheek that she woke. For a moment, she had no idea where she was.

"Are you hungry?" he asked. "Mrs. Hayworth has invited us to stay for dinner."

"Yes, I am," Sophie said and climbed out of the wagon. She tucked a few stray strands of hair into her cap and shook out her skirts.

"Sophie, I told them my name is George Holland," Teddy warned her.

"Why would you do a thing like that?" Sophie cried.

"Because Holland is a common name, and as long as they believe us to be a married couple, no one will make the connection should they ever come to hear of George Holland's wife trouble. Besides, I prefer not to give my own name."

Sophie stared at Teddy, her mouth open in surprise. "Whyever not?"

"Because I mean to buy my own ship, Poppet, and hire my own crew. Why do you think I need access to the Atlantic?"

Sophie glared at Teddy, furious that she hadn't realized what he'd been planning, but this wasn't the time or the place to hash out their differences. She plastered a smile on her face and walked into the house, greeting Mr. and Mrs. Hayworth and complimenting them on their home, which was indeed very nice.

"Your husband said he wants a house just like this one," Mr. Hayworth said as he passed Sophie a plate of warm bread rolls while his wife ladled out oyster stew. Sophie's mouth watered at the promise of a homecooked meal. Besides the stew, there was pork pie and apple fritters for after. "It's a good thing he came to me now, after the harvest," the man said. "I'm a builder, but I'm also a farmer. Living out here, we can't rely on others to provide for us. We must have our own milk and meat, and we grow wheat, barley, and corn as well," he boasted.

"How long does it take to build a house this size?" Sophie asked, wondering what Teddy had told the man. Mr. Hayworth didn't seem suspicious in the least; in fact, he'd been most effusive in his welcome.

"Normally, it takes about two months, but given that Mr. Holland wishes to build atop a hill, it will take longer since the land needs to be cleared first. I'd say we should be finished by the end of the year. Lucky for him, most men have brought in their harvest already, and there are plenty who'll be glad of the extra income this undertaking will bring. Without extra workers, it would take six months at the very least."

"Mrs. Holland, I pray you take no offense, but you look exhausted," Mrs. Hayworth said. "Stay the night. We've got a spare room and our boy will take care of your horses."

"We have five sons," Mr. Hayworth explained, grinning. "They're helping our neighbor with the haying at present, but they will be home for supper."

"Thank you kindly, but we must be on our way. Our own boy is waiting for us to return," Teddy replied, disappointing Sophie greatly. She would have liked to sleep in a proper bed and maybe even wash her hair before setting off for home.

"Why did you refuse?" she asked Teddy once they were on their way again. She felt even more sluggish after the meal, her eyes refusing to stay open.

"Because there's no one nosier than a young boy. With five of them snooping around, our secrets wouldn't stay safe for long."

Sophie nodded at the wisdom of this. Teddy was right, as usual. "Did Mr. Hayworth not question your method of payment?" she asked. Teddy had given Mr. Hayworth a large deposit, promising to pay extra if the house was indeed completed by year's end. Teddy had handed over a dozen gold doubloons, which Mr. Hayworth had pocketed with obvious glee.

"No man will turn down gold, Poppet," Teddy replied. "Currencies come and go, but gold is gold."

"Did he not ask how you came by it?"

"He was too afraid to lose the commission. The price we agreed on will keep his family in pork pies for decades, as well as the rest of this community. With winter coming, they're only too happy to put by a little extra something should their provisions not last till spring."

"Will we be able to travel up here in the dead of winter, Teddy?" Sophie asked.

"We won't have to. We'll remain in Sandwich until the end of November, then make our way here before the heavy snows come. Should the house not be ready, we'll stay with the Hayworths. Jacob and I shook on it."

"You've thought of everything, haven't you?" Sophie said, smiling. She was always impressed with Teddy's resourcefulness.

"I always do, Poppet. I always do," Teddy replied, and wrapped his arm around her. "Just a few more days and then you can sleep for a week, if you like. You do look worn out," he said, looking at her with concern. "Are you feeling all right?"

"Just tired," Sophie replied. Several nights in a proper bed wouldn't do her any harm.

"Make yourself comfortable in the back," Teddy said. "I know how eager you are to get home, so I'll drive through the night and then you can take over come morning."

"Teddy, are you sure?" Sophie asked, her heart lifting at the promise of seeing John Theo sooner than she'd expected.

"Absolutely. Go on."

Sophie climbed into the back of the wagon and was asleep within moments.

Chapter 54

December 1728

Sophie clapped her hands in delight when she walked through the door of their new home two days before Christmas. The whole settlement had pulled together, and, according to Jacob Hayworth, every able-bodied male had lent a hand to complete the building before the end of the year, eager to share in the gold Teddy was spreading around so liberally. The house still smelled of fresh wood, paint and polish, and someone had hung a pine wreath on the door, adding a bit of festive spirit to the place. The new home would take time to furnish, but they had the basics, provided by Timothy Ogden, the carpenter, who'd benefited handsomely from Teddy's generosity. There were sturdy beds, a pine table in the kitchen that could be used for cooking as well as eating, complete with four chairs, a matching pine dresser for the crockery, and several shelves in the narrow pantry. The dining room and the parlor were still empty of furniture, but they had the essentials and would manage for the time being.

"Do you like it?" Teddy asked, his gaze anxiously searching her face.

"Oh, it's wonderful, Teddy."

"Come look at the view."

Teddy pulled her out the back door, which led from the kitchen to a square yard. The ground was covered with snow and every branch was decorated in shades of silver and white, but just beyond the bay, the Atlantic shimmered playfully, the sun's reflection on the water like a pathway of gold coins carelessly strewn by a generous hand. It was breathtaking.

"You were right, Teddy," Sophie said. "This is the perfect place."

"We'll be happy here, Poppet," Teddy said. "You'll see."

Sophie shivered, and they went back inside.

"I think we have our first visitors," Teddy announced.

Mr. and Mrs. Hayworth had arrived, bringing a large canister of milk, a wheel of cheese, and a pumpkin pie. "Welcome to your new home," Mrs. Hayworth said as she followed Sophie into the kitchen. "I hope you have everything you need. If there's anything you require, just send your servant, and we'll do our best to help you out."

"Thank you, Abigail. We'll be all right. The pantry is stocked with supplies, and we have eiderdowns to keep us warm. I'll see to the rest in the coming weeks."

"Don't overexert yourself," Abigail Hayworth said, giving Sophie's middle a meaningful look. Sophie's cheeks grew warm. "You must remember to rest."

"My husband makes sure I do. He worries about me," she said.

"He's a good man," Mrs. Hayworth replied. "Your arrival has been an unexpected blessing for this community."

Teddy made sure everyone in the surrounding area benefitted in some way. He purchased something from nearly everyone in the village, even if he didn't immediately need whatever they were selling, and even made a foray into the Puritan settlement, returning with fresh eggs, a can of cream, and a jar of blueberry preserves.

"I'm cultivating goodwill, Poppet," Teddy explained. "We are newcomers, and people are always suspicious of newcomers, be they rich or poor. But if people benefit from having us here, they are more likely to dismiss their reservations. I want to know you'll be safe here, among these good folk."

Teddy was right. His generosity was returned tenfold. Over the next weeks, several families called by. They were curious to see the house and meet Mrs. Holland, but they also brought gifts, which were thoughtful and came in handy. Mrs. Appleton had made sunshine-yellow muslin curtains for the kitchen window. Mr. Carter brought a rocking chair for which his wife had sewn a checkered cushion. The Lewises were kind enough to part with several jars of honey, and Mrs. Hoffman brought a container of sauerkraut. Sophie welcomed everyone and sent them on their way feeling full and appreciated. Her Quaker neighbors had taught her how to make a cup cake. Its name came from the recipe, which was easy and delicious. Sophie mixed one cup of butter, two cups of sugar, three cups of flour, and four eggs, and set the cake to bake. She then spread several tablespoons of the blueberry preserves on top, which added a lovely, fruity flavor to her cake. Served with tea, it was a wonderful way to greet her new neighbors.

"You are so isolated here," Mrs. Lewis said as she sipped her tea. "It will be difficult for you in the coming months. We do get quite a bit of snow in January and February. Sometimes even in March."

"As long as we have sufficient supplies, we'll be all right," Teddy assured her.

"But what about coming to church?" she persisted. "Surely you won't want to miss Sunday services."

"We will do our utmost," Teddy replied smoothly.

Neither one of them had set foot in church since J.T. had been baptized in Sandwich in October. Teddy had lost his faith, and Sophie felt unworthy of entering the house of God, given that she was living in sin on money they'd come by through murder, and was now expecting a child that wasn't her husband's.

"We'll have to start attending services," Teddy said once the Lewises had departed.

"But Teddy—" Sophie began, but he shook his head.

"People who don't attend church arouse suspicion, and we want to be a part of this community, Poppet. Besides, I think going to church will do you good."

"It feels wrong," Sophie argued.

"Sophie, nothing I say will erase the guilt you feel, but once God welcomes you into his church, you will begin to feel more at peace."

"Sure, are you?" Sophie asked, feeling like lightening would strike her as soon as she walked into the church.

"Yes, I'm sure. Besides, J.T. and the new baby will need stability in their lives and belonging to a local parish is one way of achieving that."

"And what would members of the local parish say if they knew the money they'd so gladly taken from you had come from death and plunder?"

"They know," Teddy replied evenly.

Sophie stared at him, stunned into silence.

"Sophie, these folks might not be educated, but they are not stupid. They know a foreign coin when they see one, and they also know that I didn't come by it through honest work."

"And yet they have welcomed us," she mused.

"They're afraid."

"Of what?"

"Of me," Teddy replied.

"Why would they fear you?" Sophie demanded, outraged Teddy would suggest such a thing.

"Because they don't know what I'm capable of. It's safer to keep me sweet and beholden to them because of their kindness than test my patience."

Sophie covered what was left of the cake and walked out of the kitchen into the frigid January night. She knew she was young, but there was so much she didn't understand about people and human nature. Teddy had changed, more than she cared to admit, but he'd always been the clever one, the one who recognized an opportunity and seized it, while she had blindly believed whatever she was told and did what she thought was expected of her. Her naivete had nearly ruined her life. Perhaps it was time she took the blinders off and saw life for what it was: hard, often cruel, and not nearly as straightforward as she'd been taught to believe.

Teddy came outside and draped his cloak over her shoulders. "Sophie, it's all right," he said softly. "As long as you don't fear me, we're all right." When Sophie didn't immediately reply, he asked, his voice trembling with apprehension, "Do you fear me, Sophie?"

Sophie turned to face him and smiled. "No, I don't. I love you, and always will."

"I'll do anything for you, Poppet," he whispered into her hair. "Anything."

"As I will for you," Sophie replied. "You're my reason for being, Teddy. My life. You and our children," Sophie amended, placing a hand on her swelling belly.

Teddy pulled her closer and kissed her. "What have I done to deserve you?"

"You made me a dolly," Sophie replied, smiling at the memory. "You made me feel special."

"I'd have made you a hundred dollies if it made you feel less sad after your mother died," he replied.

"One was all it took. Oh, Teddy, don't ever leave me," Sophie pleaded.

Teddy didn't reply. He pulled her so close she could barely breathe, but she didn't push him away. She rested her head on his shoulder and they remained like that for a long while, gazing out over the starlit bay.

Chapter 55

The months passed quickly. For the first time since leaving George, Sophie had her own home and was surrounded by family. J.T. had turned two, and after nearly a year of living with them, he knew no other parents but the ones he had. Teddy was there, every day and every night, and she fell asleep feeling peaceful and safe knowing that he was by her side. Even Caleb was happy. He was sweet on a girl in the village, and she seemed to return his affections.

"I think Caleb will leave us soon," Sophie mused as she and Teddy lay in bed one night. "He'll want to get married."

"Would be nice if they came to live here with us," Teddy replied. "I trust Caleb, and it would be nice for you to have female companionship."

"I'm sure they'll want a home of their own," Sophie replied.

"We've plenty of land here, but you're right; they'll probably want to settle in the village, close to her family."

"So, you will not oppose the marriage?" Sophie asked. She wasn't sure how Teddy felt about Caleb leaving his service. Caleb was the only person Teddy truly trusted.

"Of course not. Why would I?"

"What if you have to leave?"

"I don't have to go yet," Teddy replied.

"Teddy, where is it, the loot?" Sophie asked. She had no idea where Teddy had stashed the booty from Hog Island.

"It's buried in the south corner of the tool shed," Teddy replied. "Come spring, I'm going to travel to Boston. I'd like to see my mother and sisters, and while I'm there, I'll try to sell some of the jewels. It's high time we put that money to work."

Sophie knew what he was referring to. She wished she could talk him out of leaving, but the money wouldn't last forever, and Teddy was in no position to seek honest employment. "I'm frightened, Teddy," she said.

"You've nothing to fear, Poppet. No one will trouble you," Teddy replied patiently.

There were things Sophie was afraid of that had nothing to do with their neighbors, but she chose not to speak of them. She feared for Teddy's soul and what captaining a pirate ship would do to him as a man. Killing and plundering on someone else's orders was bad enough, but to be the one who ordered the killing and the plunder was something else entirely. A part of Teddy's humanity had been stripped from him on Captain Martel's ship, but he was still her Teddy, he was still a good man at heart. She wanted to hold on to that man, to keep him from selling his soul to the Devil.

Teddy turned on his side and propped his head with his hand, looking down at Sophie. "I won't hurt anyone, Poppet, if that's what's worrying you," he said.

"What will you do, politely ask them to give you their valuables?" Sophie asked sarcastically.

"Why not?" Teddy asked with a grin. "People know what happens if they don't. Usually, all they care about is staying alive. Besides, there are other ways of being persuasive."

"Such as?"

"Such as tickling," Teddy replied.

Sophie yelped and began to giggle madly as Teddy performed a credible demonstration. "Stop!" she cried, laughing. "Please, stop!"

"You see. Works like a charm," Teddy said, still grinning.

"Teddy, I'm serious."

"So am I. I'm not a murderer, Soph. I don't want the deaths of innocent people on my conscience."

"What about Roy Smith?"

"He wasn't innocent," Teddy replied, no longer smiling. "Look, I know you're scared, and you'd be a fool not to be, but everything will be all right. You'll see."

"Teddy, do you know what they're saying about us? Reverend Martins says we're sinners and heretics. He's called on his congregation to shun us and boycott our custom."

Teddy considered this for a moment. "I'm not a big fan of the reverend, but he has a point. We are sinners, and heresy is a matter of opinion. I wager he sees anyone who doesn't share his views as being a heretic. Pay him no mind, Sophie. We've friends aplenty in the village."

"They fear us. You said so yourself."

"They fear me," Teddy corrected her. "No one blames you for anything. You're only a helpless woman who must do as she's told or she'll feel the sting of her husband's belt on her backside."

Sophie blanched at Teddy's words, instantly reminded of her treatment at George's hands.

"Oh God, Sophie, I'm sorry," Teddy muttered. "I didn't mean—"

"I know what you meant. Let's go to sleep, shall we?"

Teddy made a move to touch her, but Sophie slapped his hand away. "Not tonight," she said firmly, and turned her back to him.

"I'm sorry," Teddy said again, but she ignored him. Sophie rested her hand on her belly, comforted by the ripples caused by the child inside her. As a man, there were certain things Teddy could never understand. Come what may, he was still master of his own fate, but her entire existence depended on him. She was an adulteress, a liar, and an accomplice to murder. Reverend Martins might see sin behind every bush, but he was someone who had the power to hurt them. He could bring the authorities down on their heads if he laid his hands on anything that could serve as evidence.

Teddy fitted himself to Sophie's back and laid his hand over hers. They lay like that in silence, their hearts beating in unison.

"I'm sorry if I laughed at your fears," Teddy said at last. "I'll never let anyone hurt you."

"You might not have a choice in the matter," Sophie replied.

"As long as there's breath in my body, Soph, I will protect you and our children. Say you forgive me for my unspeakable idiocy."

"I forgive you," Sophie said. *I'll always forgive you*, she thought drowsily. *Because you're my life.*

Chapter 56

Lauren

Lauren frowned as she read the text from Ryan on Saturday morning. *Wear sneakers and bring a jacket.* Was he taking her on a hike? She'd assumed they were going somewhere romantic, but this didn't sound promising at all. They'd spoken several times since their make-out session on the couch but hadn't seen each other, and Lauren was beginning to wonder if she'd misread Ryan's feelings since he hadn't alluded to what happened between them. Maybe he only wanted a hook-up but having been in a relationship with Alicia since his early twenties no longer knew how to go about finding one. As far as he knew, Lauren was leaving at the end of the summer, so any awkwardness between them would be short-lived if things turned sour. Or perhaps she was overthinking the whole thing and reading too much into a hot kiss. She'd been in a relationship for over a decade as well and hadn't gone out with anyone since Zack's death. She was out of practice and possibly out of her depth when it came to embarking on a new relationship. What she needed was advice from a pro.

Lauren reached for her cell and selected Brooke's number. Brooke sounded sleepy when she answered but seemed glad to hear from her.

"Hang on a minute," Brooke muttered. There was a momentary silence, then Brooke came back. "What's up?"

"You're not alone, are you?" Lauren asked.

"Nope," Brooke replied. Lauren could hear the smile in her voice. "Your charming brother is asleep in my bed."

"Stop right there. I don't need to hear any more," Lauren replied with a grin. "Are you happy?"

"Deliriously," Brooke purred, then her tone instantly changed. "I'm sorry. I didn't mean—"

"It's all right. I'm happy for you guys. You don't need to feel guilty about being in love, especially with Xav. He's crazy about you."

"Really? He told you that?" Brooke sounded like an insecure teenager, but Lauren could understand her need for confirmation. Xavier wasn't always good at expressing his feelings.

"He did," Lauren said.

"You won't be alone forever, Lori," Brooke said, correctly reading her mood. "I think it's good what you're doing, selling your place. You need to move on, and you'll never get over Zack if you're surrounded by constant reminders of your life together."

"I know."

"So, what's the plan?" Brooke asked. "I hope you're staying in Boston."

"That depends."

"On what?"

"I met someone," Lauren said, her voice cracking with nervousness. She hadn't told anyone about her feelings for Ryan.

"Lori, that's great. Who is he? Tell me everything," Brooke gushed. Lauren heard the hiss of the espresso machine in the background. Brooke needed copious amounts of caffeine to function at full capacity.

"He's a veterinarian. He's widowed, like me, and has a three-year-old son." Lauren's statement was met with silence. "Brooke, are you there?"

"I'm here," Brooke replied. "Lori, are you sure you want to get involved with someone like him?"

"Meaning?"

"Meaning, the man's got baggage. Lots of it."

"So do I."

"Your combined baggage might be too heavy to carry," Brooke explained. "Relationships are hard enough without two dead spouses to compete with, and a little boy who'll always take priority over you."

"So, what do you suggest?" Lauren asked, deflated by Brooke's assessment of the situation.

"I suggest you have some fun before you settle into a relationship. Join Tinder, meet a few guys, figure out what it is you really want from a man. And most importantly, see if you're ready. If you find yourself comparing every guy you meet to Zack, then there's your answer. Does this guy remind you of Zack?" Brooke asked.

Lauren took a moment to consider Brooke's question. "No, he doesn't," she said at last. "Ryan is nothing like Zack."

"Are you sure about that? Could he be Zack-point-two that comes with an insta-family upgrade?"

Lauren bristled at Brooke's insinuation. She'd meant what she said. Ryan was nothing like Zack, and she didn't see Tyler as a way to get a jumpstart on the family she'd never started with Zack. "Brooke, I called you for moral support, not a lecture," Lauren snapped.

"Then tread carefully, will you? Make sure he's ready to be a partner to you in every sense of the word and he's not just looking for someone to play mommy to his kid."

"Thanks. I will. I'll call you later," Lauren said, sorry she'd told Brooke about Ryan.

"Lori, wait," Brooke wailed, but Lauren ended the call and tossed the phone onto the couch. She had hoped Brooke would give her a pep talk, but instead Brooke had made her feel even more uncertain. Perhaps she was right, and Lauren and Ryan didn't stand a chance.

Lauren ignored the incoming call from Brooke and went to make herself a cup of coffee. She'd work on the outline for her book until it was time for Ryan to pick her up. A jilted husband and star-crossed lovers weren't enough to make her book a compelling read. The story needed a plot twist, something the reader would never see coming, Lauren decided, her mind already in author mode.

Chapter 57

Lauren worked until half past four, then changed into a pair of jeans and a hunter-green silk top and applied some makeup. She made sure Billy had enough food and water, then put on her sneakers, grabbed a windbreaker from a coatrack in the hall, and was just reaching for her purse when a text popped up on her phone.

Meet me at the dock, Ryan wrote.

"What are you up to, Ryan Kelly?" Lauren muttered to herself as she locked the door and walked around the house and toward the steps that led to the water.

She was surprised to see a sleek sailboat bobbing gently at the dock, the name *Paramour* stenciled in flowing script on the side. Ryan stood on deck, smiling at her as she approached the boat. He held out his hand and helped her onboard. He wrapped his arm around her and kissed her lightly on the lips, but then let her go and directed her toward the stern.

"Is this your boat?" Lauren asked as she took a seat.

"No. It's my dad's."

"It's beautiful," Lauren said.

"It's a Harbor 25," Ryan replied.

Lauren shrugged. The model number meant nothing to her, but she found the name of the boat amusing. "Why is it called *Paramour*?"

"Because this boat is my father's other great love," Ryan replied with a smile. "My mom says that if he had to pick one, he'd go with the boat."

"Would he?" Lauren asked, curious to be offered a glimpse into the relationship between Ryan's parents.

"Possibly. He loves the old girl."

"I hope you're not referring to your mother," Lauren joked.

"No, I'm referring to this pretty lady. She's been in the family since I was a kid."

"Where are we going, Captain Kelly?" she asked.

"We are going for a sunset cruise," Ryan replied. "So sit back and enjoy the scenery."

Lauren knew little about sailing, but she could tell Ryan was an experienced sailor. He expertly guided the boat through the bay and then into open water. Lauren zipped up her jacket as a stiff breeze filled the sail and whipped her hair about her face. She pulled a hair tie out of her bag and pulled her hair into a ponytail, glad she'd brought her sunglasses along. The amber rays of the late-afternoon sun were still bright enough to make her squint.

"Do you take her out often?" she asked as she took in the endless sea and the golden clouds that sailed lazily overhead. Several other boats were on the water, including a high-speed ferry that was probably heading to Nantucket or Martha's Vineyard.

"Not anymore," Ryan replied, sadness etched into the lines of his face.

Lauren ignored the pang of jealousy she felt at Ryan's words. What he had done before and with whom was none of her business. He was here now, with her, and that was all that mattered. Everyone had a past. *And baggage*, her mind unhelpfully added.

"Where's Tyler?" she asked.

"Tyler is spending the weekend with my parents," Ryan replied softly, giving her a look that made her insides quiver. Lauren turned her face into the wind, grateful for the protection the sunglasses afforded her. She understood only too well what Ryan was suggesting, and her heart beat faster in response. He was still watching her when she turned to face him.

"Then I guess there's no reason to hurry back," she said.

"None whatsoever."

Lauren tried to ignore the butterflies in her stomach by focusing on what she did best, transporting herself to another world. She closed her eyes and let her mind take her to the aquamarine waters of the Caribbean. In her mind's eye, she saw an eighteenth-century ship, its prow slicing through the waves as it bore down on an unsuspecting merchant vessel. Lauren could almost hear the creaking of timber and the snapping of the sails in the wind. A handsome man stood on the bridge, his blue gaze directed toward his prey as the pirate ship steadily gained on the merchantman.

"Open the gun ports and prepare to fire!" he bellowed as soon as they were within range. The crew instantly obeyed, going about their business with calm and skill born of experience. Lauren could almost see the terrified faces of the merchantman's crew, several sailors crossing themselves as they prayed for divine intervention.

"What are you thinking about?" Ryan asked as he came to sit next to her. He had anchored the boat near an isolated cove, leaving him free to spend time with her.

"I was just imagining Mad Ted on his pirate ship. I wonder what it was called."

"Is that what I make you think of? Mad Ted?" Ryan asked, clearly taken aback by her answer.

You make me think of all kinds of things, Lauren thought, her belly clenching with desire, but she kept the sentiment to herself. "Sometimes I visualize a scene I plan to write when I'm nervous," she admitted.

"Are you nervous now?" he asked softly.

"Yes," she admitted.

"Why?" His breath caressed her face.

"Because you make me feel things I haven't felt in a long time, and it scares me," Lauren replied. She hadn't meant to show such vulnerability, but she couldn't bring herself to be coy. She wasn't in the mood for playing games. She'd been sad and lonely for far too long, and she was ready to take a risk, even if things didn't end as she hoped.

"It scares me too," Ryan admitted. "I've felt dead inside for so long."

"And now?" Lauren whispered as she looked into his eyes.

"And now you're all I can think about."

His lips came down on hers and she gave herself up to the kiss. Her earlier nervousness dissipated, white-hot desire flowing in her veins as she kissed him back. Brooke's warning echoed in her mind, but Lauren pushed it aside, her need to be closer to Ryan obliterating all reason. She had no way of knowing how things between them would change after this night, but she didn't care. She wanted to live in the here and now, and what she wanted was Ryan.

The crimson orb of the sun skimmed the horizon, bands of vermillion and gold painting the sky in the vivid hues of a northern sunset, but neither of them paid much attention to its breathtaking glory.

"Is there a cabin?" Lauren asked. She barely recognized her own voice. It was sultry and seductive, her meaning hard to misinterpret.

Ryan pulled her to her feet, led her inside, and shut the door. The cabin was filled with the violet shades of twilight, darkness pooling in the corners and turning something that'd look ordinary in bright daylight into a shadowy private world Lauren longed to inhabit. She unzipped her jacket and shrugged it off, her hands trembling as she slid them beneath Ryan's T-shirt. His skin was hot and smooth, the muscles in his stomach clenching beneath her touch. He kissed her hard, his intentions clear. He wanted her and he would have her and she was his for the taking. Ryan lowered her to the narrow bed, Lauren's fingers fumbling with his belt as he unzipped her jeans and pulled them off.

His hands were gentle and experienced, his mouth hot and hungry as he explored her body inch by inch, bringing her to heights of pleasure she'd forgotten she could attain. Lauren returned the favor, eager to please him as he'd pleased her and relishing every moan and intake of breath as she devoted herself to his pleasure. When their bodies finally came together, she was on fire, every nerve ending tingling with ravenous need. The first time didn't last long, their long-starved bodies giving in to the exquisite pleasure of their lovemaking, but neither of them minded. They had all night, and they meant to make the most of it.

When they reemerged on deck several hours later, the sky above them was strewn with stars, an almost full moon hanging above the horizon, its silvery light painting a narrow path on the inky waters of the Atlantic.

"We missed the sunset," Lauren said, a silly grin on her face.

"What sunset?" Ryan replied, wearing a matching smile. "Are you hungry?"

"Starving," Lauren admitted. Ryan disappeared into the cabin and returned a few moments later carrying a large hamper basket.

"I had it all planned, you know," he teased as he took out a bottle of wine, a crusty baguette, and an assortment of cheeses, cold cuts, and pâté. "A romantic dinner as we watched the sunset."

"Well, you know what they say about the best-laid plans," Lauren replied, and reached for the wineglass he was holding out to her.

"No, I don't. Why don't you tell me," he invited. Lauren just smiled. She was suffused with happiness, a warm glow spreading from her core to the rest of her body as the reality of what they'd done finally penetrated her consciousness.

Ryan opened the wine and poured her some before filling his own glass. He sat down next to her on the blanket he'd spread on the deck and lifted his glass to her. "What are we drinking to?" he asked, his gaze caressing her face.

"To new beginnings," Lauren replied.

"I like that," he said, his smile slow and full of promise.

Lauren leaned back and looked up at the stars. She felt ridiculously happy and filled with hope, something she hadn't experienced since Zack died. "What would you say if I told you I was thinking of buying Holland House?" she blurted out.

"I would ask you why you wanted to do that," Ryan replied, his eyes now serious.

"Because I want a fresh start."

"And you think that house will give you that?" Ryan asked, his head cocked to the side as he studied her moonlit face.

Lauren's happiness evaporated like morning dew. "Were you hoping I'd leave when my lease was up? Is this a summer fling for you?" She hated how hurt she sounded, but her emotions were bubbling dangerously close to the surface.

Ryan looked shocked by the accusation but bit back whatever he was about to say. Instead, he reached for her hand and threaded his fingers through hers, speaking to her as if she were a frightened animal. "Lauren, I don't do flings. I never have. I don't want you to leave, ever, but I don't think you can truly have a new beginning until you're ready to face what's been haunting you."

"You mean Sophie?" Lauren asked, taken aback.

"No, I mean Zack. There's something still holding you back."

"There's something holding you back as well," Lauren retorted, unsettled by his words. She willed herself not to cry, but she could already feel the sting of tears at the back of her eyes.

"Alicia will always be a part of me, but I've accepted her death and I'm ready to move on. I know a new relationship won't be easy to balance with being a single dad, but I will do my best to be fair to you both. I want to be with you, Lauren," he said softly. "I love you."

Lauren's gaze flew to his face, the breath she'd been holding escaping in a soft sigh. Now that he'd spoken the words, she knew them to be true. She felt the same. She loved him and she didn't want anything to come between them, especially not the past. "You're right. There is something I haven't told you," she admitted. "I was too ashamed."

"Ashamed of what?" Ryan asked gently.

The moonlight cast its silvery light onto the deck, its embrace comforting after the harsh glare of reality. Lauren sighed. She hadn't told anyone, not even Brooke, with whom she'd shared everything since her college days. Ryan sat quietly, waiting for her to say something, and she knew she was going to. She needed to talk about it, and perhaps sharing with someone who hadn't been connected to her previous life was the best way to unburden herself. She gazed up at the indifferent stars and began.

"Many people attended Zack's funeral. Some I knew; some I didn't. Everyone came up to me and offered their condolences and said something nice about Zack. Mostly I just nodded and thanked them, unable to engage emotionally on a day when my husband was being laid to rest. I just kept thinking that I had to get through the day, see it done, then I could go home, lock myself away from all these prying eyes and kindly sentiments, and quietly fall apart. I tried to fix my attention on minor details in order to keep some degree of detachment from what was happening. It was all too much, too soon. I'd just learned Zack was dead a few days before and had accompanied the funeral director to the airport the day before the funeral to take possession of Zack's casket. My parents had come with me. If they hadn't, I might not have survived the moment his coffin was unloaded from the plane, the top covered with an American flag, a tribute to a fallen hero," she said caustically. "I wanted to snatch that flag and rip it to shreds. It had taken my husband from me, had stolen my future."

Lauren wiped away the tears that had begun to fall. "Of course, I knew it wasn't anyone's fault. It had been Zack's decision to join the army, and to sign up for another tour. The government wasn't to blame. At least the powers that be had returned him to me and given me the opportunity to say goodbye and bury him in a place I could visit, but I hadn't had enough time to process and get a handle on my grief," she explained.

Ryan silently handed her a paper napkin, and she wiped her eyes and blew her nose before continuing. Speaking of that day still hurt. It was as if her lungs were suddenly empty of air and her stomach hurt, but now that she'd started, she had to get to the end.

"There was a woman at the funeral. Pretty. Mid-twenties. She didn't seem to know anyone and took a seat at the very back, crying quietly as if embarrassed by her emotions. I wondered who she was, but then the funeral service began, and I had to work hard to keep it together. I know people expect to see tears and naked grief, but those things were for me alone, not for anyone else, and I simply couldn't bare my soul in that way. I sat there, stiff and tense, willing myself not to howl or rage at the unfairness of it all."

Lauren reached for her wineglass and took a healthy swig. This was proving harder than she'd expected. "I saw the woman again at the gravesite, but she didn't come to the house afterward. Many others did, and they stayed for hours, talking and eating, and refilling their cups of coffee as if this was a party and they were there to be entertained. I heard people laughing, talking about the stock market, showing off pictures of their kids. It seemed that Zack was already well on the way to being forgotten. It was a relief when everyone finally left and I was able to tear off my dress, pull on comfy pajamas, and crawl into bed. My mom offered to stay, but I didn't want her to. I just curled into a ball and lay there, staring at nothing."

"Did you see the woman again?" Ryan asked gently.

"Yes. She came to see me a few months ago. Harper Mills, her name is," Lauren said, the name still bitter on her tongue. "She said she needed to speak to me about something important."

Lauren stopped speaking and peered at the sky, wishing she could erase that day from her memory, but it was burned into her brain forever. "That day changed everything, in some ways even more than Zack's death had. She told me she'd had a baby in November. Finn. She even attempted to show me a picture, but I couldn't bear to look at it. She felt that as Zack's son, Finn was entitled to a part of Zack's estate. Zack would have wanted that, she said."

"She could have been trying to scam you," Ryan said. "For all you know, she approached every new widow in Boston."

"I thought so too, especially since she'd waited nearly a year to come forward. Most people would have gotten rid of their spouse's personal effects by then, so no chance of a paternity test unless the widow was willing to have the body exhumed. I said as much, and she said she hadn't planned on approaching me, but she'd lost her job and she was struggling. I still had Zack's things, including his hairbrush and razor, so getting a sample of his DNA wasn't an issue. She agreed to a paternity test immediately, probably because she already knew what the results would show."

Silent tears coursed down Lauren's cheeks, blurring her vision. The words came out barely audible, her voice sounding strangled. "It came back positive. Finn is Zack's son. Ninety-nine percent match."

"So, you came out here to hide and lick your wounds?" Ryan asked as he wiped her tears away.

"Something like that. I couldn't bear to remain in that apartment, not after everything I believed to be true had been shown to be a lie. When I received the results of the test, I called Harper and asked her to meet me. I needed to talk to her, to understand why Zack had chosen her over me. I wanted to hate her, to rage at her and call her names, but I couldn't. She is a nice woman, the type of woman I might have been friends with had we met under different circumstances."

"It could have been just a one-night stand," Ryan suggested, perhaps thinking that would somehow minimize the extent of the betrayal Lauren had felt.

"It wasn't," she replied. "Harper said they met a year and a half before Zack died. He'd come in for a mandatory physical and she'd been the one to draw his blood. They chatted and he asked if he might take her to lunch since he was her last patient before her break. She agreed. She said he wore no wedding ring and didn't tell her he was married until several months later. Of course, he said he was separated, and it was only a matter of time before he filed for divorce. He simply hadn't had a good enough reason to rush things along. Until he'd met her."

"Did you believe her?" Ryan asked.

"Yes. I could see in her eyes that she was telling the truth. She looked too earnest, too guilt-ridden. I don't think she would have pursued a relationship with him had she known he was married, but then what do I know? I never imagined Zack would cheat on me and risk the life we'd built together, and, of course, Harper could have ended things with him when she found out he wasn't separated, but she didn't."

"Had Zack known she was pregnant?"

"She said she hadn't realized she was pregnant until after the funeral, and she'd intended to bring up the baby on her own."

"You owe her nothing," Ryan said, but Lauren could hear the slight tremor in his voice. As a single father, he could probably relate to Harper's plight.

"I know that, but Finn is Zack's child. It's not his fault his father turned out to be a lying, cheating bastard. I told Harper I'd have a decision for her by the end of May, but I listed the apartment before leaving Boston. Even if I refused to help her, I couldn't bear to remain. Everything I had believed to be true was a lie, and our home was now a testament to that. I needed to get away from everything and everyone I knew in order to see clearly."

"And do you?" Ryan asked softly.

"Yes, I do. I have a buyer for the apartment; I'm going to sign a contract on Monday. I am going to give Harper half the money and then I will never see her or her son again. I think that's the right thing to do, for all of us. I need to start fresh."

"And Zack? Are you ready to let him go?"

"I already have," Lauren said, smiling through the tears. "Once I had time to think, I realized that his lies hurt me more than his death. I would have learned to live without him in time, but I could never forgive his betrayal. He carried on as if nothing was going on, spoke of our future, the children we were going to have, while all the time he was sleeping with someone else and making promises to her. She showed me some of the pictures on her phone. They looked like any other couple: kissing, holding hands, strolling through the park, having a picnic, taking selfies in bed. She was no blip on the radar. She was his partner, possibly his future. And who knows, there might have been others," Lauren said, her voice devoid of feeling. "He might have been cheating on me the entire time we were together. I'll never know unless someone else comes out of the woodwork, claiming to have had his kid."

"Lauren, you can't think like that," Ryan implored. "You must let go of your anger in order to truly move on."

"Yes, I know, but everything I believed to be true had proven false. The man I trusted, had bound my life to and planned to have a family with, had lied to me at every turn. There were no signs, Ryan, that's how good he was at lying. I never felt a sudden withdrawal or a lack of affection. Our sex life hadn't changed. He was the same old Zack, the guy I'd fallen in love with. He made love to me, talked about his dreams for the future, and made plans. Never once had I suspected that his mind was elsewhere or that he was doing the same thing with someone else. I checked his phone records after Harper came to me. Nothing. Clean. He used another phone to speak to her. He covered his tracks well."

"Don't let this change you," Ryan said. "His behavior is no reflection on you, only on him."

"I know that, but how can I ever trust someone that way again? He's tainted every future relationship I will have."

"He can't taint anything unless you allow him to. Not every man is a liar and a cheat, and not every man will take you for granted."

"No, but how will I ever know if I can't trust my instinct? How can I give my trust when I don't know if it will be betrayed?"

"You won't. No one does. Falling in love is a leap of faith. A happy outcome is not guaranteed. But if you want to be with someone, you must take the risk, again and again, until you find a person who's worth it and who will cherish you and love you for the rest of your life."

"You make it sound so poetic."

"It is. That's why countless poems and songs have been written about love, but also about heartbreak. It's the flipside of the romance coin. Heads or tails? It's a tossup."

"Is it really?"

"Seems to be, since nearly half the marriages end in divorce. But people keep getting married because they believe their relationship will be the one to survive and flourish."

"Are you ready to risk it all again?" Lauren asked, turning to face him.

"Yes, I'm ready to risk it all," he said softly. "With you."

Ryan's arm snaked around her waist and he pulled her close, his lips brushing against hers. The kiss was feather-light, but it was full of hope and tenderness, and affection, just like Ryan himself. Lauren wrapped her arms around his neck and kissed him back. She would always carry the scars of Zack's betrayal and view every man's actions and words through the lens of his lies, but as the kiss deepened, she realized that she trusted Ryan and was willing to take a chance on him, as he clearly was on her. After more than a year of loneliness and grief, she felt like a bud opening to the sun on the first truly warm day of spring.

As they pulled apart, Lauren looked into Ryan's eyes, and what she saw there was love and trust. Lauren took him by the hand and pulled him back into the cabin, her intentions clear.

Afterward, as she lay next to Ryan, her body sated and her soul at peace, Lauren felt as if a heavy burden had been lifted. Nothing had changed, but everything was different. She was different. She felt reborn. As Ryan pulled her closer and her eyelids began to grow heavy with the need for sleep, an unexpected thought flitted through her brain. *Goodbye, Zack*, she thought drowsily, and knew that this farewell was final.

When Lauren finally drifted off to sleep, she dreamed of Holland House, and Sophie.

Chapter 58

Sophie

March 1729

Sophie hoisted a basket of laundry onto her hip and walked out the back door. It was a cool, breezy day at the end of March, perfect for drying laundry. She needed Caleb's help with washing the bulkier items, like bedlinens, but she washed shirts, hose, and her shifts once a week, preferring not to wait for Caleb to bring buckets of hot water and then empty the tub when she was finished. She'd gladly do it herself, but she was wary of picking up anything heavy for fear of losing the child. She was about six months along, her belly swelling noticeably beneath her apron. This child was calmer than J.T. had been, kicking halfheartedly only when Sophie went to bed. During the day it remained quiet, probably sleeping in its dark, quiet world.

Once she finished hanging the laundry and emptied the tub, she'd have a cup of tea, Sophie decided. She was tired and hungry, and it was hours yet till dinnertime. Teddy had gone into the village to look at a new horse, and Caleb had tagged along, eager to see his sweetheart. They had 'an understanding,' according to Caleb, which basically meant that he'd speak to her father when he was ready to provide for his bride. Caleb had been diligently saving his wages, so the big day couldn't be far off.

The strong tea revived Sophie somewhat, and she nibbled on a piece of buttered bread spread with honey. With J.T., she'd craved meat, but with this one she constantly wanted something sweet. Having appeased her sweet tooth, Sophie mended several pairs of hose before going to check on the laundry. In this type of weather, it dried quickly. She set the basket down and began to take the hose off the line. Her skirts whipped against her legs and her shawl did little to protect her from the biting wind. Spring came late to Cape Cod.

Sophie smiled when she saw a pair of boots appear below Teddy's still-damp shirt. "You're back early," she said. "Was the horse not to your liking?"

When Teddy didn't immediately respond, she moved aside the shirt and came face to face with George Holland. Sophie let out a strangled cry as her hand flew to her breast in terror. She took a step back, only to discover that George wasn't alone. An older man, whippet-thin and unusually tall, had come around the side of the house and was now positioned squarely behind her. His light blue eyes were narrowed, and his lips stretched into a smile of satisfaction.

"I take it that's her, Mr. Holland?" the man asked, coming even closer.

"It is, indeed, Major," George replied, his gaze fixed on Sophie's face. "You look well, wife." His gaze slid down her body, dark fury flashing in his eyes when it settled on her rounded belly.

"Wh-what do you want, George?" Sophie stammered. Her heart was hammering, her bladder threatening to let go.

"What do I want?" George echoed, clearly surprised by the question. "I want to wring your scrawny neck and toss you into the bay, but I'll content myself by beating that bastard out of you," he said savagely. "Then, I will take you back to Boston, where I will legally rid myself of you once and for all. And when your mangled body happens to turn up in some gutter shortly after the divorce, I will rejoice and take a new wife, one who'll be obedient and grateful," he hissed.

Sophie's legs nearly gave out as George took a step toward her. This was no idle threat made in anger. George meant what he'd said. He would punish her for the humiliation she had caused him, and then have her killed once he was legally free to marry again. If he killed her while they were still wed, suspicion would fall on him, but if she happened to die once they were officially divorced, no one would think he had any reason to commit murder and jeopardize his future. Sophie's gaze flew toward the house, but all was quiet. J.T. was sleeping upstairs. He'd been under the weather and had stayed abed.

Please don't wake up, my darling, Sophie silently pleaded with him. *Don't make a sound.*

"If you think your lover will save you, you're wrong. We saw him in the village. It'll be hours before he returns, by which time you'll be long gone."

"George, please, there's no need for violence," Sophie said. Her trembling voice seemed to give George great satisfaction. His smile was positively reptilian.

"Isn't there? You made me the laughingstock of the colony. Not a single person who walks into the shop doesn't know that my wife ran out on me, probably with her lover, which happens to be true. You've denied me the chance to get on with my life and have had the temerity to declare you've had a child by me, laying an indisputable claim to my estate. No doubt your lover's idea."

"H-how did you—?"

"How did I know? Mr. Barron happens to be a friend of my father's, so when your letter was delivered to him, he did what any gentleman would do and warned his friend of the plot against his family. The Hollands are many things, Sophie, but fools isn't one of them."

No, you're much worse than fools, Sophie thought defiantly. *You're monsters.*

"How did you find me?" she asked in a fruitless attempt to forestall the inevitable. It had been more than a year since she'd fled, and her letter made no mention of where she and Teddy had planned to settle. What had led George to Eastham?

"The major here is a very talented man," George replied conversationally. "He haunted the docks, thinking he might pick up some gossip that might lead him to you, and sure enough, he met a man named Roy Smith. Ring a bell?" he asked, smiling viciously. "That's right. Seems Mr. Smith had met an old acquaintance of his, a Ted Mercer, who had happened to be betrothed to a woman named Sophie Brewster before his rather inconvenient disappearance. Mr. Smith hoped to claim the reward, but Father said he wouldn't see a penny of that money until you were apprehended."

"What happened to Roy Smith?" the major asked, coming closer. "The man seems to have vanished without a trace, a consequence of getting mixed up with your lover, it seems. No one has seen him since they left Boston together six months ago. I wager he's dead," the major said, cocking his head to the side. "Yet another crime to add to your man's growing list."

"I think I'll let you live long enough to see him swing," George said with relish. "Won't that be fun? We can attend the hanging together, as husband and wife. It will be our last public outing before your untimely demise."

"George, I implore you—" Sophie began, but she never got to finish the sentence. George hit her face, hard. She staggered backward and nearly fell, her ears ringing with the force of the blow. Blood from her split lip trickled into her mouth and ran down her chin. She covered her face, but George wasn't interested in hitting her there again. Instead he punched her in the stomach, making her howl with fear and pain. She felt the child shift inside her, her belly growing taut. Sophie wrapped her arms around her belly, desperate to protect her baby, but George was far from finished. He hit her again and again, relishing her cries of pain.

Teddy! Sophie's muddled mind screamed. *Teddy, help me.*

Changing course, George hit the side of her head, and colorful stars exploded before her eyes as she went down, falling as if in slow motion. Sophie didn't feel the cold as she landed on the hard ground, nor did she hear what George said. His mouth opened and closed, but she was deaf to his threats. She was floating, the pain kept at bay by her failing consciousness. The child inside her had grown perfectly still, as if sensing the danger. *Stay with me*, Sophie begged. *Stay with me.* She rested her forehead against the ground. The cold jolted her out of her stupor, but it also seemed to wake her senses. Pain tightened around her belly like an iron band, squeezing hard and leaving her breathless. George must have cracked her ribs.

"Give her a moment to recover, Mr. Holland," the major said, his voice deep and gravelly. "You won't enjoy the beating if she's not awake to appreciate it," he added smugly.

"I don't think we should tarry," George said, his bloodlust abating. "I can have another go at her later. Right now, we need to leave. Mercer is just foolhardy enough to follow and try to get her back."

"He's one man," the major replied with an indifferent shrug.

"He's got that pup with him."

"Those two are no match for us. Mercer's not even armed. I'd love to blow his head off, but I'll leave that pleasure to you."

"You can have the boy," George replied. "Mercer is mine. I'd like her to watch him die, helpless in the knowledge that he won't be there to save her, not this time. Perhaps I should remain married to her a little longer," George mused. "Enjoy my husbandly rights. I was cheated of the pleasure the first time around. She didn't care for my methods." He laughed and kicked Sophie with the toe of his boot. "You there, my sweet? Time to wake up."

Sophie curled around her belly and covered her head with her hands. She knew it was futile, but she'd make it as difficult as possible for the men to move her and inflict a few injuries of her own. George's boots came closer. "Get up, you worthless whore," he said. "Don't make it more difficult than it has to be. You're coming with us."

When Sophie didn't budge, George tried a different tack. "Get the child, Major. He must be in the house. I'm not leaving anything to chance."

"Traveling with a child will take longer," the major replied.

"I have no intentions of taking him with us. Slit his throat and stuff him down the privy. It'll make my day to know that Mercer is shitting on his own brat."

The major walked toward the house and opened the back door, disappearing inside.

"No," Sophie cried. "Please. He's just a little boy."

"Little boys die every day. Comfort yourself with the knowledge that he'll go to Heaven," George replied with a chuckle. "Now, get up. I won't tell you again. If you refuse, I'll have the major torture the little bastard. I don't think you'd like me to do that."

Sophie sobbed as she staggered to her feet. She'd do anything to protect J.T. from unnecessary pain. He was only two—a baby, really. George came to stand in front of her. His face swam before Sophie's eyes as she swayed with dizziness. She thought she was going to be sick. A warm trickle had started between her legs, and severe cramps rolled through her stomach, making her double over.

"Quit stalling," George hissed. He grabbed her arm and yanked her toward him, making her lose her balance.

Sophie stumbled and nearly fell, but George caught her and pushed her upright. Darkness hovered at the edge of Sophie's vision, her body threatening to shut down as wave after wave of pain assaulted her abdomen. Only her fear for J.T. tethered her to the world, forcing her to remain conscious. She had to be there for him in his final moments. She had to tell him she loved him.

George suddenly released his grip on her. His eyes opened wide, a look of surprise transforming his features. Sophie sank to her knees, and it was only then that she noticed another set of boots behind George's. Blood dripped onto the ground, the droplets blooming like flower buds as they soaked into the snow. George fell to his knees in front of her, revealing Teddy standing behind him, a blood-covered dagger in his hand.

"Sophie!" he cried as he shoved George's body aside and knelt beside her. "Sophie, can you hear me?"

Teddy's warm hands were on her face, the desperation in his voice willing her to look at him, but she couldn't. Whatever strength she'd been holding on to had seeped out of her body, leaving her as weak as a newborn kitten. She felt so battered, she couldn't manage to keep her eyes open or form a coherent word. She slipped into the welcoming darkness where nothing hurt, and she wasn't terrified for J.T. any longer.

When Sophie came to, she was in her bed, J.T. asleep next to her. Teddy was sitting in the rocking chair, his feet firmly planted on the floor, his shoulders hunched as he leaned toward her, watching her.

"Sophie," he whispered. "Thank God."

"J.T.," she muttered.

"He's all right. Caleb got to him in time."

"The baby," Sophie moaned, her hand going to her battered stomach. She winced when her hand met with tender skin.

"You were bleeding, but it seems to have stopped. I will send Caleb for the midwife as soon as he returns."

Sophie wanted to ask where Caleb had gone, but fatigue overpowered her, and she fell back asleep, grateful for the painless embrace of oblivion. The next time she woke it was dark, the shutters closed against the night. Teddy was still there, a half-empty bottle of rum next to him on the floor. He looked ashen, his mouth drooping with fatigue.

"Teddy," Sophie whispered. It hurt to talk. Her lip had swollen, and her cheekbone was tender. She couldn't bear to touch her stomach. The skin was on fire and the pain of the bruises was excruciating. Sophie felt a wave of relief when she felt the baby shift.

"The midwife was here. She said the child is all right," Teddy said, as if reading her mind.

"Thank God," Sophie murmured. She turned toward J.T., but he was no longer beside her. "Where's—"

"He's fine. Caleb is telling him a story."

"And what story will you tell?" Sophie asked softly. Having seen the state of her, the midwife would know something awful had happened.

Teddy leaned back in the chair, closing his eyes as if too exhausted to speak. "I'm going to have to leave, Poppet. I killed two men, there's no getting away from that."

"But they attacked me. Surely you were justified," Sophie argued.

"George Holland was your husband. No one would blame him for coming after his wife. If taken, I'll be charged with murder."

"We'll leave here. We'll go away. No one will find us."

Teddy shook his head. "No, love. You and our children need a home. You're a widow now and no one can harm you. George Holland is dead, and so is that major."

"What did you do with them?"

"I had Caleb row them out into the Atlantic. The current will carry them further out to sea. In time, George Holland will be pronounced dead, and you will be free of him forever. J.T. will inherit his estate."

"But what about you? What about us?" Sophie cried. She tried to raise herself on her elbow, but fell back on the pillows, gasping.

"Sophie, George Holland and Major Boothe had been asking about us in the village. That was the last place they were seen before coming up here. Our neighbors alerted me to the danger, but they will not cover up a double murder. I must go. Tonight."

"Where will you go?"

"I will find passage to Wilmington, then go about purchasing a ship and hiring a crew. I will always look after you, Poppet. Always."

"When will I see you again?" Sophie wailed.

"Soon. Have Caleb build a dock. I'll come when I can."

"Please, don't go yet," Sophie begged. "I can't manage without you."

"You can and you will. Word's already spreading through the village that the two men who'd been asking after us have not returned to the inn. I don't know if George had given his real name, but if he had, they'll also quickly realize that one of us might not be who he claimed to be. It's only a matter of time until they come for me, especially if Reverend Martins has anything to say about it. He's been looking for a way to drive us out."

"And Caleb?"

"Caleb didn't kill the major; I did."

"You saved us," Sophie whispered.

"I would kill a dozen men to save you," Teddy said, brushing a stray curl away from her face. "I will be back, sweetheart. I won't desert you. Remember, there's gold buried in the shed should you have need of it."

Silent tears slid down Sophie's cheeks. It was as if God himself didn't want her and Teddy to be together. She was now a widow, but they would never wed, never live together as man and wife. Teddy would be a fugitive for the rest of his days, a man whose name would inspire fear and disgust.

"Please, look after yourself, Teddy," Sophie said, her hand going to his chest.

Teddy covered it with his own and smiled sadly. "I always do. Don't you worry about me. You just take care of our babies, and don't let Reverend Martins intimidate you."

"He frightens me with his talk of witchcraft, Teddy," Sophie said.

"Reverend Martins won't trouble you again," Teddy replied cryptically.

"Teddy, what have you done?"

Teddy shook his head. "Nothing, Poppet. Everyone has their price, and Reverend Martins is no different. Seems the good reverend has an eye to getting his sermons published. I've volunteered to cover the cost of this endeavor and he was quick to accept my offer in return for leaving us alone."

"That greedy toad," Sophie sputtered, amazed Teddy had found a way to defuse the man's hatred.

"That he is," Teddy agreed as he reluctantly got to his feet.

He was smiling, but Sophie could see the pain in his eyes. She wanted to cling to him, to beg him to stay, to refuse to be left behind, but she didn't do any of those things. This was painful enough for them both, and she had no desire to make things worse. She cried softly as Teddy kissed her and left, his footsteps echoing through the silent house.

Chapter 59

Lauren

The sun was already dipping below the horizon by the time Lauren pulled up to Ryan's house. He'd invited her for dinner, but she'd texted him a few hours ago to let him know she might not make it and to go ahead and eat without her if she wasn't there in time. Ryan smiled when he opened the door and pulled her close, giving her a lingering kiss before ushering her inside.

"Sorry I'm late. I made a detour," Lauren explained as she walked over to say hello to Tyler, who was sitting on the floor, surrounded by toy cars.

"To your apartment?" Ryan asked.

"Daddy, I'm hungry," Tyler wailed. "When are we going to eat?"

"You shouldn't have waited for me," Lauren said, secretly pleased they had. "What's for dinner?"

"Actually, I just ordered a pizza. It should be here in a few minutes. Ty, let's wash your hands, buddy."

"Okay," Tyler mumbled, and allowed Ryan to lead him to the bathroom.

Lauren walked into the kitchen and began to set the table. She was starving, not having eaten much at lunch. The chiming of the doorbell announced the pizza delivery almost as soon as Ryan and Tyler returned to the kitchen, and Ryan went to pay the deliveryman while Lauren settled Tyler at the table.

"Did you go to the zoo?" Tyler asked once he had a slice of pizza in front of him. "Daddy took me to the zoo in Boston. I liked it a lot."

"Would you like to go back?" Ryan asked. "Maybe Lauren would like to come with us."

"Would you?" Tyler asked.

"I'd love to. I haven't been to the zoo in ages."

"What's your favorite animal?" Tyler inquired.

"I like monkeys."

"Why?" Tyler asked, giggling.

"Because they're funny. What's yours?"

"I like bears, because I like Winnie-the-Pooh. What's your favorite animal, Daddy?"

"I like dogs," Ryan replied.

Jack came into the kitchen, as if on cue, and rested his head against Ryan's thigh. Ryan patted him absentmindedly.

"They don't have dogs at the zoo," Tyler protested. "It has to be a real animal."

"Well, then I like lions," Ryan replied patiently.

"Because of *Lion King*?" Tyler asked. "Am I your Simba?"

"You sure are."

Tyler smiled happily and turned his attention to the pizza, devouring the slice in record time before turning to study Ryan, a thoughtful expression on his little face.

"Are you going to kiss Lauren again?" he asked, nearly making Ryan choke on his pizza.

Lauren lowered her head and smiled into her napkin, amused and embarrassed in equal measure.

"If you're finished with your dinner, I think it's time for bed," Ryan said, doing his best to look unperturbed, but the telltale blush staining his cheeks gave him away.

"But I want to stay up," Tyler moaned.

"You have preschool tomorrow, and I have to go to work," Ryan said. "Come on."

"Can I have a story?"

"Of course."

"Can Lauren read me a story?" Tyler glanced at Lauren, whose cheeks heated with pleasure at being asked.

"I'd love to read you a story."

"I want the one about dinosaurs," Tyler said as he slid off the chair.

"Let's get you ready for bed, then Lauren will read you the story about dinosaurs," Ryan said as he scooped up Tyler and carried him from the kitchen.

Lauren smiled as she cleared the table. She enjoyed feeling like a part of a family. She could certainly get used to this.

"All right, he's all yours," Ryan announced as he came back into the kitchen. "Teeth brushed, pajamas on, storybook ready. Don't let him con you into reading more than one story."

"I won't, but it's hard to say no to such cuteness."

"Don't I know it," Ryan replied, smiling. "Hurry back," he whispered as he pulled her close and gave her a kiss.

**

Lauren snuggled closer to Ryan, a contented smile spreading across her flushed face. The dinosaur story had worked like a charm, and once the son was in bed, the father had been eager to go to bed too.

Ryan turned on his side and ran a finger between her breasts and down her belly, making her shiver. "Tell me about your day," he invited. "Did you sign the contract?"

"I did."

"Any regrets?"

"None whatsoever. It actually felt very liberating. I can't wait to close on the apartment and move on to the next chapter of my life. I think this new chapter will be titled 'Ryan.'"

"I think it will be a full-length novel," Ryan replied, grinning confidently. "Did you meet Xavier and Brooke for lunch?"

Lauren nodded. "I told them everything about Harper. They were a bit shocked, but they both think I'm doing the right thing in helping her. Now all I have to do is tell my parents, which will be a little more difficult. I briefly considered not telling them, but I think they have a right to know the truth."

"They do," Ryan agreed. "As a parent, you always want to know what your child is going through, even if it's painful. Were your parents close with Zack?"

Lauren nodded. "They loved him like a son. They'll feel almost as betrayed as I did."

"I think they'll be proud of the way you've handled the situation," Ryan said.

"I hope so. They might think I'm a fool for agreeing to Harper's demands, but I'm not doing this for Harper; I'm doing it for Finn. He's innocent in all this."

"You're a good heart, Lauren Masters. So, where did you go afterwards? I thought you were coming straight back."

"I stopped by the Boston Archive and then spent a few hours at the Library of Congress."

"Did you find what you were looking for?"

"It's what I couldn't find that's important," Lauren said, grinning.

"You lost me, Masters," Ryan said with an amused smile.

"I wasn't able to find dates for either George Holland or Ted Mercer's deaths, which only confirmed my suspicion that I was on the right track, so I moved on to the Library of Congress to search for answers. They have newspapers dating all the way back to the seventeenth century, but the content isn't available online, which is why I couldn't find anything when I did a search."

"So, what did you discover, Miss Marple?"

Lauren playfully nudged Ryan in the ribs. "After trolling through hundreds of newspapers, I came across several very interesting articles that helped me piece together this story that's begging to be written. Sophie Holland ran out on her husband after less than a year of marriage. Just vanished one day. Lionel Holland, George's father, offered a substantial reward for any information on his runaway daughter-in-law, but I found no articles that mentioned her return. And we know she didn't because she wound up here, we think with Ted Mercer. Now, at first, I thought she'd met Ted after her marriage to George, but her eldest child was born several months before she married George, and his name was John Theo."

"Theo as in Theodore?" Ryan asked, catching her excitement.

"Bingo. So, it stands to reason that Sophie was in love with Ted Mercer before her marriage. I don't know why she married George or what happened to her infant son, but I think it's safe to assume it wasn't a happy marriage. Ted suddenly came back into her life and she couldn't pass up a chance at happiness."

"And what of George?" Ryan asked.

Lauren turned onto her side and propped up her head with her hand. "That's the really interesting part. There was no mention of Sophie or George for over a year, but then, I found several articles dating between April 1729 and October 1729 which covered the disappearance of George Holland and Major Elijah Boothe."

"And who was he?" Ryan asked, his eyes glowing with curiosity.

"It seems Major Boothe was something of a colonial bounty hunter. I found several references to him online. He was instrumental in apprehending a serial killer in Upstate New York and had also helped track down a missing heiress in Boston."

"So, you think George Holland hired this Major Boothe to help him find his wife?"

Lauren nodded enthusiastically. "I think they did find her."

"And Mad Ted dispatched them," Ryan concluded.

"It would make sense, wouldn't it? Ann Oliver mentioned that two men had disappeared after arriving in Eastham. They could have been George Holland and Elijah Boothe."

"Yes, they could have," Ryan replied, his expression thoughtful. "Do you think Sophie haunts the house because she feels responsible for their deaths?"

"No, I think she haunts the house because she's waiting for her Teddy," Lauren announced triumphantly.

"Were you able to discover anything about his whereabouts after the disappearance of the men?"

"No, I didn't have time. The library was closing, but I will find out what happened to him, Ryan. I need to know how this story ends."

"How do you think it ends?" Ryan asked.

"In heartbreak and tragedy," Lauren said, suddenly subdued. "We always think past generations were so prim and proper, but their lives weren't all cotillions and church fetes. Deep passions ran beneath those buttoned-up exteriors, and the secrets they took to their graves still have the power to scandalize, even after all these centuries."

"People are people," Ryan said. "Some things never change. So, do you have enough to write your book now?"

"Yes. I know exactly how it will end."

"How?"

"I guess you'll just have to read it to find out," Lauren replied, and straddled Ryan, bending down to kiss him.

"I know how this will end," Ryan said huskily, flipping her onto the mattress and pinning her down with his body.

"Not in heartbreak and tragedy, I hope," Lauren joked.

"No, not this time," he said. "This story will have a happy ending."

Chapter 60

Sophie
November 1729

Sophie's heart fluttered with excitement when she glanced out the window. A boat was approaching the dock, the lone man rowing steadily as he looked up at the house on the hill. Putting five-month-old Cynthia in her cradle, Sophie ran down the stairs and out of the house, skipping down the wooden steps that led to the water. She threw herself into Teddy's arms as soon as he stepped out of the boat, holding him as if he might vanish. She hadn't seen him in nearly eight months and had begun to think he'd never risk coming back.

At last, Sophie stood back and took stock. Teddy wore the golden tan of the Caribbean, but there was a wariness in him that was hard to hide. His eyes searched her face, his worry abating when she smiled broadly and took him by the hand.

"Come inside," she said. "You must be chilled to the bone, being out on the water so late in November."

Teddy pulled her close and kissed her soundly. "I missed you, Poppet."

"Not as much as I missed you," she replied. "Oh, Teddy, you have to see Cynthia. She's getting so big. She's the spitting image of you."

It was only when Sophie saw the relief in Teddy's eyes that she understood the fear she'd glimpsed in his gaze. He'd had no way of knowing if the child had survived George's attack and had been too afraid to ask outright.

"She's fine, Teddy. She's lovely," Sophie gushed. "Born on time," she added to reassure him. "She can't wait to meet her father."

Teddy followed Sophie into the house. His gaze seemed to take in everything from the new settee in the parlor to the clock on the mantel.

"Caleb brought that from Boston," Sophie said, following Teddy's gaze. "He bought it with his wages."

"Where is Caleb?" Teddy asked.

"He went to the village. He and Bethany live here with me, but they go to visit her family at least twice a week. Bethany is expecting their first. She's due in February."

Teddy didn't reply. He drank Sophie in, his eyes misting with tears. "I hate being away from you, Soph," he said hoarsely. "I miss you and J.T. How is he?"

"He's well," Sophie said proudly. He'll be so pleased to see you."

"I don't know if I can bear to leave again," Teddy said miserably.

"How long can you stay?"

"For as long as no one knows I'm here. Can Bethany be trusted?"

"Yes, she can be," Sophie assured him. "Come and meet Cynthia."

Teddy followed her up the stairs and into their bedroom, where Cynthia lay wide-eyed in her cradle. Teddy removed his hat and unbuttoned his coat before reaching for the baby. She didn't cry. She rarely cried. Instead, she studied him with all the seriousness a baby could muster, taking him in as if she were an adult. Teddy cradled her head and kissed her softly.

"She's wonderful," he said.

"Daddy!" J.T. cried as he ran into the room. "Where have you been? I missed you."

"I'm here now," Teddy said, avoiding the question. He handed Cynthia to Sophie and reached for his son, swinging him up into the air. "You are so big. I can't believe my eyes. I hardly recognize you."

"I'm going to be three," J.T. announced. "Will you stay until my birthday?"

"I will try," Teddy replied as he set the child down.

"Did you bring me anything?" J.T. asked.

"J.T., it's not polite to ask people for gifts," Sophie chastised him.

"He's not people, he's my father," J.T. replied archly.

"As it happens, I did bring you something," Teddy said. He reached into his pocket and extracted a retractable spyglass. "Let me show you how it works. You can use it to look at birds and stars."

"I can use it to watch for your ship," J.T. said, his innocent comment nearly undoing Sophie. Was this to be their life from now on, seeing Teddy once a year, if they were lucky?

"You must be hungry," she said instead, striving for normalcy.

"Starving," Teddy replied as he helped J.T. on with his coat and took him outside to test out the spyglass.

Settling Cynthia on her hip, Sophie went into the kitchen to fix Teddy something to eat. Had she known he was coming, she'd have made something special, but she didn't bother to cook on days Caleb and Bethany went into the village since they always returned with bundles of food sent by Bethany's mother. There was usually a steak pie and some sort of sweet for after supper.

Sophie sliced some bread and ham and pushed the kettle hanging on the hook into the flames to boil water for tea. Her vision blurred as she watched Teddy and J.T. in the backyard, taking turns with the spyglass and looking out to sea. J.T. needed his father, and Sophie needed her man by her side, but she was no fool; she knew it wasn't safe for Teddy to stay. Rumors had been rampant after he left, the attack on Sophie discussed at length since the reason for it was unclear to the villagers. The only blessing was that George hadn't given his real name at the inn, making the connection between them difficult to establish.

Lionel Holland was still looking for his son; Caleb had told her as much when he returned from Boston, where he'd gone to visit his sister. Sooner or later someone would recall seeing the two men on the road or meeting them at an inn, and their information might lead the authorities straight to Eastham. Sophie felt no guilt about George's death, nor did she feel bad about Major Boothe, but their deaths would forever remain a stain on her relationship with Teddy, what happened that day a painful memory neither one of them wished to talk about.

Sophie smiled brightly when Teddy and J.T. came back into the house, their cheeks ruddy with cold. J.T. was clutching the spyglass to his chest, thrilled with his gift.

"Can I have some?" he asked, looking at the food on the table.

"You've had your supper," Sophie replied.

"But I want to eat with Daddy."

"All right. Come and sit down."

J.T. waited to see which chair Teddy would take, then sat down next to him, desperate to be near his father. He looked up at Teddy, his eyes shining with love. Teddy reached for a piece of bread and put a slice of ham on it before handing it to J.T., who smiled. Then Teddy took some food for himself.

"Come and join us," he said to Sophie.

Sophie didn't think she'd be able to get any food past the lump in her throat, but she poured herself a cup of tea and sat down with her boys, happy for them to be together, even if it was only for a short time.

Later, when they lay in bed together after getting thoroughly reacquainted, Sophie finally broached the subject that had been on her mind since Teddy's arrival. "I want us to be married, Teddy," she said. "I want to be your wife."

Teddy turned onto his side and propped his head with his hand, looking down at her. "I'm a wanted man, Poppet. My recent activities have not gone unnoticed by the authorities. As soon as I walk into town, I'll be turned over to the nearest magistrate."

"Then we can be married right here at home."

"By whom? Do you expect the minister to walk up the hill and perform the ceremony? He'd as soon smite me as marry me. I'm a murderer, Sophie, and a pirate. I have my own ship now, and my own crew. I'm well known to the authorities."

"Where is your ship?" Sophie asked.

"Moored off Nantucket. Once I return, we're off to Jamaica."

"Then you marry us," Sophie said, surprising them both. "You are a captain, are you not? A captain can perform a wedding ceremony."

"I don't think a captain can marry himself."

"He can in an emergency."

"Is this an emergency, then?" Teddy asked, laughing softly. When Sophie didn't reply, he leaned down and kissed her. "I've wanted to marry you since you were a slip of a girl. You are right; it's time we were wed, but our marriage ceremony will have to be a bit unorthodox."

"I don't mind."

Teddy reached for her hand and smiled. "I, Theodore, take thee, Sophie, to be my wife, to have and to hold from this day forward, for better, for worse, for richer, for poorer, in sickness and in health, to love and to cherish until death do us part, according to God's holy ordinance, and therefore I pledge myself to you."

Sophie gaped at Teddy, surprised that he'd recalled the words of the marriage service so precisely, but her shock didn't last long. She took his hand and made her own vow. "I, Sophie, take thee, Theodore, to be my husband, to have and to hold from this day forward, for better, for worse, for richer, for poorer, in sickness and in health, to love and to cherish until death do us part, according to God's holy ordinance, and therefore I pledge myself to you."

"I now pronounce us husband and wife," Teddy said. He leaned down and kissed her tenderly. "I love you, Sophie."

"I can tell," Sophie said with a giggle as Teddy's love pressed against her thigh. "At least we don't have to wait for the wedding night."

"Every night will be our wedding night," Teddy said as he rolled on top of her. "Until I have to leave again."

Sophie ignored that last part. She'd learned that happiness came in moments that had to be seized and cherished. There'd be time enough to fret and lament, but tonight, she was a bride, and she would enjoy her wedding night.

Chapter 61

June 1731

The child at her breast burned with fever, his face flushed, his gown soaked with sweat. Sophie rocked the baby gently, humming a song her mother had sung to her when she was small. At nearly a year, Benjamin was sturdy and strong, but this fever had left him weak and lethargic. Sophie smoothed back his damp curls and pressed her lips to his forehead. Still hot. She stood and began to pace, needing to do something other than sit and await the fate of her son.

After about a half hour, Benjamin finally fell asleep, his breathing shallow and ragged. Sophie stopped before the window and looked out over the moonlit expanse of the bay. Its savage loneliness was as beautiful as ever, the horizon devoid of any living thing. What she wouldn't give to see a ship on the horizon or a rowboat gliding toward the dock.

"Where are you, Teddy?" she whispered into the night. "Please, please come home."

She sighed deeply and turned away. Teddy hadn't come back since the week they married and Benjamin was conceived. He'd never seen his son, had never held him in his arms or kissed his round cheek. She prayed every night that Teddy would return, but deep down, she knew he wasn't coming back. Not this time.

Sophie settled the child on her bed and covered him with a down quilt despite the warmth of the June night. She prayed he'd sweat off the fever and feel better come morning. She couldn't lose her Benny too. She simply couldn't. Sophie lay down next to the baby, her gaze on the full moon staring balefully from the pitch-black sky. Silent tears coursed down her cheeks as she held her baby close.

"I'll never stop waiting for you, Teddy, not as long as there's hope. I promise I will never leave this place. Please come back to me," she whispered into the night. Eventually, she drifted off to sleep, her tears leaving dried tracks on her cheeks.

Chapter 62

Lauren
Labor Day

Gentle sunshine streamed onto the patio, the late afternoon cool and pleasant. A lovely breeze ruffled the leaves and several boats glided by. Tyler laughed merrily as he chased Billy around the patio, trying to get back his ball, but Billy wasn't about to give it up. He was having too much fun. Merielle watched her nephew, an indulgent smile on her face as she leaned back in the deck chair. Lauren's mom was admiring some photos Ryan's mother was showing her, and their dads were deep in discussion about fishing. The smell of sizzling burgers and barbecued chicken filled the air, making Lauren's mouth water. It was almost time to eat.

She left Xavier to help Ryan grill and walked into the house, where Brooke was putting the finishing touches on the salad. Lauren took out the side dishes she'd prepared earlier from the fridge and set them on the counter.

"I'll take those outside," Brooke offered.

"Thanks. I think we're running low on lemonade. There's some in the fridge."

"Okay, I'll come back for it," Brooke replied, and stepped outside.

"Can I help?" Ryan asked as he walked into the kitchen.

"No, everything is ready. Would you like a beer?" Lauren asked.

"Sure."

Ryan took a sip of beer and smiled at her. "You look happy."

"I actually have some news," Lauren said, smiling from ear to ear. "My agent has submitted my book proposal to my publisher, and they loved it. They've offered me a three-book deal."

Ryan kissed her sweetly. "I'm so proud of you. Are you ready to say goodbye to Sophie?"

"I'll miss her, and I'm grateful to her for giving me the inspiration and the desire to write something new and different, but if there's anything I've learned from this experience, it's that if you hope to find happiness after heartbreak, you have to grieve and then allow yourself to move on. I don't think Sophie ever let Teddy go. She mourned him for the rest of her days, and even after her death, her spirit wasn't able to leave this place."

Ryan leaned back against the counter, his expression somber. He understood grief, but if the last few months were anything to go by, he also understood the value of letting go and moving on. He hadn't mentioned Alicia once since their night on the boat, and although he'd left the family portrait on the mantel, he'd moved his and Alicia's wedding picture into the office, where Lauren wouldn't have to look at it every time she came over.

"Do you think it was grief that kept her tethered to this world?" Ryan asked.

Lauren shook her head. "No, I think it was hope. Perhaps, somewhere deep down, she still believed that one day he'd come back. Had she been able to mourn him, she might have been able to make peace with losing him."

"Did you ever find out what happened to him?"

Lauren had spent hours at the library, using her research as an excuse to take a break from packing up the apartment. It had taken several visits, but she'd eventually found what she was looking for in a book about the Golden Age of Piracy and its impact on the American colonies. Lauren was surprised to learn that Mad Ted's ship had been called *Vengeance*, a name possibly directed at those who'd tried to take Sophie away from him.

"Yes, I have," Lauren replied. "Ted Mercer was mentioned in one of the books on piracy in the 1700s."

"Was he eventually apprehended and executed?" Ryan asked.

"No. He met with a rather less dramatic end," Lauren said, feeling strangely sympathetic toward the man. "He died of malaria at the age of thirty-two. It was rampant in the Caribbean during the eighteenth century. He's buried in a cemetery in Port Royale."

"Surely someone would have informed Sophie of Teddy's death," Ryan said, his beer forgotten. "He was notorious. He was Mad Ted."

Lauren smiled. When it came to pirates, Ryan was still a star-struck groupie.

"You'd think so, but in those days, letters frequently got lost, ships went down with their entire crews aboard, and there was no Google," Lauren joked.

"Hey, you two, quit canoodling. We're hungry," Brooke called from the doorway.

"Come on," Lauren said. "Let's enjoy our last barbecue at Holland House."

She was about to walk toward the door when Ryan caught her wrist. "It doesn't have to be."

"My lease is up at the end of the month. I suppose we can squeeze in one more get-together," Lauren replied.

"Let's buy this place," Ryan said, his eyes alight with excitement. "You love it here, and so do I. Let's fill this house with love and joy and hope. It will be a new chapter for us both."

He pulled her to him, drawing her into his fantasy. Butterflies took flight in Lauren's stomach. They'd talked about the future, and she'd even considered extending the lease, but nothing definite had been decided, other than that they would continue to see each other as often as they could should she decide to return to Boston.

"What about Tyler? How will he feel about leaving his home, his only connection to his mom?"

"I will never allow Tyler to forget his mom, but I couldn't ask you to live in another woman's house. You have to grieve and then allow yourself to move on if you want to be happy," Ryan said, repeating Lauren's words to her. "I love you, Lauren, with all my heart. Please say yes," he urged her, his voice husky, his lips close enough to her ear to give her shivers.

Lauren took Ryan's face in her hands and smiled into his eyes. "I love you too, Ryan, and I have already moved on. It happened when I wasn't looking. Yes, I would love to buy Holland House and make a home here with you and Tyler. But can we keep the name?"

"You mean you don't want to rename it the Kelly House?"

"That sounds like an Irish Pub," Lauren joked. "I want to keep the name to honor Sophie."

"I'm all right with that," Ryan said, wrapping his arms around her waist as he lowered his face to kiss her.

"We're hungry," Xavier bellowed from the patio.

"Coming," Lauren and Ryan replied in unison and went to join the others.

Epilogue

Sophie stands in the kitchen, watching Lauren and Ryan from her favorite place by the window. Their eyes are glowing with love and hope for the future, and she envies them. There was a time when she looked at Teddy like that and thought their life together would be long and beautiful. They had their moments, but fate wasn't kind to them—or maybe it wasn't fate, but the people they loved and trusted. Sophie wipes away a tear that slides down her cheek when she thinks of Teddy's lonely grave in Port Royale. She still mourns for him, but now that she knows what became of him, she can finally let go. She can move on.

Sophie's face is transformed as she smiles through her tears. "I'm coming, Teddy," she whispers as her hand unconsciously goes to the necklace Teddy gave her all those years ago. "I'm coming, my love."

Lauren and Ryan don't notice anything; they're too caught up in each other and their shiny new love, but the spot by the window suddenly looks brighter, the sun filling the kitchen with the golden glow of the late afternoon. They feel a lightness they can't explain, and a shimmering joy that fills their hearts.

Cherish your love is Sophie's last thought before she flies into Teddy's arms and buries her head in his chest. *As we would have.*

The End

Please turn the page for an excerpt from The Lovers

Notes

I hope you have enjoyed The House on the Hill. If you've read any of my other books, you know how much I love historical mysteries and dual-timeline stories. I also enjoy a good pirate story. I decided not to delve too much into the more colorful aspects of a pirate's life, but I have sailed past Hog Island many times and wondered if Captain Kidd's treasure is still there somewhere, just waiting for the right person to find it.

I love hearing from you. You can always reach me at www.irinashapiroauthor.com or irina.shapiro@yahoo.com.

If you'd like to join my mailing list, please subscribe at http://irinashapiroauthor.com/mailing-list-signup-form/

You can also find me on Facebook at https://www.facebook.com/IrinaShapiro2/ or on Twitter at https://twitter.com/IrinaShapiro2

If you've enjoyed the book, reviews on Amazon and Goodreads would be greatly appreciated.

An Excerpt from The Lovers

Echoes from the Past Book 1

Prologue

The darkness was absolute, the interior of the chest smelling rank and damp. Their bodies were pressed together, crammed in an unnatural position, limbs stiff after hours of immobility. At first, there was still hope, but it had run out, as had the air, as the tight-fitting lid prevented even the smallest amount from seeping in. His arms felt like lead, but he gathered what was left of his waning strength and lifted his hand to her face. He didn't need to see it; her features were burned into his brain, as were those of their child. *Please, God, keep the babe safe.*

Her skin was still warm, but she was already gone, as surely as he would be in the next few minutes. His lungs were already burning, a sheen of sweat covering his face. He pressed his lips against her unresponsive mouth in a final kiss as a last thought flashed through his dying brain:

It was all worth it.

Chapter 1

October 2013
London, England

Sean Adams leaped from the cab of his digger and pushed his way through the crowd of men gathered around a large opening. For a moment, he thought it was a sinkhole, here in the middle of London, but what he was looking at was some kind of subterranean chamber that had been uncovered as a result of his efforts. The ceiling of the chamber—nothing more than a thin layer of rotted wooden beams—had caved in, revealing a narrow space beneath, the walls of which were solid stone. The men peered into the hole, curious to see what it held.

"Step aside, step aside," Foreman Milne bellowed. He stood at the edge of the opening and shone a torch into the dark recess of the chamber. "What have we here?" he asked no one in particular as he removed his hard hat and scratched his egg-shaped head. Foreman Milne was a good-natured man most of the time, not averse to joining his crew for a pint and singing loudly and off-key once he'd had a few, but at this moment he was vibrating with irritation. He had no time for delays; he was on a schedule, and the management was breathing down his neck.

"What is it, boss?" someone called out. "A buried treasure?" The men chuckled. They found all kinds of rubbish at every new site: bits of furniture, rusted prams, sometimes even old cellars that had been used as air raid shelters during the last war, complete with tin cups, wooden benches, and old newspapers. But this looked different. The chamber was completely empty, except for one large rectangular object.

"Bring me a ladder, lads. A long one," the foreman called. "Adams, you're with me since we have you to thank for this 'fortuitous' find."

Sean reluctantly followed his boss into the dank hole. The roof was mostly gone, but the walls were still intact, built of rough-hewn stone nearly a foot thick. They were cold to the touch, even on a pleasant day like today. The opening looked like it might have been a large well in its day, but there was no indication that it ever contained any water. The walls were not covered with mildew, and the packed earth at the bottom was dry as bone.

"Toss me down a pair of cutters," the foreman called out to the men gathered at the top. "This thing appears to have a lock on it."

The two men stood awkwardly next to what appeared to be an oversize sea chest. It took up most of the space, leaving barely any room for Milne and Adams to stand. The chest looked sturdy and was secured with a chain and an old-fashioned padlock, which was rusted with age and neglect. Foreman Milne gently kicked the chest with his foot, and the two men heard something rattle within. He then ran a finger along the lid. It came away dusty, but the wood beneath appeared to be in good condition. The chest was elaborately carved and painted, the colors still vibrant despite the layers of grime.

Sean was bursting with curiosity and wished Milne would just get on with it. His brother, Joe, worked on a site where they'd found a leather pouch full of antique coins. The story had been in all the major newspapers and even on the telly. Joe had been interviewed, and the segment appeared on the news. The coins were now part of an exhibition at the British Museum, and Joe still told the story of his historic find every time he had a captive audience.

"Shall I do it, boss?" Sean asked the foreman, his voice quivering with excitement. The older man shrugged and moved aside as much as the small space would allow, his face creased with displeasure. He handed Sean the cutters and leaned against the wall, his arms crossed, his posture indicative of the impatience that he was trying to keep in check. Foreman Milne wasn't the type of man who suffered from acute curiosity or an overactive imagination. He assumed they'd found some rubbish that would need to be cleared away, resulting in wasting several hours of their time. To him, it made no difference who opened the chest.

Sean cut the rusty chain and kicked away the lock when it clattered to the stone floor. He took a shaky breath before lifting the lid and peering inside.

"Jesus, Mary, and Joseph," he breathed out as he quickly crossed himself. Sean stepped back, nearly colliding with Foreman Milne, who'd taken a step forward to shine a light into the chest. It was full of bones, the skulls grinning eerily out of the gloom.

The men above were craning their necks for a better look, blocking nearly all the light in the process. Someone already had his mobile out and was snapping pictures of the chest, the flash blinding in the dark space.

"No photos," Milne bellowed as he stood in front of the open chest. "Get away with you."

"Sean, call the police. Now!"

Chapter 2

October 2013
Surrey, England

Quinn threw another log on the fire and went to pour herself a cup of tea. A steady rain had been falling since the night before, bringing with it a howling wind and a bone-chilling damp, which seemed to seep into the stones. The room was lost in shadow, the lowering sky and pouring rain having leached all light out of the October afternoon. But the fire glowed in the hearth, casting shifting shadows onto the stone walls and filling the room with a welcome warmth, the crackling of the logs momentarily blocking out the moaning of the wind.

Quinn sat down on the sofa and wrapped her hands around the hot mug. The heat felt good, so she held the mug for a few minutes without drinking, absorbing the pleasant warmth, which brought her a welcome sense of comfort. Despite the cold and the rain, it felt good to be home, even if that home wasn't quite as she had left it. She'd returned to England only a few days ago, landing in Heathrow on a golden autumn morning. She'd collected her cases from the carousel and made her way out the door toward the queue of taxis waiting at the curb.

She filled her lungs with crisp air and smiled at the brilliant foliage, which stood out in jarring contrast to the cobalt blue of the cloudless sky. After months of relentless heat and merciless sun of the Middle East, it was lovely to feel a cool breeze on her face and the nip of the coming winter already in the air. Quinn looked as if she'd just come back from a tropical holiday, her face and arms tanned to a golden glow. Still, the six months she'd spent on a dig in Jerusalem had left their mark, both physical and emotional, and she was relieved to be home at last. No one paid her any attention as she waited patiently in line for her turn at a taxi. To anyone who bothered to notice her, she was just an average young woman, casually dressed in jeans, T-shirt, and a worn leather jacket. Her dark hair was pulled into a messy bun atop her head, and her face was devoid of any makeup, except for some lip balm she'd put on before disembarking the plane. She looked like any other tourist, but in archeological circles she was a star, at least until the next big find.

Unearthing the Roman sword dating back to the Great Revolt of 66 CE was a tremendous coup. The sword had been discovered lodged in the drainage system running between the City of David and the Archeological Garden, and it was found only a few feet away from an ancient stone depicting a menorah. The menorah had been etched into the stone with something crude and sharp, like an old nail or a chisel, but it was close enough to Temple Mount to be of tremendous interest and confirmed what the original menorah might have looked like. Researchers from the Israel Antiquities Authority put forth various theories on the significance of the find.

Quinn had to admit that she had been more interested in the sword. It was still in its leather scabbard, which was miraculously well preserved. The scabbard kept some of the decorations from being obliterated by time and the elements, allowing a glimpse into Roman craftsmanship of the period. The sword likely belonged to a simple infantryman, but it was so much more than a sharp hunk of metal. It was not only a tool but also a work of art, a lovingly crafted weapon that would have been treasured and well maintained by its bearer. The sword would remain in Jerusalem, but Quinn had published her findings and had agreed to interviews with CNN, the *British Archeology Magazine*, and the *Archeological Journal*, scheduled back-to-back for the day after her arrival. The sword might be thousands of years old, but the news of its discovery would fade fast, and the interviews had to be published while public interest was still at its peak.

And now she was finally at home, having fulfilled her obligations and free until the spring semester began just after the new year. She'd intended to pick up a few classes at the institute, devote time to research, apply for new grants that would fund the next dig when they came through, and spend time with Luke. At least that had been the plan while she was still in Jerusalem—but things had changed.

It felt strange to walk into the house and face all the empty spaces. They glared at her like hollow eye sockets, eerie and blank. Luke had cleared out before she returned, partially to avoid awkwardness and partially because he'd been in a rush to leave. He hadn't even given her the courtesy of breaking up with her in person. He'd dumped her via text, telling her that he had accepted a teaching position in Boston and would be gone by the time she returned. This was no longer their house, their little love nest, but it was still her home, and despite the sadness that filled the quiet rooms, she loved it.

Quinn snuggled deeper into the sofa and gazed with affection at the familiar room. The house had once been a private chapel, built by some devoted husband for his devout Catholic wife, but it had been confiscated by the Crown during the Dissolution of the Monasteries and allowed to fall into disrepair once everything of value had been stripped, sold off, or melted down. It stood empty for centuries, forgotten and desolate, before being offered to Captain Lewis Granger, a distant cousin of the family that still owned the estate at the beginning of the nineteenth century.

The young captain had been embroiled in a scandal involving the young wife of a well-respected general, dishonorably discharged from the army just before Waterloo, and sent home to England. He had disgraced himself to the point where he could no longer show his face in London, at least for a time, and so he appealed to his cousin, begging for sanctuary, which Squire Granger reluctantly offered. Lewis Granger might have been a libertine and a gambler, but he had a penchant for architecture and history. He turned the ruin into a home, rebuilding the crumbling structure with his own two hands and the help of a few lads from the village, who were more than happy to earn a few quid during a time when well-paying jobs were scarce and returning soldiers tried to pick up the pieces of their lives and find any employment going.

Squire Granger had been so impressed with Lewis's efforts that he bequeathed the chapel to Lewis in his will, and it had remained in the family until the last descendant sold the house to

Quinn three years ago. Niles Granger was a young man who was thoroughly at odds with Lewis's legacy. His spiky hair was dyed platinum blond; he wore unbearably narrow trousers and horn-rimmed spectacles, proclaiming himself to be a hipster and an artist. Niles had no interest in history or architecture, and he wanted nothing more than to get away from all that "old shite," as he so eloquently described it. He unloaded it gleefully and never looked back, using the profits to buy a dilapidated loft with space for a studio, where he created works of unfathomable modernity using splashes of bright colors, bits of trash, and phallic symbols strategically displayed for maximum shock value.

The rest of the estate had been bought years earlier by an eccentric millionaire who converted the huge manor house into Lingfield Park Resort. Despite its proximity to the resort, Quinn's house felt completely private. The chapel was nestled in the woods at the edge of the property; none of the guests ever ventured in that direction, warned off by the "Private Property" sign nailed to a tree and a lack of a walkable path. There was a narrow lane, just wide enough for one car to pass on the other side of the house, which led into the village, but the lane saw so little traffic that Quinn felt as if she were living alone in the woods.

Now, three years later, Quinn was still charmed by the stained-glass windows set high in the stone walls and vaulted ceilings painted with an image of the heavens. Not much had remained of the original chapel, but there was something about it that always made Quinn feel welcome and at home. She supposed it was all the hopes, dreams, and prayers that had been absorbed by the stones over the years. Prayers didn't just dissipate into thin air—they soaked into the walls, buttressing the structure with their strength and healing energy. As an archeologist, she found it immensely appealing to live in a place that was imbued with so much character and steeped in history.

When originally built, the chapel had been one large open space, but Lewis Granger had divided it into two rooms, the back room serving as a bedroom and furnished with an antique four-poster bed and carved dresser, which Niles had been only too happy to throw in as part of the deal. The dark wood was polished to a shine, the bed hangings made of embroidered damask in mauve and gold. Once that bed had been the center of Quinn's universe, the place where she spent lazy afternoons with Luke as they made love, shared their dreams, and made plans for the future. Now, the bed was used only for sleeping and reading when sleep wouldn't come.

Quinn still felt fragile and bruised by Luke's sudden desertion, but now being on her own didn't seem as frightening as it had two months ago when she suddenly found herself single. She'd felt adrift for a while, remembering several times a day that she no longer had anyone to return to. But like all shocks to the system, the knowledge eventually became part of her new reality, and Quinn threw herself into her work, eager to feel like her old self again. There had been a few offers and casual flirtations at the dig but nothing that blossomed into anything real; she supposed she hadn't allowed it to. She hadn't been ready to move on.

At first, Quinn managed to forget about Luke for a few hours at a time, then for whole days, but now she was back home, and her loneliness was suddenly sharper and so much more oppressive than it had been in Jerusalem, where she was surrounded by people. The silence of the chapel, which she normally found soothing, weighed heavily on her, its density disturbed only by the sound of the falling rain and the ticking of the clock.

Quinn took a sip of tea and closed her eyes. She hated rainy days; they forced her to stay indoors. On fine days, she went for long country walks, walking until she exhausted herself enough to enjoy a few hours of dreamless sleep. But on a day like today, there was nothing to do but brood. She didn't even have a dog. Her job demanded frequent absences, and it wouldn't be fair to leave a puppy behind to be looked after by someone else for months on end. She did wish for a companion, though. Perhaps she could get a little dog and leave it with her parents when she went overseas. The thought cheered her up as she imagined a furry little ball of affection snuggled in her lap, making her feel less alone.

Quinn nearly spilled her tea when there was a loud knock at the door. She wasn't expecting any visitors, not so soon after arriving at home, and there was no one she could think of who'd just drop by unannounced. Quinn set her mug down and went to answer the door. Perhaps it was one of the guests from the resort who'd ventured too far off the path and got lost. Quinn opened the door, surprised to find an actual visitor.

"May I come in, or do I have to stand here in the rain?" Gabriel Russell asked as he smiled down at her.

"Of course. Sorry, Gabe. Come on in. May I offer you some tea?"

"You sure can. And add a dollop of whiskey, for medicinal purposes," he joked as he took off his wet coat and hung it on a coatrack before taking a seat on the sofa in front of the roaring fire.

Quinn held out the mug to Gabe and reclaimed her spot on the sofa. The melancholy that crept up on her earlier was gone, and she was suddenly grateful for the unexpected visit. Gabriel Russell wasn't just her boss but also one of her closest friends. They'd met years ago on a dig in Ireland when she was just a student and he was the dig supervisor and had remained close ever since, always staying in touch even during the most tumultuous moments of their lives. Gabe invited her to join the faculty at UCL Institute of Archeology when he accepted the position as head of the Archeology Department, and they shared a nice, comfortable relationship unmarred by stodgy professionalism or academic rivalry. They wanted different things, and Gabe, who preferred a desk job to digging in the dirt, supported Quinn and rejoiced in her success. Luke had taught several classes at the institute as well, using Quinn's friendship with Gabe as a way in.

Gabe was in his late thirties, with shaggy dark hair worn just a little too long and dark blue eyes fringed with ridiculously long lashes. His nose was a trifle long, and his eyebrows curved like wings above his hooded eyes, making him look stern and unapproachable at times, but that was only until he smiled. Gabe had a radiant smile that made him look sheepish and endearing at the same time. He could probably charm the knickers off Her Majesty, if they ever had occasion to be in the same room, which was why he was as popular with the faculty as he was with the students.

Few people knew this, but Gabe could trace his roots back to the Norman invasion, having descended from Hugh de Rosel, who'd accompanied William the Conqueror to the shores of England and had been rewarded for his loyalty with estates in Dorset. Gabe's family still lived in Berwick, although Gabe was the only male left of the noble line. It was Gabe's grandfather's obsession with history that influenced young Gabe and led to a degree in history and archeology.

Quinn folded her slim legs beneath her and turned her gaze to Gabe as she took a sip of her own tea, eager to hear what brought Gabe to her door on such a filthy night. He'd never been one for unannounced visits, so whatever it was had to be important.

"It's really coming down out there. I nearly missed the turn; I didn't see the sign for the village. Are you over the worst of the jet lag?" Gabe asked as he studied her features. Gabe had always detested small talk, but after several years of interdepartmental politics, he learned not to blurt out what was on his mind, as he had done when he was younger. Quinn smiled into her mug. She found this newfound political correctness somewhat amusing but went along with it nonetheless. Gabe would get to the point eventually, and she was in no rush for him to leave.

"It took about two days to adjust, but I'm back to my usual routine. It's nice to be home."

"Oh? Looking forward to a nice long winter, are you?" he joked.

"After roasting in the desert for six months, a cold winter sounds like a dream come true. I won't even complain about snow."

"We'll see about that. I wouldn't say no to a couple of weeks in a warm sunny place. Haven't had a holiday in longer than I can remember. Ibiza would do me very well right about now."

"Maybe you can take Eve after Christmas," Quinn suggested. Gabe always spent Christmas with his parents, but liked to take off for a week after the holiday, having had enough family togetherness, particularly since his mother had a long list of chores for him to complete before returning to London. Being an only child, it fell to him to see to the never-ending repairs needed to maintain the family home. His father was getting on in years and could no longer manage the upkeep on his own, but was too stubborn to hire a handyman.

"Actually, Eve and I are no longer, but that's not why I'm here," Gabe said but didn't elaborate. Eve had been the latest in a string of women in Gabe's life, an editor at a fashion magazine who was glamorous, vivacious, and dangerously independent. She was the type of woman who had lovers, not partners, and Quinn strongly suspected that she'd moved on to someone else while Gabe wasn't looking. Quinn never could understand why a man as intelligent and warm as Gabe always went for women who could never quite give him their full attention and bailed at the first sign of trouble. She had never known Gabe to be truly in love with any of his amours and wondered what kept him from finding someone who could really touch his heart.

Perhaps he feared commitment, or was wary of getting hurt. After her experience with Luke, Quinn could commiserate. She'd always craved a relationship that could sustain her, but her choice of partners hadn't been any wiser than Gabe's. There had been a few men who professed to love her, but sadly, she'd never become their number one priority and was discarded as soon as something better came along, as it had with Luke. The future she offered him couldn't compete with a professorship at Harvard University.

Quinn was actually surprised that Gabe made no mention of Luke's departure. Luke would have informed him since he'd been on the faculty and would have had to give notice. *Perhaps Gabe even warranted a phone call or an e-mail, and not just a text*, Quinn thought bitterly.

"So, why *are* you here on a rainy Friday night?" Quinn asked, her expression coy. The last thing she wanted to do was discuss Luke or Eve, but she was too curious to remain silent any longer.

"Have you seen the news?" Gabe asked as he took a sip of his whiskey-laced tea and sighed with pleasure as the alcohol hit his bloodstream.

"No, why?"

"Human remains were discovered yesterday at a construction site in Mayfair. They'd just broken ground a few days ago for another building of luxury flats few of us can afford. It seems there was a hidden chamber below ground that never appeared in the blueprints."

"And they called you?" Quinn asked, unsure of why exactly Gabe was involved. "Hardly your area of expertise."

"The foreman called in the Met and the coroner, but they quickly ruled it out as a recent crime."

"So, why's it on the news? Don't skeletal remains normally get reburied or left where they were found?" Quinn asked.

This wasn't the first case of human remains being found during excavation. The ground beneath London was full of surprises. Workers routinely came across remains of plague victims who'd been carelessly thrown into pits and buried en masse. At times, they even dug up what used to be whole cemeteries and reburied the dead in another part of town. Unless the remains belonged to someone of historical interest—like Richard III, whose remains had been resting under a parking lot for centuries—they didn't get much press. These were nameless, faceless relics of another time, a time when people were buried in paupers' graves and plague pits and forgotten about. There wasn't much to be learned from these remains, historically speaking, so they were usually just left in their final resting place as a sign of respect or moved somewhere safe.

"This find was special," Gabe replied with a sigh. "The remains were in a large chest of some kind, padlocked and chained. The two skeletons inside were lying face-to-face, as if sharing a final kiss as they lay dying. Clearly, they didn't die of natural causes, especially since there are scratch marks on the inside of the lid. Those two were murdered, their bodies hidden and denied proper burial."

"Do you think they were someone of historical significance?" Quinn asked, her interest piqued.

"I have no idea, but some tosser took pictures with his mobile and sent them to the media. *The Globe* picked up the story, and it went from there. The skeletons are now being referred to as 'the Lovers,' and they've become a real human-interest story. The public want to know who they were and what happened to them," Gabe said with a faint lift of his eyebrows. "If the media runs with this, we'll have another Romeo and Juliet on our hands."

"They'll lose interest in a few days," Quinn replied. She was very familiar with the fickle nature of the public. Unless the find was significant, people's attention very quickly strayed to something more current.

"I don't think so. I've actually had a call from someone at the BBC just this morning. They're thinking of doing a program based on various finds of historic interest that have cropped up all over the country these past few years. Think of them as historical scavenger hunts, if you will, like *Time Team*. Interest is high since Richard's remains were found earlier this year. People are intrigued by the notion that they are going about their daily lives and not suspecting for a second that they might be walking over the mortal remains of a royal."

"In all probability, those poor people in the chest were as far from royalty as one can get," Quinn said. Modern people didn't invent crime; murder had been around as long as humans themselves, and many a murder had gone unsolved, especially in times before the creation of a police force or forensic science.

"It's still good publicity for the institute and might result in some generous grants from the powers that be."

"Why do I have the feeling there's more to this?" Quinn asked with a smile. She could see the sheepish look on Gabe's face as he met her gaze. He was getting to the good part.

"I want you to take on this project, Quinn. You are the best forensic archeologist I've ever worked with, and you can use your gift to learn about the victims," he added softly.

Quinn's eyes flew to Gabe's face in alarm. They never discussed her "gift." She'd told him about it a long time ago, in a bout of alcohol-infused self-pity in a pub in Ireland, and now she couldn't take the revelation back. Gabe had respected her confidence and never brought it up again, allowing her to forget that there was one other person out there in the world who knew of her uncanny ability to see into the past. She'd never told anyone else, not even Luke, frightened of the implications the knowledge might have on her life and her work. It was her ability to see into the past that had influenced Quinn's choice of career—that, and a desperate need to tell the stories of people who could no longer speak for themselves. But she could hardly use the information she'd gleaned as scientific research. Every bit of information had to be documented and supported by fact, so Quinn kept a lot of what she saw to herself, using her secret knowledge as a road map to finding out more about the people whose possessions she came across and dressing the information up as scientific discovery.

Quinn had been able to learn quite a lot about a twenty-two-year-old man called Atticus, a dark-eyed, handsome youth who came to Judea from a province of Rome in search of glory. He died far from home and left behind a child born to a Jewess who'd been married off in haste to hide the disgrace of having lain with a Roman soldier. The sword that belonged to Atticus had been rescued from the clutches of history, but not his story; it would die with Quinn since there was no one she could share it with without betraying her ability—no one except Gabe.

Gabe came to her because he was fully aware of the limitations of this particular assignment. In all probability, historians might never be able to put a name or a face to the two skeletons in the chest, and his only hope of making this project appealing to the BBC was to truly dig deep and find out who the victims were. He was using her most treasured secret against her, knowing that she was likely the only one who could find out the truth about the two people locked in an eternal embrace in that dark chest.

"Why are you doing this to me, Gabe?" she asked warily, her voice devoid of any hint of accusation. She knew why. Gabe would give anything to possess her gift, if only for his own academic ends. He genuinely loved history, and to see into the past as it had really been rather than as it had been imagined was something that, as a historian, would send him into raptures.

"Quinn, your ability is nothing to be ashamed of. You've been given an amazing gift, one that's invaluable in your chosen profession. You can not only use physical evidence to find out more about your subjects but actually see into their lives, hear their thoughts. Why are you so reluctant to use it?"

"Because publicly admitting to it would make me look like a quack and destroy my credibility as a scientist. Can you just imagine me discussing my *visions* on BBC? People would go from calling me a historian to calling me a psychic, a label I don't really care for."

"But you are psychic, and you are the real deal."

Quinn shook her head. She'd fought her ability ever since she was a child, resentful of the responsibility it placed squarely on her skinny shoulders. She didn't want to see people who were long dead going about their business, nor did she want to hear their thoughts or feel their joy and pain. She just wanted to be a normal kid, if such a thing were even possible. Her life could never be normal anyway, given the way it had begun.

"I'll think about it," she replied with a grudging half-smile.

"All right, do. I'll be going now. I'll wait for your call. If I don't hear from you by Sunday night, I'll give the project to someone else—like Monica Fielding, for instance."

"Like hell you will," Quinn retorted, suddenly furious. Gabe knew offering this find to Monica would shake her out of her complacency. Quinn supposed that every person eventually came across someone who got under their skin for reasons they couldn't quite explain. It wasn't just professional rivalry that pitted the two women against each other, it was a personal one as well. Monica genuinely disliked Quinn and made no secret of it, actually going as far as to question Quinn's credibility in television interviews and periodicals. She had some sort of personal score to settle with Quinn and wouldn't be satisfied until Quinn became a laughing stock and a pariah in the scientific community.

"I'll do it," Quinn blurted out without thinking. "I'll take it on."

"I thought you might." Gabe's victorious smile said it all. "I'll give BBC a call and tell them you're on board."

Chapter 3

December 1664
London, England

Elise de Lesseps smoothed down the skirt of her gown and patted her hair into place, suddenly reluctant to enter the room. She'd been in her father's study countless times, to tidy up mostly, but this morning she felt strangely nervous. This summons felt different, more official somehow. She wasn't here to restore order but to be spoken to on a matter of some importance; she was sure of it.

"Oh, stop being such a ninny," she said sternly to herself under her breath. "There's absolutely no reason to be frightened."

But the brave words did nothing to dispel her sense of foreboding. She'd seen the young man come and leave this morning, had heard the thunder of hooves on frozen earth, and knew that something of significance had occurred. She just couldn't imagine what. Elise refused to entertain the notion that it was bad news. They'd had more than enough of that lately. The anxiety of not knowing made her hand shake as she finally raised it and knocked on the solid oak door.

"Come," her father called out. He stood with his back to the room, gazing out the window. The diamond-shaped panes glittered in the morning light, bright winter sunshine filling the room, which was freezing cold, the fire having been laid but not lit per her father's instructions. Hugh de Lesseps conserved firewood whenever possible; his own comfort was of little importance to him these days.

Elise stood just inside the room, waiting for her father to speak. He finally turned around, his expression unreadable. Elise couldn't help noticing the stooped shoulders or the stern set of his lips. Her father had aged drastically during the past year. His once-dark hair and beard were now streaked with gray, and his powerful frame had shrunk, making him appear older than his forty-seven years. Hugh de Lesseps's deep-set eyes studied his daughter, his head cocked to the side, as if he were listening to some inner voice.

"What is it, Father?" Elise asked, now even more worried than before. "Are you ill?"

"Sit down, child," Hugh said. "I would speak with you."

Hugh lowered himself into the carved hardback chair behind the massive desk and clasped his hands, his fingers intertwined. Normally, her father leaned back, but today he was hunched forward, his shoulders stiff with strain. His eyes slid away from Elise toward the cold fireplace, as if he was reluctant to speak, and he remained silent for a few moments before finally facing her again.

"Elise, I've had a messenger this morning," he began.

"Yes, I saw him leave," Elise replied. "What news?"

Her father took a deep breath as his eyes met hers over the breadth of the desk. "I won't beat about the bush. You're old enough to know the truth, and since your mother died, you have been the lady of this house and a mother to your sisters."

Her father sighed, as he did every time he mentioned his late wife, who'd left them only last February. Nothing had been the same since. The house seemed cold and empty, even on the warmest and sunniest of days. The laughter had died, as had the music. Hugh often called his wife frivolous while she was alive, but he always said it with a smile, glad to see his wife laughing and dancing with her daughters. Their two sons were grown men now, one living in Massachusetts Bay Colony and one in Port Royal, Jamaica, where he was most useful to his father.

Caroline de Lesseps had been a child bride, a girl of fifteen when Hugh married her, and she'd retained something of that innocence and joy, a quality he loved above all else in a woman who never aged in his eyes. She'd been only thirty-six when she died, but to him she was still the young, beautiful girl who took his breath away the first time he saw her. It had been a marriage of convenience arranged by the families of the couple, but the relationship had blossomed into one of love and respect and became a true partnership. Many men married again once the period of mourning was over, but Elise was certain that her father wouldn't look at another woman for a long time to come, if ever. No one could replace his beautiful Caroline, and secretly she was glad.

Hugh de Lesseps pinched the bridge of his nose, as if he had a terrible headache, then looked up at his daughter, his expression one of utter misery.

"The messenger was from Lord Asher. I owe him a great deal of money since the cargo he'd paid for is now at the bottom of the sea. I am not in a position to repay him, at least not at this time. Since the sinking of the *Celeste*, our financial situation is dire, Elise."

The *Celeste* went down in a storm just off the coast of Jamaica in September, taking with it all her father's precious cargo and its crew. Hugh de Lesseps owned one more ship, the *Sea Nymph*, but no ships crossed the Atlantic during the winter, and it would be nearly a year before Hugh saw any profit from the sale of the cargo the crew would bring back from the West Indies.

"Is Lord Asher demanding payment?" Elise asked carefully. She had more of an education than most girls of her station and understood only too well the ramifications of losing the cargo and the vessel. Her father would need ready capital to purchase goods, which would be shipped to Jamaica and sold, the profit used to purchase Jamaican goods that would then be transported to the American colonies. A third cargo would then be loaded on the ship for the voyage back to England, the hold loaded with tobacco, furs traded from the savages, and wooden spars, which would be sold to the Navy for the building of masts. Only once the cargo was sold in England would a profit be realized and the debt to Lord Asher repaid.

"Lord Asher has offered to allow me a grace period of two years to pay the debt, but on one condition. He wishes to take you as his bride."

"Me? Why? I hardly know the man," Elise exclaimed. Lord Asher was a wealthy and powerful man who had the ear of the king and could choose any woman for his wife. Elise had neither title nor fortune, and the dowry her father had set aside for her was hardly enough to tempt a man of Asher's wealth and position. Why would he want her?

"Lord Asher has offered to forgo the dowry," her father added, his expression pained. "It seems he has no need for it."

Elise slowly rose to her feet, her legs suddenly too wobbly to hold her up. She grasped the back of the chair for support as she faced her father. "I don't have a choice, do I?"

"I'm sorry, Elise. I promised your mother that I would see you happy, but if Lord Asher calls in the debt, I will be ruined. Your brothers will lose their livelihood, and your sisters will have no dowry once they come of age. I can't afford to refuse."

"I understand," Elise breathed. She felt faint but remained standing upright, her knuckles white on the back of the chair.

"You will be the wife of a great man. Your sons will be of noble birth, and you will be received at court. I know that Edward Asher is not your heart's desire, but you will benefit from this union, as will your sisters. Our family will weather this crisis."

"Yes, Father," Elise replied woodenly. "May I go now?"

"Go on. You need some time to absorb this news."

"When does Lord Asher wish to marry?"

"In three weeks' time, at the New Year."

"That soon?" Elise willed herself not to cry, but her voice sounded shaky.

"You will be ready." It wasn't a question but a statement. She would be ready; she had no choice. The bargain had been struck and she was the chattel that would be transferred as payment of debt—human cargo replacing material goods.

Elise didn't bother to shut the door behind her as she fled the room. She needed time alone to sort out her tumultuous feelings and prepare a story for her sisters. Amy and Anne were only thirteen and nine, too young to understand the implications of the *Celeste's* sinking. They'd lost their mother less than a year ago, and now they would lose their sister as well. To show them the depth of her despair would only make the inevitable separation more difficult for them, so Elise had to put on a brave face and make them believe that this match was of her own choosing.

Elise climbed the stairs to her room and shut the door, locking it behind her. The girls would be expecting her in the parlor, but she couldn't bear to face them just yet. She couldn't calmly work on her sewing when she was battling rising hysteria. In three weeks, she would be married off to a man she barely knew. Elise had met Lord Asher once when he visited her father on a matter of business. She'd seen him twice more since then, but no words had been exchanged besides a curt greeting. Lord Asher had bowed to her, his eyes never leaving her face as his lips stretched into a half-hearted smile. Elise assumed he was just being polite, although a man of his station had no obligation to be polite to the likes of her.

Elise sat in front of the cold hearth and pulled a warm shawl about her shoulders, but it did little to warm her. She closed her eyes and tried to picture herself standing next to Edward Asher in church as a vicar bound them for eternity, giving her new husband complete control over her life. Edward Asher was an imposing man, to be sure, but old enough to be her father. *He has to be at least five and forty*, Elise thought miserably. She shuddered and opened her eyes. The only way to accept this new reality was to focus on the positive things about her future husband. Elise was hard-pressed to find any, but she had to, so she began with his looks.

Lord Asher was of above-average height, and despite his age, he was still in good physical form. He didn't run to fat, nor had he lost his hair. She supposed he wore a wig when at court, but when he'd come to visit her father, he wore his own hair, which was a rich brown with only a few strands of gray silvering the temples. His gray eyes were not unkind, and he did smile easily, which spoke of a good temperament. As far as Elise knew, he had no children, at least not ones still living.

Elise supposed that any girl of her station would be honored to marry a man like Lord Asher, who would pluck her from complete obscurity and elevate her practically overnight to become one of the ladies of the royal court. To be wealthy and titled and received by His Majesty Charles II was the stuff of dreams for young maidens, but that had never been Elise's aspiration. She'd never been inside the palace, but she had seen courtiers out and about, carousing in the Strand and enjoying pleasure cruises on the river. They were like peacocks, draped in yards of exquisite fabric and lace, painted like whores, and adorned with bows, ribbons, and ridiculous curly wigs, which made even the most masculine of men look like overgrown poodles. Most people gleefully accepted the new fashions when Charles II took the throne, tired as they were of the black and gray of Puritan rule that had been the order of the day for so long. The theaters had reopened, music and color burst into people's lives with a gaiety most had forgotten, and suddenly, life was good again. Everyone, from the wealthiest nobleman to the poorest wretch, was glad to be alive.

But now, after half a decade of excess and frivolity, the unbearable glitter of royal glamour had begun to fade, and the common people were beginning to tire of the careless spending of their new king, their lot in life still not much better than it had been during the reign of his father and the tyranny of Oliver Cromwell.

Elise had no desire to become one of the cheap, painted ladies of the court, who indulged in sinful games, thinly veiled sexual innuendo, and provocative masques, the only purpose of which was to showcase their charms and catch the interest of a new lover. Elise was a good, Christian woman, and she wanted nothing more than to be like her own mother: a faithful wife and loving mother, with a husband who was loyal and devoted even after decades of marriage. And she'd come so close to achieving that dream.

Elise had been nursing a tender affection for Gavin Talbot, her father's clerk, for the past two years. Gavin was kind, thoughtful, and hardworking. He would never be rich, but through hard work and careful planning, he would surely be able to offer his family a comfortable living. And he was handsome. Gavin had sandy hair and wide blue eyes that shone with good humor. He'd always had a kind word and a smile for Elise, even when she was still a young girl and beyond his notice. Now that she was a woman of seventeen, Gavin was in his mid-twenties and ready to start his own family. No betrothal had taken place, but there was an understanding between them that with her father's permission, they would marry once the year of mourning for her mother was over. Elise had never spoken to her father of her feelings for Gavin, but she was sure he knew. Hugh de Lesseps was an observant man, a man who was a devoted father to his girls, and who, she believed, genuinely wished for their happiness. He would have consented had this catastrophe not struck their family, Elise was sure of it.

And now Gavin was as far removed from her as the moon. Her father had a debt to repay, and she was the currency. There was no one else. Elise bit her lip to keep from crying. She had no choice. If she refused, her father and brothers would be ruined, and her sisters would have no chance of a respectable marriage. It was her duty to honor her father's wishes and make a good marriage that would benefit the whole family. Few girls had the luxury of choosing their own husbands, and even fewer had expectations of a happy marriage. Lord Asher would be good to her, and she would want for nothing. Perhaps she could even help Amy and Anne make an advantageous match when the time came.

Elise sprang to her feet when she heard footsteps outside her door and the excited voices of her sisters. She forced a smile onto her face just as the two girls burst into the room. "Father says there's to be a wedding," Amy exclaimed. "Oh, that's so exciting. I can't wait until I am a bride." She sighed dramatically and did a little pirouette.

"Father says there's to be dancing and a great feast. Do say we can come, Elise," Amy pleaded.

"You'll have to ask Father. You two are too young to attend, but perhaps you can watch from the gallery, if the wedding is to be held here."

Amy continued to perform dance steps as she gazed at herself in the cheval glass, but Anne stood quietly by the door, her eyes shiny with unshed tears. She was the more sensitive of the two and had taken their mother's death very hard. Her grief was still as fresh as it had been when their mother breathed her last, and Elise worried how she would cope once her big sister was gone. Amy was too young and frivolous to give her sister the support she so sorely needed.

"You're going to leave us," Anne whispered as she ran to Elise and wrapped her arms around her waist. "Oh, what are we going to do without you?" she said and began to sob.

"Come now, Annie. It won't be so bad. I'll be a great lady, and you might be able to visit me in my house across the river. Just think of it."

Anne's eyes grew round with wonder. She'd never been across the river. There was no call for the girls to leave their house in Southwark; everything they needed was right there. But Lord Asher lived in the Strand, where Elise's new home would be. She'd never seen Lord Asher's house, but she'd heard her father speak of it. Grand, it was, he said, and well appointed, with tapestries on the walls, carpets on the floors, and fine furnishings. There were many servants: maids, cooks, grooms, and gardeners. Perhaps Hugh de Lesseps viewed this turn of events as fortuitous. Elise only wished she could bring herself to feel the same.

Printed in Poland
by Amazon Fulfillment
Poland Sp. z o.o., Wrocław

57159529R00223